For us, it was an old game:

Me racing to get out of the jungle with my orchids, Lawrence Daley, my one serious rival, racing to catch me and steal what I had in my backpack.

Now, looking down through a break in the midstory's dense leaves, I noted with some satisfaction that my wait had not been wasted.

"Jessica!" Daley called. What he said next was incomprehensible, but it didn't matter because anger made him boring. And predictable.

I released the slipknot and plummeted. The rope sang through my gloved fingers. Vines and branches whipped my legs. My boots thumped into the thick forest floor, raising the rich, heady scent of moist earth. The backpack whacked my rump as it caught up. I quickly hauled the remaining rope up and over the branch, then stepped back to let the bitter end slap the ground like a whip.

His hat had fallen back on his neck, the leather strap tight on his throat. His sweaty face was tanner than I remembered, and his blue eyes shone with anger.

"You'd better be careful," he said. "There are other collectors far more ruthless than I."

"Yeah," I said. "That's why we're more successful."

Dear Reader,

You're about to read a Silhouette Bombshell novel and enter a world full of excitement, suspense and women who stand strong in the face of danger and do what it takes to triumph over the toughest adversaries. And don't forget a touch of thrilling romance to sweeten the deal. Our bombshells always get their men, good *and* bad!

Debra Webb kicks off the month with *Silent Weapon,* the innovative story of Merri Walters, a deaf woman who goes undercover in a ruthless criminal's mansion and reads his chilling plans right off his lips!

Hold on to your hats for *Payback,* by Harper Allen, the latest in the Athena Force continuity. Assassin Dawn O'Shaughnessy is out to take down the secret lab that created her and then betrayed her—but she's got to complete one last mission for them, or her superhealing genes will self-destruct before she gets payback....

Step into the lush and dangerous world of *The Orchid Hunter,* by Sandra K. Moore. Think "botanist" and "excitement" don't match? Think again, as this fearless heroine's search for a rare orchid turns into a dangerous battle of wills in the steamy rain forest.

And don't miss the twist and turns as a gutsy genius races to break a deadly code, trap a slippery terrorist and steal back the trust of her former CIA mentor, in *Calculated Risk,* by Stephanie Doyle!

Strong, sexy, suspenseful...that's Silhouette Bombshell! Please send your comments to me, c/o Silhouette Books, 233 Broadway Suite 1001, New York, NY 10279.

Sincerely,

Natashya Wilson
Associate Senior Editor, Silhouette Bombshell

Please address questions and book requests to:
Silhouette Reader Service
U.S.: 3010 Walden Ave., P.O. Box 1325, Buffalo, NY 14269
Canadian: P.O. Box 609, Fort Erie, Ont. L2A 5X3

THE ORCHID HUNTER

SANDRA K. MOORE

BOMBSHELL

Published by Silhouette Books

America's Publisher of Contemporary Romance

SILHOUETTE BOOKS

ISBN 0-373-51349-6

THE ORCHID HUNTER

Copyright © 2005 by Sandra K. Moore

SANDRA K. MOORE

has been a technical writer, poet, martial arts student and software product manager, occasionally all at the same time. Although she obtained her master of arts in English from the intensely literary University of Houston Graduate Creative Writing Program, she has happily embraced the fact she's a commercial fiction writer at heart. She lives on the Texas coast and when she's not writing action-adventure novels, she can be found hovering over her lone *Phalaenopsis,* trying to get it to bloom. Visit her on the Web at www.sandrakmoore.com.

Acknowledgments

Many thanks to Laurie C. Skov, President of Orchids
and Tropicals, LLC of Houston, Texas,
for his technical information about the fascinating
Orchidaceae family; to John E. Erickson for allowing me
to use his gorgeous orchid photographs on my Web site;
to Heather Giles for her information about the
pharmaceutical industry; and to Richard Shepley and
Emerson Ricci for their help with the Portuguese.
A complete bibliography is available at
www.sandrakmoore.com/orchidhunter/.
Any outstanding errors of fact are entirely mine.

Chapter 1

On the northern ridge of Mount Aiome, not far from the highest point in Papua New Guinea, just inside the province of Madang, a broad stone ledge juts out from a sheer cliff. Carpeted with lichen, the ledge overlooks a handful of majestic emergent hardwoods poking out from the dense canopy of the rain forest below, hardwoods similar to the one a tomboyish woman like me might choose as her vantage point for keeping watch.

She'd be high enough on this ledge and in this tree that on a clear, predawn morning she could see in the far distance, just over the coastal ridge that hid the swamps, the Bismarck Sea's great darkness. If she waited long enough, the sun would rise over the water and the archipelago islands would gleam like emeralds on a silky topaz bed. The howling nocturnal cacophony would steadily give way to the brighter tones of the dawn chorus. The light mist fingering the treetops would scatter and disappear beneath the sun's abrupt heat, and the woman might wish she'd worn a lighter-weight pair of canvas pants.

She might also wish she'd used a wider strap to fashion her climbing harness because her ass was, quite literally, in a sling and gone dead as a doornail. After another twenty minutes, she'd wonder if there was any good reason for suspending herself here like bear bait, her backpack full of carefully packed rare plant specimens. A little while later, she'd start wondering if there might be a better way for a woman of her talents to make a living, since she was bored as hell now and her butt was starting to tingle.

But I'm getting ahead of myself. The truth is I'd been up in the tree for a good hour because Lawrence Daley, my one serious plant-collecting rival, had been tracking me all yesterday and last night. For us, it's an old game: me racing to get out of the jungle with my orchids, him racing to catch me and steal what I've got in my backpack. We'd pretty much been enemies since grad school, when Daley's idea of a good time had been trying to one-up me with graduate advisors and on lab projects, generally making a nuisance of himself. He craved competition. I craved adventure. I guess that's why we both gravitated to exotic-plant collecting, the only adventurous, competitive niche in the otherwise ho-hum world of botany.

So I was stuck there, roughly ninety feet up in the canopy in the predawn darkness, my butt starting to tingle. I could have tried climbing down the ledge in the dark, but the nocturnal jungle is far more dangerous than the daylight one, and I've had one too many run-ins with boa constrictors, poisonous ants and loose rock to be cavalier about it. Back in the golden age of orchid hunting, the Victorian era, hunters died of dysentery or malaria, or disappeared without a trace, or killed each other over a plant. The killing part had slacked off some, but the rest of the experience was intact. Stay sharp or get dead. I tried to stay sharp.

My plan from here on out was simple. If Daley didn't show by first light, I'd drop from the canopy and head down the ledge. From there, it was twenty miles to the airstrip where a decrepit Douglas Dakota and a genuine muscle-bound Aussie bush pilot waited for me.

Looking down through a break in the midstory's dense leaves at the string of utterly silent Maisin natives filing along the path below, I noted with some satisfaction that my efforts had not been wasted, because there, in the back as always, was a white man wearing a ridiculous Australian bush hat, the left brim tacked up in rakish style. I cursed the selfish bastard for abandoning me in Sierra Leone last year after stealing my prize orchid, the luscious *Cymbidium archinopsis* (or at least what he thought was a prize orchid; I'd actually switched it for the rather pedestrian *Cymbidium parthenonae*), and my passport (okay, the passport was fake but he didn't know that, did he? and okay, I'd been wearing my real passport taped to my back but it'd still been tight threading through the paramilitaries and diamond smugglers to get outta there), and then how *dare* he pretend nothing had happened when I saw him in Stockholm at a private black-tie orchid party two weeks later?

It was enough to make even a well-bred girl want to hock a lugie down on his arrogant head.

This well-bred girl didn't, though. Instead, I checked my gear.

The rope tied to my climbing harness ran up over an evergreen branch. It came back down where it ran through a stainless steel figure eight at my stomach, and then around my waist to run through a carabiner at the small of my back. It finally got tied to itself in a slipknot at my left side. The remaining rope wound in a loose coil at my belt. I held the business end of the coiled rope in my left hand, and my right hand—the braking hand—tucked comfortably around the rope behind my back. Hanging here all morning wasn't a problem. Except for the butt-going-to-sleep part.

Now I just needed Daley and his pals to move on down the

ridge, discover there wasn't an easy way off the ledge, and then go back to wherever they had come from. After that, I'd ease down and be on my way, straight down that lovely ledge—the shortest distance from Point A to Point B.

I was still daydreaming about the muscle-bound Aussie pilot when the Maisin spotted me.

Daley barked a sic'em order. The natives swarmed up tree trunks, climbing bare-handed, barefoot, toward me. Daley leaned back to look up.

"Jessica!" he called. "Come on down, luv, and give us the pretty plants."

I can tolerate almost anything about Lawrence Daley except that affected English accent. Why did a guy from Baltimore feel the need to pretend he was from Blackpool?

"Up yours," I called down.

"From this angle, it looks more like up yours, luv." He laughed, hands on his hips. "And a very nice yours it is. What has von Brutten sent you after this time?"

I shrugged, one eye on the natives. "Same old, same old."

"*Cattleya astronomis,* perhaps? *Dendrobium peristansis?*"

"*Rudbeckia hirta,*" I called back. Wildflower. Black-eyed Susan, to be precise.

"Don't be a smartass, dahling. We could be a great team—"

"Right, like in Sierra Leone. You nearly got me killed!"

"You're far too resourceful for that. And look what's happened since. You've been so intent on beating me to the good plants that you leave a trail a mile wide. I can track you anywhere."

"Correction. *The natives* can track me anywhere. *You* can't find your own ass with both hands and a flashlight."

"I hear von Brutten's got a bug in his ear."

"What? Have you been begging for your old job back? You should know by now that I keep my employer's little green thumb *very* happy."

Daley's sneer echoed in his cocked hip. "Getting fired by Linus von Brutten was the best thing that ever happened to me."

"Sounds like sour grapes. Everybody on the planet knows he's been the best orchid breeder for decades. Maybe you should have spent more time in grad school thinking about your future instead of how fast and how bad you could screw me over. Speaking of, did you ever get your degree?"

The stiff got even stiffer. "Paper means nothing these days, dahling."

"Oh, I don't know. I kinda like having a degree. Keeps my employment options open. How many botanical gardens passed on your résumé, *dahling?*"

His snort was audible from here. "Collecting for an eminent European orchid breeder is employment enough."

It should be. Constance Thurston-Fitzhugh had money to burn and an ax to grind with von Brutten. Von Brutten, thanks to my fieldwork and his own high-tech knack for hybridization, had swept top honors at the World Orchid Conference two years running and dumped Thurston-Fitzhugh from her orchid-breeding throne directly onto her glamorous tush. Daley and I were just the latest weapons in a dirty little two-decade war going on underneath the glitz and highbrow of more-money-than-God orchid collecting.

I glanced over. The natives were about halfway up, rustling leaves and scraping bark with bare feet that must have been just as rough. Thank God for Rockports. Watching the climbers made my arches itch.

Daley wasn't done taunting me yet. "I'm surprised von Brutten hasn't told you about his heart's latest desire."

I waited for him to tell me his rumor about my employer. He always seemed to think that keeping me waiting would make me wet my pants in anticipation. He never learned.

He gave in. "The Death Orchid."

I burst out laughing. The natives froze and looked at each

other, apparently debating the sanity of a white woman, suspended by a rope in the rain forest, cackling her ass off.

The Death Orchid? It was beyond legend. It was myth.

"Debunked!" I shouted down.

Daley's hat twisted as he shook his head. "O ye of little faith."

"I'm a scientist. Discredited jungle native accounts of miracle cures do not constitute a *clue*."

"Harrison was wrong when he published that report!" Daley shouted.

No way. Terence Harrison was a taxonomic god, my dissertation advisor and mentor my entire grad school career. The man always knew exactly what he was doing. If he said the Death Orchid didn't exist, it didn't.

"Harrison proved everyone in the orchid-collecting community was nuts," I shouted back. "Except me. I didn't believe those rumors were true. That supposed Death Orchid he tested wasn't some kind of miracle cure and he proved it. Scientifically. In a lab!"

Daley stamped a few steps away, then back. "Harrison lied!"

"Willful ignorance is the last bastion of the faithful. Harrison's too straitlaced to lie and you know it. Do the facts confuse you? Or does Mrs. Thurston-Fitzhugh just hate losing to my boss so much she's convinced you this crap is true?"

"Connie has reason to believe—"

Connie? I laughed, interrupting him. "On a first name basis with your employer?"

Daley stopped pacing and shoved his hat back from his forehead. I couldn't see the grin, but I could the signs of one in his cocky stance. "I'm doing rather well in the bedroom, if that's what you're asking."

The Maisin were close enough now to distinguish as individuals. Time to think about leaving.

"You're all talk, Larry." I unhooked the coil of rope at my

belt and held it loose in one hand, ready. "Do you suppose she fakes it like your girlfriends in school?"

"You little—" The rest was incomprehensible, but it didn't matter because anger made him boring. And predictable. And American.

A rail-thin native, a jet-black adolescent wearing fierce ocher and white face paint, a necklace made of oyster shells, and a pair of department-store shorts, grasped the branch below my dangling feet. I raised one boot as his chin came level with the branch. He looked at the beefy no-nonsense sole, then at me. I shook my head at him. Behind me, the others scrambled across narrow branches. They were closing in and I really didn't want to break this young man's nose. His deep brown eyes—I'm a sucker for brown eyes—widened.

I glanced down. Daley waited. Alone.

Dumbass.

I released the slipknot and plummeted. The rope sang through my gloved fingers. Vines and branches whipped my legs as I dropped through the midstory leaves. Above me, the natives fell into the sky. Below me, Daley's mouth hung open in his usual expression of slack-jawed surprise. I gradually tightened my grip over the last twenty feet, slowing. My boots thumped into the thick forest floor, raising the rich, heady scent of moist earth. The backpack whacked my rump as it caught up. I quickly hauled the remaining rope up and over the branch, then stepped back to let the bitter end slap the ground like a whip.

"Leave me the hell alone," I grated at Daley, rapidly coiling the rope over my bent arm.

His hat had fallen back on his neck, the leather strap tight on his throat. His sweaty face was more tan than I remembered, and his blue eyes shone with anger.

"You'd better be careful," he said. "There are other collectors far more ruthless than I."

"Yeah." I glanced at the natives struggling to hurry down without killing themselves. "That's why we're more successful than you."

"Give it to me." He made a grab at my backpack's left shoulder strap.

Hopping back out of reach, I slapped his hand away. "Why don't you dig your own orchids for a change instead of trying to steal mine? It didn't work at school and it hasn't worked since."

I strode to the ledge and quickly fed my climbing rope around the stout and stubby palm tree I'd scoped earlier. I backed over the edge. Just as I started seeing rock instead of foliage, I heard the first of the Maisin hitting the forest floor. Their feet pattered on lichen. Broad brown faces peered over the edge.

Kicking off from the cliff, I touched the rock here and there. It was a long way down to the lowland rain forest but there was no need to hurry.

"Come on, luv!"

The warning tone in Daley's voice made me look up. He lay facedown on the ledge, arms extended, pistol aiming. "Get back up here!"

Would he shoot me? I doubted it, but I shortened my strides anyway, darting back and forth in an irregular pattern while letting miles of rope slide through my fists. Daley's shooting sucked but I'd made him mad, and some people's aim got better when they were pissed. Tree branches raced toward me. I couldn't see the ground. There was only the dark, mottled green of trees waking up as I crashed through the canopy on the lower ridge.

Several more feet, and the end of climbing rope not tied to my harness slipped through my braking right hand. I clamped down hard on the bitter end with my left hand, nearly yanking my arm out of its socket. Two hundred feet of rope and it was too short. Way too short. Dangling like bait on a hook, I glanced up through the leaves. The more intrepid Maisin pursuers leaned far over the cliff, looking for handholds. One had pulled his machete and was hacking away at my climbing rope. Daley took aim. Doing a buttplant on the forest floor didn't sound like much fun but, as I reflected before letting go, it might be something I could tell my grandkids.

Two branches clipped my shoulder, then I broke through leaves like an airplane descending through clouds. Almost immediately my feet hit thick moss and I rolled hard for some distance. Either I'd fallen the last couple of dozen feet really fast or, more likely, I'd fallen five feet through the leaves of a short but elegant ficus. As I was still conscious enough to register landing pain in my shins, I gathered it was the latter.

I sat up. No nausea, no concussion. Not yet, anyway. With any luck, the rare orchids in my pack weren't concussed, either.

A whistling hiss warned me to scoot to my right. The climbing rope shot down through the midstory, undeterred by the branches, and slapped the ground a foot away, raising a huge cloud of murky dust that danced in the filtered sunlight. I looked around to make sure the hissing I'd heard had merely been the rope. Nothing slithered.

Ignoring the days-old stink of rotting mammal from somewhere nearby, I tested fingers, toes, arms, legs and shoulders. All good. All ready to go, if a little sore. I coiled the rope and tied it off. The high-speed drops and the machete action had rendered it unsafe, but I live by a simple rule: pack in, pack out.

As I threw the coil over my head and shoulder, I spotted the remains of what looked like a canopy-dwelling spider monkey, its neck definitely broken. I preferred to think of it as a "lesson" rather than as a "warning." Thank you, God.

Above, I could hear Daley shouting instructions at the Maisin. It sounded like they were fed up and ready to go home. If Daley had a map, he might be able to find his way to the airstrip. I didn't need a map. And from my survey of the area, I knew it'd take him four hours to get down to me by way of the southwestern trail. Unless he wanted to free-climb down the sheer cliff face.

If I knew Daley, he didn't and wouldn't.

"Up. Freaking. Yours!" I shouted to him, and headed north-north-east for the airstrip and my muscle-bound Aussie.

Had my great-uncle Scooter ever bothered to put any money into it, the Slapdash Bar and Grill could have been a full step above the average East Texas honky-tonk it was. The dilapidated front porch showed Scooter's optimistic view that a good time didn't mean you couldn't navigate three tilting steps down to the parking lot. These same steps seemed, as I put my pickup's nose to the hitching rail out front, to be complicating the efforts of a drummer hoisting his gear onto the porch. His next obstacle was the life-size, paint-flaked wooden palomino pony just outside the front door. And I'm sure there's some law against having an attached firing range, but the local sheriff hadn't yet seen fit to enforce any regulations and in fact he was knocking back a Bud by the jukebox when I threaded past the sweating drummer and stepped inside.

"Jessie!" Hank boomed, standing to bear hug the air out of me. What little breath I had left at the end got hijacked by his aftershave. "About time you came home."

"It's good to be back," I said.

He slammed his beer bottle down on the worn oak table and looked at me, his gray eyes warm with affection. "It's good to see you again, little girl."

I set my brown paper bag, containing a glad-to-see-you present for Scooter, on the floor. "I haven't been gone that long."

"Been over six weeks." A frown's shadow crossed his tanned forehead but disappeared almost immediately. "What'd you do to your hair?"

I guiltily ran a hand through it. "Long and red didn't suit me. Shorter and brown's better for my line of work."

"Didn't suit you, my ass."

"I'd shave it all off if I had the nerve."

Hank grinned. He knew I wouldn't, but it'd give him something to rib me about later.

"Scooter around?" I asked.

"Don't you go nowhere. I'll fetch him." He stalked his broad frame up to the bar where Marian, the homely blond barkeep, did her best not to pass out from lust. The fact Hank was pushing fifty didn't seem to bother her twenty-something hormones. But, as Scooter liked to say, every pot has a lid.

What he meant was, every pot except the ones he used in the back to cook up his four-alarm chili. Hell, if he had more than a ladle and six spoons in the kitchen I'd be surprised. He'd probably worn his trademark black-iron pot down to tin-foil thickness by now.

And he wouldn't let me replace the damn thing with a new one. A stickler about borrowing, he'd nearly had a heart attack when I'd told him I was going to get a student loan to pay for school. Hank and I had a tough row to hoe when we talked him out of selling the Slapdash to pay for my education. Hell, it wouldn't have covered much more than tuition and books for the first two years, anyway. The money I'd made working for von Brutten let me pay off the entire loan in a year and two months.

Hank cracked the kitchen door and shouted, "Scooter! Your lady friend's home!"

Looking around at the clean, well-worn tables, the gleaming bar, the glittering beer mugs, and the black-and-white photos of who knows whom on the walls, I felt the first thrill of seeing him again. This place was so like him—beat-up and characterful and comforting—where you could go and feel at ease and let the world slip by outside.

Being with Scooter always felt safe. When I first came to live with him after my parents died, he made me feel like I belonged here. Even though he didn't have kids of his own, Scooter somehow knew how to guide me through my parents' deaths in that car accident. It felt like he'd always be here, always just through the kitchen door, no matter what else was going on in my life.

I guess I was about nine when he blindfolded me and took me into the middle of a neighbor's cornfield. He set me down between two rows and told me to count to a thousand, then take off my blindfold and come home. Maybe I counted to a thousand or maybe not, but I remember pulling off that navy-blue bandanna, squinting into the bright noon sky, surrounded by the smell of hot corn leaves going dry with summer sun, and thinking, "I better go that way." Thirty minutes later, I was back at the Slapdash, not knowing how I'd known where I was or where I ought to head. I was just glad Scooter was waiting for me on the front porch with a glass of cold grape Kool-Aid and a hug. He'd patted my head and chuckled, then bragged about how sharp and capable I was to all his friends that night as they sat around the gleaming mahogany bar.

Now, beside the bar, Hank swung the kitchen door wider and Scooter barreled through, shoving his walker out in front of him like a battering ram. Two shuffling steps, shove. Two shuffling steps, shove. I noticed immediately the hair sticking out from under the baseball cap had silvered a lot. His face, a dull gray under a surface flush of either excitement or freshly chopped jalapeños, broke into the broad, toothy grin I remembered from the day I came to live with him. I'd been seven then and the teeth had been real.

When he cleared the door, I went to him and hugged him over the walker, feeling his loose-skinned old-man shoulders through his plaid cotton shirt. Two-day stubble scratched my ear and his arms tightened shakily around my back as he said,

"Well, well. How 'bout that." He smelled like garlic and moth-balls and spearmint. If I could bottle that scent I'd remember him forever.

"Hello, old man," I said.

"'Bout time you came back. I thought you'd done forgot me." He winked one watery hazel eye to show me he didn't mean it. "Marian! Bring my girl a beer."

"What'll you have?" she called.

"Saint Arnold."

"You want a mug?"

"Nah."

Scooter gestured to a table close to the kitchen. "You tell me where you've been this time." He let Hank guide him into a wide-backed chair sporting a seat cushion. So Scooter had finally broken down and set himself up a receiving table. Hank settled in at Scooter's right hand.

"I'll do better than just tell you." I set the brown paper bag on the chair next to me and took out *Phalaenopsis donerii,* a delicate beauty whose petals gleamed a pure, bright yellow. The lip—the insect pollinator's landing platform—resembled a leopard's skin, dark brown and golden. "Fresh from Micronesia," I said. "She's small, but she's fertile. I made sure of that before I turned her siblings over to the boss."

Scooter's liver-spotted hand stopped trembling as he touched the plant's shiny leaves. Just like some stutterers can sing flawlessly, so his hands became steady as a rock around an orchid.

"Wide leaves. Understory t'rrestrial," he murmured, turning the pot gently. "Monopodial. Better not keep your feet wet, lovely girl." His fingers lightly traced her lines. "What pests?"

"The usual. And spider mites on the underleaves."

"Pollinator?"

"The male leopard moth. She blooms for two weeks before the female moths hatch."

"So the gents make love to her until their lady friends show up." He shook his head. "Somethin' else, ain't it?"

"Timing is everything," I admitted.

"This is the prettiest since my *Laelia anceps*. My first orchid." His voice softened. "Long time ago now."

"What about the Draculas I brought you last year? Or the *Brassia verrucosa* the year before that?" I'd nearly broken my neck for the blood-red *Brassia*.

"There ain't nuthin' like the first." He seemed to want to say more, but didn't. His eyes sharpened when he tore his gaze from his orchid to look at me. "Couldn't catch me a couple of moths?"

"You know I don't do moths. I'm only licensed for plants."

He nodded. "Appendix One?"

He was referring to the CITES, pronounced *sigh-tees*, regulations about transporting animal and plant products across international borders. Had I been caught in customs with Scooter's little *Phalaenopsis*, I'd be in jail and facing a hundred-thousand-dollar fine. It would have been fun because I'd had four of them packed in my luggage at the time.

I shrugged, noncommittal. Best I not admit to anything in front of Hank, who was, after all, the law. Better for Scooter, too. U.S. Fish and Wildlife raids on orchid growers, even here in the free United States of America, weren't unknown. Heck, a well-respected Florida botanical garden got nailed a few years ago because they neglected to tell Fish and Wildlife they were *preparing* to formally register the previously undiscovered *Phragmipedium kovachii*.

Abruptly, Scooter smiled. "Good girl," he murmured.

I swigged my ice-cold Saint Arnold while my gut warmed with pleasure. Getting rare orchids into the States under the noses of customs and wildlife agents satisfied us both—me because of the challenge and ultimate monetary payoff from von Brutten, and Scooter because he was a true conservationist.

Scooter had explained to me how the CITES rules worked when I first decided at the ripe old age of ten I wanted to find orchids for a living. It's simple. You can't take a plant listed in CITES Appendix One out of its country of origin. It doesn't matter whether you want to conserve it, study it or clone it. It doesn't even matter if everybody knows that same country of origin is about to bulldoze the last one under to build a road. That plant can be the only one in existence, and CITES won't let someone like me save it by taking it out of the country. It's just one of those things: good intentions gone bad.

Scooter got me started on orchids with his collecting hobby, but I've never had the love of the things he does. I like the grittier side. Ever since he told me the horror stories about the Victorian hunters—Roezl losing his arm but tramping across the Americas for the sake of a single orchid, the intrepid von Warscewicz hunkering down in the wildest Colombian floods with his foul-smelling guide—I've wanted to be a field collector. For me, it's the chase, the challenge. If I have only the foggiest idea of what I'm looking for, nothing grabs my gut more than trying to track it down in the middle of a choking jungle. And the tougher the job, the better.

"What else you got for me, Ladybug?" he asked.

I spread five plastic sleeves across the table like a winning flush. As I named the powdery seeds inside them, Scooter's smile got wider and wider until I thought his jaw must hurt.

"Marian!" he called. "Take these into the greenhouse office for me."

"The plant, too?" she asked, sweeping up the sleeves.

"No." He caressed the orchid's pot with a tremorless hand. "I wanna look at it for a while." He raised his liquid gaze to my face. "I'm glad you came to see me, Ladybug."

"Me, too, Scooter."

An hour later, I watched Scooter row himself to the office

for his late-afternoon nap. Marian hovered over him like a hummingbird, carrying his orchid.

"His Parkinson's is getting worse," I said to Hank, "and his color's bad. His skin's gone gray. He was barely stage three when I left and now he seems like he's gone all the way to stage four. Have you talked him into seeing the specialist yet?"

Hank tapped his beer bottle on its coaster. "You managed to do that your last visit." He took a deep breath, his barrel chest broadening under a short beard just starting to grizzle, his craggy face grim.

"Thank God. One more trip to that witch doctor and I thought he'd start howling at the moon."

"He's dyin', Jess."

I waited a few seconds for him to add *just kiddin'*. Or to say that we're all dying and Scooter is seventy-four, after all, so he's just a little ahead of the game.

But when he continued, Hank said, "The doctors gave him a cocktail that was supposed to help the Parkinson's, but it's damaged his heart."

"Okay, so they can fix that—"

"It's irreversible."

Tears stung the backs of my eyes. "Is that what the cardiovascular surgeon said?"

"It's what a team of specialists—heart surgeons and neurologists—said."

"They took an oath," I protested. "What happened to 'do no harm'?"

"They did their best."

"No, they didn't. They broke him." My gut tightened. I knew the question to ask, but waited until I wouldn't cry when I asked it. "How long?" I said finally.

"A month at the outside."

After the next wave of pain passed, I asked, "What are they going to do?"

Hank shook his head, squeezing my hand once before letting go. "Nothin'. He's too old." Before I could get up a good head of steam, he added, "He wouldn't let 'em do anything about it now even if they wanted to. You know him."

"Yeah, I do. He'd rather waste his time and money carrying around rabbit's feet and drinking herbal concoctions Old Lady Fenster cooked up in her backyard than take a vitamin." I shoved away from the table and stood. "I need to have a talk with that old bat."

Hank grabbed my arm. "Don't, Jess. There's nothin' wrong with what she was doing. It may not have helped him, but it didn't hurt him none, neither."

"Didn't hurt him? You mean when he didn't go to the doctor early enough to get help or when she gave him false hope that she could stop the Parkinson's?"

"It's Scooter's choice. It always has been."

His grip felt like iron, completely unlike Scooter's feeble grasp earlier. The contrast made my throat ache. "She had no right filling his head with that crap," I said. "If he'd listened to me years ago and gone to a doctor then, they could have prescribed L-dopa to slow the symptoms."

"It's more complicated than that," Hank replied, his voice soft. He let go of me as I sat back down to listen. "This drug treatment they gave him is in trials."

I stared at him for a moment while my brain struggled to work. "He let them *experiment* on him?"

"Only because he's already so far gone. But now they know more about the side effects—"

"Let me get this straight," I snapped. "The doctors turned a non-life-threatening disease into a death sentence because they wanted to test a cocktail that hasn't seen FDA approval yet. And when that clinical trial failed, they decided to wash their hands of him and let him die because he's old. Is that what you're telling me?"

Hank's shuttered expression told me I was wasting my breath. He was a bottom-line kind of guy, but I guess the bottom line I'd reached didn't sit well with him.

"Look," I argued, "I just wanted him to see if anything could be done. Not to throw himself into a bad science experiment."

Hank nodded thoughtfully with the air of a parent letting his ten-year-old finish up a tantrum. It pissed me off. I clutched my sweat-slick beer bottle as he said, "He's a grown man, Jessie. He's gonna do what he's gonna do. It's not up to you to go tearing up Old Lady Fenster or parade over to San Antone to yell at the doctors. Especially since he's been workin' with 'em ever since you left."

My radar went off. San Antonio wasn't the Parkinson's capital of Texas. Houston was.

"Talk to me about San Antone," I said, shedding my anger a hair. "Why'd he go there?"

Hank toyed with a coaster. I knew I wasn't going to like what came out of his mouth. "Your great-uncle decided last year he'd check into a cure on his own. He found a lab that was workin' on one and talked to 'em."

My heart sank. "Don't tell me. They agreed to make him a guinea pig." At his nod, I added, "And he chose them because they're using an extract of some damned insect saliva in the formula."

Hank looked at his hands as he said, "They're still workin' on the cure. The head guy at the lab, Dr. Thompson, he said the drug had been tested on mice okay. The San Antone fellas just need a little more time."

I got mad all over again. "It doesn't sound like they have time. What's this outfit called?"

"Cradion Pharmaceutical."

"And they're hooked up to Scooter's regular doctors how?" I demanded.

"They offered the trial drug and assigned Dr. Thompson to his case. His G.P. just oversees his checkups."

"Did his insurance pick up the cost?"

"Not much of it. The Slapdash is mortgaged up to its neck."

I bit my lip. Damned old fool and his damned fool ideas. "He should've paid a hit man. It would've been cheaper and faster."

"Ever'body did their level best, Jessie. Sometimes it just don't work out."

"I should have tried harder."

"We all could have."

"No. I mean I should have gone to court, got him declared incompetent, and then put him in decent care when he was first diagnosed. I should have been here to make sure the doctors were going to help him, not hurt him."

Hank stared at me, mouth tightening with what might have been anger. "He'd never forgive you for doing that to him. You got no call to be trying to run his life when he's still kickin' around like a mean old hoss." His bearded chin stuck out a little as he said, "He wouldn't have tried to tell *you* what to do."

I waited for Hank to finish. Behind him, the band's guitar player slipped the strap over his head and twanged a string, prompting a pretty brunette in tight jeans and boots to drag her man onto the scraped-up dance floor. A group of cowboys in the corner laughed over a hand of cards.

When Hank ran out of things to say, I stood. "See you around." I headed for the door.

"Jessie," he warned.

"It's okay. I won't bother anybody." I threw a few bucks on the bar for Marian on my way out.

On the porch, cool wind brushed my cheeks. Only then did I feel the sticky wetness of tears. The man I knew as a father was dying because he was too stubborn to do anything else. A homeopath had given him false hope and some bogus pharmaceutical company had made him a guinea pig and thanked him for it by killing him.

But I was the one who hadn't been here. I hadn't done what needed to be done.

If anybody had put the first nail in Scooter's coffin, it was me.

Chapter 2

Hammarbya paludosa. The Bog Orchid. Officially extinct in Britain, the last wild one had been stolen in December of 2001 from a secret site in the Yorkshire Dales and sold on the black market, probably for around ten grand.

Normally when you think of orchids, you think of the gorgeous, vibrantly colored petals of *Phalaenopsis,* or the pure seduction of *Paphiopedilum,* commonly known as lady's slipper. Orchids are the most blatantly sexual flowers of any on earth, rampant in their attractions, decadent in their enticements.

The Bog Orchid is a runt. It's a dull stunted foxglove of an orchid—long spikes studded with greenish, waxy-looking leaves that are actually flowers. Ugly thing.

Kew Gardens never succeeded in reproducing it despite their best efforts. There may be a few in Northern Ireland, but no one's saying if or where.

Most orchid collectors have a couple of rare orchids like this one to trot out at flowering parties and green their guests with envy. The idea is to have lots of different orchids to show one's taste, one's style, one's sensibilities.

Linus Geraint Newark von Brutten III has over fifty Bog Orchids.

I knew because in the thirty minutes I'd been kept waiting in Building 6, I'd counted them: fifty-seven ugly plants, fifty-seven ugly flowering spikes, 942 ugly flowers.

Tardiness is the privilege of the billionaire who feeds me. Ordinarily I wouldn't mind. It kept us honest; we always knew where we stood. But von Brutten had pulled me away from Scooter, and I was ready to get this show on the road. In the time I'd not been counting, I'd been mulling over how to tell him I wasn't going on a fishing expedition for him, at least not while Scooter was still around.

"Dr. Robards."

I turned. A bow-tied, black-jacketed butler stood in the greenhouse's doorway. His high forehead sprouted a light humidity sheen. The Bog Orchid does need, after all, a bog.

"Hullo, Sims," I said. "How's it going?"

He bowed. "Mr. von Brutten requests your presence in the morning room."

Well, hell. That'd be a twenty-minute walk. "Then why did he send me here when I arrived?"

"I am afraid I cannot say, Dr. Robards, but I am sorry for the inconvenience."

I wondered if all butlers were taught to speak without either expression or gesticulation. Sims might be being truthful about what he didn't know, or he might not, and I'd never know. Couldn't help but like the guy. "Lead on," I said.

Von Brutten's estate, fancifully called Parsifal, was a sprawling thousand-acre ranch fetched up against a low ridge about an hour outside Spokane, Washington. The ranch had two lakes and a great view of the Columbia River. I'd been in about half of von Brutten's greenhouses, Buildings 1 through

9. The other half he kept to himself. It rankled, not being trusted. But if I'd been robbed blind for my plants as often as he had, I might be a little picky about my buddies, too. The only reason I knew those greenhouses were there was because I'd seen the satellite photos. Sometimes it helps to date the right people.

When it came down to it, as much as I hated to admit it, I owed Daley for getting me this job. My first year out of grad school, I managed to track down *Cattleya turneris* in Costa Rica, a rare blue orchid the year blue was all the rage in collecting circles. Plucked it right out from under Daley's nose, in fact. I got the call from von Brutten within a day of arriving back in the States: he wanted to hire me as Daley's replacement. "Daley," von Brutten had breathed over the phone line, "has not lived up to expectations." I'd been collecting for von Brutten ever since.

The morning room faced east, and light cast down through the glass roof for only a couple of hours. I liked this room because it opened onto a little shade garden surrounding an irregularly shaped man-made pond. Von Brutten's orders must have been to make the garden look like a jungle, with its bowing palms and water-loving bromeliads. It didn't. This garden looked like a place you'd want to rest in, maybe take a nap.

The word *jungle* is from the Sanskrit *jangala,* meaning "impenetrable." The jungle smothers you with noise and odors and fear. Its trees tower, woody vines dangle, insects bite, birds screech, monkeys howl, jaguars stalk, and the whole time heat rises through the air like somebody threw water on a griddle. You don't penetrate the jungle. It penetrates you.

"Dr. Robards," Sims announced, his deep voice echoing under all the glass.

Were he true to the stereotype, von Brutten would have been huddled over a *Dendrobium,* clutching a watering can and muttering diabolically to himself about humidity. Instead, he relaxed his small, elegantly suited frame into a Lucien Rollin chair and smiled a frosty smile over his silk jabot.

"Dr. Robards," he breathed. "Please, sit and enjoy a little something." He snapped his fingers. Food and juice appeared, carried by silent bow-tied wait staff.

"Just tea for me, thanks."

A French press of tea sat at my elbow. *Poof.* Just like that. Maybe *money* was the secret of Houdini.

"Did you enjoy your flight?"

"I always enjoy the Lear, thanks," I said. "Very nice."

While we traded meaningless social niceties, I studied him. His pale, even features seemed vaguely threatening in repose, but I'd gotten used to that. He resembled the guy who'd share his last smoke with you before smiling benignly and dropping you headfirst into a shark tank. Small eyes, aquiline nose, a thin-lipped mouth, a closely trimmed goatee. In some circles he might be considered genteelly attractive. I didn't move in those circles. As far as I knew, there was no Mrs. von Brutten, nor was there a boy-toy wandering around. Von Brutten appeared to be either extremely celibate or extremely circumspect.

Or maybe he just got his rocks off pollinating nearly extinct orchid species.

After he asked me a polite question about my limo ride from Spokane to Parsifal, I realized he was desperately excited about something.

The more excited he was, the less likely he was to act that way. But I needed him to hurry up so I could get back to Scooter. The trick was to hustle him up without appearing to want to.

"Your jet's much nicer than the crate I took out of Micronesia," I said casually. I wished I smoked, so I could blow a stream negligently into the air while glancing away.

"A successful trip." His hand strayed in the general direction of Building 3, where the siblings to Scooter's *Phalaen-opsis* were being studied in a high-tech laboratory.

"I'm glad to hear it."

"Did you…have fun…in Micronesia?"

I shrugged carelessly. "I ran into Mrs. Thurston-Fitzhugh's errand boy."

"And you took care of him."

"He came away empty-handed, as usual."

A smile fled across von Brutten's silvery eyes.

I waited. You can't push someone like von Brutten too hard. And he was enjoying my news too much for me to rush him. Mrs. Thurston-Fitzhugh had consistently beaten him to the punch until I came along, and von Brutten had made sure I knew he was pleased with my performance. My ability to outwit and outcollect the handful of professional field collectors in the world meant von Brutten stayed top dog in the insulated and obsessive world of ultra-high-dollar orchid collecting. We had a gentleman's agreement: he paid me generously and I didn't work for anyone else.

The ten or so other professionals tended to freelance, sometimes for private collectors like von Brutten and sometimes for legitimate botanical institutions. Not that the institutions would admit to being party to breaking the CITES Treaty. The only other monogamous employer-hunter relationship I knew of was Mrs. Constance Thurston-Fitzhugh and Lawrence Daley.

I sipped my excellent tea, poured for me by someone I hadn't noticed.

An irregular chuffing noise started up from von Brutten's direction. I glanced over to see him holding an embroidered handkerchief to his mouth. His eyes wrinkled at the corners. Was he choking? I nearly got up to administer the Heimlich, but the chuffing stopped and he removed the hanky from his mouth.

Laughing. He'd been laughing at my dumping Daley. I felt bizarrely honored.

"Hmm," he said, then surprised the hell out of me by saying, "Tell me about your great-uncle."

"He's not your business," I replied.

"He's ailing, is he not?" Von Brutten's left hand twisted a gold ring around his right hand's index finger. "Victim of a pharmaceutical experiment?"

"That's not—"

"It's a shame that someone who raised you after your parents died—car accident, wasn't it?—should now be facing imminent death as well as the loss of everything he owns."

I stood up, tossed the linen napkin onto the table. "Thanks for the Earl Grey. I'm glad you liked your flowers." I walked toward the door.

"I know what it's like to lose all of one's family," he called.

He could go screw himself. I kept walking.

"My sources tell me Cradion has a record of concealing its failures no matter the cost." And when I didn't stop, he added, "I can repair the damage they did to your uncle."

I spun. There was no point in shouting *How do you know about Cradion? How do you know about Scooter?* because of course this was Linus Geraint Newark von Brutten III. I kept my mouth shut and glared at him instead.

He inclined his head toward me. A conciliatory gesture. "But I need your help to do so."

"Surprise me."

"Bring me back the Death Orchid and I'll see your great-uncle has the best chance at living out his full span of years."

"What do you mean?"

"It's everything it's rumored to be." He spread his hands as he said, "It's the elixir of life."

He was out of his mind. As nuts as Lawrence Daley and his nutty high-society employer. As nuts as any nutty botanist, taxonomist, or nursery owner who longed for glory in the insulated, isolated, nutty world of rare orchid collecting.

Before I could open my mouth, von Brutten said, "I have proof the orchid exists."

He snapped his fingers. Sims glided in with a thick padded envelope, laid it on the table, bowed and vanished.

"Please." Von Brutten's long fingers gestured to the envelope. "See for yourself."

I didn't budge. "What about Cradion? What proof do you have of their wrongdoing?"

"Let me handle Cradion."

Fair enough. My agenda was pretty narrow. "What will you do for my uncle?"

"I have controlling interest in Lexicran Pharmaceuticals, which directly competes with Cradion. I can…encourage…a particular kind of research."

"You're way behind. Cradion's already in phase two trials. The drug'll be on the market in no time."

"My company has been developing a similar treatment for Parkinson's."

"Maybe so, but my great-uncle's problems are a little bigger than that now."

"A Parkinson's cure is not the only endeavor my company pursues. Heart medications, like the one that may restore your guardian's damaged tissues, are also of interest to us. The Death Orchid is the difference between our drug getting FDA approval in two years and Cradion killing off more old people."

"You just want to see Cradion go down the tubes so your company won't have any competition. You don't care about its ethics. Or the Parkinson's patients."

Von Brutten's silver eyes flashed with what might have been humor. "Of course I don't. I care about the bottom line. So do you. You only want your guardian to survive. You don't care about the patients who might die because Cradion can pull the wool over the FDA's eyes."

"That's pretty harsh," I began, but he kept going.

"Stop pretending we're not the same, Dr. Robards. If you were perfectly honest with yourself, you might find you don't even care that much about your great-uncle because you're too busy hating Cradion."

"Bullshit!" I reached for the doorknob.

He raised his voice. "I can take Cradion down with your help. And save the old man."

The door handle's coldness penetrated my palm. I was too much of a pragmatist to obsess over ethics or consequences, but I resented his assumption that my hatred of Cradion overshadowed my love for Scooter. Being successful had made von Brutten arrogant. And offensive. On the other hand, experience had taught me he was also a man of his word, twisted as it was.

He turned my pragmatism against me to get what he wanted: the Death Orchid. And he'd use my bottom line—Scooter's life—to get it.

Damn.

I let go of the doorknob. "Show me," I said.

"The Death Orchid is real. I'm told it contains the compounds necessary to create a lifesaving heart medication."

"Terence Harrison published a paper that refuted claims the Death Orchid exists."

He inclined his head. "He did so at my request."

"You mean he *lied?*"

"I mean he massaged the data so we could continue our work with the plant unmolested by competitors. But that's old news, Dr. Robards. My researcher ran out of specimens for testing and I need you to bring me another." His lips quirked. "Or two."

He opened the envelope and slid its contents onto the table as I walked over to see what he had. It wasn't much. A blood-streaked, ripped-out page of a spiral notebook. A brass key.

I raised one eyebrow at him.

"Harrison's last work," he replied.

"Harrison's been on sabbatical for a year."

"I know. He was working for me."

"What?" My brain struggled. "Harrison isn't the kind of guy to give up his precious scientific detachment to squander his talents in a commercial effort."

Von Brutten beamed a pitying look my direction. "If you only knew how many idealistic academics I have on my payroll. Harrison was your mentor, wasn't he?"

I nodded. "Plant Biology, specializing in taxonomy and biochemistry. And he works for you now?"

"He did, yes."

"Did?"

"May still do. I'm not sure."

"Why not?"

"He's missing."

A chill shot through my gut. The mild-mannered and anal-retentive Dr. Harrison was physically no match for one of Scooter's nursing home girlfriends, much less a hired thug. The shock subsided a little in time for anger to take over. Harrison was harmless. They didn't have to get rough, whoever *they* were.

I turned the notebook page over, studying the brown stain's irregular edges sprawled on top of scribbled black ink. The writing beneath was illegible, partly because of the blood and partly because of Harrison's trademark chicken scratch and the torturous, self-invented shorthand he'd used. Shorthand I'd spent long hours deciphering, keying his lab observations into the best taxonomy and morphology database in the country.

My mind flashed on Harrison's characteristic fastidiousness, his fondness for bow ties and cheap cologne, his weirdly pale green eyes. Dedicated to the cause. He wouldn't work for von Brutten unless he had to, no matter what von Brutten had said. I'd sat through too many ad hoc lectures about ethics and the purity of intellectual scientific pursuit to believe otherwise.

But there was that day I'd come back to his office early from lunch and settled down in my cubicle to catch up on some tedious cataloging. Over the high wall that separated my desk from Harrison's, I heard the door snick shut and him pace quickly to his desk. We worked in silence for a few minutes until I popped up from behind my cube to ask a question. His desk faced mine. Behind it, he stared intently at his computer screen, like a kid lost in a video game. When I spoke, his eyes snapped to mine and his face flushed. Caught. I couldn't understand what he said to me then, he was stuttering so badly. It'd taken most of the day for his hands to stop shaking and his face to resume its normal pallor.

I'd never cared to know what he was looking at and I still didn't. All I knew was that beneath the hard core scientist lurked something weak, maybe even shameful. But hell, we all had our weaknesses, our frailties. What had happened to make Harrison sell out his principles, to work for someone like von Brutten? To possibly get him killed? The anger took on an edge of sadness as I ran a finger over the stain's edge.

"Harrison's blood, perhaps," von Brutten offered.

"And he's missing." I swallowed. "Or do you really mean dead?"

"Kidnapped is another option."

Great. I was not Nancy Drew. "Right," I said, "and he could have nicked himself with a penknife, thought, 'to hell with it,' and is now stretched out in a hammock in Belize. I can't find him based on this information."

Von Brutten pressed his silk hanky to his upper lip. "Dr. Harrison's whereabouts don't interest me, Dr. Robards. I want you to find another Death Orchid."

"You want me to find a phantom orchid at the possible expense of my life, Mr. von Brutten. I know you play your cards close to the vest but I need you to flash me an ace here." His mild eyes flickered when I looked at him hard and asked, "Is Harrison dead?"

"I honestly don't know. He hasn't reported in, and this is what was brought to me when I made inquiries."

It wasn't brain surgery to figure out the henchmen von Brutten had sent hadn't found either Harrison or Harrison's corpse. "Is this the best your goons could do?" I waved the page. "Where's the rest? And what's it from?"

"It's from the project notebook he used during new lab tests. He was double-checking his initial results before heading into the field to obtain another Death Orchid. My associates didn't find the notebook."

So whoever did something, whatever it was, with Harrison probably had the bulk of the research. I struggled with the image of Harrison frumping around the forest, red bow tie and green cardigan, a trowel in one hand and bug spray in the other. As far as I knew, the closest he'd ever gotten to a jungle was a springtime stroll through Edgerton Park.

"Where is 'the field'?" I demanded. "South America? Africa? The Pacific Rim?"

"I don't know."

"That's crap. If the Death Orchid was so important to you, you'd know where it could be found."

"Dr. Harrison disappeared before he could convey that information to me. He was working in San Antonio." Von Brutten picked up the brass key and dangled it from his elegant thumb and forefinger like a gift. Or bait. "His lab."

"Will whoever jumped him be waiting for me when I get there?"

Von Brutten's shoulders lifted a quarter of an inch, then dropped. A shrug, I interpreted.

"For a guy who knows everything, you don't know much,"

I informed him. "You know what happened to him, and you know whether I'll be next if I use this key."

The smile that briefly tipped up the corners of his lips chilled my blood. "You won't be next. After all, I'm counting on you to bring back my orchid."

His orchid. Right. Keep your priorities straight, girl. This ain't 'bout nothin' but the flower. Remembering that might keep me alive.

"You do know Thurston-Fitzhugh knows you're after it," I said.

Von Brutten's sculpted eyebrows rose slightly. "A leak." The brief flash of steel in his eyes said heads would roll within the hour. "There is a detail of which you should be aware," he added.

I didn't like it already. "What's that?"

"My lab will require a week to produce the serum that will save your great-uncle."

Fear clutched my stomach, choked my lungs. "And my great-uncle will last a month at the outside. So you're telling me I have a little over two weeks to figure out what Harrison knew, get to wherever he was headed, find the orchid and then get back?"

Von Brutten shrugged. "Sixteen days, technically, if you leave today. And if the old man hangs on."

Shit.

There was no way. Finding a plant you'd never seen took months, not days. But I had to try.

"You have copies of these things?" I asked as I shoved the evidence back in its envelope.

His smile suggested I was terribly naive. "Have a good trip, Dr. Robards. Keep me informed. I'll have the lab on standby, awaiting your return."

I leveled a look at him meant to tell him bad things would happen if he didn't honor that promise. His own expression was mild, vaguely fatherly, the look of a man who had nothing to lose.

And because I had everything to lose, I grabbed the envelope and left.

Not one to walk into trouble blind, I decided to call in a couple of favors before heading to Harrison's lab. In a previous life, I'd done a little contract work for the CIA, helping them with the Danube violet poison case. Nearly getting killed then would come in handy now: this particular science office owed me some serious favors. I planned to get the straight story on Cradion Pharmaceutical and my missing graduate advisor. If anybody could dig up the real dirt, it was these guys. After a short conversation with the Man In Charge about some pharmaceutical industry snooping, I took the elevator to the basement to find Marcus Donovan.

Marcus's wizardry with all things clinical had broken the Danube case open wide and made him the leading expert on plant-based poisons. Before the CIA wags could start speculating on my joining their little hazplant team and before Marcus could start speculating on whether I'd move in with him, I'd bailed. As far as I was concerned, getting involved with *anything* for the long haul was bad news. This time I needed to keep things between me and Marcus professional.

I had to remind myself of that as I leaned in his lab's doorway, watching him do his secret agent thing. Tall, he had to lean way over to look through his microscope, spilling locks of long, black hair over his forehead. His broad, white-coated shoulders made him look more like a sanitarium orderly than a scientist. His movements were large but precise. The impression I got was of a pro running back repairing an antique watch.

He must have sensed my presence because he said, "Not you again," without looking up.

I waved the plastic envelope von Brutten had given me,

Harrison's bloodstained page safely sealed inside, and pushed off from the doorjamb.

The lab was stainless steel, glass, and bitterly cold. I wished I'd brought a sweater. Maybe it was why Marcus and his crew were confined to the CIA's basement, leaving the innocuous, stucco-fronted HQ upstairs looking more like the San Antonio Visitors Bureau than the software company it purported to be.

"How'd you get in here?" He removed the slide from the microscope and filed it carefully in sequence on a tray.

"Everybody in this office owes me for the Danube incident."

Marcus looked up finally, meeting my gaze. "I think I've already paid my dues."

My face went hot. "You're right," I admitted.

"You could at least have left a note on my pillow." His keen blue eyes sharpened. "A Dear John works better for me than a vanishing act."

I nodded. I needed to apologize—for leaving without saying goodbye, for being scared, for hopping in the sack with him in the first place—but the words stuck somewhere around the base of my throat. *Dear Marcus, I'm sorry I'm a selfish bitch. I'm sorry I left after one night and never looked back.*

He nodded, apparently accepting the words I didn't say. A deep breath later, he relaxed into his old teasing ways. I was forgiven. "What'd you do to your hair?"

I shrugged, felt the ponytail just brush my shoulder. "I needed a change."

"You see the boss?"

"I did indeed. He wished me well."

"He wished you to hell, you mean."

"Yeah, but only after I've got what I came for. He's checking into a pharmaceutical company for me."

"A pharma?"

"It's personal."

He nodded, taking that in and leaving it alone. "I thought you'd moved far, far away," Marcus said, rounding the gleaming worktable and smiling a little as he did it.

He was still a hunk, but I wasn't here to resurrect ghosts. "I did. Now I'm back."

"For how long?" He crossed one muscular arm over the other, prompting a nice burn of remembrance in my sweet spot.

"Long enough for you to tell me what this is." I handed him the plastic envelope.

He took it, glanced at the page. "It's a new excuse for not having your homework."

"I'm serious."

When Marcus smiled, that dimple quirked in his cheek.

"I'm really serious," I said firmly, trying to ignore the dimple. "This is evidence and I need to read what's under the blood."

He exhaled loudly for my benefit. "All right." He pulled the page out of its protective plastic to examine it. "I don't see how you can read this scribble even if I can clean it up." He frowned. "But it's not blood. It's something else."

"What?"

"I'll have to get back to you."

"I'm short on time," I said. "Can you at least make the writing visible?"

"Wait here." He went through a side door that had a red bulb over the doorway, like a photography dark room.

While I waited, I took out Harrison's brass key. Under the harsh lab lighting, the key looked crisp around the edges, like it'd been superimposed on my vision. I evaluated what I knew at this point. Harrison had set up a research lab in San Antonio and worked on some kind of miracle cure for von Brutten. Whoever had kidnapped or killed Harrison had probably already been to his lab since von Brutten's henchmen had come up with nothing more useful than the stained page Marcus was working on. If the bad guys had taken Harrison's project notebook, that meant they had some idea of what they were looking for. But as far as I knew, there weren't that many assassin botanists running around, so I stood a chance of finding something the bad guys wouldn't think important. Otherwise, I'd have to widen my search to Harrison's house.

The dark room door opened and Marcus came back with what looked like a Photostat on clear film. It was.

"Here's the page sans blood as best I can get it for now. If you want to know what the blood actually is, that'll take a little time." He leaned his hip against the lab table and smiled charmingly at me. "Can I call you?"

"Better leave me a voice mail," I said, handing him my card. "I'm in a hurry."

I froze, my hands in Harrison's drawers.

Down the town house's single flight of stairs, low voices burbled. Men's voices. Two of them. Steps creaked as the men climbed up. Fortunately, I'd pushed the upstairs bedroom door nearly shut before starting my little rampage through my old mentor's underwear.

My luck never runs good for long. They must be cops. Had someone seen me breaking and entering an expensive condo in broad daylight?

The men passed up the bedroom and went directly into the home office across the hall, like they knew where they were going. Shuffling, papers flipping, footsteps. They weren't cops. Harrison's latest graduate students, maybe? Did they work in his lab? Something glass shattered on a hard surface and one of the men cursed.

"Shut up!" the other hissed.

"Why? Nobody's home." A pause. "It stinks in here."

"So?"

"It's gross."

"Keep your voice down. Leave that alone and help me look through these binders. It's got to be here somewhere."

I straightened. Funny how fear evaporates when I know the other guy is just as much in the wrong as I am. It kind of levels the moral playing field. Gives a girl back her spunk.

The Dr. Terence Jasper Harrison I knew was a Grade-A neatnik. A place for everything and everything in its place. His office could have been the poster child for anal, scientific academia. He didn't go out looking for plants; plants came to him to be studied to death.

One look at Harrison's lab on San Antonio's north side an hour ago had told me he'd either gone off his meds or the bad guys had beaten me there. After scrounging around the broken glass, strewn papers and emptied specimen cabinets, I'd gotten out before the cops could show up and pin the damage on me.

Next stop: his downtown two-story condo, where I now knelt, up to my elbows in socks carefully bundled into color-coded piles, except for a mateless stray exiled to the bottom right corner.

The second-floor home office now being ransacked by the jokers had yielded nothing for me but a bunch of old notebooks, an array of dried specimens, a few bottles of herbs in preservative alcohol, and one very nasty dead mouse behind the bookcase. Dr. Harrison had been out for some time. Nothing even remotely resembling a clue had been left behind.

That was my advantage in having been his graduate assistant. I knew he may have kept his technical notes in his office, but he always kept a memento of his current big find close to home. Kind of like a souvenir. Or a security blanket. Or a good-luck charm.

Hence the sock drawer. Alas, nothing but socks. I took another look around.

Harrison's full-size bed sported a manly plaid bedspread undimpled by hands or head. The plain oak nightstand was held down by two neat stacks of books, biology texts in one and true crimes in the other. The oak dresser sat forlornly against the near wall, its surface empty except for a lone comb, a homemade ashtray and a fine layer of dust.

I flipped silently through the books on the nightstand. Nothing. The nightstand didn't have a drawer. The stray sock's mate lay limp under the bed. I felt between the mattresses but came up with nothing. I picked up the heavy wooden ashtray, hoping for a key underneath. Nada.

I was about to put the ashtray back when its design caught my eye. The pattern under the varnish gleamed pearlescent black on matte black, almost like raku. Had they smoked the wood somehow to make it look like that? I looked closer. The ashtray was homemade all right, but not by Harrison's niece in art class. The inside bottom bore a miniature stylized jaguar pawprint.

Last time I saw something like that was in an ethnobotany presentation on how particular plants and herbs had been used for hundreds of years by shamans. Into the bowl goes crushed leaves and monkey spit, out comes a medicine to cure earache. The bowl itself was blessed by the shaman. A blessed bowl imbued the plant matter ground in it with magical powers.

Harrison wasn't the type of guy to keep knickknacks around, not even precious mementos from past projects. Hell, there was barely anything in the condo that didn't look like standard hotel fare. And Harrison didn't smoke.

The bowl's presence suggested two things: First, Harrison really *had* been in the field to collect the Death Orchid and brought this little talisman back recently, as a souvenir. Second, if I could find out where the bowl came from, I could figure out where Harrison had found the orchid.

The bowl fit in my shoulder bag. Now to wait until the jokers left.

"We could get Noah to go after the orchid, you know," one

said to the other. It sounded like he was standing in the office doorway.

"I don't want to pay him if I don't have to."

"Well, no, but why should we have to contract malaria when we can hire someone else to do it?"

Indeed. I'd often asked myself the same question. My answer was always that I knew my job better than anyone else. These clowns might be after the Death Orchid, but they were probably armchair botanists. Sort of like Harrison without the single-minded pursuit of taxonomic perfection. This Noah guy might be another collector for hire, like me or Lawrence Daley. Heck, these guys might even be locals working for Constance Thurston-Fitzhugh, trying to track down the Death Orchid for her.

As it was, Noah was a nice alias. Most of us used stage names to hide our identities from Fish and Wildlife and Customs. I'd already had six last names in the past three years, with passports to match. "Robards" was my favorite so far. I'd hate giving it up in a few months.

Then there was a crash and thunk, like they'd pulled the desk apart. Scrabbling. A creak. Nails being ripped from boards.

"Wait, I've got it!" the one inside the office said.

"This isn't a map—"

"No shit, Sherlock."

Silence for a long moment. Annoyance flared in my chest. It was unfair. So I'm not Nancy Drew. I got here *first*. I just don't bust up the furniture to find the loot.

"What are all the numbers?" the whiner asked.

"He wrote everything in code. I'll get one of his students to translate it. Let's go."

"So we don't need Noah?" the whiner asked as they passed the bedroom on their way out.

"Not if this turns out to be a map."

I waited until they closed the front door to slip downstairs after them. They headed off the condo's grounds and further into town, toward the River Walk. I followed, playing native San Antonian out for an early evening stroll.

The one I assumed was the Whiner was a thin little guy about my height sporting a bad haircut and a limp. The other one, the Brain of the outfit, needed to take an iron to his Dockers and was losing his hair in back. He was kind of cute if a girl could ignore the haughty look he threw at her as he shrugged on his light windbreaker. Jerk.

They crossed the Crockett Street Bridge and dropped down to the River Walk below, where the trees, flowering shrubs and flowing green water lowered the temperature several degrees. I hadn't been on the Paseo del Rio since the Danube case three years ago, but a glance at a walk map refreshed my memory. The restaurants and shops might have changed hands, but the river itself was still the same.

Fair enough. The dinner crowd was just picking up. Bumping into the Brain and the Whiner would be a cinch.

I eased down the stone steps to the Paseo del Rio, letting them get a little ahead so I could judge their purpose without being spotted. It seemed weird that they would have lifted the map leading to the Death Orchid and then just meandered down the River Walk for an evening meal. Where was their sense of professional urgency? Maybe I was feeling enough urgency—because of Scooter—for all three of us.

They stopped at a pink oleander-shaded menu stand and stood with their hands in their pockets, browsing. A gang of teenagers migrated past, jostling the Brain, who glanced up in annoyance. Then his attention went back to the menu.

Better to approach them one at a time. The Brain walked on. The Whiner lingered over the appetizers. I strode forward, turned my head to look at Boudro's Texas Bistro, and gave the Whiner a full-frontal press.

"Oh, I'm sorry," I spewed, smiling my sweetest smile as I pawed his trousers as though trying to cop a feel while maneuvering my shoulder bag. Nothing in his pockets. The map had to be on the Brain.

"That's all right." The poor guy looked almost grateful to have been groped.

Then the Brain turned to look for his buddy and stared me in the face. His eyes widened. He clearly recognized me from somewhere, but I had no idea where. His face—innocuous, bland, shocked—meant nothing to me. In a split second, he pivoted and sprinted away, one hand reaching for his left windbreaker pocket.

Eureka.

"Hey! Wait!" the Whiner yelled behind us.

The Brain didn't slow. He dodged through the walking crowd alongside the river like a freshman running back. I got hung up around a waiter carrying a tray of steaming seafood, slid underneath his arm, and took off again. The Brain's distinctive bobbing head kept me posted amid the sun visors, suits and golf shirts.

He abruptly turned up a steep stone staircase to Commerce Street. I took the steps two at a time, jostling a bevy of well-dressed tourists and earning a chorus of "Hey!" A guy wearing a navy sports jacket and a power tie with green accents—not a good combo—grabbed my arm but I twisted free. The interference slowed me down enough to let the Brain make the street without me and lose himself in the shopping crowd spilling onto the sidewalk.

Damn.

I jogged further south, thinking he wouldn't be so stupid as to double back to pick up the Whiner. At the Market and Alamo intersection, I came upon another set of steps leading down to the River Walk. From the Market Street bridge, I could see a good bit of the river and the people walking along

both sides of it. On the north side, not much happening except for a maintenance barge puttering south and a bright
pink river barge loading up with dinner passengers. On the
south side, the terraced Arneson River Theater seats had filled
up with spectators for whatever was going on onstage across
the river, which was loud salsa....

Bingo.

Thinning hair, beige windbreaker, and a furtive look over
one shoulder. Had he not looked, I'd have had to think twice.
I swung down the stairs, jumping the rail on the last five steps
to land next to a startled restaurant hostess with flaming red
hair and a Clinique-ly perfect face.

"Sorry," I mumbled.

I was nearly on him when the Brain caught sight of me and
bolted toward the stage. On it, several brilliantly costumed
Mexican dancers wheeled in some traditional hoedown. Mariachis jammed on a little platform behind the dancers. Across
the river, spectators sprawled on the terraced seats leading up
a steep hillside. A tourist barge moseyed in our direction, the
driver giving the usual historical spiel as he steered his boat
between the stage and the seating area.

Perfect place for a takedown.

The Brain jumped a barricade blocking off any pedestri-
ans who might wander onto the stage and caught his trailing
foot on the wood. He nearly fell, taking the barricade with
him. Great. He was tiring. I sprinted over the downed barricade. He catapulted onto the stage. The crowd gasped. I
jumped up after him. Dancers scattered like gorgeous tropical birds spooked by a cat. A running leap and I tackled him,
shoving him down face first onto the wooden flooring.

"Gotcha!" I shouted over the mariachis. The Brain wriggled like a worm on a hook. "Hold still a minute, will ya?" I
reached for his map pocket.

I caught a glimpse of dark green uniform in my peripheral

vision as the Brain wrenched himself loose, throwing a much lighter me to one side. I scrambled to my feet. Dark green uniform meant the Parks and Wildlife cops. The dancers faded back when I lit out after the Brain again, chasing him up the walk toward Presa Street.

The Brain threw a frightened glance back at me and then did something I'll never forget: he jumped from the sidewalk onto the oncoming river barge, skidded behind the driver, hopped from there onto a maintenance scow headed the other direction, and then finished with a mad leap to the other sidewalk. A second later and the boats had passed each other, leaving me looking at twelve feet of water between us.

Nice trick. And there wasn't a footpath close enough to cut him off. I watched him scramble up a retaining wall. He disappeared.

The dark green uniforms pounded my way, so I took a page from the Brain's book and skedaddled up an ivy-covered wall. On the other side, I sprinted over Market Street to the River Bend parking garage and my first floor Rent-A-Wreck. Thirty seconds later I motored sedately out into evening traffic.

Only after I knew I wasn't being followed did I pull over so I could study the paper the Brain had so graciously given up, unbeknownst to him, in our scuffle amid the gorgeous dancers.

Harrison's proprietary code covered the page. I scanned through the gibberish, finding nothing but lots of notes to self about insects, repellants and allergies. The poor Brain had got himself bamboozled. Then a set of letters and numbers caught my attention. I translated, tried not to get too excited.

Oh, yes, Harrison had been in the field. That little encoded phrase at the bottom of the sheet told me exactly where he'd been.

Roraima, Brazil, here I come.

Chapter 3

The Hotel Imperial in Boa Vista crouched at the city's edge, its clapboard sides weathered and unpainted for most of a decade. Chico, the Brazilian contact I'd inherited from Daley when he got dumped from von Brutten's payroll, had set up both my flight from Boa Vista into the jungle and my guide. He'd also booked the Imperial for me. Doing me a favor, he probably thought. I could tell it was usually a brothel but, for the sake of the International Conference on Environmental Protection and Sustainable Living being held that week, it had temporarily become a true hotel. Just grungy, sleazy and cheap.

Thanks for nothin', Chico.

The conference was being held in one of the legitimate hotels in the city's heart. Strange city to have a conference, I thought as I collected the old-fashioned church key to my no doubt dingy and bug-ridden room. Why not Manaus, which at least had a cosmopolitan air? The greasy hotel landlord smiled a greasy smile and wished me a good stay. At least I'm pretty sure that's what he said; my Portuguese isn't what it should be.

As I trudged up the narrow stairs, I heaved my canvas duffel bag over one shoulder. The pain about doing what I do isn't the scraping around in the jungle. It's having to buy all your supplies at the local open-air market—rice, beans, a cooking pot, matches, mosquito netting, a hammock, tins of cooked meat, bottled water (which is incredibly heavy after you've carried it around for a while), and rum or whiskey for trading with the Indians. Bickering prices with wily natives whose language I imperfectly speak and hear is no fun. I walk away suspecting I've been robbed.

I usually bring with me the real basics: my day pack, two sixty-meter climbing ropes and assorted climbing hardware, a collection of Hefty OneZip bags in various sizes, a first-aid kit complete with snakebite antivenin and antimalarial prophylactic, several cans of mosquito repellant, three changes of cotton underwear, tincture of iodine, tampons and garlic. I know. Garlic. But I swear, the jungle grows fungus better than any place on earth with the possible exception of a woman's vagina. One clove used as a suppository can kill the beginnings of a yeast infection. Cross my heart. Garlic is a natural antibiotic.

Life in the jungle doesn't get really hairy until about the second or third day. You count on being able to wash out your undies in a stream at least once a day; when you can't, you turn them inside out or go grungy until you can find a stream. When the bottled water runs out, you boil enough local water to fill a canteen, doctor it with the iodine and hope for the best. You try not to get bitten by snakes, and Brazil has plenty. You also learn real fast how to tie mosquito netting around your hammock so the little bastards don't eat you alive in the night. The mosquito netting also keeps the vampire bats off you. And no, the garlic won't help in that situation.

Normally all this stuff would get carried around by lackeys I'd hired. But Daley decided this time last year his best bet to finding good plants was to track *me* rather than the plants. Besides, an orchid stolen from me wouldn't make it into von Brutten's hands. During his first attempt, I'd had two "interns," a gun-toting guide and a burly carrier for the heavy stuff. As a result of having too many people to worry about when Daley and his little band of Merry Men struck, I nearly let him make off with a delicious *Phragmipedium*. Never again, I vowed, and have traveled with only a guide since.

I humped all my stuff down the long, dark corridor to my room. The church key went into the heavy stained-door's lock and turned. The lock *clicked* and *thunked*. I shoved. The door creaked but didn't budge. Brilliant. The damn door was stuck in its frame.

I dropped my stuff on the dirty floor and backed across the corridor—a whole step. Not much room to build up a head of steam. And in my colorful cotton *turista* dress disguise, I couldn't just pound the door down without getting the neighbors' attention. I certainly didn't want that in case Daley managed to track me this far, which he was probably working on. So I set my back against the corridor and put the heel of my flat sandal near the rickety handle. I gave a quick, sharp, satisfying kick.

The door exploded open. It swung hard and bounced off a wooden chest placed too close to the doorway. Inside, the room echoed the same gloom as the corridor. I stepped in to review the scene. Rickety iron bed, cracked mirror, dirty walls, light eeking from a bare bulb in the middle of the ceiling. Hotel California it ain't.

"I beg your pardon."

I spun. Behind the partially open door and battered bureau sat an iron claw-footed tub filled with soapy water and a handsome man. Dark hair, dark eyes, lightly flared nose, a flurry of black hair on his well-muscled chest.

"I told the manager I wasn't interested in any entertainment," he said in what I suspected was perfect Portuguese. He looked me up and down, pausing in interesting places. "But you may have changed my mind."

He stood, revealing the most splendid specimen I'd ever seen either in the hothouse or in the field. Water glistened over his dark skin, accentuating every angular muscle and darkening the dense thatch beneath his navel. An admirable addition to any garden, I thought. He reached for a towel and casually dried his back, still standing knee-deep in water and letting me enjoy the view.

Part of my brain scrambled for the proper phraseology for *I'm not a whore, you chauvinistic ass,* while another part searched for, *Take me now and be quick about it.* The sane part—the very small part with the synapses still firing—screamed to get out of there.

I struggled with my Portuguese. "You must have the wrong room."

"Inglês?"

"Yes."

He continued to study me while he lifted one powerful leg from the tub, then the other. Even the undersides of his thighs were dark. The towel made another circuit of his broad shoulders and traveled down his chest, but not far enough to obstruct my line of sight. The scientist in me took over, pondering dimensions, speed, staying power.

"I rather think *you* have the wrong room." His English was as perfect as his Portuguese. And his deep voice stung right where a girl needs it most. "Too bad."

I managed not to stutter. "I was told this room."

"Then maybe that's correct." He looked pointedly at the laughable excuse for a double bed provided by the establishment. "Do you hog the covers?"

"On that thing I wouldn't have to."

"It is narrow." His gaze lingered on the open neckline of my dress.

I resisted the urge to tuck my arms in and artificially produce more cleavage than I legitimately have.

"I'll straighten this out with the manager," he said.

He dressed as leisurely as he toweled. First he pulled on a pair of cotton trousers. I guessed underwear wasn't his thing. He shrugged into a loose shirt, then buttoned it from the bottom up, leaving me a nice swath of bulging chest to admire for as long as possible.

Evil man.

I followed his broad shoulders downstairs where he engaged in a lively debate with the greasy landlord in speed Portuguese, most of which I didn't catch. When they were done, the landlord smiled apologetically.

"What just happened?" I asked.

"The international conference has every room in this place taken. We will have to share."

"Then we should each get half our money back." It was miserly of me—half would be all of eight dollars—but it was the principle of the thing. I didn't appreciate being taken advantage of.

"He's agreed to have dinner sent up." He steered me back toward the stairs.

"Sent up? We're not honeymooning." I mentally cursed as slightly pornographic images starring my handsome roommate naturally coursed through my head.

His deep laugh sent a thrill down my spine. "Perhaps not, but I believe we may be together for some time."

"What do you mean?" I stopped on the landing, leaving him a couple of steps behind and still at eye level. Nice and tall.

"Our generous landlord told me your name. Dr. Robards?"

"Yes," I admitted warily, reluctant to give up even my stage name to this guy.

"I am Carlos Gutierrez, your pilot. Chico hired me to take you into the jungle." He smiled, and his black eyes glinted many, many promises at me.

Thank you, Chico.

I slid out of bed well before dawn and silently dressed. Force of habit. I always check all my gear before heading out. At first light Carlos and I would be at the airstrip, taking off for the deep interior. I twisted the bare bulb in its socket to turn it on, then pulled out the number-coded paper I'd lifted from the Brain in San Antonio, memorized it and burned it in a metal ashtray. When the ashes cooled, I broke them up with a ballpoint pen.

Despite the crackling and the smoke, Carlos still slept soundly, as well he should after the heroically athletic sex he'd treated me to. He lay with one strong arm thrown over his bare stomach and the other tucked under my pillow.

I tipped the ashes into the waste can on top of the used condoms. Story of my sex life, I thought, looking into the can. I always get hot for somebody and go into it thinking, *The sex is going to be great so maybe this guy is The Guy,* and the next day have a helluva casual sex hangover. Maybe it was time to stop making this mistake. The ashes cast up a question mark of smoke. I went to check my gear.

All the essentials went into my day pack, and everything else would go into the canvas duffel bag, leaving me plenty of room for the orchids. Ordinarily I'd bring a newspaper with me for drying and pressing specimens. But von Brutten needed the Death Orchid alive, so I'd brought several cardboard tubes for storing and shipping. He'd also given me a handful of forged CITES certificates to help me get the orchid back into the States. I'd have to pass off the Death Orchid, if I found it, as a different orchid altogether.

That's another irony of CITES. You can't transport a specimen across international boundaries unless it can be identified as a known species. So if you're like me, hunting down brand-new species, you're outta luck. Or else you become a criminal, as I have. What a woman will do in the name of botany.

I settled in the chair and by the dim light took another look at Harrison's notebook page Photostat. Marcus would probably figure out pretty fast what the blood on the original page really was, but my guess was I'd be in the jungle by then, out of reach of anything remotely resembling phone service. I'd just have to check messages next time I hit a city. Most of Harrison's handwriting, shorthand and abbreviations I could decipher from three years' practice working as his graduate lab assistant. The page took issue with Rudall's suggestion of a close morphological relationship between *Hypoxidaceae* and *Orchidaceae. Hypoxidaceae* are bulb plants, like lilies and amaryllis. Put simply, in order for a plant to be chemically active, it needed, among other things, to have alkaloids, and *Hypoxidaceae* don't. If orchids were like lilies, in other words, they'd be useless for any pharmaceutical company to pursue.

Harrison's notes, calculations and research were all designed to determine whether his Death Orchid specimen could indeed be used by a pharmaceutical company. In layman's terms, the answer was a whopping great yes.

A scribble near the margin, barely readable and in short-hand, caught my eye. Something about the orchid's distinctively long column. That probably meant its pollinator, whatever it was, had a distinctively long proboscis. Rain forest relationships are ancient. Sometimes, more often than you might think, a single insect and a single plant have coevolved so that one can't exist without the other. The bug drinks only the nectar provided by the plant and the plant can accept as pollinator only that bug. Or, like Scooter's *Phalaenopsis,* the flower disguises itself as the bug's mate so the males will be attracted to it. Darwin himself, after finding an orchid with a twelve-inch column, had hypothesized the existence of an insect with a twelve-inch proboscis. Turns out, years after Darwin's death, someone found that very insect.

But the idea of saying "Open wide" and shoving a microscopic tongue depressor down a bug's throat didn't appeal to me.

Then another scribble: the Death Moth.

"Up already?" Carlos's carelessly deep voice should have raised a shiver, but it merely annoyed me. I liked to work alone, in silence.

"Getting ready to go," I replied, shoving the Photostat into my day pack.

"Where are we going today?" he asked.

I dug the medicine bowl out of my day pack and handed it to him. "I need to go where this was found."

"Yanomamo," he murmured. His forefinger traced the jaguar pawprint idly.

"And that narrows down my search to what? A million square kilometers of rain forest?"

Carlos grinned. "No, *gatinha*. I can take you to someone who can tell you exactly where this came from. A scientist."

"Chico said you knew the area."

"I do," he said, flashing a charming smile that fell strangely flat. "I know every airstrip in the northern Amazon."

Great. Now I'd have to risk exposing my mission to someone who just might deduce what I was after. Someone who might give Lawrence Daley the same information. This trip was getting more difficult all the time.

An hour later we piled out of a battered taxi and strode through a scattering mist toward the airstrip. A beat-up Cessna Caravan 675 squatted behind a sheet metal shed. At least the plane looked relatively new. Riding in it couldn't be any worse than riding ten miles in a shockless Chevy over the pocked and jutted road to the airstrip. The runway, predictably, was a ribbon shaved out of the jungle, bounded by ever-encroaching forest currently being beaten back by a small army of machete-wielding Indians.

When we approached the shed, its crooked wooden door shoved open and a smallish Brazilian stepped out to yell at Carlos. Carlos started shouting back with equal verve in what I gathered was some kind of bargaining behavior.

Then a fresh-faced, good-looking young white guy bounded out of the shed, carrying a backpack, a tripod and a camera case.

"Oh no," I said to Carlos, interrupting his shouting match and thumbing at the college boy as he joined us. "He's not sharing my plane."

College Boy pushed his wire frames higher on his nose and held his hand out to Carlos. After a shake, he launched into a spate of excellent Portuguese that, judging from Carlos's raised eyebrows, surprised the pilot as much as it did me. The Brazilian stood back and grinned. Then College Boy reached into his pocket and pulled out a wad of bills that could choke a horse.

"We had a deal," I reminded Carlos. "You. Me. The plane. No one else."

"Excuse me," College Boy said in English, turning to me. "What."

His smile didn't falter. "I'm Dr. Richard Kinkaid. I'm headed out to Ixpachia Research Station." He shoved his glasses further onto his nose. "I'm an entomologist," he added, as though that would somehow make a difference.

I looked him up and down. Right. A bug nerd. A Milquetoast bug hunter with an oversize camera and no idea how to take care of himself outside a graduate school laboratory. I read the tea leaves and didn't like what I saw.

"No," I said to him. "You may not share my plane."

"If the pilot's willing to take me, it's not your concern."

"And I won't take you to your research station, even if I knew where it was."

"I have a map—"

"And I won't pull your ass out of the jungle when you get burned by fire liana."

"Fire liana?"

"Or stung by Dresk's beetles."

"I have an antidote for that—"

"Or get a limb chewed off by a hungry jaguar."

"Jaguars don't—"

"Or get shot with a poisoned arrow by one of the several hostile indigenous peoples."

At that his strong face solidified to stone. Arrogant jungle newbie on his first field trip. His presence was an unacceptable risk. We glared at each other.

"Not interested," I clarified.

"But I am," Carlos cut in. "Ixpachia Research Station is where we are going. However, my rates are rather steep."

The bug nerd turned his back on me to juggle his tripod under one arm as he counted out bills. Carlos's eyes widened.

"Hey," I said to Carlos, grabbing his sleeve to take his attention off the cash. "I paid for your *exclusive* services."

"You got those last night," he said with an intimate leer.

My face heated up. "I paid you good money for a solitary trip. A flight in, five days working in the jungle, a flight out. I'm not sharing my plane."

"But his money's as good as yours." Carlos's perfect white smile would have dazzled me yesterday. Today it just made me mad. "And the flight is dangerous, is it not? Should I not be paid for the work as much as I can get?"

"We had a deal."

He chuckled. "*Gatinha*, my word is true, but money is life." He waved at the bug nerd. "Bring your gear, *amigo!*"

The Brazilian cackled as I stumped along behind Carlos and the bug nerd, fuming. I'd have a word with Chico next time I saw him. For now, I'd deal with it. But I didn't have time to baby-sit anybody. Scooter was my priority. Everybody else would just have to get by.

Carlos jerked the Cessna's cargo door open for us. A *whoosh* of stifling hot air fell out. The plane was just this side of a stripped-down drug runner: a pilot's seat, electronics and little else. Even the passenger seats were gone. Good old Carlos must have a day job flying snow. Maybe dodging the joint Brazilian-American drug-enforcement guys had made him arrogant with the average sightseer. He was used to flying much richer cargo than what I'd bring back.

"Let me get that for you." The bug nerd reached for my duffel bag.

Hell, why not let him play gentleman and throw out his back? Maybe I'd make this trip alone after all. But he easily swung the heavy duffel bag into the cargo bay with one arm. Then he hopped into the plane after it, holding out his broad hand for my day pack and smiling at me like this was a Boy Scout jaunt to Camp Okefenokee.

"I got it." I kept my day pack and climbed into the plane. I settled down across from the open cargo door and hoped he wouldn't start talking.

Up front, Carlos flicked switches and turned dials. A few minutes later, the Cessna's single engine fired up. The bare metal wall I leaned against vibrated from my neck all the way to my butt. Even my ankles tingled from the jarring.

The bug nerd shoved his gear against one of the plane's exposed steel ribs and scrambled up to the cockpit.

"The engine doesn't sound right to me," he shouted over the guttering noise.

Carlos shook his head. "This plane is safe, my friend. Go take a nap."

"But the mechanical clatter—"

"It's nothing!"

The nerd's firm jaw tightened, then he yelled, "So where are the parachutes?"

Carlos flashed the nerd a dark look and jerked his head toward the cargo bay. *Get out of my face.* I could read the message from halfway down the plane. Carlos might be a good guy as far as illicit dealings in the jungle go—meaning he wouldn't kill anyone without a good reason—but, like me, he was a mercenary who needed to eat. Mouthy pip-squeak "experts" got tossed out the cargo door at seven thousand feet.

Besides, the bug nerd had given him the full payment up front. Dumbass.

The nerd flopped down again across from me, mindless of the open cargo door to his left. He closed his eyes, apparently taking Carlos's nap suggestion seriously. He wore pristine trekking gear that looked like it'd been ordered out of a Whole Earth Catalog: heavy canvas pants, a shirt a size too big for him, what had to be day-hiking boots made by Birkenstock. His dark brown hair lay longish on his collar, highlighting prominent cheekbones, a strong jaw and chiseled lips. I wondered briefly what he'd look like with a ponytail but decided "tasty" wasn't a word a woman like me should use. The wire frames slipped a half inch down his nose. He didn't move.

I turned my attention to the shed. The Brazilian who apparently acted as the local air-traffic controller was nowhere to be seen. Nothing out there but trees and bugs and already-intense heat.

The plane lurched forward. The Cessna stuttered and jerked toward the dirt runway. Deep jungle green rolled by. Workers' arms rose and fell, blades slashing and hacking. Carlos turned the plane's nose due west and the shed came into view again. A very dark man, maybe half Negro, half Indian, stood beside the shed, staring at us. Carlos stopped the plane to check something.

The staring man strode toward us purposefully, his gaze unwavering. A chill shot through my veins. Carlos fidgeted with controls, and still the man walked, unhurried and deliberate. How could someone stare so long without blinking?

Then the man grasped the open cargo doorway and leaned in. Twin puckered scars etched his face, neck, and the part of his collarbone I could see beneath his ragged shirt. Around his neck, a leather cord held a single jaguar tooth—a canine. His huge hands gripped the doorway with such strength I had no doubt he could bend the metal if he chose. Black eyes stared at me.

Directly at me.

The chill in my veins dropped to a freeze. He didn't glare; his eyes were as emotionless as those of the jaguar he'd killed for its tooth.

Endless darkness welled up in my periphery. The plane's metallic clatter heightened into deafening howls and screams and roars. The world dropped away from my feet, leaving me standing in utter blackness, alone. I no longer hunkered down in a Cessna waiting to go into the jungle. The jungle had come for me, and what hunted me breathed hot and heavy on my neck. I spun. Nothing. I spun again. Nothing. Panicked, I struck out with both arms, swinging wild. If I could just see.

As if in answer to a prayer, a dim yellow light grew near my feet, filling the darkness with itself, illuminating nothing. A single sound cut through the cacophony: a slithering hiss that singed my spine with fear and brought bile into my throat. I knew what it was. The yellow light sharpened into two flat, slitted, alien eyes. Pit viper. The kind of venomous snake whose head would chase you *after* you'd severed it from the body. Low words, words I didn't understand but whose meaning I knew instantly, told me to leave this place. What waited for me in the trees was hissing death.

Abruptly, the vision disappeared.

The empty cargo-bay door yawned. Outside, trees and undergrowth lurked behind the sagging shed. The shaman—if that's what he was—had disappeared.

Once the Evil Eye has its grip, you're lost. The open cargo door tempted me to leave. I could jump out now before my curse found me. Jump out, go home, save myself. My fingers itched for my day pack.

I shook my head to clear it. Medicine man tales, I said to myself. Shaman lies. I'd had a hallucination due to fatigue and stress. I lived in a world of science and technology. The Evil Eye was like the boogeyman, meant to scare and intimidate you into doing what someone else wanted. It couldn't catch me or keep me. It couldn't prevent me from going deep into the jungle.

"Let's get this show on the road!" I called up to Carlos.

He gave me a thumbs-up. The plane jerked twice, then bumped down the strip, gaining speed. Straight brown tree trunks and masses of green leaves flitted by. Carlos pulled back on the stick and abruptly we were up, over the treetops, heading northwest.

Heading to a place where I wasn't welcome.

But I'd survive.

Scooter's life depended on it.

Chapter 4

Stuttering. It's not a good sign at five thousand feet, whether it's the pilot or the plane. In this case, it was the plane.

The bug nerd's eyes opened, glared briefly toward Carlos's broad back, and closed. I knew that look: *You're the tough man, you handle it.*

Brilliant emerald treetops fluffed the ground. From above, the canopy shows you a solid-looking mass with an occasional peep-show peek at the really good stuff underneath. To see the real wealth of species—the dozens of monkeys, thousands of birds, bazillions of insects—you have to go in from the bottom.

North-north-west, where we were headed, the canopy abruptly rose and fell with the stubby Guiana Highlands. The high point, Serra do Apiau, was only around 3,300 feet, not even as high as most of the hiking in the Great Smoky Mountains National Park. And nothing like the Rockies.

But the terrain wouldn't make a nice landing pad. By the increased clattering of the engine and the intensity of the frown the bug nerd cast in Carlos's direction, maybe we were going to need one.

On cue, the Cessna fell several feet, tossing my stomach up around my ears. Carlos's right hand felt around over his head for some controls. The bug nerd got up, grabbed a steel rib and leaned out the cargo door. His hair whipped his left ear. He held his glasses in place with his free hand. Not a good place to be sick, I thought, but he levered himself back into the plane and headed to the cockpit.

I didn't catch his first shouted words, but there was no mistaking the pale grimace of fear Carlos shot him in response. Time to be worried, I gathered. I got up and joined them, hanging on to a steel handhold over my head like a professional New York commuter.

"What's going on?" I yelled over the chatter and chuff.

"Bad fuel!" the nerd shouted. "The engine's about to quit!"

"Over my dead body!" Carlos spun dials. I could see his feet working some kind of pedals. "She hasn't let me down yet!"

"If it's bad fuel, you don't have a choice!"

"Come on!" Carlos yelled at the plane. "We're less than thirty miles from the strip!"

An earsplitting screech went off somewhere near my head.

"Shit!" Carlos shouted.

The plane shuddered, nose tipping. *Chuff, chuff,* a slower *chuff,* then the prop wound down like a bad dream. The engine spat and quit. The alarm screamed.

"Hold on!"

Carlos kept one hand tight on the W-shaped wheel and flipped some more switches. The one gauge I recognized— the altimeter—confirmed the hard lean pulling me forward. The nerd braced himself where the copilot's seat should be and grabbed the matching wheel.

Out the window by Carlos's head, various trees were rapidly becoming recognizable to my naked eye. Another bad sign.

"You'd better get back!" the nerd yelled at me. "We're going to have to make an emergency landing! Find something to strap yourself down with!"

"Emergency landing?" I shouted back. "Where?"

"Airstrip ahead!"

I looked out the front windshield. A tiny airstrip, much tinier than the tiny airstrip we'd left an hour earlier, had been scraped out of the jungle. To my untrained eye, we looked way too high to land on that little ribbon. Next to it, a bevy of shacks and huts surrounded a huge, muddy gouge in the hillside that spewed brown water down a channel, feeding into a natural stream off the Rio Branco.

A gold mine. Probably illegal. Definitely dangerous. All male, all testosterone, all heavily armed.

"Get back!" the nerd shouted again, his eyes intense behind his lenses.

I hand-over-handed my way back down the twelve feet of cabin space and looked around. No parachutes. Nothing to use as a tie-down. In frustration I kicked my day pack and duffel into the tail area, then settled into my original seat, across from the open cargo door. The wind gushing in smelled greener, more lush, wetter. My shoulder fit snugly against the plane's rib cage. The plane bucked and wobbled. My only comforting thought was that if I whacked my head good and hard during the crash landing, I'd at least be unconscious during the rape later.

Sudden tears stung my eyes. Dammit. A girl in my position wasn't supposed to be afraid. *Where's your guff?* Scooter's voice chided gently. *No girlie of mine is goin' cry,* he had said over countless jammed fingers (softball), skinned knees (tree climbing), and a broken arm (off-road motorcycle). *No ladybug I know is goin' be skeered,* he told me during storms (including two tornadoes), as I rode The Demon (his meanest adopted mustang), and after falling fifty feet down Eagle's Nest while tethered to a threadbare rope (rock climbing).

No, sir. I scrubbed the tears away. I ain't skeered.

The Cessna skittered sideways and dropped. When my butt made contact with the floor again, I grabbed the nearest tie-down ring. We bore down on the trees. Thick, humid wind flushed the fear stench from the plane. My mind flashed on tree limbs snagging our landing gear to pluck us from the sky.

That was my cue to worry about one thing at a time. No need to wear myself out over everything at once. Worry about the airplane end-over-ending first, a crash landing second, and getting raped third. Got it. I gritted my teeth.

The plane shuddered. Up front, Carlos knelt by an open compartment door, fiddling with something inside. The nerd wedged himself into the pilot's seat and leaned on a control. I felt a glimmer of hope. Speak immaculate Portuguese *and* fly a plane? We might get out of this yet. The nerd shook his head, then hit the control again. Out the cargo door, I started seeing branches instead of leaves. We were dropping into the airstrip ribbon way too fast. The engine spat, choked, then rumbled.

Outside, the propeller hitched a couple of times before catching a groove to spin smoothly. The Cessna's nose picked up just in time for its landing gear to smack the ground with the delicacy of a brick. I lost my grip on the tie-down ring and rolled toward the tail, my ribs grinding over protruding metal bits. The bouncing plane sailed up, fishtailed, hopped sideways, straightened out. We whacked the strip again and started to slow.

I looked up. The forest grew taller and taller and taller toward the windshield. The nerd stood his ground. We'd lose this game of chicken, no doubt about that. I took a deep breath and tried not to panic.

The Cessna abruptly skipped, wheels barking on the dirt, and jerked to a halt. I skidded face-first several feet and stopped where I'd started this trip, near the cargo door.

There was no sound other than the engine's stutter and the rumble of generators filtering through the trees. From my sprawled landing position, I surveyed the crew. Carlos crouched next to the pilot's chair, his arms curved over his head. Kinkaid sat in the chair, his hands still locked on the wheel.

The propeller whirred innocently.

Just freakin' typical.

Kinkaid reached out, killed the engine. The prop wound down and stopped. Its three blades cast a shadow of the peace sign onto a copse of rubber trees inches away.

"Are you okay?" Kinkaid asked me over his shoulder.

I sat up. The ribs hurt, but didn't move when I pressed them with my palm. I also took comfort from the fact I could stand and hadn't thrown up yet. "Yeah. Nice landing."

He unwedged himself from the pilot's chair. "You all right?" he asked the floor, where Carlos was starting to unfold himself.

"Yes."

Carlos and I looked at each other for a long moment.

"You're fired," I said.

I could hear shouts in the distance, growing closer. Time to start worrying about staying alive. I grabbed Kinkaid's arm as he staggered to the tail section to check his gear.

"We're scientists," I said. "We're just going to the research station. We are *not* journalists."

"What?" He picked up his camera case.

"That stays here," I said.

"No, it doesn't—"

"If they think you're a journalist, they'll kill you." When he stared at me, I added, "Don't provoke anything. We're going to the research station. That's it. Nothing else."

"Why would they kill us?"

"Because the mine is illegal," Carlos answered from the cockpit. "This is Yanomamo land, and the miners have dug without government permission."

"They're paranoid about being stopped," I said to Kinkaid. "Or robbed." The voices outside grew louder. The distinctive, heavy, *shung-clunk* of a shotgun being racked made me lower my voice. "Don't be stupid and we might get out of this alive."

He nodded.

"That means keep your mouth shut," I clarified.

He nodded again, shoving his glasses back onto his nose.

I shrugged into my day pack, ignoring my tender ribs. Showing weakness to a dog pack just feeds the frenzy. I needed to get out of this with Harrison's ashtray, my forged CITES certificate, one cardboard tube for storing a Death Orchid, and my life.

Everything else was negotiable.

A strong brown hand gripped the door and a short man stuck his head through the cargo door. *"Saia do avião!"* Behind him, the shotgun's nose beckoned us.

We climbed out and lined up beside the plane. Four men with rifles slung over their shoulders clambered in. In a moment, I heard my duffel unzipping and my stuff being pulled out. The short guy who'd spoken to us appeared to be in charge, probably the head *donos,* the mine foreman. Security would be part of his job. A much younger man held the shotgun on us, his face pasted with a "just doing my job" expression.

The *donos* smiled, revealing an archetypical gold front tooth. "You have come visit us," Goldtooth said in English.

I felt Carlos tense beside me. "Bad fuel," he replied. "We were lucky."

Not quite as lucky as we might have been, I thought. The *donos* studied Carlos for a moment.

"We took bets whether you crash." He slapped one broad hand into the other and grinned. "I lost!"

A tinkling bang inside the plane heralded the end of Kinkaid's camera. In my peripheral vision, I saw Kinkaid's jaw tense, but he kept his mouth shut. The *donos* shrugged. "Accident," he said. "Too bad."

When Goldtooth turned his attention to me, I dropped my gaze to his feet. I'm proud, but I'm not stupid. I'd save the I Am Woman tirade for when I was the one holding the shotgun.

"What you doing here?" Goldtooth asked. "What a woman need here?"

"I'm a scientist," I replied. *"Científico."* No, dammit, that was Spanish. *"Cientista."*

I let my eyes wander from his muddy boots up worn work pants to his stout white cotton shirt. A few wiry hairs sprouted from the shirt's open neck. "Studying *plantas.*" I chanced a glance at his face.

His black eyes had narrowed. I was starting to feel pretty good about those eyes not looking like a snake's when I realized his nonviper gaze had settled below my neckline. Never mind my bulky, buttoned-up canvas-shirt look. This guy was interested in what lay beneath, which was a white cotton muscle tee, a white cotton sports bra—a not-too-shabby C—and a lot of sweat. Bugs buzzed my ear, but the deet kept them at bay. Too bad they didn't make lech-repellant.

His fingers twitched. Abruptly he grinned. "Come to office!" he said. "You need Coca-Cola!"

The sullen young guy with the shotgun waved us down the airstrip toward the collection of hovels that served as mine headquarters. As we trudged along the airstrip's rutted surface, the clatter of generators rose over the sheet-metal buildings. Now, at around ten in the morning, the sun was ready to bake us into crispy bits. I shrugged off the stray notion that we were descending into hell. I hadn't been searched, I'd been allowed to keep my day pack, and the worst they'd done to my person was ogle.

All things considered, things were looking up.

The shotgun-toting guy stopped at an outlying building beside the airstrip. Beside the building, three Yanomamo women wearing brightly colored T-shirts and bowl-cut hairdos loitered in the shade, one holding an infant in her arms. A Yanomamo boy who looked about twelve chased a toad, aiming boy-sized arrows at it from his boy-sized bow.

The Shotgun Kid swung open the door and waved us inside the building. I'm glad I wasn't expecting a blast of cool air because I didn't get one. If anything, the heat was worse. Goldtooth motioned for us to move on through a small anteroom to the large office and sit down on the floor, then he disappeared.

A large metal utility desk sat square in the middle of the room with a wide wooden chair squatting behind it. A neat stack of papers held down one edge of the desk. A two-drawer metal filing cabinet hunched in the corner. Overhead, a ceiling fan vigorously flung stale air onto our heads.

I took the corner where I could see the door and the Shotgun Kid filling it. A third Brazilian lingered just outside the door. Kinkaid settled cross-legged next to me. For the first time I noticed he'd brought his own day pack with him. Good Boy Scout. Too bad his camera hadn't made it. A thin trickle of sweat slid down his temple but he seemed calm. I wasn't surprised. Landing the little plane the way he had took more nerve than I had.

Carlos hunkered down next to Kinkaid like he was sitting around a campfire. He looked a little too at ease for my peace of mind. Of course, he wasn't one of two Americans in the room. Or a woman. My guess was that before this was over, he'd end up cutting a deal with the miners to make some of their supply runs into Boa Vista.

Goldtooth returned with three open glass-bottled Cokes. Refrigeration was too much to hope for, but a wet drink was a wet drink. He handed them out, let his thick, rough fingers scrape mine when I took the bottle from him. His grin, stretching through a fleshy face, made me think twice about taking a sip. I set the bottle's warm butt on my knee.

"Now!" he announced, perching on the edge of the desk. "What you doing here?"

I didn't volunteer anything and neither did Kinkaid. The question had clearly been addressed to the man the *donos* would assume was the pilot.

"Engine trouble," Carlos said after a moment. "Bad fuel. We were forced to land here."

"Yes," the *donos* agreed patiently. "What you doing here?"

Sweat broke out on Carlos's upper lip. Not good. If you act guilty, you are guilty.

"We hired him to bring us to the jungle," I said.

The *donos* turned his black eyes on me. Maybe I'd spoken out of turn and it would get me in trouble, but it was better than watching Carlos get us all killed by taking too long to think about his answer.

"You had a video camera."

"It was mine," Kinkaid said.

"You a journalist?"

"No." Kinkaid looked at the *donos* a moment before switching to textbook Portuguese and adding, "I study insects and how they work in your rain forests. The camera was for photographing them at night."

Goldtooth nodded thoughtfully. Had the camera survived, Kinkaid might have been able to play back the film he'd already taken to help make his case.

"*Plantas,*" Goldtooth said abruptly, still in Portuguese. "Which?"

I took a deep breath. "Bromeliads, lichen, moss," I said in English. At his puzzled frown, I said, "Weeds."

That he understood. Bromeliads to a guy like him *would* be weeds. If he had to clear it to make room for an airstrip or a mine, it was a weed. He nodded and looked down to shuffle through the desk's papers, ignoring us. I got it: he was a busy and important man. I set my untouched Coke bottle on the hard wooden floor next to Kinkaid's, also untouched.

The *donos* sniffed and traded a glance with the Shotgun Kid. "Out," he said to Carlos.

Carlos slowly stood. "Out?"

The Shotgun Kid pointed the muzzle at Carlos's shins and then gestured to the door. Carlos took a few steps, but hesitated when he passed the Kid. I didn't blame him. I knew the skin of his back was crawling, waiting to be pumped full of shot.

"Take your plane," the *donos* said.

"It won't fly on bad fuel," Carlos objected.

Goldtooth nodded at the Brazilian lurking outside the door. "Get him fuel." The Brazilian left. "We will talk, eh?" he said to Carlos. "Maybe we do business. Now go."

Carlos spared me a rueful glance, a shrug of apology, then turned and walked out, taking my hope for getting out of here with him.

That seemed about par. Guy screws you and leaves without looking back. My luck, which had been on the upside briefly today, was headed straight down the toilet again. It was just me and Kinkaid and no transportation. Brilliant. My heart started pounding my chest wall, wanting out. I couldn't blame it. Things couldn't get much worse.

The Shotgun Kid suddenly backed into the room, a hint of fear on his impassive face. Then a stout, uniform-clad man wearing jet-black sunglasses stalked in, his cane thumping the floorboards. The colonel—at least that was what his uniform's shoulder boards said—looked ridiculously like an elderly Manuel Noriega, his thick curly hair sticking out from beneath a gold-braided cap. Goldtooth shot off the desk like a rocket and stood at attention.

The big cheese had arrived.

Kinkaid leaned forward as though to stand, but I clutched

his arm. Prisoners did what they were told. Standing might be construed as an affront to the colonel's authority. Better to take a chance on playing dumb Americano. Just when I thought I couldn't get any more scared, I did.

The colonel's full lips pursed as he studied the frozen *donos*. I got the impression Dad had gone off for the weekend and unexpectedly returned in the middle of his son's unauthorized house party. This wasn't Goldtooth's office after all. I hoped Kinkaid and I wouldn't end up paying the price for the head foreman's cheekiness.

The colonel spat something in rapid-fire Portuguese I didn't understand. Goldtooth hurriedly ordered, "Stand!" so we did. He patted us down, enjoying my chest and thighs a little too long despite Dad's hovering presence. I concentrated on worrying about the colonel. Worrying about the inevitable rape came later.

"Journalists," the colonel muttered in disgust, waving us to sit on the floor again. He snapped his cap from his head to the desktop, revealing more shaggy, curly hair going a dirty white. "Why do you come here?" he demanded, leaning on the desk and shaking his cane in our general direction. "To tell us how to treat our land? To tell us we cannot dig here, we must dig there?" He erupted into a coughing fit that sounded like it'd bring up a lung.

I squeezed Kinkaid's hard forearm to remind him to keep quiet.

Recovering a few moments later, the colonel put his cane on top of the desk. He grabbed his sidearm from its holster and waved it. "We bring food and work to the Indian," he continued, stamping a little groove back and forth in front of us. His hands quivered. "They do not work. They do not help. We take less than what we give. We make roads into the jungle." He jabbed the gun at Kinkaid. "We tame it and make it useful to men and commerce. We bring medicines." He jabbed the gun at me. "We clear timber for farms. We do all of this with best of intention." He stopped jabbing and pacing to stand in front of us, eyes sparked with fury. "And *still,* you Americanos try to tell *me* what I can do, where I can do it."

I held my breath. Probably no Americano had ever told this sociopath anything, with the possible exception of the CIA operative who had trained the colonel's paramilitary organization, whatever it was. His beef was probably with the environmentalists, specifically those conscientious internationals in Boa Vista, and I definitely didn't help fill those ranks.

But Kinkaid might. He looked the type. The colonel glared at us. A quick twist of fear stabbed my gut. I gripped Kinkaid's arm tighter.

Maybe it was the colonel's nonviper gaze that made me brave. A snake would take me out. Not this guy. Maligning the natives seemed to be what he wanted to hear, and the safest thing to say to make him think we were on his side. "With respect," I said in my best bad Portuguese during his pause, "I see you bring food and money to the Indians here. If they wanted to work, they would work."

"Yes!" the colonel agreed loudly, shakily waving the gun. "Yes! We give them clothing. We give them food. We give them better life. Still, they do not work." His next coughing fit doubled him over.

Goldtooth made as if to pat his back, but retreated, a sneer gracing his face, as the older man waved him away. The colonel straightened, cleared his throat. Then he stared at the wall next to me as though gathering his thoughts. He nodded. He sniffed. He looked at the *donos,* then at the Shotgun Kid. When he glanced over at me and Kinkaid, he frowned.

The old man, I decided, was losing it. Alzheimer's? Hardening of the arteries?

"Americanos," he muttered. "Stupid Americanos."

The colonel holstered his weapon and crossed his arms

over his barrel chest to survey his subjects: two nervous Brazilians and two nervous Americanos. He abruptly uncrossed his arms, apparently remembering what he was doing.

He said something I didn't understand to Goldtooth. The Shotgun Kid motioned for us to stand. I got up, careful to hold my day pack by the strap without making any sudden moves. Kinkaid echoed my actions.

"I will take those." The colonel gestured to our packs.

Well, hell. I handed mine out, and the Shotgun Kid took it. Kinkaid did the same. Then Goldtooth nodded for us to follow him, leaving the colonel and the Shotgun Kid behind.

So we'd survived the crash, the preliminary interview and the colonel's whim. I wondered what was next on our to-do list.

"Come, I show you we bring money to jungle!" Goldtooth said as we blinded ourselves by stepping outside.

Down the far end of the airstrip, a huddle of men stood around the Cessna, Carlos among them, smoking. I ignored the spilt milk. Time to forget being scared and start thinking about getting outta here.

Following Goldtooth through the camp's maze, I counted seven large huts—administrative buildings, various living quarters, what passed for a cafeteria where fish was being grilled on an outdoor spit. All the while, the thick smell of water permeated the air, like steam lifting from a hot summer day's asphalt. The generators, wherever they were, rattled and rumbled. Smoke rose over the trees we were walking toward. A loud, rushing hiss abruptly started up ahead, became a roar. Goldtooth led us down a narrow path cut into the forest and stopped at a gigantic hole in the ground I hoped was not our grave.

Standing on the hole's crumbling edge, I looked down. Some twelve feet below, a drenched man carrying a fireman's hose aimed the nozzle at a chunk of earth that held out for a good five seconds before it fell apart. Mud-covered men immediately pounced on the earth. They broke it apart to pluck out large chunks of rock that they passed down a line of more mud-covered men. At the end of this human conveyor belt, the rocks got put on a real, mechanical mud-covered conveyor belt and carted up out of the hole into an open-air processing area opposite where we stood. These were the *garimpeiros*, literally "gold robbers," who had moved from poverty in the south to take whatever jobs they could find.

The generators' deafening rattle made Goldtooth shout. "We give jobs to men who work! Do you see any Yanomamo there?" he yelled. "They stupid and lazy. We offer jobs."

I nodded knowingly. Right. Men slopping around for twelve hours in mud for ten cents a day: smart. Men lying in hammocks in the jungle after hunting two days out of the week: stupid.

"What's that?" Kinkaid pointed to the murky brown wash flooding from the processing area. A little waterfall spilled down the eroded hillside and pooled at the bottom, then flowed out of sight.

"There we take gold from earth." Goldtooth pointed like a proud papa showing off his firstborn son.

Smoke belched from the open-air processing area, where I could see bandana-masked men leaning over large flat pans set over fires. Chunks of gold-mercury amalgam were being heated up in those pans. Occasionally a workman tipped a pan to pour the quicksilver off into the channel. Some of the mercury would be reclaimed and used again. Most of it would be washed into the little waterfall and travel downstream where it would be consumed by unknowing Indians and Brazilians. Birth defects and mysterious cancers were sure to follow.

Kinkaid opened his mouth but closed it when I shot him a glance. I knew where he was headed and he didn't need to go there unless he was heavily armed.

"Come! I show you quarters!" Goldtooth yelled over the racket.

We walked back to the compound. I was glad just to get a little distance from the noise. When we reached the hovel apparently reserved for drop-in guests, I stopped.

"We have associates, other *cientistas,* waiting for us," I said. "When will we be allowed to leave?"

"Leave?" The *donos's* gold tooth mocked me. His eyes drifted south, to my chest, and I stifled a shudder. "You leave when I say you leave."

Though that wasn't in my plans, I nodded and went inside.

"Is he insane?" Two feet away, Kinkaid lay on his back in the stifling little hut. He hadn't moved in a while or said much, for which I was profoundly grateful. I'd been thinking up ways to get out of the mining camp without being seen, and most of them were lousy.

"Which one?" I asked.

"The military guy."

"Probably. My guess is El Capitan was given this mine as a perk for a shoot-'em-up somewhere."

"Massacring the Indians, you mean."

I shrugged. "No telling."

My butt was starting to ache from sitting propped up against the hut's timber frame. I wanted to stretch out like Kinkaid, but there are times when matching someone's posture—in this case, lying next to Kinkaid on the floor—seemed too intimate. Too familiar. I wriggled a little straighter instead.

Through the gap between the door and its frame, I could see a burly wrestler type standing guard outside. Powerfully built, he was still shorter than me. Compact stock, these Brazilian Indians. The thick scent of cooking meat wafted into the three-inch gap between the hut's bark wall and the bare earth floor. Above us, the hut's thatched roof had a single dinner-plate-size opening through which I could see kapok tree leaves.

I was still puzzling over how to take out the wrestler when Kinkaid asked, "Do you think he believes what he was saying?"

"About what?"

"Mining being good for the Indians."

"Probably."

Kinkaid sat up. "They use mercury to process the gold. That was mercury they were dumping into the runoff."

"Yeah."

His glasses glinted at me. "Doesn't it bother you they're poisoning everybody downstream?"

"What bothers me right now is the fact that I'm in here, and I want to be out there."

He didn't say anything to that, but merely drew his legs in to sit cross-legged again, his back ramrod straight. After a moment, he asked, "What can we do?"

I sighed. "To get out or to save the world?"

"Let's get out first, then save the world."

"How about *we* get out, then *you* save the world."

"Okay. Then we head for the research station?"

Since the research station was where Carlos, as my plant-hunting guide, had planned to take me, I could only assume that it was in the general vicinity of the Death Orchid. He'd probably planned to approach someone at the station to identify Harrison's medicine bowl. "Yep," I said, "we head directly for your research station. First we get out."

I remembered how easily Kinkaid had one-armed my fifty-pound duffel bag into the plane. "You're pretty strong. Do you think you can take this guy out?" I nodded toward the doorway and the guard.

"Knock him out?"

"Yeah. Knock him out."

Silence.

Please don't tell me you're a pacifist.

"Sure," he said hesitantly. "I guess I can do that."

"I don't think I can do it," I replied. "Not without a weapon."

His back straightened more until I thought it would crack. "Of course I'll help."

I plucked a stick from under the hut's wall and started drawing the mining compound in the dirt between us. "Here's the airstrip, and here's the mine. The compound lies in this direction, with the main concentration of buildings here. We're here in this little side complex—"

"How can you tell?"

I looked up from my maze of squiggles. "What do you mean?"

"I thought we were on this side." He pointed to the due south side of my drawing.

"No, that's where the dirt track heading back to Boa Vista is. We're not far off from the mine, which is tucked into the hillside on the southeast."

"But I thought the road ran perpendicular to the airstrip."

I shook my head. "The airstrip lies north-west-west. You probably couldn't see the compound layout from the air when you were landing the plane. Too many trees." When he frowned again, I added, "I always know where I am."

"Photographic memory for terrain?" he asked in a faintly disbelieving voice that sounded like sarcasm.

"Close enough," I retorted, thinking about Scooter and endless rows of corn and grape Kool-Aid. I drew a strictly defined escape path between the buildings and out into the jungle.

Kinkaid gestured toward the little map. "Look, I'm thinking maybe we can go this way—"

"You have to trust me on this," I said. "You landed the plane and saved our lives. I'm grateful, believe me. But I know better on the ground." When he still looked doubtful, I added, "I do this all the time."

His lenses caught a narrow band of sunlight, shielding his eyes from me for a moment. Then he nodded. "Your way then."

I drew a nice big X near the airstrip's end. "I'll meet you right there. The most important thing is not to draw attention to yourself on the way out."

"Okay."

"I'm going to get the guard to come in," I said. "When he does, be ready to hit and run."

Chapter 5

Caterwauling. Laughing. Crying out in pain.

None of these seemed like a good idea to get the guard's attention.

But fire did.

Unfortunately, my lighter was in my day pack. The fear of fire would have to do.

"Stand over here across from the door," I said to Kinkaid, "and answer my questions. Then get ready to hightail it."

I hopped up to grab hold of the single crossbeam securing the hut's roof. It felt like it'd hold my weight. "When I was a kid," I said, "I used to climb trees all the time. I loved climbing trees."

"Fascinating."

"Isn't it?" Still hanging from the beam, I bent at the waist to swing my feet up to my hands, then pivoted up onto straight arms like a gymnast on the high bar. "But I was awful with languages. Still am." From my straight-arm position I leaned my body over the beam and got a foot on top. Simple matter then to hoist myself up, balancing on the stout wood. I turned slightly so I could see the guard through the crack in the hut's doorway. "So tell me," I asked Kinkaid, "what's the Portuguese for *fire?*"

"Fire?" He frowned a moment, but I couldn't tell whether he was searching for the word or searching for the reason I asked. "It's *fogo.*"

"Sorry, I didn't catch that."

"Fogo," he said louder.

The guard shifted his weight.

"Okay, so if I wanted to start a *fogo,* what would I use?"

"Matches or a lighter, I guess."

"What's *matches* in Portuguese?"

"Fósforo."

The guard did more than shift his weight. Now he turned and I could see his rough-shaven face as he peered through the door's crack.

"That's promising," I said to Kinkaid. "I've learned two new words today. Use them in the sentence, 'I want to start a fire with these matches.' Maybe you should kneel down while you say it."

Kinkaid's smile spread slowly across his face. He knelt and swept his hand through my dirt map, then cupped his fingers together and said, slightly louder, *"Vou provocar um incendio com os fósforos que tenho aqui."*

Bingo. The guard silently unlatched the door, jerked it open, and charged inside directly underneath me.

"Pare!" he ordered, brandishing a shotgun.

In the time it took him to remember there were supposed to be two prisoners, I dropped behind him and laid a game-winning field goal kick between his legs. He hunched and groaned. Kinkaid's eyes widened in sympathetic response, then he laid a right hook to the guard's nose. Cartilage crunched. I grabbed the rifle from the falling man's limp hands. The beefy guard thunked onto the earthen floor.

Nighty-night.

The rifle turned out to be an ancient bolt-action single-barrel like the one Scooter kept behind the freestanding cupboard in his trailer. I'd shot at and missed many a rabbit while Scooter was in town or busy at the bar. While Kinkaid shook out his hand, I opened up the gun. Empty. So Goldtooth didn't trust the hired help. Well, you work with what you're given. Maybe we'd run across a box of shells somewhere. I snapped the gun closed.

"Let's go," I said to Kinkaid, slinging the rifle over my shoulder. "Remember your route?"

"Yeah. What about the mine?"

I stopped in the doorway and looked back. "What about it?"

"Aren't we going to do something to stop it?"

"Against a dozen armed men?"

His strong lips pressed into a thin line. I could sympathize. I didn't like the mercury dumping, either, but now wasn't the time to deal with it.

"Look," I said, "maybe you can get some of your friends together to come back later and do something. For now, I'll meet you at the end of the airstrip. If they come after you, keep running. I'll find you."

"All right."

Kinkaid bolted off along his assigned route, quickly disappearing. I headed into the compound to try to locate my gear.

Five smallish buildings lay between our hut and the office where we'd been robbed. Most of the *garimpeiros* were out on the job, and the handful of guys loitering in the open-air food court were consumed by their card game. I threaded my way between buildings and through trees, keeping low, keeping my head down, keeping my empty rifle ready to swing.

At the building where we'd been questioned, low mur-

murs told me there were at least two men inside. Probably the principals—El Capitan and Goldtooth, which meant the Shotgun Kid wasn't far away. Was my gear inside or had it been taken someplace else?

I crept around front. When I poked my head around the north corner, the three still-loitering Yanomamo women and the kid looked at me curiously, then ignored me. I eased the front door open, and when no one came running to stop me, slipped inside.

The small anteroom held nothing but a chair and a closed door into the big man's office. Eavesdropping is something I do when it's necessary and I don't feel particularly guilty about it. Especially when the eavesdroppees have held a gun on me. I forgot about eavesdropping when they started yelling. Fortunately, these guys enunciated for effect when they yelled and my Portuguese was up to the task.

"The only way to handle them is to get rid of them!" Goldtooth shouted.

My blood warmed all over. Good thing Kinkaid and I hadn't waited around to be shot. My nerves hummed.

"Do that and start a war!" yelled someone else who was not El Capitan. "We can find a better way."

"They are stupid Indians," the *donos* spat. "What do they know? What do I care about them?"

"The village leader will work with us if we—"

"He is a stupid old man. They will not do as they're told. They come beg for food and whiskey and give nothing in return. I'm through with it. Get out of my sight."

I slipped back outside into the relative cover of the next building. In a few seconds, the sullen Shotgun Kid stamped out and headed toward the food court, clearly put out.

So the Shotgun Kid showed some spunk against authority. Interesting development. Didn't help me find my gear, though.

I edged to the building's backside and found another little

room stacked floor to ceiling with supply crates, mostly dry beans, rice and glass bottles of Coca-Cola. True to my luck, no shells. And no day packs. No duffels. No nothing.

I didn't like the idea of being out in the jungle with no gear whatsoever, but it looked like I didn't have a choice. First things first. Rendezvous with Kinkaid. Better there were two of us against the world if it turned out we couldn't get our gear.

Outside, a wave of muffled shouts caught my attention. Darting along the compound's edge, I made my way toward the noise, following the wave to the rumbling, hissing hell of the mining pit. I skidded to a stop at an outbuilding near the pit's edge. Between the leaves and slender tree trunks to my right, I saw two camouflaged gun-waving types running toward the mine. Ahead of them, Kinkaid's crisp beige shirt flapped as he sprinted full tilt to the edge, took off, and leaped into the gaping, twelve-foot-deep hole.

Fear clenched my gut as Kinkaid flew, arms pinwheeling forward like a long jumper's. No way, I thought as he sailed, stopping time, defying gravity. Then Mother Earth decided she'd been denied long enough and he arced, impossibly graceful, into the pit, aiming for the moving conveyor belt.

He missed.

His leap fell a good two feet short of its mark; his body dug knee-deep into the mud. The miners howled with laughter, pointing and shouting. The man working the firehose shut off the water and stared. The *pistoleiros* stopped at the pit's crumbling edge to tee-hee. Kinkaid struggled to pull himself out of the sucking mud, his glasses askew on his face. He got one leg out before the *pistoleiros* quit chuckling and raised their guns.

You know those moments when your body overrides your brain and you do the next thing in front of you even though it seems insane?

Adrenaline surged through my chest and arms, making me unsling the rifle from my shoulder. My legs sprinted toward the *pistoleiros*. On them before they saw me, I swung the rifle like a softball bat and clobbered one on the back of the head, knocking him out cold where he stood. The other turned, mouth open in surprise. He grabbed my shirt collar with one hand, nearly pulling me off my feet. I fought his grip, swinging wildly at his face. He dropped his rifle and caught hold of my upper arm just as the pit's edge gave under our combined weight.

I lost my stomach. Mud flew as we plunged down the muddy side, rolling twice. We whacked bottom, me on top, and slid through the slime into a shin-deep puddle where the fire-hose guy stood. The *pistoleiro* lost his grip on me as I wriggled off and scrambled to my knees. He crawled after me. The useless rifle tangled in my legs. I fell on my butt. I heard a heavy clunk, then the *pistoleiro* stared blankly over my left shoulder and fell face-first into the mud.

The firehose guy standing over the *pistoleiro* waved the heavy hose nozzle and smiled. I heaved for breath, rocket fuel in my veins.

The *garimpeiros* were really laughing their asses off now. On the other side of the pit, Kinkaid had freed himself from the black mud and waded slowly but single-mindedly for the conveyor belt.

"Don't!" I yelled as I gained my feet. "That feeds a rock grinder!"

"I know!" he shouted back.

Above me, Kinkaid rode the conveyor belt's long slope to the top, about halfway to the point where he was about to become ground round. I started to yell again but a gunshot cut me off. Kinkaid ducked and spun. I glanced up at the pit's edge. The *donos* had a rifle aimed at Kinkaid.

The fire-hose guy shoved the hose under my arm and cranked the lever. A blast of water shot out of the nozzle—no arc—and plastered Goldtooth with several hundred gallons a minute of filthy water, blowing him off his feet and me off mine. The fire-hose guy leaped back. My butt hit the ground and I slid a few inches back, driving more muck under my shirttail and into my pants. Somehow I held on to the hose, spraying water into the air. Laughter, dampened by the soft mud, echoed thickly in the pit. When Goldtooth looked like he wasn't going to reappear, I jumped up and threw the hose down where it writhed like a snake, firing everywhere at once.

The conveyor belt hadn't shut down yet and Kinkaid had nearly reached the grinder. I hightailed it over and climbed onto the belt, sprinting to the top where Kinkaid jittered like a nervous cat trying to decide exactly how far that jump really was.

The noise fell on my head like an anvil. The belt emptied into a massively toothed roller grinder, which had been rigged to sit at a forty-five-degree angle. A few small rocks danced in the hopper, chewed off of larger rocks and waited their turn to be caught in the teeth and ground to powder. A work platform had been built about six feet away from the hopper. Between the hopper and the platform was nothing but empty air down a few feet to where the fuel tanks that fed the generators sat. We steadily backpedaled on the conveyor belt to stay out of the hopper.

"The ledge!" I yelled over the clatter and crunch. "Get a running start!"

Kinkaid shook his head. "Let's take out the generators!" he yelled. "Stop the gold processing!"

"We don't have time!" I shouted back. "We gotta get outta here!"

"Come on!"

He jumped down through the gap. The fuel tank *ponged* when he landed. Then he disappeared.

Well, hell. I drew the line on this one. There was no way I'd help him with his little sabotage activity when I should be concentrating on getting out alive. I backed up a few steps, glancing behind me to see how much space I had for the jump. Movement on the pit's opposite side caught my eye. More *pistoleiros* had arrived, and El Capitan stood next to the dripping Goldtooth, who shouted and waved his arms. At least ten rifle muzzles pointed at me.

Shit.

I dropped into the gap after Kinkaid, where the conveyor belt provided a wide swath of cover from the rifles. Kinkaid hunkered a few feet away, twisting off the tank cap.

"You gonna water down the diesel with spit?" I asked.

He flashed a cheeky grin. "Nope." He turned away from me slightly and unzipped.

Good grief.

"You're gonna need a full bladder," I informed him.

"Fait accompli," he replied. After a moment, he zipped up, then started grabbing handfuls of mud off his boots and cramming them down the nozzle for good measure, smearing muck all over the tank in his hurry.

His hurry was the only thing I agreed with. While he did his best to foul the generators' blood supply, I watched the fresh batch of *pistoleiros* figuring out how to get to us without crossing through the mud pit. Our way out was simple: duck under the shed housing the generators, which would probably render us both deaf, and slip out over the runoff spillway. One of the gunmen started down the slippery slope while El Capitan motioned the Shotgun Kid to run the long way around the pit to cut us off.

"Are you done yet?" I yelled over crunching rocks and growling generators.

"That's it!" Kinkaid shouted.

"This way!"

I was right about the path under the generator shed: the noise reverberating down onto my head made my eyes water.

But the path was also dry, at least here, so we scrambled along relatively easily until we came to the shed's backside where the spillway vomited its mercury-tainted waterfall.

Mercury doesn't smell, which is what makes it so dangerous—you can't tell poisoned water from safe water. I felt a twinge of gladness Kinkaid had taken the time to sabotage the generators. It wouldn't stop the mining for good, but it'd slow it down a little.

Kinkaid jumped over the spillway and turned to wait for me. I'd already committed, was in the air, when I saw the Shotgun Kid step out from behind a boulder, his gun trained on Kinkaid. No time to react. I landed, held up my hands and, heart pounding, waited to be shot.

"Come with me! Quickly!" the Shotgun Kid said in English. He motioned with his gun and didn't try to take my useless one.

If the Shotgun Kid held a grudge against El Capitan and the *donos,* I reflected, Kinkaid and I just might have gotten very lucky.

I nodded at Kinkaid. We followed the Kid deep into the forest, well away from the struggling *pistoleiros.* When we were some distance up the hillside and the noise of the now-gagging generators had become a dull grumbling, we hunkered down behind a stone outcropping. The Kid put down his gun. Kinkaid took off his glasses and started wiping at the mud smears with his surprisingly clean shirttail tugged out of his pants. I tried to wipe some of the muck off my legs to disguise the fact my hands were shaking uncontrollably. Helluva adrenaline kick.

"My name is Porfilio," the Kid said. "You must take a message for me to the Yanomamo village. You a friend of the Yanomamo, right?" he asked Kinkaid.

Kinkaid's eyes narrowed, wary. "I'm a scientist," he said, "and I don't like what the gold processing does to the water. It's illegal."

"So is destroying someone else's generators," I remarked.

"Yes," Porfilio said, ignoring me. His gaze, wide-eyed and earnest, latched on to Kinkaid. "I know. I want to bring the Yanomamo and the mining together, not to fight. The colonel will destroy the village. He will not listen to me. Which is why I must fight him myself."

"Why would he destroy the village?"

"To stop the Yanomamo from being in his way. The little villages are banding together to come destroy the mine. Rumors of fighting everywhere. The Yanomamo want their land back."

Kinkaid nodded. "So you want to negotiate a truce."

"More than a truce," Porfilio said solemnly. "A partnership. Stop the mercury. Stop the tearing up of the land. Stop the killing of Yanomamo, of miners."

Kinkaid put a hand on Porfilio's shoulder. "What's your message?"

I stared at the two of them while they kept talking—two idealists out to save the world. If my hand hadn't been so slimy I would have slapped my palm to my forehead in disbelief. Time to excise myself from this little do-gooder club and be on my way.

Then Kinkaid nodded, shot me a quick glance...and nearly knocked the breath out of me. His angular face intense, his longish hair slicked back, glasses off, and an eight-hour beard scruffing him up, he could have passed for a bedroom fantasy involving black leather and scented oil.

And dammit, his eyes were a deep, deep brown. My very fave.

"I'll take your message," he said to Porfilio. "I'll help in any way I can." They shook muddy hands on it. Friends of the Earth, I thought, in more ways than one. What next? Cut their palms and become blood brothers? But Kinkaid's hand, grungy as it was, looked strong and capable, like it could accomplish anything he wanted it to.

I cleared my throat. "We gotta get outta here. What'd they do with our stuff? The stuff from the plane?"

"I took it," Porfilio said proudly. "I bring it to you tonight."

I shook my head. "With your friends looking for us everywhere? No good. I plan on being miles into the jungle by nightfall. It's now or never."

Porfilio's face darkened as he considered this. It obviously bugged him not to give my gear back, but was it worth the risk? Then his black eyes cleared and he nodded. "Go to the other side of this hill and wait for me in the little cave. I meet you there soon."

I didn't like the wait, inevitable as it was. But the prospect of spending twelve hours in the open jungle at night without my first-aid kit or fresh water didn't appeal to me, either. The research station might be able to provide supplies, but we had to get there first, and it was a good fifteen miles away.

"Okay," I said finally. "The little cave. If you don't show up in an hour, we're going anyway."

Kinkaid put on his glasses, ruining the fantasy. "It's not safe to leave without our gear."

"No, but it's not safe to stay for long. We can't afford to hang around until the bad guys find us."

"I will hurry," Porfilio said. "Here." He dug into his leather ammo pack and plucked out a handful of shells. "In case they catch me and come after you."

I took the shells, suddenly feeling like hell for making him go get my gear. If El Capitan suspected the Kid of screwing him over on our behalf, El Capitan would doubtless de-capitate him. Based on the conversation I'd heard earlier, Porfilio already walked a thin line with Goldtooth.

But Scooter came first. I'd been fooling myself to believe I could get by without my climbing gear. I needed that stuff, bad, or else Scooter didn't have a chance.

After Porfilio took off, Kinkaid and I hiked around the hill.

It took me a half hour to find the little cave, which turned out to be an oversize cleft in the rocky northern face. Still, there was room to wedge ourselves inside. A good-size manioc tree shielded the entrance. Kinkaid shoehorned himself in to sit sideways, his long legs stretched across the cave. I followed, sitting to face him. If I pressed my sore ribs hard against his calves, I could just stay in the shadow, out of sight. I loaded up the rifle, then laid it across my lap.

"I don't know your name," Kinkaid said after a while.

I picked up a stick and started digging mud out of my boot soles. "Robards."

"Is that your first name or your last?"

"My first is Jessie."

"Short for Jessica?"

"Yeah."

"You study bromeliads, huh?"

"Look, you don't have to make small talk."

He fell silent. The dim light threw his cheekbone into sharp relief. Just under his lenses, that pinup bad boy impression lurked, taunting me. Okay, he'd landed the plane and saved my life. He'd made a helluva jump into a mining pit, was cool as a cucumber under gunfire, and managed to single-handedly shut down the compound's generators. But I didn't want to be his friend.

I guess that didn't mean I had to be an ass, though.

"Sorry," I said. "Busy day."

"I know what you mean."

"So you're an entomologist," I said. "What are you doing at the research station?"

"That's base camp. I'm here looking for the *Traça do Corpse*." He sat up a little straighter. "A colleague of mine spotted it last week. It's huge—" and here he demonstrated with his hands "—a wingspan of nine inches, and pollinates an orchid—"

"Wait," I interrupted. "What is it? A bee? A beetle? What?"

"*Traça,*" he said, pushing his glasses up his aquiline nose. "A moth. The Corpse Moth."

Not the Corpse Moth. The Death Moth.

According to Harrison's notes, that moth was the Death Orchid's sole coevolved partner. Sighted last week, it would have been out pollinating the Death Orchid, which itself would have been blooming. And the shortest distance between two points is a straight line.

I looked at the man who happened to be the straightest line I had at my disposal.

My days of working alone were over, at least for now.

Chapter 6

After Porfilio brought our gear, we took a few minutes to re-arrange. Without his camera and tripod, Kinkaid was travel-ing light, so he took on some of my climbing gear to even up the weight distribution. I strapped on my lightweight head-lamp for the hike. Kinkaid's map showed his research station to be about fifteen miles away, and if we hiked the rest of the evening and all night, we'd be within spitting distance of it by dawn. I hoped he was up to it. I didn't want to hang around while he caught his breath.

Hiking through the jungle at night even under a full moon isn't particularly easy. You think the jungle's alive during the day, but it's ten times more that way when the sun goes down. Every creeping thing that creeps upon the earth creeps out, and at the pace I set, there wasn't time to make sure every stick was actually a stick before stepping over it. For the sake of speed, I'd take my chances getting stung and bitten. Come daylight, I'd have thirteen days left.

If Scooter was hanging in there. Not knowing how he was doing gnawed at me.

We stopped around two in the morning for a break and something to eat. When I eased my duffel off my aching shoulders, my sudden ravenousness surprised me. On the move, I don't really think about anything except where the next foot goes. I dropped my duffel between my feet on a moss-covered rock and dimmed my headlamp so I wouldn't blind Kinkaid.

"Here." He held out some kind of granola-based tree-hugging vegan Buddhist energy bar, which I accepted without an ounce of shame.

"Thanks."

He hadn't said a word since I struck out into the forest, and he had kept pace over some messy ground, even without his own headlamp. I was starting to doubt he was a jungle newbie.

"Do you always know where you're going?" he asked as he tore into his energy bar's recycled paper wrapper.

"I always know where I am, and I guess that's the real issue."

"How do you do that?"

I shrugged. "Internal compass, I guess. My great-uncle once took me blindfolded out into the middle of two hundred acres of cornfield, but I found my way home almost immediately."

"How old were you?"

"Nine."

Kinkaid meticulously folded his wrapper and tucked it back in his bag. "That's kind of young to be left like that in the middle of nowhere."

I shrugged again. "He knew I'd find my way home. It was an experiment. I bet he was never more than fifty yards away the whole time."

His glasses glinted as he nodded. The contrast of darkness and dim light made his angular features stronger, more classically handsome. After a while he said, "How far do we have to go?"

"I'm figuring another eight miles. Are you up for it?"

"Sure."

"Not like hanging around the gym, is it?"

I sensed more than saw his smile in the dim light. "I don't hang around a gym, but I know what you mean."

He shifted his weight to put a hand against a *Tachygalia myrmecophilia* tree but suddenly jerked away. Kinkaid really did know his field stuff, I gathered. The *Tachygalia myrmecophilia* has one of those coevolving relationships with a vicious biting ant. There isn't enough deet in the world to stop those ants when they think their home is threatened.

"What does your moth look like?" I asked, trying to sound casual. If the moth was attracted to the orchid's coloring because the flower looked like its mate, I'd have another clue about what I was looking for.

"My colleague told me it looks remarkably like a *Laothoe populi,* except several times larger." Excitement tinged his voice. "I want to see for myself, though."

I could relate. There's nothing like poking around the woods and swamps for endless days and nights looking for any clue—a tiny sprout in a tangle of weeds, the whiff of a scent you'd never smelled, a leaf shape that didn't look quite like it fit. The thrill of the hunt was my favorite part. Then to discover that the little clue you've been looking for is gravy. It was one reason I was glad to be traveling at night. During the day, it's too easy to get distracted by the decadent display all around me. I couldn't afford the luxury of distraction on this trip.

The good news was that *Laothoe populi,* if I remembered what few bug facts I'd learned in grad school, had the pearlescent black wings whose color had been smoked into Harrison's medicine bowl. It sounded like I was on the right track.

Trying to tamp down another excitement-provoked adrenaline surge, I hitched my duffel onto my back. "Ready to go?"

"Why are you doing this?" Kinkaid asked.

"Doing what?"

"Taking me to the Ixpachia station."

"It's the same general direction as where I'm headed." I dialed up a brighter beam, shooting a swath of light into the darkness.

"You don't seem the kind of person who'd do this out of the kindness of your heart."

"I'm not. But two things. First, I owe you. You saved my life." And I always try to pay my debts. "Second, there might be a botanist at your station who can help me out."

"With your bromeliads."

"Yep." I started off, but looked back when I didn't hear him behind me.

"Bromeliads," he said again.

"Bromeliads," I replied.

We looked at each other for a long moment. Then, even though he must have known I was lying, he followed me.

The Ixpachia Research Station was a considerable step up from the mining compound in terms of amenities. The buildings that ringed its large open area had screened doors and freshly thatched roofs. There wasn't a mess hall, so to speak, so I had to assume it was every scientist for himself when it came to cooking. Sometimes if you park near a village, an Indian will cook for you in exchange for rum or whiskey. As long as you didn't look too hard at what was in your soup, you'd eat pretty good.

Speaking of, I was starving. And what I wouldn't give for a shower and a mudless set of clothes.

Those thoughts dropped out of my head when a contingent of intellectual types piled out of the buildings at our arrival.

A tall, bearded guy who looked to be in his robust sixties strode out from the crowd. His white, bushy hair stuck out all over his head and bobbed as he walked toward us. A grin broadened his face.

"Rick!" he said, shaking Kinkaid's hand heartily. "Glad you made it!"

"Thought I wouldn't for a while there."

"You look like hell. Have you been wrestling with a wild hog?"

Kinkaid flashed that bad-boy-having-fun grin. "Jessie, this is Dr. Darrin Yagoda, an old professor of mine from the University of Florida. Darrin, this is Jessie Robards, the lady who got me here."

I got the impression Yagoda summed me up in one word: trouble. His handshake lacked both enthusiasm and warmth. What? Was I treading on someone's toes by showing up?

"Don't worry," I said to Yagoda. "I won't be around long."

His gray eyes widened at that. "You're welcome to stay as long as you need," he said quickly. "I just didn't expect Rick to have company."

"Neither did I," Kinkaid said, smiling, "but I'm glad I did. Where's breakfast?"

"Come on." Yagoda hooked an arm over Kinkaid's shoulder and ushered him toward one of the buildings, leaving me standing there.

Unsure whether Yagoda intended me to follow, I did. I wanted breakfast and I wanted it now. No amount of our host's pretending I didn't exist changed how loudly my stomach was growling. When they reached the building, Kinkaid dropped back and waited for me while Yagoda went on inside.

"Be patient," he said in a low voice. "He's rough around the edges, but he's okay."

"Old friend of yours?"

"My doctoral dissertation advisor eight years ago or so."

Eight years? That put Kinkaid in his early thirties, just a few years older than me. No way. He looked all of twenty-four. Maybe he was a prodigy.

"All I want is something to eat and someplace to crash for the day," I said. "Then I'll be on my way."

"That's what I can offer," Yagoda said from his makeshift fireplace. "Come on in, Ms. Robards."

"I suspect it's *Dr.* Robards." Kinkaid's eyes sharpened behind his glasses. "Though she hasn't admitted it."

I smiled at Kinkaid but didn't answer yea or nay. A good plant collector, especially a mercenary like me, doesn't tell anything more than she absolutely has to. The last thing I needed was these people to try to stop what I was doing because they hated private collectors. Or worse, carry stories about me to other drop-in visitors who happened to be my competition.

Which got part of my brain wondering if Lawrence Daley was on his way down to Roraima while another part took note of Yagoda's posh setup.

The main area consisted of a cooking fireplace where something delicious-smelling stewed merrily, a worktable cluttered with a microscope, mounting board, and several bottles of alcohol, and a couple of hand-built bamboo chairs. Yagoda must be big man on campus to rate a hut with a separate sleeping room. A doorway on the back wall led out to a little patio deck where a rusty pipe dribbled water. The bathroom, I gathered.

"Have a seat." Yagoda gestured to the chairs, which Kinkaid and I took. "I hope you like *agouti.*" He raised a challenging brow at me as he dished out of the cook pot to fill a bowl.

"I love jungle rat," I said, then leaned conspiratorially toward Kinkaid. "Tastes like chicken," I assured him, prompting a thin bark of a laugh from Yagoda.

"Tell me about the Corpse Moth," Kinkaid said as Yagoda

walked over to hand him a wooden bowl filled with stew and a palm-size piece of bread to eat with.

Yagoda shook his shaggy head. "Why don't you eat first. You look like you've hiked all night."

"We did." Kinkaid tore off a piece of bread and tucked it gingerly into the stew.

The big man paused in the act of handing me my bowl to stare at Kinkaid. I reached up and took the bowl out of his hand but he didn't notice. The rich aroma rising off the stew got my stomach growling again.

"Why did you do that?" Yagoda asked. "That's dangerous!"

While Kinkaid talked and Yagoda tried to wrap his brain around our little trek, I got up and tore myself a hunk of bread off the loaf by the fire. I scooped the bread into the stew and tasted. Heavenly. I sighed and headed back to my chair but Yagoda had sat down in it.

"Hey," I said to him.

He gave a start and popped out of my chair, then sat cross-legged next to Kinkaid's chair to continue their conversation about the trip to the station.

Ah, yes, scientists. Yagoda didn't have a clue how insulting he was being. He was just a one-topic kind of guy. All the brilliant ones are like that. Harrison certainly was. Had been. The stew was magnificent.

"Have you heard anything from the Yanomamo about it?" Kinkaid was asking when I scraped bottom and tuned in again.

Yagoda shook his head, throwing a few wispy hairs off his white-bread afro. "We have three Yanomamo workers, but none of them have mentioned fighting the miners. Are you going to talk to the village leader?"

"Yes." Kinkaid pulled off his glasses and scrubbed his eyes with his fingers. "I need some sleep first. And a shower."

"You're in luck," Yagoda said. "Bernard is back in the States for a semester, so you can have his hut."

We picked up our gear and followed Yagoda along the circle to a smallish hut that housed a cot, a table, a chair and a cooking fireplace. No separate sleeping room for Bernard. But the screens were in good shape, and the walls went all the way to the floor, which meant our chances of being crept upon were slimmer than usual. Yagoda produced a spare cot and a couple of blankets. The little stone-floored patio area had a full-fledged solar-heated hot-water bag shower suspended above it. Things were looking up again.

But lying down after a fifteen-mile overnight hike, finally clean, in clean clothes, in a relatively comfortable bed, under shelter, with a full stomach, my brain refused to shut up. My body wanted to crash, but my mind raced as I lay staring at the ceiling beams.

Was Kinkaid's moth the secret to my finding the Death Orchid, or was I on a wild-goose chase? No, it had to be the same insect. Corpse Moth, Death Moth. The moth's coloring matched the medicine bowl. The medicine bowl had been in Harrison's apartment along with his notes pointing to this area. I was in the right place.

What had happened to Harrison? What would have caused him to leave academia and go to work for the arch-capitalist von Brutten? I couldn't shake the feeling that Harrison had been coerced somehow into working for my employer. Some weakness had made him a victim, possibly of von Brutten, possibly of someone else. Maybe he'd gotten scared or depressed and run away. I could see him doing that. Or had he actually come down here to harvest a Death Orchid only to get himself killed, perhaps by another orchid collector?

Speaking of, what about Lawrence Daley? He knew von Brutten wanted the orchid, and he would have followed me to steal it. I'd used yet another alias when I made my travel plans, so it was possible I'd given him the slip. I shook my head. No, Daley was too motivated by cash and revenge and downright orneriness to let me get away with this orchid. He was a known quantity and I'd dealt with him before.

But who was the Brain, the guy I tackled on the River Walk in San Antonio? Where did he know me from? Was he one of Harrison's grad students? It could be he was working with Harrison on von Brutten's Parkinson's project, but I couldn't envision a mild-mannered medical research scientist pulling a desk apart looking for a map to the Death Orchid. If he'd been working with Harrison, it made sense that von Brutten would have known about him and told me. No, the Brain must be working for someone else. But who?

That brought me to the not-blood-stained notebook page. Marcus Donovan, using the considerable resources of the CIA tech lab, would be able to figure out the stain in next to no time, at least according to his reputation. Had he left me a voice mail like he said he would? I'd have to wait until I got back to Boa Vista to check my messages.

I could call Scooter then, too. Was he doing okay? Hank and Marian were probably taking good care of him, like they always did while I was away. Marian worked for her room and board, so at least with the barmaid living in Scooter's trailer, he'd have someone with him day and night. And home-cooked meals.

The last question I had was whether von Brutten was doing something about Cradion already, or was he waiting for me to return with the Death Orchid, playing the games powerful people play when they're orchestrating world events from on high?

"Are you okay?" Kinkaid's voice startled me out of my near-comatose reverie.

"Yeah. Why?"

"You were making little noises. Like a bad dream."

I threw one arm over my eyes, playing drama queen. "I was whimpering, wasn't I? How humiliating."

"No—" and there was a chuckle behind the word "—you just seemed…disturbed. Upset."

I sighed and put my arm back down. When I turned my head, I looked up close and personal into the face of that naughty bedroom fantasy. Bug nerd, I reminded myself. Appearances aren't everything.

Right, another part of my brain laughed. *Carlos's appearance had nothing to do with jumping into bed with him.*

"I have a lot to do and not much time to do it," I replied.

"Same here."

"What's your timetable?"

Kinkaid heaved a sigh, then rolled off his back to lean on his elbow and look at me. He wore a white muscle-tee undershirt and the bit of chest I could see was smooth skinned, unadulterated by even a hint of hair.

I like my guys burly, I thought, calling up images of Carlos's perfect body. Burly with nice chest hair a girl can run her fingers through.

"The Corpse Moth is kind of an unknown species," he said. "I can only guess how long it lives and what its mating behavior is like. Dr. Yagoda first spotted it five days ago, so I'm counting down. I hoped to be looking for it last night." He shrugged his smooth shoulder. It was evenly tanned, dark against the white T-shirt. "What about you?"

"I have to be back to start a new job in a couple of weeks," I lied.

"What do you do?"

"Nursery work. Breeding, crossbreeding, that kind of thing."

"So this is a research trip for you?"

I nodded, wondering what his smooth, tanned chest felt like to a girl's cheek. Warm, probably. Too warm in this heat.

"I have the feeling we're looking for the same thing," he said.

My lungs froze up. "What do you mean?" I asked, trying to sound casual.

"You know, the one great find of your career—the find that gets you noticed by universities."

"Oh."

"We'll both find what we came for," he said confidently, rolling onto his back again and stretching. "What we were meant to find."

Great. Kinkaid was a split personality: entomologist and Pollyanna. And gymnast, if you counted the wild stunts he'd pulled at the mine. Stunts that could've gotten us both killed.

Scooter, I thought to the old man, you'd better be around when I get back because I'm going to a lot of trouble for you.

As my brain finally gave in to exhaustion, I heard Scooter's chuckle. *Don't you worry none 'bout me, Ladybug,* he said. *You just worry 'bout yerself.*

Good plan.

"Dammit!" Kinkaid said, staring into what I suspected was an empty trap. The trap rested on a tree branch, baited with some kind of scent he insisted the Corpse Moth found attractive. Where he got that information, I have no idea. Probably Yagoda.

"Didn't get one, huh?" I asked.

"No."

"Dammit," I agreed.

We had plenty to curse about. Two days of getting drenched with rain, two nights of finding not even a suggestion of the Corpse Moth. Even Kinkaid's Pollyanna side seemed subdued today. Maybe it was the last thunderstorm's positive ions. Those have an ill effect on the human animal.

The positive ions certainly had me feeling a little on edge. For the past half day or so I'd had the distinct, hair-on-the-back-of-the-neck impression we were being watched. But every time I glanced behind me, nothing but vines and palm fronds and deep green.

"Maybe the moth's habitat is another part of the forest," I suggested.

"If anything, I'm not putting the trap high enough. The Corpse Moth usually doesn't venture out of its strata."

"Maybe it was slumming."

"Dr. Yagoda was very specific about where he last saw the moth." Kinkaid picked up his backpack.

"Yeah, well, my science gods have been wrong before, so maybe yours is this time."

He shot me a hard glance as he shrugged on his pack. "Hero worship isn't my style."

"I'd believe you if every other word out of your mouth wasn't the man's name," I remarked.

"I respect his judgment," Kinkaid said testily.

"So do I."

My innocent look must have been working because he said, "Will you do me a favor?"

I smiled my sweetest smile. "Where do you want your trap?"

He glanced up without moving his head.

"Canopy, huh?"

"If it's not too much trouble."

"Hey, I was headed up there anyway. Besides, I owe you. You save my life, I save your career."

He turned away too late. I saw his grin and answered with a genuine smile he didn't see. As he moved off, I noticed his oversize shirt had shrunk with the washing he'd given it at the research station. Now it barely fit shoulders that were broader than they'd first looked.

We started the trek back up the mountainside to the hollow where I'd left my climbing gear. Over the past two days, as Kinkaid hunted the Corpse Moth and I pretended to hunt bromeliads, we'd worked our way some miles away from the Ixpachia Research Station, which was fine with me. I didn't much care for His Highness Yagoda or the Stepford grad students he'd brought with him. Rick was much more real, more human, than those cookie-cutter geeks.

On the other hand, our little treasure hunt took us back toward the mine, which I didn't like because it kept me on high alert for the *pistoleiros*. And backtracking slowly over the miles I'd covered at high speed a few days before was annoying. It felt like wasted effort.

But we'd worked out a schedule that suited us both, traveling in the morning and setting up camp in the early afternoon. Then while Kinkaid loaded his bug traps, I'd climb to the canopy and spend the afternoon looking around. Early the next morning he'd check his traps and we'd be off again to the next likely site. Hiking as fast as we did, we were a good seven miles away from the station even moving just a few hours a day.

I guess I worked so well with Kinkaid because he was a scientist with his mind on the prize and nothing else. It felt like the camaraderie I'd had in grad school when a few of us struggled to identify one of Harrison's ambiguous specimens or do a genetic analysis. Intellectual equals with no funny business to get in the way.

"What do you like best about your work?" Kinkaid asked as we hiked around a fallen tangle of liana vines and richly composting plant matter.

That was easy. "The chase."

"I prefer the find."

"Why the find? It's all over at that point."

"It's only over if you value the hunt above all else. I like everything that comes after the find. The study, the understanding. Learning everything there is to know."

"Well, yeah, but what about the excitement?" I glanced back at him. "The thrill of something new?"

He shrugged. "It's still there. The more you learn, the more you learn you need to learn. I never get bored." His bad-boy look lurked under his lenses again. "There's always something new if you know how to look for it."

I let that ride without comment.

"So you only hunt?" he pursued.

"Usually."

"Ah." His tone of voice said, *That explains a lot.*

I shot him a glance. The grin was back. I ignored it. Cheeky boy.

Climbing gear comes in handiest when you're already up a tree. A botany lab I saw in Peru last year was practically a canopy-based city, a complex of lines and pulleys and even wooden platforms anchored in the emergent hardwoods to hold scientists, rudimentary equipment and specimens. Very neat stuff, and if I hadn't been heading off with a pair of rare *Brassias* at the time I might have lingered to appreciate the engineering that went into building it.

But the first task was to get up the tree.

"Do you want the headset?" Kinkaid asked.

I looked at the miked headset he'd borrowed from Ixpachia and shook my head. "I'll be up and down in no time. Let's not bother."

I buckled up my harness and used a piece of flat webbing to make my running anchor. The hardwood I'd picked to climb was a kapok with massive flying buttress roots—a kissing cousin to the swamp cypress but with a much wider base. I hooked a coil of rope across my chest and clipped some additional webbing to my harness, then fed the running anchor around the tree's huge foot. Kinkaid waited quietly.

Walking up a tree is kind of like rappelling down a cliff—you have to do exactly the opposite of what instinct tells you to do.

Here's how it works. You've got a running anchor rope that goes around the tree trunk, with both ends attached to your harness. You toss that rope up the tree trunk a little ways and walk up the trunk to it.

But the trick is that your legs are stuck out nearly in front of you, like you're sitting down. Your weight holds you tight against the anchor line and you don't slip. In theory, you can brace your feet on the trunk and kind of lean there all day long. Next time you're in a narrow hallway, try bracing your hands and feet against opposite walls and hanging off the floor. Same general principle.

When you're ready to move up the tree, you have to lean forward just enough to give you the slack to hike the anchor up the trunk a little. It's scary the first forty times you do it, but after that it gets to be old hat. Years ago, telephone repairmen who worked the poles used the same technique to climb before some bright spark thought of installing those metal L pieces in the pole to make a ladder.

My only real challenge, one the telephone repairmen didn't have, was the ubiquitous tree branch. I had to string a second running anchor over the branch, lean on it, then release the first running anchor that was below the branch. Piece of cake.

As I passed from the midstory into the canopy, sweating like a pig, I suddenly wondered if the Evil Eye was going to catch up with me. If Scooter were here, he'd be warning me to watch for snakes "extry careful." Hell, if Scooter were here, he'd have me wearing some kind of herbal charm around my neck to ward them off. I'd probably catch the damned thing on a branch and choke myself to death.

I'd reached the canopy. Time to concentrate on setting my sling. I tossed a line of webbing over a stout branch and pulled hard. When the branch didn't give, I clipped a locking carabiner to the line. Then the same procedure on a different branch, for safety's sake.

I hooked a new anchor line through the carabiners and attached it to my climbing harness. This anchor would take all my weight. Yanking on the anchor didn't budge the slings. Good.

I passed the climbing rope through the two independently hung carabiners. It would take me home when I was ready to leave, and I'd leave it overnight for tomorrow's trip up to check the trap.

"Rope!" I yelled down to Kinkaid.

"Ready!"

Under most circumstances I'd handle the rope work myself, but I was kind of glad to have him belay me while I set the trap. I don't have enough hands to maneuver and hold myself steady and set bug traps all at once.

I dropped the rest of the coil. Ordinarily a hundred feet of rope would tangle on itself or catch on something, but it fell straight, unmolested, through the midstory to land near Kinkaid's feet. Things were looking up.

Kinkaid grabbed the rope and took up the slack. The other end I tied to my harness. Then it was a simple matter of unhooking the running anchor line holding me to the tree and stepping into the air.

This is the part where it's best not to look down. Even now, after years of climbing cliffs, ledges and trees, my calves tingled when I looked down. Why does fear go straight to the knees?

I swung, breathless, away from the kapok. A hundred or so feet below, Kinkaid leaned back, ready to catch me if one of the two slings broke.

Everything held.

I had to admit to myself, as I strapped the bug trap on a tree limb directly above me, that it was nice not to have to go it alone for a while. My nightmares aren't about falling. They're about landing. And lying there. Indefinitely. Starving to death, or maybe being picked on by scavengers. Vampire bats. Or being gnawed by a jaguar while still alive.

I pulled out my field glasses and surveyed the botanical wealth. Bromeliads, yes, everywhere. A half-dozen orchids of various identifiable persuasions, endless vines, a cautious capuchin monkey watching me while it chewed a piece of fruit.

A flash of white that wasn't light caught my eye and I

paused. Below me, woody liana vines crawling across the midstory treetops had made themselves into a giant hammock filled with what my colleagues call biomass. Don't let the fancy name fool you. Basically, biomass means "living matter." In this case, the biomass was "a compost pile."

But compost piles that hang in trees make great places to find epiphytes—plants that grow on the tree but aren't parasites. Oddly, the biomass doesn't smell too awful because everything breaks down so fast. Beetles burrow through the rotting leaves, the epiphytes anchor their roots, rainwater leaks through from top to bottom. It's just mucky.

True epiphytes, like bromeliads and some orchids, survive off whatever sheds onto them, whether rain, bugs or dead leaves. And if they happen to get lucky enough to be seeded in a hanging compost pile, so much the better for them.

Right now, my heart started to pound as I scanned the biomass for that white flash. A flower would be too much to hope for and my luck wasn't ordinarily that good, but it didn't hurt to give the compost pile a once-over.

"I'm coming down a few feet to check something out!" I called down. "I need about two inches of lift."

"Got it."

Kinkaid pulled hard on the rope to raise me, taking the pressure off the anchor line. I unclipped the anchor and let it swing.

"Slack!" I shouted.

Kinkaid started paying out the rope. I guess he'd taken climbing lessons somewhere, because he knew what to do without my having to tell him. I still controlled my descent, but he belayed me like a good climbing partner.

I came even with the biomass hammock. The white stuff might be mold or high-flying mushrooms for all I knew. I pulled my machete from its holster and prodded into the mass. Plenty of material there, but where was that flower? I stuck the machete under a largish branch and shoved it to one side.

Yellow, alien eyes speared me. Pit viper. A fer-de-lance. Its coiled brown-gray body unwound as it eased toward me, tongue flicking, its head the size of a big man's fist.

It struck.

Chapter 7

I jerked back, twisting away. The wedge-shaped head snapped past my right shoulder. My machete hand was in the wrong position to hack. I grabbed at the snake's body with my left hand.

And missed.

It slithered off the hammock and fell onto my lap, its tail writhing around my dangling legs. Its head angled toward me.

"Drop me!" I screamed to Kinkaid.

Instantly the rope jerked into motion and I fell, crashing through air, through banana, cassava, bitterroot, palm. A branch clipped the machete, knocking it from my grip. I grabbed the viper's warm, dry body with my good left hand and my stunned right. My fingers didn't even begin to go around the snake, it was so huge. Its tail clung stubbornly to its death grip on my left calf, squeezing the muscle. Head reared back, it showed me its extended fangs. My heart tried to pound its way out of my chest. I had to do something.

Then my harness jerked, biting into the backs of my thighs and throwing me forward. The fer-de-lance jolted, hissing and writhing. *Please,* I prayed. I slid my right hand up its body toward its massive head. I couldn't feel my left foot anymore. But my right boot toe grazed the ground.

I tried to pry the snake off my leg with my left hand, keeping my right arm locked straight and the snake's head as far away as possible. It was stronger and faster than I was. Much faster. I wouldn't avoid another strike if it broke free of my grip.

"Cut it in half!" I shouted to Kinkaid. "Hurry!"

He cursed, then in my periphery I saw him stoop to grab the dropped machete where it had landed, blade dug into the earth. I held the viper stretched out between my hands. Kinkaid raised the machete to swing.

The fer-de-lance twisted from my grip and sprang at Kinkaid, sinking its fangs deep into his bare forearm.

"Dammit!" I yelled.

Kinkaid backed up, stumbling over tree roots and uneven ground, dragging the fer-de-lance with him. The viper released my leg. Its heavy body thumped on the forest floor but it didn't let go of Kinkaid's arm.

"Stop moving!" I shouted. "If you keep moving you'll get more venom!"

He pushed the machete blade tip into the viper's mouth. Abruptly the fer-de-lance broke away, slithered into the jungle underbrush, out of sight. Kinkaid panted, staring at his arm.

My sling held me hostage, just off the ground. The rope had caught on something, dangling me. *Damn my luck.* "Sit down!" I called. "Sit down and don't move!"

I yanked on the rope above me. It didn't budge. *Dammit!* With my good hand, I got a tight grip on the rope and raised myself, taking pressure off the harness carabiner. I tried to squeeze the carabiner's lip open to release the climbing rope. My fingers were too shocked, too weak. Like in a dream, I heard myself gasping with frustrated tears. I squeezed the carabiner again. Got it. The rope slipped through and I fell hard to the ground.

I scrambled to gain my feet. I scooped up my day pack and ran to Kinkaid where he sat against a tree, holding his forearm.

"Let me see," I said.

He took his hand away. Two perfect punctures, one still filled with fang. His skin already reddened and puckered as his body responded to the venom. And, true to my luck, the viper had struck deep into the muscle, which would carry the neurotoxin through his system faster than a hit into fat.

"It stings," he remarked calmly.

"I'm going to take this fang out and then give you the antivenin."

"Okay."

"Keep your forearm below your heart." I dug through the day pack for the antivenin kit. Thank God I'd bought a fresh one before flying down. But I had to hurry. The sun was fading and I was losing the good light.

My hands were shaking so hard I couldn't hold the tweezers steady to pluck out the fang.

"Jessie. Jessie." Kinkaid's deep voice swept over me in a soothing wave.

I grabbed a fistful of his sleeve and held on, not meeting his gaze. If I did that I'd burst into tears right here. I was freakin' useless. "Okay," I said after a moment, steeling myself. "I'm ready."

This time my hands were calm enough to snag the fang with the tweezers. I put the fang into a small specimen jar. "For a souvenir," I told him as I screwed the cap on.

"If I last that long."

"Shut up. You'll last." He had to. That snake was meant for me, not him. I tore open the antivenin kit. "Are you allergic to horse serum?"

"I don't know." Sweat glistened on his forehead.

"How do you feel?" I asked. "Dizzy? Faint?"

"A little nauseated."

I nodded as if that were routine. In reality, the venom was working much faster than it should. The viper must have pumped a lot of poison into him. "I'm going to use the extractor to try to remove some of the venom," I said as casually as I could. I still sounded terrified.

The Sawyer extraction syringe sucked out a few cc's of blood along with some clear venom. But the fact Kinkaid was already nauseated suggested he was extremely susceptible to the poison. I kept up the extractor for a few minutes until messy fluid soaked the washcloth I was using. I didn't get anything significant and the wound was starting to swell.

On to the big guns. "Let's give you the serum sensitivity test."

He leaned his head back against the tree, watching me. "The station is a long way to hike."

"Yeah, it is. Hold still." I scraped his unbitten arm with the kit's test pad.

The station was so far away, in fact, that if Kinkaid turned out to be allergic to the antivenin, given his sensitivity to the venom, he didn't stand a chance. To get him to the station, we'd have to violate the first rule of snakebite: don't move. This wasn't an outing to Camp Okefenokee. No road. No telephone. No life flight choppers. No cavalry riding over the ridge. No help anywhere except what I could give. And I couldn't carry him the seven miles over rugged terrain. In the coming dark.

But if it came to it, I'd try. My teeth clenched against tears. This was my fault, my snake. He was a good guy and he wouldn't die on my watch if I could help it.

"That was a potent thought you just had," he remarked. "You tensed up pretty hard."

"Thinking about strategy." I tossed him a quick smile that felt like it didn't go anywhere.

He nodded. "When will this test be done?"

I glanced at the watch I'd clipped to the day pack's strap. "Another five minutes."

"It's itching."

"The scrape or the wound?"

"The wound's just numb. The scrape itches."

"Let's give the test its five minutes." I swallowed hard, knowing it was useless.

He was allergic to the horse serum.

He was going to die.

I turned away and started shifting stuff around in my packs. Everything nonessential went into the duffel. Water and food went into the day pack. After a moment's hard thought, the vial of morphine—seventy milligrams, more than enough to shut down a grown man's nervous system—went in as well.

Kinkaid's good arm looked like road rash. He wasn't just a little allergic to the serum. I cut a thin strip of climbing rope to tie snugly around his upper forearm, then made sure I could slide a finger under it. Tourniquets for snakebite had fallen out of favor years ago.

"Okay," I said, strapping on my day pack, "here's what we'll do." I knelt next to him. His eyes, steady behind the lenses, were calm and still. Trusting. "We'll hike for an hour and rest for ten minutes. We've still got plenty of water, so we can keep you hydrated."

"How long?"

I slid my machete into its holster on my back. "We should reach Ixpachia by—"

"No. How long do I have?"

"Every case is different," I began, but something in his warm, brown eyes stopped me. He deserved what truth I could give him, even if I didn't want to give it and he didn't want to receive it. "I'm not sure, but you seem pretty sensitive to the poison. I'm guessing four hours."

"So if we averaged two miles an hour, we'd make it back. That's just a walk."

A walk through jungle doesn't equal a walk in the park and he knew it. "The faster we go, the faster the poison works through your system." My throat tried to close up, but I said, "I'll get you back. The station plane can fly you to Boa Vista in no time."

"Can you give me the serum anyway?"

"You'd go into shock, then cardiac arrest."

He took off his glasses with his good hand and wiped his face with his sleeve. When he looked at me again, his eyes were soft. "My brother Jake lives in Australia, in the west country. Will you get a message to him for me?" He paused, studying me, and the masculine strength in his cheekbones and dark eyes caught me off guard again. "Or if you don't want to do it, will you tell Yagoda and have him contact Jake?"

"I won't let you die," I said gruffly, thinking about the morphine overdose in my pack. Men in the final throes of fer-de-lance venom screamed in agony, begging to die. I wouldn't let Kinkaid suffer that death. Not while there was a single damned thing I could do about it. "If it looks like you're going to pop off, you can give me your message then. Let's get going."

He put his glasses on and nodded. He stood, steady on his feet but sweating more in the past ten minutes than I'd seen in the past two days of hard work.

"Here." I handed him a bottled water, which he started sucking down greedily. "Are you good to walk for a while?"

He nodded underneath the bottle. Then he lowered the water and stood perfectly still, looking over my right shoulder. My hand itched for the machete.

"Is it a snake?" I asked softly.

"It's a boy."

I turned. A Yanomamo boy, the one I'd seen at the mining

pit three days ago shooting toads, stood a good distance away, watching us with unfathomably deep black eyes. He wore only a string tied around his waist, the traditional bowl-cut hair—and the dead fer-de-lance around his neck. Both ends of the snake touched the ground.

He picked up the snake's huge head in both hands and shook it at us. Then he dropped it to the ground and beckoned.

"He wants us to go with him," Kinkaid said.

"We don't have time to come out and play," I snapped. "We have to go."

Then Kinkaid shot off a few words I'd never heard before. The boy shot back at least two paragraphs. It suddenly dawned on me Kinkaid had been in this part of Brazil before, and for some time. Nobody picks up Yanoman by listening to *Learn Yanoman in 30 Minutes a Day!* tapes.

"He'll take us to the shaman," Kinkaid explained. "His village isn't very far away, and the shaman is an extremely wise man."

"Right," I said, "and Santa Claus lives at the North Pole."

"It's worth a try, Jessie."

"Is the village on the way to the station?"

Kinkaid spoke briefly with the boy.

"No, it's back toward the mine," he said to me.

"Forget it. If the shaman doesn't kill you, the time we lose getting you to civilization will. Let's go."

I turned away but stopped when Kinkaid said, "I'm going with him."

The words knifed through me. I was responsible. I was the best hope Kinkaid had to survive, and he wanted to go traipsing through the jungle to a witch doctor? His life was at stake. The only word that would get past my tight throat was, "Why?"

"These people live here," he said evenly. "They have their own medicine."

"That's crazy!" I said, suddenly angry. "You want to go

drink some herbal tea and then writhe on the floor bleeding from every pore? Because that's what the fer-de-lance poison does. It's a screaming, bloody, agonizing death. Is that what you want?"

"Hey. Hey." When Kinkaid took my hand, the tears stinging the backs of my eyes squeezed out and fell down my cheek.

"I can get you to the station," I retorted, blinking hard.

Kinkaid stepped closer and dropped my hand to grip my shoulder. "You don't have to save me," he said in a low voice.

"That snake was meant for me."

He frowned. "I don't follow that, but let's not get into it. Marcello says the village is close."

I opened my mouth but Kinkaid cut me off.

"It's my choice," he said firmly. "My life." His fingers felt hot, feverish on my neck. "My choice," he repeated. "I'm going to the shaman."

"Fine. Go to the shaman," I said, throwing up my hands. "But you're not going without me."

We followed the kid's winding path through the darkening jungle, Kinkaid first, then me humping all our gear. At least from the back I could keep an eye on Kinkaid's condition, how he walked, whether he stumbled or swayed.

I fumed with every step. Kinkaid was making exactly the cock-eyed choice Scooter had made over this herbal crap. And just like Scooter, he didn't listen to reason. The old man I could understand—he'd been raised on old wives' tales and granny witches and rabbits' feet—but Kinkaid was a freakin' scientist. He ought to know better. Sure, I was a botanist and knew that sometimes native medicine could do the trick. But what about when the patient was as sensitive to the neurotoxin as Kinkaid? Where were the documented cases of success and failure? There were none, because there's no one around keeping count.

Dammit, he was as good as committing suicide. If we'd

tried hiking to the station, I could have pretended, at least for a couple of miles, that he'd make it.

Now he'd die for sure.

My throat started to ache again.

Just like Scooter, it was my fault. My snake, my curse. Rick was a bystander who happened to get in the way, like the wrong man in the wrong doorway of a drive-by.

What's up with that? I prayed irreverently. *Why him?*

Kinkaid had said we'd find what we were meant to find, and now I wanted to know what the hell he was meant to find in this situation.

We walked into the Yanomamo village just as all light receded. A small group of men wearing only strings around their waists met us at the perimeter holding torches, raised bows and machetes, but the moment they saw the kid, they parted to let us into the clearing. The kid spoke to them for a few minutes while what looked to be his proud father stroked the fer-de-lance hanging around his neck. One of the adults took off into the jungle, presumably to get the shaman.

Then the father beckoned us to the *shapono,* a large circular hut that was basically a tall, inward-leaning wall around an open dirt courtyard. The entire village lived under the wall, each family grouped together and having its own cook fire. He pointed to a low-strung hammock where Kinkaid lay down shakily, his face white beneath his tan.

Kids clustered around him, trying to touch his glasses and his watch. I put my gear down. Shooing the brats away did no good whatsoever. I ignored them and got busy stringing mosquito netting from the palm branch rafters. After a couple of minutes, a bare-breasted woman I took to be the kid's mother helped secure the netting over Kinkaid. Then she went back to her cook fire and quickly coaxed it from embers into flame.

I ducked into the mosquito tent. At least the annoying kid-

diewinks were out there and not in here. I settled cross-legged at Kinkaid's hip. "How are you feeling?"

"Okay, I guess. A little dizzy."

I nodded. Dizziness meant the venom was racing through
his body. "How about your face?" I asked. "Anything feel
weird?"

"My cheeks are numb."

I fished a clean cloth out of his pack and wiped his face
with it. "Are you thirsty?"

He shook his head. He raised his good hand to loosen his
shirt at the neck, but his fingers didn't want to work. I unbut-
toned his shirt and opened it up. In the dim light, his skin glistened with sweat even though the temperature had dropped
with the sun.

"You'd better tell me what you want me to tell your
brother."

His shadowed gaze locked on mine. Still no fear. Just a
calm acceptance, like he always knew he'd die this way, in
the wild, among strangers. So damned Hemingway.

"Tell him I finally understand. And give him this." He dug
a chain from around his neck and slipped it off. It had a single gold pendant, small, flat, round, with writing on it I
couldn't read in the dimness. "It's not important," he said,
sounding apologetic. "But it means something."

"Then it's important." I took the chain from him and put it
around my neck, tucking the pendant under my shirt.

Rick looked like he wanted to say something else, but the
kids outside the net parted like the sea for a man headed our way.

The native wore nothing but a string around his waist that
was tied to an elaborate, feathery penis-covering. Rather than
a bowl-cut, his hair fell to his shoulders except for the short
bangs cut straight across his forehead. A red braided cord was
tied around his left bicep and its ends held beads that clicked
faintly when he moved.

He stared at Rick through the mosquito netting for fifteen seconds, then left.

That guy might be the village doctor, but I didn't much care for his bedside manner. I got mad all over again.

"You should have let me take you to the station," I said sharply.

"I wouldn't have made it that far," Rick replied.

"No, you wouldn't," said another stranger who threaded his way through the children to reach us.

This new guy was a tall, middle-aged Brazilian, wearing thick plastic-frame glasses that made his eyes the size of my fist. His long hair was tied back with a hank of leather over western jungle gear. It wasn't until he removed the colorful bandana from his neck that I saw his white collar.

A priest? Living here? Sure, missionaries were all over the jungle busily rearranging the indigenous peoples into manageable groups, but this guy didn't give me the impression he was interested in rearranging anybody. In fact, he had Jesuit written all over him—gentle, intellectual, pacifist.

He slipped under the mosquito netting and knelt next to Rick. "The shaman will be back soon," he said in English as he placed a hand on Rick's forehead. "His remedy has never failed."

I kept my skeptical thoughts to myself. It was bad practice to dis the local wise man.

"I'm Father Dswow."

It took my brain a minute to translate that bizarre word into what it actually was: João. And saying it wouldn't be easy. Portuguese phonetics were beyond me. I wondered if I could get by with just calling him "padre."

Then a black thought occurred to me. "You're not here to administer last rites, are you?" I demanded. I didn't even know if Rick was Catholic.

Father João smiled, radiating peacefulness through his

thick lenses. "No. I'm here to keep you company until the shaman returns," he said gently, soothingly. "Don't worry. He
won't be long."

If I could have freeze-dried and shipped this guy's serenity to the States, I could've made a fortune off the corpo-
rate world.

"How long have you lived here?" Rick asked weakly, ever
curious.

"Years and years," the padre said, waving his hand as if to
conjure aeons. "I came when I heard outside people were
bringing disease to the villages. I inoculate the villagers
against us and our 'civilized' diseases." He raised a brow at
me as if he sensed I was a big fan of civilization.

"Against us?" Rick's slow smile drew his mouth into a pale
imitation of his grin. "As in 'corrupting cultural influences'?"

The padre shrugged. "Cultural influence is inevitable."

"But it doesn't have to be destructive."

"Not intentionally, no."

I got the impression they could go on for hours discussing
cultural issues—if Rick had hours—but Rick suddenly said,
"I need to see the village leader. One of the mine foremen, a
man named Porfilio, wants to negotiate a partnership between
the villages and the mine."

The padre's eyes narrowed. "The headman will be glad to
hear it. You may talk to him when you're better."

Better? I wanted to yell. What kind of idealistic universe
did these people inhabit?

The shaman stalked across the communal hut carrying a
black medicine bowl, a cup and a nasty-looking stick.

The shaman motioned me and the padre out from the mosquito tent. Once inside, he gave Rick the cup and made a
"drink up" motion. Rick did, grimacing. Then the shaman
emptied the contents of the bowl over Rick's head, shower-
ing him with horrific smelling crushed leaves and herbs. He

shook the stick at the doorway, then at Rick's arm, then raised it over his head, his eyes closed. I took a step toward the tent but the padre grabbed my shoulder. The shaman's stick swung down with breaking speed toward Rick's arm, then abruptly stopped a mere inch from the wound.

The shaman stepped back. He stared hard at Rick for a moment, then nodded decisively and swept out of the mosquito tent. The vile smell followed him. He barked a few words at the padre. Then he left.

"What did he say?" I asked Father João.

The padre smiled. "He says your friend has the heart of the jaguar."

"Did he mention anything about surviving the snakebite?" I asked curtly, "or is 'what is the sound of one hand clapping' the best we're going to get?"

"O ye of little faith," Rick chided from his hammock.

"Damn skippy," I retorted. I shook off the Yanomamo kid hovering at my elbow, the one who'd led us to this village, and brushed into the tent.

The herbs' stench set my eyes to watering. "What's he trying to do, make you smell so bad that Death will take a holiday?" The joke sounded awful to my ear and I regretted it the minute I said it.

"Whatever works." Rick managed a weak shrug. "I need to sleep."

"Okay."

I sat next to him. I kind of wanted to hold his hand while he drifted off, but it seemed too sentimental. Things like this happen, I told myself. You can't get too attached to people because one day they'll up and leave, and then where will you be? Isn't that the way it always works out? Except for the annoying people. They seem to always be just around the corner. But the ones you love? You wake up in the middle of the night and your neighbors are crying and patting your head and

telling you how sorry they are that the people you love most
are dead. I know how that works.

And I couldn't afford the distraction from Scooter, who
was my number one priority, anyway. On the other hand,
Rick was my responsibility, at least while he was alive and
bitten by my snake. On the other hand—

On the other hand, I have five fingers. Give it a rest.

I gave up and took Rick's cool hand in both of mine as he
fell into a fitful sleep. The padre left at some point, but I don't
know when. Rick stopped pouring with sweat and in the next
hour or so eased into a peaceful sleep. The kids finally got
bored and wandered off to their family areas. The shaman
came back once to put a noxious-smelling poultice on the
snakebite, but ignored me. I tried to get a look at his medicine bowl, to see if it matched Harrison's, but he kept it moving and I figured he wouldn't give me a peek, even if I knew
the Yanoman words to form the question.

The kid's mother brought me a hunk of cassava bread and
a mug of cassava beer—definitely an acquired taste—which
I consumed automatically. There are times when food is
merely fuel. As evening wore into true night, I knew I should
go check the bug traps at first light. I just didn't want to leave
Rick alone with the witch doctor and pacifist padre to do it.

The villagers never really settled in for the night. Some
slept, some wandered in and out, two talked in their normal
voices for a while. One picked up a hatchet and stepped outside to hack up firewood to feed his cook fire. Each family
appeared to have enough space to lie down in, their few be-
longings stacked neatly against the structure's supporting
poles. How they ever got a good night's sleep was beyond me.

I checked Rick's forehead, which was cool for the first time
in hours, and stretched out beside him on a kapok-fiber pallet
the kid's mother had given me. Sleep laughed at me, though, and
I kept having to get up to make sure Rick was still breathing.

As dawn threatened, I checked Rick's arm. The swelling had gone down under the nasty poultice. I rolled the sleeve back to get it over his elbow and out of the goop. I remembered this arm tossing a fifty-pound duffel into the plane, but hadn't noticed its lean, hard muscle at the time. His chest lifted slowly, easily, and for grins I put two fingers on his wrist. Jeez. Cross-country runners had resting heart rates in the mid to upper thirties, and his was right down there with them. Or maybe that was just an herbal effect and he actually was dying, right here in front of me. But he'd lasted far longer than he should have. He must have responded to the witch doctor's doctoring.

I'd have to leave him to check the bug trap. What if he woke up and needed me? What if the shaman tried to give him some concoction that really did manage to kill him? But I couldn't afford to lose another day. Heaven only knew what would happen to the moth if I left it in that trap all day. Bake in a box, probably. After a moment's further arguing with myself, I headed into the darkness.

It was daylight when I reached the trap area. Even the Ya-nomamo kid, following me again and staying just out of sight, didn't annoy me too much. I was too anxious to check the trap and get back to the village. As long as he stayed out of the way, he could watch all he wanted. And his shy eagerness kind of tickled me, in a tomboyish way.

Clipping the running anchor onto my harness, I felt a stab of loneliness that made me pause. Rick ought to be here. I pushed him out of my mind. I've never been lonely. Ever. I started to climb. I guessed I could blame that feeling on Scooter's condition and me getting ready to let go of him. But that wouldn't have been the truth. The truth was I'd gotten used to having someone else around. But I'd been fine working alone before and I would be again. Once Scooter was on the mend, my life could go back to normal.

I hit the canopy in record time and transferred over to the main swing. The trap, a high-tech polyurethane and high-density plastic affair, clamped on to the branch directly over my head. I unfastened the straps. Holding my breath, hoping against hope, I drew the trap down to eye level.

A huge moth, its body half my palm's width, fluttered harmlessly inside the trap. This sucker could easily have been mistaken for a small bird from a distance. No wonder people hadn't seen much of it, or recognized it if they did.

And it was black as night, with pearlescent black markings on its wings.

Just like Harrison's medicine bowl.

Heart pounding, I took my time scanning the canopy but saw nothing the moth might have been attracted to other than the trap's scent. No blooming plants. Certainly no flowering orchids.

But if this bad boy was in the area, the Death Orchid would be, too. It was just a matter of finding it.

I clipped the trap on to my harness and dropped from the canopy. My high-speed descent brought the wide-eyed Yanomamo kid close. As I detached from the climbing rope, his busy hands ran all over the shiny carabiners. Infernally curious, these Yanomamo, with no sense of privacy whatsoever. The kid may never have seen anyone whiter than Father João and he certainly had never seen a white Americano before, especially a female rigged with climbing gear that lowered her as fast as I liked. I unfastened my harness to remove it, but paused when Marcello fingered the wide webbing and looked up.

"Do you want to climb up there?" I pointed to the canopy.

His black eyes widened. Did he understand what I'd said?

I fastened my harness again and grabbed one of the running anchors. "Here's how you do it," I said, wrapping the anchor around the tree's broad trunk. I walked up a couple of steps. Below me, Marcello's grin lit up his nut-brown face and the whole darned morning.

"Come on. You try." I hopped down.

Marcello pointed to my harness, then at himself.

"I know. I'm going to make you one." I dug through my pack for a spare piece of webbing, then gestured to him. "Come here."

I wrapped the webbing around Marcello's tiny waist and threaded it into a makeshift climbing harness, careful not to crunch his little nuts with the leg straps. It would've been easier if his people wore clothes. After the webbing was secure, I stepped back. Yep, Day-Glo green webbing wrapped around a nude kid's groin looked pretty funky.

After I'd made sure his reproductive future was still intact, I shortened the running anchor to match his leg length. Then I held it out to him. Marcello studied the anchor and its carabiner, turning it in his hands. He brought it to his face and sniffed it. For a moment I thought he was going to gnaw on it to see what it tasted like.

What wheels were turning in this kid's head? He came from a people whose lifestyle was Stone Age. Did he understand the carabiner's clasp mechanism or was his brain stuck relying on tools that could be woven from bamboo or carved with sharp stones?

A slow grin that reminded me of Rick's spread over his little face. He pressed the carabiner's lip with his thumb and opened it. After snapping it open and closed for a minute, he clipped the carabiner on the harness. The pleased, questioning look he gave me—so open, so innocent—made me wish I spoke his language.

I motioned him over to the tree and ran the other end of the anchor around its trunk. He grabbed the free end and snapped it in place on his harness. Quick learner. I smiled at him and got back a cascading laugh in return. The Yanomamo, I was beginning to see, laughed at just about everything.

"Go ahead."

He put one bare foot on the tree's trunk. I pushed back on his bare chest to get him to lean away from the tree. He batted his eyes at me. Flirt. Where did he learn that? I tapped his other leg and pointed at the tree. He picked up that foot and promptly fell on his butt. He would have rolled over laughing but the anchor held him tight. As it was, he lay on the thick moss and cackled.

When his giggles subsided, I said, "Try again."

He wrenched himself to his feet, then made a show of putting his foot on the tree, testing the spot, batting his eyes at me, smiling. Little ham. This time I stood behind him and wrapped an arm around his waist to hold him up. That set off another round of giggles. I couldn't resist and tickled his ribs. Suddenly I had seventy pounds of squealing, bouncing, squirming little kid in my arms. I let him go and stepped away.

He motioned me to come back, but I didn't know whether it was to tickle him again or help him climb the tree. Whichever worked for me. Climb the tree, it turned out. He settled down once I got my arm around him, and he put both feet on the trunk. All at once I caught his young-wild smell, musky, full of rain and sunshine, like someone coming indoors on a clear autumn day. I tipped him back until the anchor caught. He took a single, cautious step up the tree, then seemed to understand almost instinctively how to keep his weight back against the anchor. I watched him walk up until he reached the limit of his running anchor and looked down at me, just over my head.

"Come back." I gestured. "I have to go. See how Rick is doing."

He obediently stepped back down into my arms. I unclipped him and gave him the running anchor to carry for me. He seemed to want to keep his harness on, so I let him. I didn't need that extra piece of webbing anyway.

"Let's go," I told him.

Leaving the long climbing rope hanging in the canopy made the most sense. The next logical step would be to bring the moth back and turn it loose. With any luck, it would lead me to the Death Orchid.

As soon as I convinced Rick that releasing his precious moth to find a Death Orchid was in his best interest.

Shouldn't be too hard. He was, after all, a bug nerd. No, an entomologist. Entomologists understood the delicate balance between the objects of their lives' pursuits and the rest of nature.

But when I returned to the village, I realized he knew a lot more about delicate balance than I could have guessed.

Chapter 8

The crowd standing in a circle on the village outskirts was mostly children. I started to go around them, but then caught a glimpse of dark brown hair—not black like the Yanomamo—and white T-shirt. What was Rick doing up and around? Had he collapsed? Why wasn't anybody helping him? I jogged up to the circle and looked over the kids' heads.

Rick sat on the ground in lotus position, his thumbs and forefingers pressed together in okay signs that rested on his knees, his eyes closed. After a moment, he smoothly bent forward to place his forehead to the ground, untangling his legs as he did so. Then he rolled into a headstand, his legs straight up, his hands placed at a comfortable distance to give him a three-point stand.

I gathered he was feeling better.

The twenty or so kids planted their heads on the ground and flung themselves into the air. A small forest of feet sprouted around me, wavered, then collapsed in a chorus of laughter and squeals. None of the ruckus seemed to bother Rick.

He moved his hands a little, arched his back and lifted himself into a handstand. I could have pegged him for a yoga boy, sure enough, but I had no idea yoga boys could do push-ups from a handstand like he was doing now. Or balance themselves so easily while they did it.

His long, lovely leap into the mining pit suddenly made a lot of sense, and it kind of got me wondering about those smooth shoulders and that smooth chest. His arms were as strong as advertised, so didn't it make sense the rest of him would be strong?

But he was foolish to be pulling this stunt after being bitten by a viper last night. I cut through the confusion of flailing limbs, fuming.

"What the hell do you think you're doing?" I demanded.

He paused mid-push-up, then dropped his feet gracefully to the ground and straightened his strong torso to meet my gaze. Pumped up with the exercise, what I'd originally thought was his thin chest strained his T-shirt. Not bulky like a weight lifter, but lean, sculpted, sexy. He'd taken off his glasses and his inner bad boy grinned at me. Dammit. I suppressed the sudden images of Kama Sutra flexibility that flashed in my head.

"I feel good," he said, smiling at me.

He looked good, too. Too good.

Even the color had returned to his face. He held out his snakebite for my inspection like an obedient patient. The fang holes had closed and pinked, healing with new scar tissue. No sign of infection. And his skin was cool, fresh, as though he hadn't nearly died.

"Damn," I said despite myself, turning his arm this way and that, amazed.

"Good medicine," he said softly, but he was looking at me when he said it.

I dropped his arm. "How long have you been awake?"

"Long enough to see the headman." He turned and we started walking back to the village. The children scattered. "He's interested in talking to Porfilio if I can set up a meeting. I'll send a message to the mine arranging the time and place by Marcello."

"Since when did Marcello become your errand boy?" I glanced back. The kid followed, still wearing his Day-Glo green climbing harness and twanging his bowstring at bugs and leaves as he pretended to shoot them. Pretending, of course, not to be interested in what we were doing.

"I think he's got a crush on you," Rick observed.

"I seem to have that effect on men. Have no idea why."

"Don't you?"

I didn't dare meet his eyes. "Maybe he's just not used to seeing a woman out of her customary realm of duty," I said. "So why are you using him as errand boy?"

"He's the adopted son of the headman's favorite warrior. And he'll be a *huya* soon—"

"A who?"

"*Huya.* Young man of responsibility."

I glanced at Marcello's tiny self. It made sense. Kids in the jungle got married at twelve, were grandparents at thirty and died around fifty. Life just happened faster here.

"You think Porfilio will be able to do anything?" I asked, thinking about the colonel's temporary insanity.

"The colonel can be forced to cooperate," Rick said firmly.

"Forced? Isn't that a bad idea? I mean, you don't want to start a range war."

"I'm not talking about a war. I'm talking about a clear assessment of facts. The Brazilian government has to start backing up its laws with enforcement. That's all I'm saying."

"Ideally, yeah," I said. "But the National Foundation of The Indian is underfunded and understaffed. You know how big the Amazon is. How can they possibly—"

"Sometimes it takes will to get the job done."

I recognized the gleam in Rick's eye. Scooter got it sometimes when he was talking about conservation. No matter what came out of my mouth, Rick wasn't going to hear it. Time for me to keep my trap shut on the subject.

"Check this out," I said instead.

I unclipped the trap from my belt and handed it to Rick. His eyes widened as he took it and his steps slowed to a halt. In true entomologist fashion, he started mumbling to himself about the tympanum, proboscis, labial palps, wing venation and so forth. After watching him a minute or two, I wondered if I got as hot and bothered looking at orchids.

I hoped not.

"I need my glasses," he said abruptly, tearing his attention away from the moth and walking again. "We have new quarters. We got kicked out of the communal living area. The headman said we should stay in our own hut from now on."

"Nice of him to make us so welcome," I said dryly.

"He figured we foreigners needed our own space. They built us a hut this morning."

"Yeah, but does it have a shower?"

"No, but they told me where there's a pond to bathe in."

"Is that communal, too?"

Rick cast me that grin. "Only if you issue an invitation."

"Like that'll happen," I retorted. "Where's this hut?"

It wasn't bad for emergency living quarters. The walls didn't meet the floor, so the creeping things might be an issue, but if we kept the deet sprayed on we'd be okay. Besides, they'd strung hammocks up for us. And since we were in Death Orchid territory, I wasn't going to complain too much. Somebody had already moved my duffel bag inside.

Rick collected his bug gear and went outside to study his moth. I was surprised to see a bunch of electronic equipment emerge from his big duffel: a handheld Global Positioning

System like mine, a transmitter, a couple of small-screened monitoring devices, and a closed tray of what looked like tiny computer chips that must have been bug trackers.

"The *pistoleiros* didn't break your stuff?" I asked.

"Not the stuff that mattered." He settled on the ground and took out a slide gauge. The moth fluttered as he slipped his gauge through specially designed trap holes to get his first measurement. He jotted notes in a half-size notebook.

I eyed the computer chips. "Is that homing equipment?"

He nodded, not looking up from his notebook.

"To track the moth?"

Rick glanced at me. "Yeah. You curious about it?"

"After all the trouble we went to to catch it, I want to know everything about it. In detail."

He was silent for a moment, scribbling, before he asked, "Have you found your bromeliad?"

I shrugged. "Not yet."

His lips pressed to a thin line and I could sense for the first time his disapproval. "Is it not a priority for you?"

"I've been busy helping with your moth," I said, feeling annoyed. "And sitting by your bedside hoping you wouldn't die."

"Thank you. I appreciate that."

His tight-lipped formality pissed me off. Where was his attitude coming from? Time to go on the offensive. "Last time I looked, my bromeliad wasn't your business."

He raised an eyebrow and finally gave me his full attention. "So far, you've been more interested in my moth than your plant."

"It's my vacation. I'll damn well do what I want."

"What are you really after, Jessie?"

"I'm actually a psychologist studying the anal-retentive nature of bug nerds," I replied. "You're my first subject."

He ignored the sarcasm. "I'm not stupid. It's the orchid, isn't it? You work for a private collector."

"My job isn't your business, no matter what it is."

"It is if you're here to steal a rare exotic at the whim of people with more money than sense."

Only idealists had that kind of nerve, strutting around trying to solve the world's problems. "I don't need a lecture from you about what I do for a living. My client is a serious conservationist."

"Because he hires you to bring him back an orchid he thinks no one else in the world has? For the prestige? Jeopardizing serious research with his egotism?"

"Because he manages to reproduce the rarest plants when the best brains in the orchid-growing business can't," I retorted, a good head of steam building up. "Because he's convinced this one is special. Because his pharma might be able to use this one to create a Parkinson's cure."

And I swear to you I heard the next words coming out of my mouth when I really didn't want to say them. "Because he'll save the life of the man who raised me. That's why I'm here, not looking for bromeliads and following your moth around. Because Scooter's dying."

His eyes narrowed. Thank God I didn't start bawling. I was mad enough to. As he set the trap on the ground, I scrambled up and headed into the jungle. Anything to get away from Mr. Idealistic Judgment.

I heard footsteps behind me, then a soft "hey." He caught hold of my arm.

I jerked from his grasp. "Don't 'hey' me. It's not your business." And then, to my everlasting humiliation, the tears came. "Just don't kill that moth," I said, glaring at him through them. "I need to use it tonight to hunt my orchid."

Then I turned away and stalked deeper into the impenetrable forest.

A half mile into the jungle, the low voices tipped me off a split second before the stench did. I crouched silently, peering through the underbrush at the three Yanomamo warriors squatting next to a small cook fire.

One dropped a handful of leaves into a black iron pot of witches' brew while another swung the pot slightly off the flame, regulating the temperature. If they were doing what I thought they were doing, no woman should be witnessing the ritual. Maybe I didn't count because I wasn't one of their women. They could be just cooking up something for the shaman, I mused.

But one man holding a jaguar-skin pouch nodded at the other two, then took a slender arrowhead from the pouch. He attached it to a notched stick and carefully dipped it in the cook pot. When the arrowhead came out, it was coated with a slimy black paste. He set the arrowhead, pointing away, on a wide fallen log to dry.

I watched him doctor a dozen arrowheads before I backed off as quietly as I could.

They were cooking curare, a poison capable of killing a man in ten minutes, a poison for which there was no cure.

The Yanomamo were preparing to go to war.

Marcello found me about thirty minutes later in a little liana forest where I lay on a flat rock, staring up at the midstory and trying not to think too much. I had to smile at the green webbing still tied firmly around his waist and legs. My throat tightened up. What would happen to him if things escalated out of control with the miners? Would this entire village be wiped out as if it were a bothersome colony of ants rather than a community with its own social rules, its own mores and religion and idiosyncrasies?

I knelt to be at eye level with him as he approached. His black eyes, fathomlessly deep in his brown face, gleamed with barely checked mischief. He grabbed my hand with his small ones and tugged me. Come on, he was saying, I have something to show you. When I hesitated, he frowned, tugged harder.

Marcello wasn't playing around. He meant business. Fear pricked my gut. Had Rick had a relapse? Had he overdone it with his yoga grandstanding earlier?

I followed Marcello down a narrow path to a remote hut identical to the one the Yanomamo had built for me and Rick. It was some distance from the village, like it might be the shaman's, but instead Father João stood outside the doorway. He beamed beatifically at me.

"Please," he murmured, gesturing to a seat on the other side of the doorway. He sank to the ground after I sat cross-legged. Marcello hunkered down next to me and draped an arm over my knee.

"Thanks for helping with Rick," I said.

The priest waved his hand. "I did nothing. But I will convey your thank-you to the shaman."

I swallowed and nodded. Yeah, that was fair. The shaman had saved Rick's life with his weird herbal concoction and I'd be stupid to ignore that fact. I just didn't like being wrong.

"Why did you send for me?" I asked.

"Perhaps I can tell you why I am here," Father João replied.

Not in the mood to listen, I still couldn't muster enough rudeness to say so. When I didn't say anything, he went on.

"I came to this village years ago, when mines started opening up all over the Amazon Basin. Poor southern men came here, looking for money and secure jobs, so they started to work for mines. Not just gold, like the one you saw, but bauxite and oil wells, too. Or they brought their families and took farms alongside the Transamazon Highway.

"I knew the Yanomamo and their neighboring tribes wouldn't survive the new diseases, so I came to give them preventative medicine. In most cases, it was good. The longer I stayed, the more I learned about their medicine. It is written in a wise book that when a shaman dies, a library is lost. This is true."

Father João nodded at me sagely before adding, "And so when someone is bitten by the fer-de-lance or touches a poisonous toad, I wait first for the shaman."

He looked at me expectantly for a long moment. "Okay," I said finally, not knowing what else to say.

"Marcello lost his village in a different way." The priest smiled at the boy fondly. "He understands some of what I am saying to you because he started learning English very young."

"Do you run a school?" I asked, startled. It didn't seem like something this particular priest, interested in maintaining the native culture, would do.

"Oh, no! Marcello was found running the streets of Boa Vista. His village had suffered attack by corrupt gold miners, so he walked down the Amazon tributaries until he found a city."

Marcello had found a city all right. Boa Vista was about a couple hundred thousand people worth of city.

"He was brought to me to bring back here," Father João continued. "The alternative was an orphanage, where he would know nothing of his culture, his language, his customs."

"How old was he when he walked to Boa Vista?" I asked, curious.

"He believes he was six."

I looked at the kid, sitting there quietly, his dark eyes soft and fathomless. He'd walked a helluva longer distance than I had during Scooter's little experiment, and he hadn't had the assurance of someone coming to find him if he got lost. Or giving him a hot meal when he got where he was going. Here was a kid with gumption I appreciated, clever and self-sufficient. And, if I were to be completely honest, he was pretty adorable to boot.

When I smiled at him, he leaned on me trustingly, still gazing at me with those wide eyes. Great. Him and Rick.

Maybe not Rick anymore. My smile died. Maybe it was just me and the kid now.

"So why did you tell me this?" I asked Father João, putting my hand on the back of Marcello's neck. The kid was just this side of purring. "Do I look like I need a history lesson?"

"It is so you'll understand when I tell you you aren't welcome here, you and your kind, Dr. Robards."

What the—? The priest's tone hadn't changed, I sensed no menace in his words. But the message was as clear as the Evil Eye's: get out and don't come back.

I stared at the padre's gentle face for a full minute, wondering if my eternal soul would go straight to hell for cold-cocking a priest.

"What do you mean, 'my kind'?" I asked softly.

"Mercenaries. Hunters. Whatever it is you call yourselves."

"How do you know what I—"

"A man came through the village yesterday," Father João said, "which is why you were taken to the communal hut. He was looking for you, Dr. Robards. And the orchid."

It must be Lawrence Damned Daley. "Was he English? Or funny English? Like he was pretending?"

Father João nodded.

"Did he have anyone else with him? Indians or Brazilians?"

"Four Brazilians. *Pistoleiros.*"

"Did you tell him I was here?"

"He passed through in the afternoon before you arrived. It's why we took the precaution of hiding you when you showed up."

"You took a chance," I said grimly. "I appreciate that."

"Don't," Father João replied. "I would have turned you over to him if I'd had to, to protect this village."

"He's not dangerous," I assured him, then paused at the memory of him leaning over a cliff aiming a semiautomatic at me. "Not to you, anyway."

"This place is a—what do you call it?—powder keg waiting to blow up. The mine's *pistoleiros* roam, threatening the Yanomamo they find. Now you and your mercenary ilk are hunting each other. All armed."

I'd hoped he hadn't noticed the rifle poking at both ends of my duffel. Ah well.

"I don't plan on hurting anyone, especially not these people," I insisted, pointing toward the village. "I just want my orchid. That's it."

"And yet you bring the *pistoleiros* in pursuit, as well." Father João crossed his arms over his chest, the first antagonistic gesture he'd shown.

"They tried to hold us when our plane went down. It's not *my* fault they're chasing me around."

No, it was Kinkaid's, pissing into the fuel tanks. But everyone saw *me,* an Americano woman, taking down the *pistoleiros* and setting the *donos* on his ass with a fire hose. Kinkaid was just a take-it-or-leave-it nuisance.

"There is another man, an American, chasing through the forest, as well," Father João said.

What?

Had some other orchid collector got wind of what I was doing? Or had Daley brought a buddy with him? No, Daley working with someone else didn't compute.

My mind finally flashed on the Brain. The Brain had told the Whiner that if they couldn't find Harrison's map, they'd have to send someone called "Noah." Was Noah here, now, looking for the Death Orchid? Or had the Brain come himself?

"Can you describe this man?" I asked.

Father João shrugged. "I saw him from a distance. He did not come to the village, but stayed away."

"How do you know he was an American?"

The padre smiled. "He was big. Very tall."

That didn't sound like the Brain. "Was he losing his hair?" I motioned on my own head to show him where.

"No. This man had light hair, cut short, almost like the military. What is that called? Crow—"

"Crew cut," I corrected absently, staring at the palm growing behind the padre's hut.

Well, dammit. It must be the man called Noah.

"It is in everyone's best interests if you leave this place and never return," Father João insisted gently. "You bring too much danger and uncertainty with you."

"The mining operation is all yours," I pointed out. "I had nothing to do with that. Whether I'm here or not, the mine will be a problem for the Yanomamo."

"Your friend sees a solution," the padre observed. "He is willing to help."

I got the message. Rick was okay but I wasn't. The fleeting stab—of not being welcome, of not belonging—annoyed me.

"I have my own priority—"

"I'm sure you do, Dr. Robards," the padre said. "I do not wish to pass judgment on your actions or motivations. I wish merely to protect the innocents around you who will only suffer the consequences should you choose to remain here."

He had a point. The *pistoleiros* were likely to shoot everything in sight to kill me, on the colonel's orders. There was no telling how dire, how explosive, that situation really was. The *pistoleiros* might have guns, but the Yanomamo had their curare-tipped arrows and impeccable aim. War wasn't inconceivable. Then the military would get involved and within hours there wouldn't be anything left of these people.

"Don't worry," I told him. "I won't be here for long. Two, maybe three days." I had only ten days left to get the orchid back to von Brutten. If Scooter was still alive.

"That may not be soon enough," Father João replied. "The village headman will meet with the man called Porfilio tomorrow. Your friend Rick will be present to help facilitate, of course."

"I won't be here," I told him. "I'll stay out of the way."

"It is for the best," Father João confirmed.

I glared at the padre's serene face for a moment. I could understand his wanting me out. Daley was after me. Some unknown military-type American was lurking in the forest. And Father João had nothing to offer me beyond what he'd already given: a bed for the night and advice.

On the way back to the hut to catch some z's, I considered my options. Daley's being so close, and with four *pistoleiros* in tow, meant I'd have to do a little fancy footwork to stay away from him. The unknown American might be friend or foe, but I guessed foe. He might be more difficult to shake than Daley.

The bottom line: Kinkaid's moth had to point me to the orchid tonight. I needed to grab that orchid and get the hell out.

"All I want," I told myself, preaching to the choir, "is the orchid I came here for. I don't want to have anything to do with the mine, the research station, Kinkaid, the pit viper, or this village."

And that was for the best, because clearly none of them wanted me.

Chapter 9

Before settling in for the day's sleep, I needed a bath. Bad. I grabbed a clean pair of undies from my duffel bag and headed into the village for someone who could point me to the bathing pool.

In the middle of the afternoon, the village seemed only a little busier than it had in the dark. The communal living building sat square in the middle of a natural clearing. Loosely grouped around the building, the Yanomamo busied themselves: the men repairing bows or carefully pressure flaking arrowheads, the women weaving slivers of palm into baskets. A couple of girls combed each other's hair and painted decorative designs on their faces. All the little boys were off somewhere doing whatever boys do, I guessed.

Entirely peaceable, and not likely to survive many more years. I felt a twinge of regret for these people. In another twenty years they'd be wearing Western clothes, and twenty years after that they'd be gone, dispersed into the cities or

sucked into slash-and-burn agriculture. It had happened—
was happening—all over the rain forest.

A woman coming out of the building came over to me.
While she pointed and gestured, I recognized her as the
woman who'd helped me with the mosquito netting the night
before, Marcello's adoptive mom. At the end of our five-min-
ute pantomime, I had a good idea where the bathing pool was.
Nice lady.

With any luck, the bathing pool wouldn't be full of either
mercury or Yanomamo.

Her instructions and my nose led me a short distance
through a liana forest where trailing vines hung like spaghetti
through the midstory. On the other side, a hill abruptly interrupted the lay of the forest. The earthy, slightly musky odor
wafting my way told me I was close.

You get used to sniffing out water's scent after a while.
When I live outside, in the weather, everything is vital and
real. Living in town, in an apartment or house, stunts my ability to do that. Four walls and a roof give me an excuse to pretend "outside" doesn't exist. In town, rain is a nuisance that
slaps the car hood as I drive through it to get somewhere. Here,
rain is a pleasure that taps my head and runs down my shoulders and arms, giving me goose bumps as my body cools. I
feel much more connected out here. Maybe that's why I've
never really felt at home in a city.

I stopped to listen. Well beneath the birdcalls and monkeys
chattering in the canopy, and under the shifting leaves as a bit
of wind sifted through the midstory, I heard water shattering
on rock. When I closed my eyes and concentrated, I could
trace the sound due east. I headed in that direction.

The waterfall's splash dropped the temperature a good fifteen degrees. Maybe that drop was in my imagination, but I
didn't care. I needed a break from the heat and even a fake
break was better than sweat trickling down my sides. Past a

banana tree, through some tall ferns, and the pool stretched out like a tropical paradise behind some movie star's Beverley Hills mansion. Large-leafed undergrowth leaned decoratively over the pool's edge. Even the moss looked landscaped.

And not a creeping or slithering or stinging thing in sight.

My boots came off first. Then I stripped my camouflage shirt off my back and dunked it into the water at the pool's edge. The canvas pants peeled from my legs inside out, they were so damp with perspiration. The muscle-tee undershirt, cotton sports bra and panties came next and I submerged all that as well. The clothes wouldn't be washed but they'd be rinsed and I'd take it. I wrung out the wet clothing, turned inside-out things right side out, and laid them on a flattish rock to dry. I dropped my fresh panties on a bowing fern at the pool's edge.

I put one toe in, kind of staring at the water in sheer exhausted mindlessness. Running seventy-two hours on about four hours' sleep can really take it out of a girl. You know when you're so tired that your brain is numb and everything moves in slow motion, but your eyes latch on to something, like the wallpaper pattern, and you don't move for a while even though you know you could just lie down? It's just too much effort to do anything other than look at whatever's in front of you. Ripples from the waterfall spread toward me in rough rings, and what little sunlight fell through the canopy dappled the clear water. I zoned.

A movement caught my attention. My eyes focused automatically on the waterfall and I saw Rick walk waist-deep through it on a submerged rock ledge, crystal-clear water sheeting over his head and shoulders. Before he could look up, I dropped into the pool.

I'm not usually missish, but flashing for Rick would be a little like walking around nude with your brother. Icky. As it was, the water felt like it'd come straight off a glacier and had

every part of exhausted, overheated little me shivering with
the cold. It wasn't exactly as clear as your rich aunt's backyard pool, but clear enough to give you a general idea of what
was under the surface. And it was deeper than I expected.

Rick dove off the ledge and made a beeline in my direction. He surfaced a few feet away, water slicking his prominent cheekbones. "This is fantastic," he called over the
crashing water, treading. "I feel better all the time."

"I'm glad." And I was. Surprisingly so, setting off a twinge
in my chest. Jeez. First Marcello and now Rick. I was going
soft in my late twenties.

Still, he'd ticked me off and I wasn't ready to give that up yet.

"I wouldn't have made it without your help, Nurse Robards," he said, grinning and conjuring up a bedroom fantasy.

I bet I'd look good in a perky white cap, no-nonsense
shoes, and nothing else. "Don't mention it."

He dove again and circled back toward the waterfall. I
wondered if his distance meant he'd shed all his clothes as
well. It made me feel better to think he was just as self-con-
scious as I was.

He was down a long time and I was just starting to get antsy
when he surfaced like a porpoise, exploding out of the water
with enough force to show me his back and bare hips. When
he raised his arms straight out at the top of his leap, like he was
going to fly, his back made a nice V shape with the long, lean,
muscular bulges made for a girl's grip. Is it just me, or is the
tan line low on a guy's hips one of the sexiest sights on earth?

Strike another assumption from the nerd list, I thought. The
geek's got a body. From every angle at my disposal.

He sank back into the water and turned, flashing me his
muscled pecs. "Come over here."

I thought about grabbing my undies but it was the moment
of truth. Which action would be more embarrassing: swimming over in the raw to discover he was actually wearing a

Speedo, or making a big deal out of putting on my bra and panties? Not being the cocktail-party type and therefore not accustomed to making this kind of "what's the least embarrassing thing to do?" decision regularly, I struggled.

Oh hell. I started swimming, determined to swagger through it. I had nothing to be ashamed of.

As I got within about five feet and stopped, he slicked the water from his face. His longish hair had formed an adorable ducktail. "I owe you an apology," he said.

"You think?"

His grin faded, but not much. "Yeah, I do. Are you interested in hearing it?"

"Why wouldn't I be?" I retorted.

"Receptivity doesn't seem to be your strong suit." He smiled just enough to take the sting out.

Cheeky boy. I wondered how well he could see without his glasses. Five feet seemed a safe distance.

"I'm feeling receptive," I said.

"Here goes." He treaded a little closer into my space—four feet and counting—and cleared his throat. "You're right. Your job isn't my business."

After a moment I asked, "Is that it? Where's the part where you prostrate yourself at my feet and beg my forgiveness?"

The sudden image of his strong hands grabbing my ankles under the water warmed me all over. Maybe I'd have to rethink the "brother" idea I'd had earlier, especially when that slow-burn smile spread across his mouth, which, if he were to dive right now and grab my ankles, would be on a level with…my sweet spot tingled.

"Screw that," I muttered under my breath, trying to stop the images in my fertile little brain from multiplying faster than I could tamp them down.

"So you *don't* want an apology?" he asked.

"I don't know," I replied, treading water with short

strokes to keep my breasts blurry, in case he was less near-sighted than I suspected. "Are you going to get around to it today?"

"Isn't admitting I was wrong enough? You didn't strike me as the type to want flowers, too."

"Maybe I'm higher maintenance than you thought."

"I guess you are," he replied, looking undaunted by the idea. The grin was definitely back, turning his good-looking features into suddenly handsome ones.

"I'm surprised flowers even occurred to you."

"Why?" His brows shot up. "You're a botanist."

"Anal-retentive bug nerds," I said dismissively. "You know how they are."

"No, I don't," he said, treading a little closer. Three feet. Definitely within my personal space now. His eyes glinted with a much more adult version of Marcello's mischief. "Tell me."

"I'd better keep my professional opinion to myself."

Likewise, I kept my gaze to myself. On a very few occasions—very few—I can resist temptation. But meeting his eyes was somehow more erotic than checking out his equipment. Those brown eyes just got deeper and deeper the longer I looked at them until I felt like I'd drown. Happily.

His voice lowered slightly. "If you won't tell me what I'm like, how will I know what to do?"

"It depends on what you want to do," I countered.

"I want to do lots of things," he said, slipping easily through the water. Two and a half feet. Another foot and my space would become our space. "I want to show you something."

I glanced down. My brain immediately spun into over-drive trying to remember if water was a magnifier or reducer.

You want to show me something? Then don't you move, big boy. I took a deep breath and affected mild interest in what he was saying.

"It's back here," he said, "behind the waterfall."

"Hey, little girl, want a piece of candy?" I remarked, treading a little faster.

Rick laughed and back-stroked away, toward the fall. His lower body rose tantalizingly in the water but didn't surface. "Hey, little girl, want to see a *Streptocarpus campbellus?*"

Damn him. I'd never seen a *Streptocarpus campbellus* in my life.

"There's a rock ledge, here where I'm standing." The tops of his shoulders gleamed wetly in the shard of light cast down through the canopy. "It's inside there."

I side-stroked past him, keeping my back to him. The waterfall deep-muscle massaged me as I stepped up on the ledge and toed my way through it.

Behind the fall, I caught my breath. A shallow cave had been dug out of the hillside where the waterfall now plummeted. Enclosed on all sides, the stony bower held shade-loving lithophytes—rock-dwelling plants—that clung to every crack and ledge. Long-fingered weed cushioned my bare feet and stroked my ankles where I stood in the waist-deep pool. It smelled fresh and wet and deep and rich. Something about the coolness of it, the darkness, the enclosed space, made it comforting. It was the kind of place where secrets were told and promises kept.

And there, halfway up, was the *Streptocarpus campbellus*. I could just reach it to stroke its leaves. It was like magic, touching this beautiful plant I'd never seen before. Several plants, actually, because this genus was unifoliate—one leaf per plant. I studied the stem structure and admired the leaves' brilliant green coloring. Buds arced gracefully, deigning to bow. Another week or two, and they'd be in full bloom, splashing nearly Day-Glo purple against the darker moss and lichen. Too bad I wouldn't be here when it happened.

"Gorgeous, aren't they?" Rick asked over the waterfall's roar as he waded to stand next to me.

"Unbelievable," I said, turning a leaf to study the underside's red coloring. "I wish I had my equipment."

"I thought for a while it might be *Streptocarpus wenlandii*."

"No way."

"Why not?"

We talked for a while, and I guess you could say at one point we actually argued over the plant's genus, our voices echoing around the small space. He knew a lot about plants for an entomologist, but I guessed he wasn't a one-subject wonder like I was. I liked plants but I wasn't crazy about them. It was tramping around in places like this that I liked. But Rick seemed as adamant about his botany as he was his entomology.

"Look, I'll take a specimen for the herbarium," I said finally, a little exasperated. "We can't make a definitive taxonomical statement until it's reviewed in the lab." I didn't add that Harrison would have been the man to consult. Kidnapped, missing or dead, he was a better taxonomist than I could hope to be.

And at that point we both kind of woke up to our situation. Well, *I* woke up at least, to him standing so close the back of my right arm felt the heat radiating from his rib cage. And there I was, all hot and bothered over a freakin' plant with my own fruits, as they were, on display for everyone to see. One glance down was all it took to tell me *he'd* noticed them. *He,* or perhaps more precisely, *it,* had been awake to our situation for a little while. And *his* blossom was more impressive than I could have guessed. No prize winner like Carlos's, but more than ample for getting the job done. The sight set off a strong hum in my core that threatened to explode into a full-fledged burn.

He met my gaze innocently enough. "Let me know what your research turns up," he said. "I'm curious. I've never known a *campbellus* to evidence characteristics of either the *wenlandii* or the *porphyrostachys*. Even de Vries would have to admit they're related."

I've got a question: what do you do when you're standing

naked with a guy who turns out to have a nice bod—scratch that—a great bod, a great bod that's clearly glad to see you, and he keeps talking about plants as though his not inconsiderable banner of desire isn't waving in the wind? What kind of message is that? Every other part of him was just so damned disinterested that I didn't know what to do other than continue the casual conversation and ignore the way his interested part bobbed merrily in the water.

While he went on about de Vries's Delineation Theory, I got to thinking. Maybe I wasn't worth jumping. Sure, other guys had found me worth jumping, but then Rick was a true scientist, and an earnest one at that.

An idealistic, do-gooding, yoga-practicing, granola-bar-eating, heart of the jaguar, occasional fantasy-inducing bug nerd.

I guess I wasn't his type.

Hell, he wasn't my type, either.

The steady hum in my core vanished when he said, "Who's Scooter?"

I was so surprised, I answered. "My great-uncle."

"You said he raised you."

"I need to get my gear together for tonight." I turned my back to him to go.

"Jessie." Rick's voice slid like a caress over my ear. He was so close I felt his breath on my shoulder.

I paused. "What?" I asked, not looking at him.

"I don't bite."

About a dozen bad and obvious jokes sprang to mind. "Okay," I said instead.

"I know he's important to you," Rick went on. "I'm just trying to get a sense of what's going on. You won't tell me anything."

"I don't want to make my problem your problem, okay?"

His fingertips touched my shoulder, making me turn my head to look at him. "We'll find the orchid."

Gratitude flooded my chest. Underneath all the excitement with the viper and the gold mine and Daley, I'd been tense about finding that orchid and getting it back to von Brutten. As much as I hated to admit it, I'd have had a hard time finding the Death Orchid so soon without Rick's help. His knowing what I was up to was a relief, because it meant I could get on with my job without tap-dancing around my motives.

He nodded. "As soon as I get the situation with the Yanomamo straightened out, we'll set the moth loose and track it to your orchid."

I stared at him. The man was out of his mind. His little campaign for peace would take years, not hours. "What are you here for?" I asked.

His eyebrows shot up. "What do you mean?"

"The first rule of fieldwork," I reminded him. "Don't get involved with the locals."

"If I don't get involved, there won't be any habitat left for my research."

"Give me a break." I crashed through the waterfall and dove deep into the clear, cold water. Parts of me that had warmed up in the cave instantly iced over again as the water enveloped them. When I surfaced, I headed for the pool's edge.

"What's your problem?" Rick demanded, splashing in my direction. "I'm just trying to secure a sustainable habitat—"

"It's not your problem. It's not your business." I hoisted myself from the water, then stepped into my dry panties while I talked. "All this stuff—the mining, the mercury, the natives—it's all theirs to fix. Not yours. Not mine." I skipped the sports bra and jerked my still-damp muscle tee over my head. "We're scientists, not working for a friggin' Nobel Peace Prize."

"I'm trying to protect my scientific interests." Rick shoved himself out of the pool, water sheening his muscles. He picked up his clothes from behind a big palm tree a few feet away.

"I want to have a place to do my research during the next twenty years," he called over.

"The Amazon will be around in twenty years," I argued as I wrestled myself into my stiff, damp canvas pants, "but you won't if you get yourself killed trying to stop something that can't be stopped."

"The gold mine is illegal—"

"And the government is letting it happen. How much more of a clue do you need here? Nothing can be done."

"I don't buy that," he said stubbornly. He zipped up his pants and stood there, water dripping down his carved pecs and abs. "I believe I can make a difference."

"You don't want to make a difference. You want to manage this thing. Has it occurred to you they don't need you to do that for them?"

He crossed his arms over his chest, making his biceps bulge. "It's better to do something than to turn my back on them. I'd rather take the chance of getting involved."

"It'll take more than a nosy Americano to get the miners to quit being greedy and the Yanomamo to want to live the American dream. Let them sort it out for themselves."

"That's the easy way out. Don't you care about what's going to happen?"

I scooped up my remaining clothes in one arm. "Look, I don't want to see the Amazon cut down and burned or the native peoples poisoned any more than you do. But there's nothing in the world that's going to stop it. If you believe you can, you need to take off those rose-colored glasses you're so fond of."

"What's really got you pissed off?"

"What do you mean?"

"You don't care about these people or what happens to them. Or even what happens to this place." He jerked his thumb at the green extravagance around us. "So you can't be pissed about my helping them." His lips clamped into a thin line.

"You're right. I don't have time to be pissed about that. I need my orchid tonight," I informed him, "so I can get out of here in one piece before you start raising hell."

"I'm due at the village for the negotiations tomorrow."

"That's not my problem. I get the orchid and I'm gone."

"What's the rush?" He jammed his arms into his sleeves and shoehorned his T-shirt over his head, for an instant becoming a faceless, sculpted body from a hot novel cover.

Jeez, how annoying. Did he not get it? "Look, I got a guy following me," I admitted. "If I get out tomorrow morning, I save myself a lot of trouble. All I need is a couple of hours of your time, and then it's all yours. Hell, show me how to use the tracking equipment and you can stay in the village for the big powwow while I get the orchid."

"No way," he retorted. "I haven't waited four years for this moth to show up just to have you lose it." Before I could object to his assumption of my incompetence, he said, "The moth flies tonight. I'll get your orchid before I come back to 'save the world,' as you put it."

Then he turned his back on me and stalked toward the village, leaving me out in the thick and restless jungle he was so afraid would disappear.

And me? I watched him go, wondering why everything that was so important to him just didn't seem that important to me. And why that was starting to bother me.

Rick and I hiked through the late evening and early night in silence. Mosquitoes clouded our heads. A throaty roar reverberated through the canopy and ended with a strangled wheeze, a howler monkey warning off a rival. Shapes flitted drunkenly in the growing darkness. Bats.

When we reached the mutually agreed upon base spot to set the moth loose, Rick busied himself with his tracking equipment while I scouted the terrain. To the unpracticed eye, the four hundred yards in all directions might look exactly the same, but to me, they were as different as night and day. It took me almost an hour to familiarize myself with the area we thought the moth might hang around in, then a little while longer to review the preliminary precautions I'd taken that afternoon when I was supposed to be napping. If Daley decided to show his ugly mug, I wanted to be ready. Everything was good to go.

"How's it going?" I asked when I returned to base.

Rick didn't look up from the monitoring equipment in his lap. "Good," he said shortly.

I'd had about enough of his holier-than-thou attitude, but I didn't want to get into it. Getting into it meant I wanted him not to treat me like I was a plague. Wanting him not to treat me like I was a plague meant it bugged me that he thought of me that way. And it bugging me that he thought of me that way meant way more than I was prepared to deal with.

"Let me know when you're ready," I said. "The sooner we get this over with, the better."

"Everything's tested. I'm ready."

He slipped the monitor strap over his neck and shoulder like a guitar player. I already wore my harness and had a two-hundred-foot coil ready to go, plus my running anchors. Rick opened the bug trap and carefully lifted the moth out. By the glow of the monitor, I could see the square computer-chip-looking transponder glued on the moth's thorax. For the first time that evening, Rick looked at me. I looked back but didn't say anything. He turned and opened his hands.

The moth instantly winged up, beautiful and wild, disappearing into the night.

Rick tipped the monitor toward his face, casting a dim red glow onto his glasses. The screen showed, among other things, vertical and horizontal coordinates for the moth. It headed further up, into the canopy, then took off east-north-east. The hunt was on.

We clambered over downed trees and shoved our way through dense underbrush, me hacking a trail a few steps ahead while Rick watched the monitor and directed me. A half hour of slogging brought us to a *Pterocarpus* with those massive buttress roots.

"Hold on," Rick said, excitement tinging his voice. "It's stationary."

I backtracked to him and stood next to him to study the monitor. "Time to go up?"

"If it acts like its cousins, you've got about fifteen minutes before it moves again."

Somewhere a hundred feet over my head, in branches I couldn't see, his moth had alighted on my orchid. We put on Yagoda's portable headsets so Rick could guide me through the trees to the moth without vocally alerting Boa Vista of our progress. I strapped on my headlamp. I didn't want to use it because it'd be a heckuva bright beacon for a sharp-eyed hiree of Daley to spot, but I wasn't sure I'd have a choice.

I got out my running anchors. Harness, carabiners and climbing rope were ready. I slipped a fresh bug trap into my backpack, since Rick would want his moth when all this was over.

The *Pterocarpus* was much thicker than the kapok I'd climbed the day before. While I adjusted the running anchor's length, I said, "I told you a guy was following me. Lawrence Daley. He wants to steal the orchid when I get it."

"Old foe?"

"Yeah. He won't mess with you unless he thinks he can use you against me. So if I see anything suspicious, I'll give you a fruit-bat call. You know what that sounds like?"

Rick nodded. "I'll take the long way back to the village."

"Are you okay with that?"

"Yeah."

I studied his angular face as best I could in the monitor's glow. He'd programmed a waypoint for the village into his GPS tracking system, so he ought to be able find his way home, even at night. But I wanted him to convince me he could make it back to the village without my help.

"We'll get your moth back," I promised.

"I don't doubt it. You're too good at what you do."

"If we find this orchid, I'll owe you," I said.

"You won't owe me."

"Yeah, I will. And I'll get your moth back. Or another one. Before I go."

"You're in a hurry. Why bother?"

"Because it makes us even," I said irritably.

"Right." His voice sounded distant, a little annoyed. "Life for life, moth for orchid."

"Isn't that a fair contract?"

"What makes you think I want a contract?"

I drew breath for a real zinger but caught his lips instead, warm and firm. His fingertips pressed my neck, points of contact that grounded me to him, energy flowing between us like an electrical current. Every ounce of blood in my body flooded my chest before it turned south. He abruptly let go and I realized he'd barely touched me, and for only a second at that.

"We're a good team," he said, still very close. "I'm sorry I've been a hard-ass."

"No worries," I replied gruffly, trying not to sound like I'd lost my breath, which I had. "I'm a bitch and I know it. Just get your hard-ass back in one piece if Daley shows up. Can you do that?"

"We bug nerds have a way of finding our way home."

I heard the grin and wished I could see it. "Maybe Marcello can help you when you get lost."

I felt a tug at my waist as he clipped a transponder to my

harness, making me a blip on his monitor. It also put my thigh against his. "That kid can outtrack us both."

I knew the affection in his voice was aimed at Marcello, but it sounded awfully good to me, especially since his knee pressed the inside of my thigh and gave me all kinds of ideas. At that point it became clear I needed to either get up that tree or get a little more of what Rick had offered a minute ago. As time was wasting and neither the moth nor Scooter were following my personal schedule, I opted for the climb.

"You can handle Daley," I said, faking confidence as I slung the anchor around the tree. "It's his Brazilian friends you need to worry about. I don't think they'll play nice."

"I'll give you a shout if the moth moves."

I switched the headlamp to its dimmest setting and double-timed it to the canopy. Laying anchors and slings was about four times more dangerous at night than in daylight. On low, my headlamp could only illuminate about five feet. But there's something about not being able to see the ground that makes it easier. I could pretend I was ten feet off the ground rather than a hundred. *Be bold, young woman,* I exhorted myself as I planted my feet against the trunk and leaned out.

I fired up the headset. "How am I in X and Y?" I asked.

Rick's voice sounded close, softly intimate, distracting. "Ten degrees south in X, up another two meters in Y."

"Roger that," I whispered, feeling ridiculously like a golf announcer. I gained the required height and said, "I'm there in Y."

"Anything south of you?"

Still tethered by running anchor to the tree, I twisted around as far as I dared. I snapped the headlamp on bright for a split second and shot a high beam into the canopy. Nothing.

"Hang on," I said. "Let me give it another blast." I turned my head slightly and punched the light on and off.

I caught a glimpse of a small bird hovering like a hummingbird in a handful of narrow orchid leaves.

Bingo.

I fought down a surge of adrenaline. Clear head, I reminded myself. Don't get overexcited. Don't lose your cool. It'd be easy to get sloppy. Getting sloppy would get me dead. Eyes closed, I tried to center my thoughts. Put on the blinders. One move at a time. In a moment, I was ready.

"I got it," I told Rick. "Give me a minute to set my slings."

"The moth's moving."

"It doesn't matter. I've got the orchid in sight."

I made shorter slings than usual so I'd have a little more maneuverability. My shoulders and back would be sore from holding myself up and working the web slings along the branches, but it was a necessary evil.

"Here comes a rope drop," I said.

"I'm clear."

I let the belaying rope go. It slapped and crashed down through the midstory, setting off a cackling mob of toucans. *Oops on the nest,* I mentally apologized.

"You're way up," Rick remarked. "Be careful."

"I just need a minute."

My feet dangled where I hung in the sling, making my knees weak even though Rick had me covered. I grabbed the *Pterocarpus* branch with both hands, praying a snake hadn't curled up on it somewhere between me and the Death Orchid, and hand-over-handed my way forward. When I had my nose on the orchid's leaves, I worked the webbing to catch up with me.

I snapped on the headlamp and dimmed it as low as it would go.

The Death Orchid gleamed, a *Laeliocattleya,* delicate and luscious, demure and sexy, the feathery ruffles on an Old West madam's nightgown. Its petals and sepals shone a brilliant white. But its lip, with which it tempted the Corpse Moth, echoed the moth's own pearlescent black.

Innocence and sin. Purity and decadence. Truth and deception. The Death Orchid, called that because it gave life.

God, it was gorgeous.

And there were two, here within reach. The adrenaline and excitement surged, warming my gut. Scooter's salvation, right here. A whoop was starting to grow in my chest. I bit it back. Time to get on with business. Stay focused.

First I removed the bug trap from my backpack and strapped it onto the branch over my head. That gave me some room to maneuver my gear. Then I carefully sliced off hunks of bark the Death Orchids clung to and packed both bark and plant in cardboard cylinders that slid into my pack.

"I've got 'em," I told Rick. "Just wait until you see—"

"Jessie—" he whispered, but suddenly the headset died.

On instinct I turned off the lamp, blinding myself.

Then drifting up through the darkness came the squeaking chirp of a fruit bat.

Damn Lawrence Daley to hell, I thought, and dropped.

Chapter 10

I hit the ground hard, boots thumping in the thick soil. Rick had disappeared, presumably headed for the village. Not too far away, a low scrabbling alerted me to someone's approach.

The climbing rope unhooked quickly from my harness and I left it hanging from the slings. It was a beacon to the Death Orchid's whereabouts, but my goal was to get the orchid back to von Brutten's lab, not prevent Daley from knowing where it had been.

I headed off toward my little homemade obstacle course, making just enough noise to get Daley thinking I was panicked. Even in the dark, I had a good idea of where I was going; the terrain played out in my brain like a movie from the little tour I'd taken during the day. And without interference from the lamp, my eyes were adjusting to the dark. As I snuck along a stream, I heard the first pursuers behind me. Someone was smiling down on me again because Daley really had hired Brazilians, not Indians.

Indians wouldn't be fooled by any of the traps I'd laid. These bozos might. Here's hoping Father João was right about there being only four of them.

I passed my first landmark, a split banana tree next to a rock, crossed the wide stream quickly and ran silently back up the stream to about where I thought the pursuers would emerge on the opposite bank. Sure enough, they called to each other over the burbling water, apparently debating whether or not to cross. I scraped my boot on a rock and flashed my head-lamp on and off.

One of them stepped my direction. A profound silence, then a grunt and the snapping of bone as he landed in the streambed.

I guess he didn't realize he'd been standing on an eight-foot-tall embankment. Bummer.

One down. Three left.

I circled back up the hillside, found the kapok tree I was looking for, crouched behind it and waited. After a while Pursuer Number Two caught up with me. When he passed the kapok at full tilt, I reached out and shoved him into a *Tachygalia myrmecophilia* tree. He hit the tree hard, face-first, and started screaming. I quickly brushed off the biting ants that launched themselves onto my arm. The rest of the colony swarmed him. Easier target. He collapsed at the tree's trunk and rolled, but the ants would leap onto his prone body as long as he stayed within a couple of feet of the trunk.

"The stream's that way," I said in my awful Portuguese, pointing.

He rolled in that general direction, scratching and clawing at himself.

Two down.

It took a while longer to pick up Pursuer Number Three. Even Daley must have caught on and was exercising caution. The pursuer and I danced around each other, around trees and over rock formations, for what felt like an hour. But though he was a wily opponent, our dance whirled us closer and closer to a nasty surprise.

Suddenly a crack—rifle shot—echoed along the ridge where I hid in the underbrush. It sounded like it originated in the valley below us. Fear iced my veins. Had Daley taken a shot at Rick? I clutched the trip rope I'd rigged.

Come on, buddy, I mentally broadcast to Pursuer Number Three. *I need to quit playin' around and get on with it.*

He emerged from a palm thicket a few feet away from me. *Another couple of steps,* I coaxed. He clutched his pistol and cautiously followed my instructions. *One more.*

There.

I pulled hard on the trip rope. Way up in the midstory, the feeble branch the rope was tied to gave, and the half-dozen fire liana vines wrapped around it fell with it. Pursuer Number Three just had time to hear the commotion and look up before the vines landed on him like a gigantic stinging net. I couldn't see them but I knew welts were rising almost instantly on his skin, welts he'd have to go to Boa Vista to have treated. A swim in a stream wouldn't help. I left him alone to grunt and whimper, feeling only a little guilty about leaving him there.

Three down, one left. And Daley.

If Daley had hurt Rick, I had an extra special surprise for him.

Halfway down the hillside, I got that hair-on-the-back-of-the-neck feeling, which I've learned to never ignore. I hunkered down next to a boulder and closed my eyes. All around me, nocturnal sounds filled the darkness—bats clicked in their curious Morse code, dozens of crickets drew one leg against another, an owl hooted and rustled. Nothing else.

That's when I knew Daley had hired Indians, as well. Good ol' Daley. He really was starting to brighten up.

I hightailed it further up the hillside. Here, about three

miles from the village, I'd discovered a great hiding place where I could while away the rest of the night until they gave up and quit looking. With the change of plans—I needed to get finished up here and go find Rick—I could still use the hiding place to lose the Indians before doubling back toward the village.

The climbing rope I'd strung earlier led to a non-stinging liana hammock anchored relatively low, about ten feet off the ground. It's conceivable for over one hundred and fifty different species of beetle to live in a single tree, and knowing my luck, they'd all be on vacation in my hammock. But I could handle being crept upon for a little while until the Indians tired of looking for me.

As long as the hammock didn't house a pit viper, I'd be okay.

A volley of shots echoed around the ridge as I hooked up my harness and started climbing. What the hell was going on down there? Had Daley lost his mind?

I reached the hammock and pulled the rope up after me. The sling on the branch above the hammock would have to come down because those sharp-eyed Indians would spot it. Hell, they could shoot a capuchin monkey in the canopy with a bow and arrow at dusk, so they'd easily see my sling, even in the dark, probably because it just wouldn't look right.

I toed the hammock gingerly, testing for creeping things and poisonous snakes. Just a few innocuous ants and the requisite handful of beetles amid the rich-smelling muck of decaying leaves and fallen branches.

It was, of course, damp.

Before unhooking the sling, I took the precaution of tucking my pant legs into my boots and lacing them up tight to prevent a lower-body attack by the creeping things. My shirt got buttoned up all the way and I tied around my neck the oversize handkerchief I always carried. Then I gathered all my gear inside the hammock with me, quickly lying down to spread my weight across as much space as possible, evening out the pressure on the vines. Just in time, too, because I heard Daley's voice below.

"Bloody hell," he said gruffly. Then in Portuguese, "Tell the Indians to fan out. She's here somewhere."

The last Brazilian said, "What about Quando and Gilberto? What about Silvo?"

"Don't worry about them, my friend. They know the rendezvous points."

The Brazilian spoke a few words I didn't understand, and a soft male voice answered. An Indian. It sounded like Daley and the Brazilian moved on. The Indians, of course, were totally silent.

Then my luck ran out.

The liana hammock creaked. All along my body the biomass shifted subtly.

Damn.

The hammock hitched, jerked and gave in to gravity, vines screaming as they tore along their fibers. The tree branches anchoring them snapped and the hammock slid sideways, tipping me over the edge.

I hit the ground hard, full out, facedown, knocking the breath out of me just before three hundred pounds of biomass hit. Buried under decomposing plant matter and heavy branches, I burrowed one hand to my right, thinking it might be the shortest way out. My fingers found hard sticks or bones, but no air. I tried the other side. The same. A shallow breath sucked silty bark into my mouth.

Now's not the time to panic, I thought. I spat dirt and drew one arm as close to my body as I could. My hand found my shirt. I bowed my back to give myself a little space and managed to get my mouth inside my handkerchief for some clean breaths. Thank God.

Up was clearly the road to take, but to go there I'd have to

forfeit the act of breathing for the time it'd take to swim my
way out. If I could wiggle forward and up against the dead
weight. Even if I managed to get my shirt over my face so I
could breath clean, the biomass would plaster the cloth to my
nose and suffocate me in place.

I was still struggling with my plan of action when I heard
voices. The biomass felt lighter as seconds passed, and then
hands broke through the muck to latch on to my arms and jerk
me out.

It was like surfacing from a muddy pool, smelly mud and
leaves and dead things spraying in all directions as I shook
off my rescuers.

Daley, damn him, was laughing. I wiped the goop from my
face, coughed hard a few times, and glared at him and his Brazilian in the dim light of false dawn.

"Oh, luv," he said when he could talk without gasping,
"you are a sight."

The Indians, who were melting out of the shadows, stared
at me with something like awe and kept their distance. I
guessed liana hammocks weren't where they were used to
hanging out. Half-hoping I'd inadvertently tapped into a myth,
I took a single step toward one of them.

The Indian didn't move, but Daley held a nasty-looking
pistol at my rib cage, his laughter abruptly silenced.

"Don't try anything, luv," he said soothingly, his voice like
milk chocolate. He held out his other hand. "I believe you
know very well what I want from you."

"I can't give them up," I said, shaking my head. "Not both
of them."

"Give me the pack."

He pressed the gun's muzzle against the ribs still sore from
the bad plane landing seven days before. Seven days? It felt
like a month.

"Come on, Daley," I said, trying not to sound like I was desperate, which I was. "I need you to cut me some slack, just this once."

His smile would have been beautiful except for the ugly look in his eyes.

"I see no good reason for honoring that request."

"One orchid," I said. "All I need is one."

"As many times as you've screwed me over?" he asked softly, that beautiful smile sliding steadily into sadistic menace. "As often as I endured your insults? Your humiliations?"

"I know I've been tough on you but it was only because I knew you were man enough to take it," I lied. "Leave me one orchid. It's personal. It has nothing to do with von Brutten or Thurston-Fitzhugh. Believe me."

I bit down on a wince when the pistol's muzzle dug harder.

"I don't believe a word that's coming out of your pretty little mouth," Daley whispered. "Give me the pack."

The desperation abruptly welled up and drowned my pride. "Please, Lawrence," I said, hating the way my voice shook. "Just this once—"

"Now."

A shrug, and the pack slipped from my shoulders into my hands. He yanked it from my grip and tossed it to the Brazilian, then stepped back.

Daley barked an order the Brazilian translated. The Indians disappeared into the forest in all directions, making sure I'd have a hard time following them. I didn't care about the Indians but there was no way I'd let Daley or my orchids out of my sight.

A rifle cracked nearby, sending us both to the ground for cover. In the confusion, I scrambled over and tried to get a grip on Daley's gun but my muddy fingers slipped. He swung hard at me. My head thudded when the pistol's butt clipped my temple. By the time I quit seeing stars, he'd stood and put several steps between us.

"Trouble in paradise," he remarked, motioning toward the Yanomamo village below us. "I shall be leaving now, and wish you a very good trip back to your employer. Perhaps we shall see each other again soon. But not too soon, I hope."

It was a clear invitation to go after him. I sat up and my eyes had to catch up with me before they could focus on Daley's back disappearing into the forest. Damn him. The shortest distance between two points was a straight line. Rick had been my straight line up until now. I could probably catch Daley on the other side of this range and then—

Another rifle crack. Shouts. The acrid smell of burning wood. I scrambled to my feet, looked down into the valley just rising into the light of dawn. Gray smoke rose over the village and amid the trees I could see faint tongues of flame. A woman screamed until a pistol shot echoed against the hillside, cutting her off. What the hell had happened? Had the Yanomamo been attacked? By whom? And where was Rick?

Daley's undisguised footsteps thumping over the forest floor faded. My orchids. As of dawn, I had six days to get the orchids and get back. Scooter came first. He always came first.

I took a single step after Daley and stopped, feet frozen.

Forgive me, Scooter.

I started running for the village.

True dawn was breaking as I reached the village outskirts. Flames shot out of the *shapono,* its framework a liquid orange skeleton as it burned. Two *pistoleiros* writhed on the ground in front of it, arrows sticking out of their stomachs. A little pile of Yanomamo dead lay crumpled at the clearing's edge. I ran to my hut. It still stood, far enough away from the main village to be overlooked. No sign of Rick. Faint screams sounded deeper in the forest. I grabbed the rifle from my duffel and slung it over my shoulder.

A volley of gunshots led me toward Father João's hut. I circled wide, trying to figure out from the sounds where the shooters were. The *whiff* and *thunk* of an arrow striking flesh, a man's cry, then a *pistoleiro* dropped like cut timber three feet in front of me.

I hoped the Yanomamo would recognize me when they saw me.

A *pistoleiro* broke cover and ran toward me, rifle raised. Without thinking I squeezed the trigger at point-blank range. He looked more surprised than hurt, clutching his stomach. I grabbed his rifle as he fell. Five Yanomamo men sprinted past me, bows ready, and flushed a handful of *pistoleiros* from behind Father João's hut. The Brazilians ran, then sprouted arrow feathers from their shoulder blades.

I followed the Yanomamo warriors back toward the flame-lit communal area. Where's Rick? my gut shouted, but I didn't have any words I could say to the men to get an answer. The women's screams became wails when we stepped into the clearing. On the far side of the burning hut, the shaman tended the wounded and Father João directed a child to bandage a woman's bloody arm. Porfilio, the Shotgun Kid from the gold mine, held a cloth to a man's chest.

I scanned the triage area as I walked closer. Where the hell was Rick? A finger of rage stroked my breastbone. If Daley had done anything to him—

Father João moved. Behind him, a man sat on a downed log with his head in his arms, blood sheening the side of his face and head, running down his forearm. Shot in the neck or face probably. The blood masked his features, made him unrecognizable. He wiped his sleeve across his eyes. Light glinted from the eyeglasses he held.

Oh God.

Rick.

I nearly had my shirt off by the time I skidded to a stop in front of him. "Don't move." I dropped to my knees, then ripped a strip off my shirttail to make a bandage. His eyes were shiny white in all the shiny red. "Where were you shot?"

The right side of his face was thick with blood, his hair clotted with it. My throat tightened up so much it hurt to breathe.

"Jessie."

"Hold still."

I gingerly ran my fingers over his temples and into his hair, feeling for the wound and praying he'd just been scraped. So much blood. And I was so damned filthy. What if the wound got infected because my hands were covered with dirt? I wiped my eyes on my muscle-tee's strap.

"Jessie." Our fingers slid greasily across each other as he caught hold of my hands and drew them down in front of him. "I'm not shot. It's not my blood."

That took a minute to register because most of my synapses had short-circuited over the thought of him dying. When his words finally hit home, I clamped my arms around his neck and tried to see how close I could get.

"I'm okay." His arms wrapped so far around me that his hands gripped my sides. "I'm okay," he whispered against my ear.

In my entire life, a full body hug had never felt so good. The blood's metallic smell, my earthy, mucky grime, Rick's slimy cheek, his glasses frames poking my head—I didn't care about any of it as long as he didn't let go for about a year.

Behind us, the wailing subsided slowly. After a moment there was only the crackling of the fire and the occasional crash when a burned hut support collapsed. Men muttered. I heard Father João's voice. Then the high-pitched, plaintive cry of a child.

I pulled back to look at Rick. "Where's Marcello?"

His forehead tensed, making three long cracks in the rime of drying blood. He bent his head, then raised it and met my gaze. His eyes gleamed with pain. My heart died.

"No," I said.

"I'm sorry, Jessie. There wasn't—"

"Where is he?"

"Father João and I took him into the jungle. It was better that way."

"I want to see him." Tears streamed over my cheeks. "Take me to see him."

When I tried to stand, Rick caught me hard against his body and made me look at him. "There's not enough left of him to see," he said quietly.

I stared, not believing. Finally, "This is his blood, isn't it?" Rick nodded.

My forehead pressed his blood-smeared neck. "What happened?" I asked his top button.

"Marcello brought Porfilio last night so we could start talks this morning. The colonel must have suspected something, because his strongmen followed them here. Porfilio and I tried to talk to them, tell them not to attack, but they didn't listen." Rick's hands stroked my back. "When they started fighting, Marcello got in the way. That's all. He just got in the way." I felt him swallow. "I tried to save him, Jess." He gave up a sob. "I couldn't."

The damned analytical part of my brain took over and I raised my head. "If he was shot, why was it so bad? Why was there so much—"

"He wasn't shot."

"You said—"

"I said he got in the way. Please, Jessie," he said, his dark eyes pleading.

He shook his head, refusing to say aloud what I suddenly knew had happened. My chest went leaden with rage. It was a technique played out around the world in every third-world jungle and savannah I'd ever been in. Save the bullets for the adults.

"Goddamn it!" I shouted, wrenching from Rick's arms.

"Jessie."

"Leave me alone!"

I stalked back out to the communal area where the two *pistoleiros* lay dead. The pile of Yanomamo were, I saw now, children.

One of the dead men held a blood-covered machete in his hand.

There are times when the rage doesn't run out, when it turns in on itself and cools to hardened steel.

Calm descended on me. I loaded the rifle and fired into the dead man. Then I reloaded for his dead buddy. Then I did it again, and again, until I ran out of shells. When that was done, I hoisted the assault rifle I'd taken from the Brazilian I'd shot and emptied its magazine into them. Finally I took the machete from the dead man's hand and leaned it up against a rock. I lifted the assault rifle, aimed and punched the stock hard onto the blade. The machete snapped in half.

I stood for a moment over the dead men and massacred children. Somewhere in the jungle, Marcello lay, broken and bloodied. Probably still wearing that Day-Glo climbing harness. *Oh, God.* I fell to my knees, holding on to the empty rifle, tears flooding over my soiled hands.

Why Marcello? Why these kids? They weren't a threat to anyone. The sheer uselessness of it pummeled my brain and heart, over and over like a relentless tide throwing itself on rock. Useless, the waves said, like Scooter's illness. Useless like my parents' deaths.

It took a while to pull myself together, but when I had, I went back to the triage area. Villagers lay or sat around the flat rock that was Father João's makeshift worktable. The shaman sat on the table, his face expressionless. The padre heated a knife over a flame. Rick limped as he walked from a villager he'd just bandaged to the operating table.

"What's this?" I asked Rick, pointing at his foot.

"Nothing serious," he said dismissively. "Twisted ankle, but nothing broken or torn."

I shot a glance at Father João, who nodded. "Getting the children into the jungle," the older man added, his eyes huge behind his thick lenses. He saw me looking at the sling cushioning his left arm and shrugged. "Broken. It does not matter." He turned to the shaman.

The shaman's shoulder had bled profusely at one point but had stopped. Rick peeled back one of the padre's precious bandages to reveal a gunshot wound. Father João said something to the shaman, who neither moved nor spoke. The padre muttered briefly under his breath, then pressed the knife tip into the wound. A few minutes later, he'd dug out the bullet. The shaman waited, impassive, apparently not feeling a thing.

Maybe he could teach me how to do that.

"We both need a bath," Rick said to me gently as the shaman moved off. "And you need some rest."

"I'm not sure I can sleep."

"I'll bring you something to eat."

"I'm not hungry," I muttered automatically.

"You're hungry, angry, and tired. I can help two of those. Come on."

He made me go back to the hut and eat a hunk of cassava bread. Then he dug out some clean clothes for me. We went to the bathing pool, walking slowly to accommodate his limp.

"Did you get the orchids?" he asked as we stripped.

I waited until I was naked to answer. "I lost them. Daley caught me."

I freed my ponytail and a quarter pound of dried mud fell out. I took the bar of biodegradable soap Rick offered and dropped into the pool, heading for the ledge where I didn't have to tread water.

"All of them?" he asked from the bank.

I nodded.

I couldn't say anything else. It was just too much right then. Standing chin-deep on the rock ledge, I dunked my hair and tried to run my fingers through the wet strands, but no dice. Too many tangles. Too much gunk. I tried starting at the ends, but they caught on my fingers, too. Two nails had split into the quick during my little jaunt and ached beneath their stinging. A dead beetle clung to a knot.

Dammit, I thought, feeling everything inside me and outside of me going out of control. The orchids, gone. Marcello, slaughtered. Rick, hurt. Scooter, dying. See what happens when you get close? Better I stay away from people. I clenched my teeth and tugged viciously at my hair. Dammit, dammit, dammit.

"Here. Let me help," Rick said behind me. I hadn't even heard him get in the pool, I was crying so hard. "Tip your head back."

I did. My body naturally rose to float. I stared up through the trees while he patiently untangled, unwound and debeetled my hair. The sun warmed my front and cold water chilled my back. My mind centered on sensation, on Rick's fingers and the green trees above me and the small swatch of blue sky shining beyond the canopy. Floating between hot and cold, feeling the occasional waterfall ripple lick up my sides to cool my skin. This was here, now. Horror behind me, horror in front of me. Tears leaked from my eyes. What if I couldn't find another orchid?

The sweet soap smell wafted over me as Rick gently worked the lather into my hair. There was only the steady pressure of his fingertips, then the warmth of his bare chest on my back as he drew me close to rest my head on his shoulder while he worked through the ends. He cupped his hand and spilled cold water over my forehead until the soap disappeared, leaving the strands clean.

"You'd better do the rest yourself," he said gruffly in my ear.

I pivoted. He'd washed the blood from his face and hair, leaving something like despair in its place. His dark eyes seemed haunted, guilty.

"Get some sleep," he said before I could say anything. "I have a few things to take care of."

He stroked away. I watched him easily hoist himself from the pool and dress, then limp off without a backward glance. I felt sorrow—for Scooter, for Rick, for the innocent villagers, for Father João, for Marcello—and all that sorrow fed directly into the core of rage that lay deep in my heart.

I nursed all that bad feeling while I finished my bath. I nursed it while I pulled on my sun-warmed clothes and strode back through the jungle. I nursed it when the shaman and a group of Yanomamo men paraded the bodies of their people to their sacred ground for the cremation ritual. I nursed it when I saw Rick leaning on a cassava branch crutch, talking with Porfilio outside Father João's hut, and saw Father João join them.

I nursed it while I lay down in my hut, pulling the mosquito netting close, as if that thin veil could prevent the world from hurting me. Or my cold rage from hurting it in return.

Chapter 11

In the dream, I felt warm and safe and comforted. I knew it was a dream, because I don't usually feel that way in real life. But my body clock was screaming to get going, so I forced my eyes to slit open, my brain firing on only two cylinders.

I lay on my side in the hammock, facing the door. The dim light coming through the hut's cracks told me it was nearing dusk. I'd have time to track the moth to another Death Orchid. That was good news. For a change.

While I drowsily ran through my mental climbing checklist, I gradually became aware of a warm weight on my side. And on my hand. And on my back. My brain finally ticked over into consciousness.

Rick spooned me tightly, his arm wrapped around me, our right-hand fingers entwined. Cheeky boy, I thought automatically, then realized he was a few steps further down the road from cheeky if the steady pressure on the back of my bare thigh was any indication. One of the several nocturnal gestures of hope every man has.

Too bad he wasn't interested in sharing that hope with me.

Ignoring the wave of hurt that thought provoked, I extended the fingers tangled with his and stretched. He roused and made room for me to roll over to face him, his arm still draped over my waist. The hammock swung gently with our movement.

"Good night," he said sleepily.

"That's morning to you and me." I straightened out my muscle tee that had corkscrewed around when I rolled over.

He inhaled deeply, then opened those brown eyes. We were nearly nose to nose, our lower bodies touching just enough to remind me of what I wanted and couldn't have. He seemed to study me for a minute, then did the most erotic thing any man had ever done. He pillowed his head on his bent elbow and started talking.

"Are you okay?"

"Yeah. Why?"

"You were crying in your sleep when I came in." His eyes wandered to my temple and he frowned. "Good God, Jess, what happened to you?" He moved his arm to stroke the hair away from my forehead, where Daley's pistol had clipped me.

I shrugged. "I lost."

"Lawrence Daley?" His voice was hard.

"Fair play."

His eyes narrowed and his arm dropped back to my waist. "And he took the orchid?"

"Yeah. I was stupid. I had two. I should have left them in the canopy and carried decoys."

"What about your great-uncle?"

Fresh pain twisted in my gut. Everything in my life had gone to hell in a handbasket in about four hours flat. "I've got six days to get a Death Orchid back to my employer's pharmaceutical company."

He frowned. "I don't understand."

I took a deep breath and broke yet again my self-inflicted rule about keeping my private business private. "The company is working on a drug and they think the Death Orchid has the compound they're looking for."

"So the hurry is…" he prompted.

"Scooter's got maybe three weeks left, if that. They can create the drug to help him after I get back with the orchid."

Rick's chiseled lips pressed to a thin line. "No lab can get a drug out that fast. It takes a year and a half at best to go from formulation to phase two trials on humans." He paused. "Well, with the new FDA regulations they can cut it to six months in some cases."

"I got the impression this pharma had a backup plan."

"Backup plan?"

"Like they had more than one iron in the fire. Take this plant out, put the Death Orchid in."

"Then they're talking about switching out the primary compound." He shook his head. "The process starts over. Not from elementary research, which could take five to ten years, but you've still got the six months to get to trials."

I'd never questioned what von Brutten had told me because pharmacology wasn't my area of interest. I knew only in general terms how pharmaceutical companies got from Point A to Point B, but had never known specific timelines. Not like Rick apparently knew them.

Had von Brutten been feeding me a line just to get the Death Orchid into his hands faster than usual? Because he had a bet going with Thurston-Fitzhugh? Sure, he wouldn't win any philanthropy awards, but he'd never lied to me about what he wanted or what he'd give to get it. My considerable bank account vouched for that.

No, von Brutten must have an ace up his sleeve on this one. Maybe he planned to market the drug as an herbal supplement or something else that didn't require FDA approval.

Or maybe the Death Orchid meant a lot more to him than he was letting on. Harrison had disappeared over it. Daley might have killed me for it. Was the orchid really that potent?

"I can't risk missing this deadline," I said. "It's the only chance I have."

"I understand." Rick was quiet for a moment, then said, "Have you lived with your great-uncle for a long time?"

"Since I was seven. My parents died in a car accident and I went to live with him in east Texas."

His eyes narrowed. "That's tough." Wheels appeared to turn in his head. "Scooter helped make you who you are." It was a statement, not a question.

"I think he let me be who I am."

"Yeah, that's different," he agreed. "When did he get sick?"

"A few weeks ago. He got into a drug trial program because the pharmaceutical was using some kind of natural extract for a drug base."

"What? The same pharmaceutical you're working for—"

"I'm not working for a pharma," I said shortly. "I work for a private collector. He's got the connections to the pharmaceutical, not me."

Rick frowned. "Working for a pharmaceutical company isn't a sin. They do a lot of good work."

"Maybe so, but right now I'm thinking they're about as trustworthy as Old Lady Fenster's rabbit feet," I retorted.

"Old Lady—"

"Don't get me started."

He sighed. "So what happened to your great-uncle?"

"He agreed to be a guinea pig for the new drug they made. Then the experimental drug they gave him damaged his heart. They pretty much said, 'Sorry, Pops, you're too old to fix.'"

"Bastards."

I followed this understatement with, "My employer has his own pharmaceutical company that's a direct competitor."

"And he thinks he can use the Death Orchid to save your great-uncle." He didn't sound convinced.

"Yeah."

He nodded, still keeping my gaze. "Six days."

"I had to haul ass from day one, but I can't keep it up." I rolled to my back, set the hammock swinging again, and thought how good it felt to be putting all this out on the table for someone like Rick. He might not like my choices and tactics, but I got the impression he'd never question my motivation. Being just his buddy was a bitch, but maybe it was for the best, because I sure as hell didn't have any idea how to be anything else with a man. Except maybe a good lay.

"It's my fault," he said suddenly.

I turned my head to look at him.

"The attack on the village," he continued, his eyes growing haunted again. "I thought if I could just talk to those guys, make them see reason—" His jaw clenched, then released. "You were right. I had no business getting in the middle of it. They don't know how to negotiate with anything other than guns."

I rolled to my side and hesitantly stroked his cheek. "Their being bastards isn't your fault," I said as gently as I knew how.

"But I should have stayed out of it. You were right about not getting involved. Marcello might still be here if I'd left it alone."

"What about Porfilio?" I demanded. "Wasn't he there trying to fix things, too? Why isn't it his fault?"

"Because I convinced him to bargain with the colonel," he said flatly. "I thought the best thing to do was to be up-front with them, make an offer for peace. I was wrong."

"Did you do what you thought was best?" I asked.

He knew where I was going and didn't answer the question.

So I badgered. "Or did you blow in with your typical arrogance assuming you knew what was best for everybody else?"

He irritably withdrew his arm from my waist and turned to lie on his back.

"I guess it was the latter, then," I said. "I hit some button square on, didn't I?"

"Look, I already feel like hell."

"I know," I said softly, raising up on my elbow to lean close. "That's why I think you should cut yourself some slack. Yes, people died." I let the tears pour, unashamed. "Yeah, Marcello died. But I don't remember you pulling a trigger or swinging a machete. You were just trying to help." I wiped my cheeks dry as I added, "You did your best, and that's the best anyone can do."

He shook his head. "No. I could have stayed out of it. First rule of fieldwork. And now Porfilio and the Yanomamo expect me to lead their war council."

I sighed. Dr. Richard Kinkaid, Bug Nerd, was the best man I knew. "Heart of the jaguar" had been a fine way of putting it.

"I should have listened to you," he continued. "You always know what you're doing."

"No," I said truthfully, "I don't." My voice caught as I said, "I could have been here. I could have dumped a decoy orchid on Daley and come back here to help. Or waited another day."

"But our agendas were different. The talks with the miners wasn't what you were doing."

"Maybe it should have been."

And I had to face that possibility. Maybe it was time to consider the idea that my determined self-interest, the ease with which I let everyone else's problems be their own, without lifting a finger to help, might not be the best plan. Not always.

Had I waited another night, couldn't I have helped the Yanomamo fight the *pistoleiros* and still gotten my orchids, perhaps giving Daley a day to get farther away without finding me? Now I was yet another day behind, with no moth to track, and would have to execute another dangerous climb tonight in hopes of finding an orchid I overlooked the night before.

Meanwhile, Scooter was dying. The villagers had died or were preparing to. People I respected, even if they didn't like me or want me around, were injured.

And Marcello was gone.

Rick rolled to face me, but instead of putting his arm over me, he stroked my face. "Did you do your best or did you waltz in believing you knew what was best?" he chided gently. "You always know where you are and what to do," he whispered. "I envy that."

He leaned forward and kissed me, as if our contact would somehow imbue him with those qualities. It started out soft, searching. The sheer comfort of being touched by a man who respected me took my breath away. It was peaceful and simple and innocent. As it always would be with Rick, who was far too good a man for me.

Then he groaned, pushed me onto my back and rolled on top. Before I could move, he lowered his head and kissed me again. His tongue thrust into my mouth and I welcomed it, tasting him, matching him passion for passion. He broke the kiss. His mouth started roaming my neck, his breath hot. The hammock's shape made him arch into me and I gave him room to settle between my thighs.

I hadn't earned it, and I certainly didn't deserve it, but my God, did I need it.

I wanted the comfort of his body and his passion and his need, as much as he seemed to need mine. And I planned to give it all to him if it would make this ache in my heart go away for a while.

My hands ran down his strong back to his hips, where those sexy black briefs he wore snugged his skin. His fullness pressed my sweet spot agonizingly, and when he barely arced his body to rub against me, I nearly came just with the anticipation.

He raised his head to kiss me deeply again, then settled comfortably along my body and gazed at me with regret.

"I can't do this," he whispered.

"Yes, you can," I replied, trying to keep the pleading note out of my voice.

He shook his head and cast a long lock over his eyes. I ran my hands through his hair to draw it from his face. The bedroom fantasy was back in full force. "You'd look great in a ponytail," I observed for the hundredth time, the first time out loud. "Now take me."

"I won't." His soft expression made me ache. "As much as I want to, I won't."

"Why not?"

"Because it's not just about us."

God, I thought, exasperated. What idealistic claptrap was he about to spring on me now?

"This hut is full of everything out there. Marcello, your great-uncle, the colonel, the villagers. They're all here. It's not just us."

"I don't care. I need this."

"This isn't how it should be," he insisted, still deliciously hard against me. Then something that looked like sadness crossed his eyes. "I don't want to be just one of your men, Jessie."

Every hot spot in my body turned to ice.

"Yeah, I'd hate to ruin a good working relationship by making you the last in a long line of bad choices," I said, levering him off me and scrambling out of the hammock.

"It's true, isn't it?" He pushed up on an elbow, the hammock swaying hard from my sudden exit. "The pilot, Carlos. You'd known him what? A day?"

"My personal life has nothing to do with you," I said, sweeping the netting aside to leave him in the sanctuary alone, "and I don't remember giving you permission to comment on it or my choice of lovers."

"Lovers?" Even through the filmy white netting, I saw every line of his body was taut with tension as he swung out of the hammock. "Is that what you call your one-night stands?"

"No. I call those fun."

"Yeah, you looked like you were having a great time when I met you, presumably the day after a little 'fun.'"

"Okay, hotshot. Interested in my laundry list?" I challenged. "Should I tell you about Marcus in San Antonio? How about Roy in Costa Rica? Or Jack in Indonesia? There're plenty more."

"I just don't want to be added to the list," he said.

I could tell all the evidence was stacked against me. Self-righteous son of a bitch. "Look, I know I don't deserve you," I said, cramming my foot into my pant leg, "so let's just let it go at that, okay? We agree that I'm not good enough for you. I knew that before you started pawing me, thank you very much." I zipped up.

"That's not what I was saying, Jess."

"The hell it wasn't."

"Be honest with me here. 'Long line.' Those were your words."

"I was honest with you about everything I could be." I buttoned my shirt up with shaking hands. "Your track record must be pristine. I guess you've made excellent choices all your life. I haven't." I whipped my hair into its usual ponytail. "Call me a slow learner, but nobody I've ever been with has lasted longer than one night. At least give me points for not giving up, no matter how bad it hurts afterward."

"One night's not much to work with."

"It was all I had."

"And whose choice was that? Who left whom?"

A sudden spasm gripped my chest. I couldn't speak.

"It's all or nothing for you," he persisted, stepping close, "except you don't give anyone anything. You think you do, but you don't."

"I know the way things work." I hated how weak my voice sounded. "People don't hang around for long. Not the ones you need."

Rick's eyes narrowed and his voice was gruff. "No, sometimes they don't. Sometimes they don't even give you a chance."

"Hey, I was interested in giving you a chance."

"All you had on offer was your body. That's all you've ever offered anyone."

Stung, I retorted, "Don't worry, I'm clean. I get my regular checkups. You wouldn't have caught anything from me."

"That's not what I was saying."

I picked up his monitor and slung it over my shoulder. "I'm going to get another orchid," I said. "When I get back, I'll be ready to fight."

I told myself that climbing alone again felt somehow right. True to who I was. The clenched fist in my chest told me I was lying. I swallowed and kept walking to the area where we'd found the orchid. Lying or not, I needed to harvest another plant and take off.

I ended up not needing to track the moth. Instead, I climbed the *Pterocarpus* I'd scaled the night before, belaying myself as I was accustomed to doing, and worked my way back to the spot where the Death Orchids had clung elegantly to their tree.

I switched the headlamp on full force in the gathering dark. No need to hide my activities. Daley was long gone. The man called Noah might be hanging around somewhere, but I didn't care. My black mood, the tamped-down rage of loss, would be more than enough fuel to handle him if he showed his face.

The image of green webbing flashed in my memory and I had to choke back a sob. *Steady, girl. Do what's in front of you.*

The lamp's bright beam scattered a handful of howler monkeys that bobbed and bounded away. My slow sweep across the area revealed a nice crop of Death Orchids—three sprayed their blossoms in short cascading falls, stark white against the tree bark but for the fathomless, pouting black lips.

I quickly maneuvered over and harvested all of them, filling the last of the cardboard tubes which fit snugly into my makeshift rucksack. The plants would keep well enough for the trip back to the States. And with the forged CITES certificates von Brutten had thoughtfully provided, I shouldn't run into any customs trouble between here and there.

Tonight I'd travel with the fighters to the gold mine. I'd gladly give the colonel something to think about the next time he wanted to slaughter a bunch of kids. Then I'd be on my way. I'd be back in the States with a couple of days to spare. Scooter would survive. And my life would go back to being how it was before I ever showed up in this place.

It felt like a good plan. Scooter, I was confident, would approve.

The voices of the war council rose like smoke through the trees. Now full night, the heat had faded and a coolish breeze filtered through the trees around the village clearing as I approached it.

The men's faces were lit only by the fire smoldering where the *shapono* used to stand. No women or children in sight. Twenty or so Yanomamo *huya,* young men, clustered in the shadows, well back from the fire, wearing red and black face paint and red-painted nut beads around their necks. Their hands bristled with arrows.

In the inner circle around the fire, the men were arguing about the best way to get near the mine without being seen. The conversation was going on primarily in Portuguese and occasionally English, and I saw Father João whispering to the shaman and village headman. The headman, a smallish Yanomamo with black designs painted all over his body, squatted next to the shaman, who meditatively chewed a hunk of bark.

On the far side from where I came into the clearing, Dr. Yagoda and one of his Stepford grad students waited. I guessed Kinkaid had called in reinforcements. He was probably going to need them.

Next to them sat Porfilio and, of all people, Carlos Gutierrez. What the hell was he doing here?

He looked up and caught my eye. His arrogant grin broadened and he bowed his head to me. When he met my gaze again, his eyes seemed softer, almost apologetic. Definitely warm. Definitely the eyes of a man interested in showing a girl a good time. His grin faltered as I stared at him. I wasn't interested. Best if he got that message right away.

Kinkaid's frown deepened when he saw me. The shadows threw his face into sharp relief and his expression gave me no clue what he was thinking. I had planned to keep to the background, not knowing how these men would take a woman's presence. The world's advance into the twenty-first century didn't mean much in places like this and I didn't care to be on the business end of a curare-tipped arrow. I'd speak when spoken to. But Kinkaid motioned me to sit next to him on a downed log. He pointed to a hand-drawn map in the dirt similar to the one I'd drawn for him for our mine escape.

"Why bring her into this?" Father João asked abruptly. "She's not needed."

"She stays," Rick said sharply.

"But I don't see—"

Porfilio interrupted gently, "She took out two soldiers and humiliated the *donos!*"

"That was an accident," I said.

"You didn't see her in action, my friend," Porfilio insisted.

"No, you didn't," Carlos murmured, but loud enough for me to hear and to attract the curious looks of men sitting on either side of him.

"Pissed" didn't do justice to the anger broiling inside. I shot Carlos a glance that could have melted bone but he wasn't looking.

Then Rick said, "If you don't care for the situation, Father João, you don't have to stay."

The padre frowned slightly and nodded. "I shall stay."

"What's the plan so far?" I asked.

Rick turned slightly. "Approach the mine, subdue the colonel. Force a negotiation."

"With what?" I asked. "How do you think you'll get him to cooperate?"

Porfilio smiled. "The *pistoleiros'* defeat last night will not make him happy. He'll be glad to talk peace."

Optimistic outlook. "How many *pistoleiros* does the colonel have?" I asked Porfilio.

"Ten, twelve, maybe, now."

I looked at him sharply. "I counted twenty-three when we left last week. Did the Yanomamo kill that many?"

Porfilio nodded respectfully at the village headman. "The Yanomamo killed several. And that English hired some away."

A teaspoon of guilt lifted from my shoulders. Broken legs, ant bites, and fire liana stings were entirely justified. And Daley, bless his cowardly heart, had diminished the colonel's little army.

"They won't expect a hit tonight," Carlos said. "We'll have surprise on our side. We can take the camp by coming in here." He picked up a stick and drew a rough line indicating the airstrip.

"Don't the main buildings front that airstrip?" I asked. "And look what we have here." I gestured to the group around the fire. "Three injured men, two academics, a bush pilot, a mine foreman, and a woman, none of whom are proficient in firearms even if we had any. And any invasion team—or whatever you want to call it—will be vulnerable to automatic weapons fire."

Even across the fire I could see Dr. Yagoda go green around the gills. "They're carrying military weapons?"

"The bad guy's a colonel," I reminded him. "Some of the *pistoleiros* are carrying military weapons, anyway."

Porfilio nodded. "And they have explosives, of course." He grinned. "But I have explosives, too!"

Yagoda shook his shaggy head. "We don't dare get involved. It's too dangerous. The university can't risk an international incident."

"What about your study habitat?" Rick demanded.

"The university won't take the risk, even to save the habitat."

Disappointment registered in Rick's clenched jaw. If he wanted to pursue this, it'd be on his own, without his science god.

Then Yagoda threw him a bone. "I can offer you access to the station's airfield. That's it."

Rick nodded, his eyes lightening a little. I didn't tell him not to get too excited about the airfield. Based on his previous performance, there was no way Carlos would volunteer to fly his crate into battle.

"Look," I said, "maybe it'd be best for the Yanomamo to leave this area until the mine is exhausted."

"Why should they move?" Rick demanded. "They were here first, it's their land, and the laws are on their side."

"But cannot be enforced," the padre said softly. "The government tries, but is spread too thin. Perhaps she is right."

"No," Rick snapped. "We have to try to negotiate a solution."

"With a madman?" I snapped. "You think his henchmen started killing children because the kids were some kind of threat? He didn't send his men here to make a statement. He sent them to wipe the village out."

"Then what do you suggest, lady general?" Carlos asked.

I ignored his sardonic eyebrow. "I suggest you figure out what your real objective here is. If you just go in and whack the colonel, you'll have a paramilitary group, which might mean the Brazilian army, breathing down your necks as soon as word gets into the city. *We* may not like El Capitan, but he's a star in somebody's eyes."

The men stared at me in dramatic silence. Hadn't they thought of this problem?

"International English, Jessie," Rick said softly.

Then he translated, which set off a round of speed Portuguese I couldn't follow.

It seemed clear to me that the primary objective was not to take out the colonel, much as I liked that idea right now. It was to stop him dumping mercury from his processing plant.

The strip-mining, ugly as it was, was negotiable. The land could be reforested to some degree by either the miners or the Yanomamo. While it wouldn't have the same value in eco-biological terms as the old growth that had been removed, it would grow into that value in a hundred years or so. It was doable.

And I had to admit Rick had had more or less the right idea with the negotiations. With the colonel connected in high places, he might very well just be performing a job for someone higher up the food chain. Tick that guy off, and you'd find yourself bombed into a state of reasonableness. Better to find the win-win.

However, a paranoid schizo minor tyrant with delusions of grandeur, by definition, couldn't be counted on to see reason. It was pointless to try to cut a deal with him. The only way reason might start looking more attractive was if the tyrant's jewels were in a vise.

The question was, What was the most expedient way of shoehorning said jewels into one's grip?

We could shut down his mine, but he'd just move the whole operation somewhere else. We could destroy his equipment, but he'd bring in more. A miner revolt wouldn't do it. Yanomamo threats wouldn't do it.

No matter what we did, he'd come back to make prostitutes out of the Yanomamo women, rape the Yanomamo land, kill the Yanomamo children, and then move on to the next likely mining spot. And any village on its periphery.

Either the Yanomamo or the colonel would have to go.

I looked at the shaman, who was already looking at me. The last time I'd made serious eye contact with a shaman, I'd had the Evil Eye put on me. Pit viper. The Evil Eye had failed to keep me away. Is that what this shaman saw in me? Or did he see something else, something far less honorable and courageous than the heart of a jaguar?

Men's voices rose and fell around us. Still, he stared. I stared back.

You know how sometimes things can fall into place when you quit thinking so hard about them? The solution to the problem happened somewhere between us while the shaman and I locked eyes.

The shaman was our ticket out. And Porfilio was our ticket in.

The shaman might be able to concoct a curare-type poison, preferably something that caused the death to look like something else—a stroke, maybe. That would take out the colonel. But what about Goldtooth, the colonel's *donos?*

"Porfilio!" I said loudly over an argument about whether to use Carlos's plane for a dubious air attack.

They hushed up and Porfilio looked at me expectantly.

"Who's the next in command at the mine after the colonel?"

He raised his brows in surprise. "The *donos.* Then me."

"The *donos* is a poser." International English, Jessie. "A pretender. Isn't he?"

Porfilio frowned. "You mean he has authority but has not earned it. The men do not respect him."

"Right."

"Yes, that is true."

"And they respect you?"

Porfilio nodded. "They see me argue with the colonel about the mercury." He made a hand motion demonstrating fumes wafting into his face. "It makes them sick. Very bad."

"Will they help us or are they too afraid of the colonel?"

"The colonel is crazy," he stated. "But they are scared. I cannot count on them to help until after he is gone."

And I knew from experience they weren't happy with Goldtooth. That seemed to clear the way for Porfilio to take over. At least until the higher-ups decided to hand the mine over to another pet colonel.

The Yanomamo headman had been talking with Father João for a while and now Father João stood. "The honored headman demands retribution from the men who attacked the village."

I understood their sentiments. Too bad getting revenge would only make things worse for the Yanomamo. "Will he be placated with the death of the man who ordered the attack?" I asked.

Father João and the Yanomamo headman spoke at some length. Rick's brow furrowed. I gathered the discussion wasn't going well. Father João needed to convince the headman not to attack the colonel or his *pistoleiros*. Doing that would seal the village's fate—they'd have to move deeper, further into the interior, and could never return here for fear of being picked up. Or slaughtered.

Father João finally finished up and turned back to us. "He says the world of the white man is strange to him. He demands revenge, and if we cannot provide it, he and his warriors will take it."

"He'll give us tonight to do what we can?" I clarified. "His warriors won't attack the mine or the miners?"

"No."

Not good enough. I needed to know the headman under-stood. "Will you ask him, just to be sure?"

The padre relayed the question. The headman grunted and said a couple of words. The padre nodded. "He understands."

I said to Father João, "You may want to leave this meet-ing now."

"Why?" Rick asked sharply.

"Because I cannot condone what she is about to suggest," Father João said evenly. "I take it you found what you were looking for."

I figured left field was as good a place to play as any on a day like today, and asked, "What do you mean?"

"You found the orchid."

"Yes, I did."

Then it hit me what he was saying. The Death Orchid wasn't the elixir of life. Far from it. I'd intended the shaman to concoct a poison, sure. But not from the Death Orchid.

Father João nodded, spoke a few words in an undertone to the shaman and village headman, and rose. "I cannot wish you God's blessing on this endeavor," he said. "I cannot in good conscience even wish you to succeed." He turned to go, then paused to look at me once more, light glinting from his thick lenses. "You will leave after this."

"Yes," I promised. "As soon as I prevent an all-out war, keep more innocent people from dying, and help the Yanom-amo get what they want, I'll leave."

He answered my cutting remark by simply walking away.

"What is he talking about?" Yagoda asked.

"He's saying the Death Orchid is called that for a good reason," I replied. I turned then to Rick. "Will you ask the shaman if the orchid can be made into a poison?"

"Jess," he said in a low voice.

"I don't like it, either," I said, "but if the colonel's death looks like natural causes, Porfilio can take over the mine. The Yanomamo will still get their revenge. And nobody else gets hurt."

If the Death Orchid could be used to kill, it would take a heck of a chemistry trick to make it a cure. I froze. Harrison was a taxonomist, the best in his class, not a medical research scientist. Had von Brutten fed me a line about the orchid's curative powers just so I'd come after it? Did he want the plant because it took life away instead of restoring it? Or had Harrison actually been working with a research partner to develop the cure von Brutten told me about?

The distinct possibility I'd been used to gain an end I wasn't aware of gnawed through my gut. If von Brutten had lied, if he'd promised to help Scooter when he knew it was impossible, if he'd lured me away from Scooter during my great-uncle's last few weeks—

I felt Rick studying me, felt naked under his scrutiny. Naked and open and as if he could see all the way down to the anger and hurt lying on my heart. He took a deep breath. I think he might have taken my hand if we'd been alone. And I would have accepted whatever he'd offered, even if it was only that single touch.

Rick tore his gaze away and spoke to the shaman and village headman. The headman said nothing in reply but his eyes gleamed. The shaman chewed his bark for a full minute, his eyes on me. He clearly wanted something from me, but I had no idea what.

Then the shaman spoke for several minutes. At the end of his speech, the Yanomamo warriors dispersed. The headman stood, surveyed us all regally, and left.

You could've sliced the unease around the rest of the circle. It was one of those times you realize just how different our cultures are—the Yanomamo could have all been headed off for a communal whiz, but it looked like we'd been diplomatically snubbed. Would the arrows start flying?

"He'll do it," Rick said quietly. "The poison provokes a heart attack. It'll take an hour to cook up, but then we'll be ready to head out. The warriors have gone to keep watch on the mine. But not attack."

Back in the hut, I carefully drew one of the Death Orchids from its cardboard cylinder and studied its white-petaled, black-lipped flower. It seemed ironic—that it represented, literally, black and white, life and death. The one who held it had life, and the one who would drink its nectar had death. Except the one holding it was me, and I lived in a world of shades of gray. Live and let live. Except, perhaps, for this one time.

Killing a man in self-defense, as a reflex, was nothing like what we were planning. None of the reasons I'd thought of could truly justify this premeditated act. While I've always treasured my innate sense of moral ambiguity, I wasn't sure I was prepared to become an assassin.

But Marcello.

As I got back to the circle with the orchid, Porfilio was saying, "I can put it in his food. Or his whiskey."

The others murmured agreement, even Yagoda. Then Rick shook his head and everyone stopped talking to look at him. "You're already compromised as a traitor," he pointed out. "We'll have to find someone else to put it in his food."

Rick was the big dog at this gathering, I realized, the man expected to lead. The glasses-wearing, granola-eating entomologist had somehow worked himself into a position of respect and authority.

I handed over the orchid to the shaman, who took it reverently, daring to stroke its lip with almost a lover's touch. Firelight flickered over his broad brow and cast half his face into darkness. Fitting, I thought, as he turned away without a word and faded into the night.

While the shaman doubled, doubled, toiled and troubled in his private lair, the rest of us worked on how we'd get the poison into the colonel. None of the miners, Porfilio assured us, would have the courage to help. They were too afraid of the colonel. We decided it'd have to be someone familiar with the mine's layout. Someone who could sneak in, do the deed, and sneak back out without being seen. The choice was inevitable.

I would head out as soon as the poison was ready.

Chapter 12

"You do this often?" Carlos asked me as we crouched under a low palm and peered at the airstrip lit up like a sports field under the compound's bright electric lights. Carlos's Cessna squatted, a fat fly, at the airstrip's edge. Next to it crouched a smaller plane.

"Murder Brazilian colonels or creep around in the jungle? No to the first and yes to the second, but it's usually in daylight." I raised my field glasses and started counting *pistoleiros*.

"No. Give your men...the cold shoulder?"

Night vision goggles would've been nice. "You're not my man. Don't disturb my concentration."

Six *pistoleiros* milled around the cooking compound, three loitered outside the colonel's office, and two headed toward our end of the airstrip, clearly on patrol. All had semiautomatic rifles slung over their shoulders.

The patrol looked tense. It was just after midnight. I wondered if the Yanomamo had made their presence known before our little group hiked the eight miles to the mine. These *pistoleiros* were edgy, nervous. And I hadn't even gotten started yet. I glanced down at Rick's backpack, which carried a couple of sticks of Porfilio's dynamite. At least I'd enjoy some of the night's festivities. Then I'd head on for Boa Vista and the quickest route back to the States, taking my beautiful, poisonous orchids with me.

One of the *pistoleiros* walking toward us bent his head to light up a smoke. The other grabbed his hand before he could strike a match and scolded him. Too late. I'd already seen them.

They kept walking. Had we been backlit, the patrol would have easily picked us out despite our greased faces and camouflage. When they got close to the jungle's edge, the bossy one turned casually to glance over his shoulder at the compound. Then they slipped into the darkness and headed east.

"Damned deserters," Carlos murmured as soon as they were out of earshot.

"Maybe we'll get lucky and the rest of them'll take off."

"Listen," he said, touching my arm, "You must let me make up to you—"

"Save it," I snapped. "I'm busy right now."

I couldn't afford to let Carlos's belated sense of responsibility get past my guard. I had shut out everyone and everything on the way here—Scooter, Rick, Marcello, my guilt, my newfound loneliness, anything that could make me weak. With each step, the black maw of anger had widened inside my heart and mind. I needed every ounce of steel in my blood and bones to do this job. And if the steel failed me, there was always the rage. If it didn't swallow me whole first.

"Do you recognize the new plane?" I asked Carlos.

He shook his head. "It must have come yesterday after I left to find Porfilio." He took the glasses and had a look. "It has no governmental or military markings. Must not be the colonel's."

"What did you tell the *donos* when you left to find Porfilio?"

"That Porfilio owed me money."

"Call him."

He pivoted and sent a low whistle into the dark. Moments later, Porfilio scooted up to join us. Once I offed the colonel, he'd handle the *donos,* probably with bribes. The *donos,* Porfilio had said to Carlos as we hiked to the mine, was a dog that needed only a few scraps to be happy. I personally thought appeasement would only spell more trouble, but Porfilio hadn't asked me.

"Is it not normally lit up like Christmas?" I asked, prepared to translate into international English, but Porfilio shook his head.

"Planes cannot land at night here. Too dangerous."

"Has this plane landed here before?" I asked.

Porfilio studied it through the field glasses, then shook his head. "It is not one of our regular suppliers. I do not know."

"The colonel looks like he's expecting trouble," Carlos muttered.

Porfilio nodded. "He could. He has been acting…strange. Insane. More than usual," he added at our stares.

"Go find your miners," I said to him, "and get them to the cookhouse. All the explosions will be in the processing area."

"What?" he protested, his broad brow furrowing. "You cannot blow up the—"

"I'm not going to blow it up. I'm going to make the *pistoleiros think* I'm going to blow it up."

Doubt still lurked in the way he held his head, a little to one side like a shy child. He nodded hesitantly, like he didn't believe me.

"I'm not going to destroy your livelihood trying to destroy the colonel," I assured him. "But I need the *pistoleiros* to leave the colonel so I can plant the poison."

He nodded more confidently then. "Good luck." He drifted into the leaves and disappeared.

"Come on," I said to Carlos.

We backtracked around the hillside where Rick and I had huddled in a cave waiting for Porfilio to bring us our gear. In the night, the generators' roar seemed louder than I remembered, echoing down onto our heads as we climbed toward them. I guess they'd recovered from Rick's personal fuel additive.

We paused to survey the scene. If El Capitan was that paranoid, the processing shed should be bristling with *pistoleiros*. This was where the wealth happened. As it was, not a soul to be seen. Interior lights filtered through cracks in the shed's walls, casting pale bars on the harmless-looking mercury waterfall. No lights shone directly outside. We'd have plenty of darkness to work in.

Had El Capitan totally lost it? Why were there no guards?

I set my orchid-filled duffel to one side and levered Rick's backpack from my shoulders. With Carlos hovering over me, I gingerly pulled the two sticks of Porfilio's Stone Age dynamite from the supply backpack. Dynamite gets unstable as it ages. Not only were these sticks old, they were probably bootleg and suspect to begin with. Porfilio had strapped the sticks together in classic Old West style and wired a timing device to it.

"Looks threatening enough," I murmured.

"Will it blow?" Carlos asked over my shoulder. His sweat smelled acrid. Fear.

I couldn't blame Carlos for being scared. He'd be closest of any of us to the old, unstable dynamite until the show got started. "Hell, it'll probably blow if you breathe on it hard."

Carlos retreated to the sluice's edge, just out of the light. "I'll keep watch while you plant it," he stage-whispered over the running water's splash.

Good idea, Braveheart, I thought uncharitably. Rick wouldn't have been cowering in the shadows. He would have been making himself useful, pissing in the gas tank again. If I'd let him come with us. His limp would have slowed us down.

Deeper into the jungle, I found a hollow log that looked about right for the diversion. I set the timer for fifteen minutes, checked my watch, then shoved the whole package down the log.

"You know what to do," I said to Carlos when I passed him to pick up my duffel and Rick's pack. "I'll be on the other side of the camp when this baby blows."

He nodded. "Don't hurt yourself," he said. Sweat gleamed on his darkly handsome face.

"Timing is everything," I reminded him. "See you after the fireworks."

He leaped lightly over the waterfall and disappeared into the darkness under the processing shed.

One more trip around this hillside and I'd leave a donkey trail, I thought, moving as silently as I could toward the mining camp's northwest edge. Carlos had been right. The well-lit airstrip suggested El Capitan wasn't feeling safe. But he had no one protecting the processing shed. His guards were deserting him.

What was going on? Had some bigger cheese shown up to wreak havoc on El Capitan's little kingdom?

I knelt and tucked my duffel next to a rocky outcropping. The orchids in their cylinders, two of them now, lay inside next to their CITES certificates and my passports. With most of my climbing equipment still hanging from trees back near the village, I'd travel home pretty light.

Then I remembered Rick's necklace, the one he'd given me to give to his brother when he was dying. It still hung around my neck. Reaching inside my shirt neck, I fingered its markings as if they were Braille, as if I could read the message engraved on it. Maybe I could send it back to him by Porfilio.

Stop it.

Yeah, I needed to quit thinking about Rick before I started regretting him. Regret was an armor chink, plain and simple.

So was wishing things had been different, and wanting what you couldn't have.

I needed to get back to basics: do the job I came to do and stop getting sidetracked by nonessentials. I'd take out the colonel, then take care of Scooter. Nothing else mattered. The anger—of being used, of being hurt—spread like darkness over my heart.

A thunderous boom punched the night air. A split second later, the ground shuddered under my feet just as every light in the mining compound died.

Kudos to you, Carlos, I thought. *You turned off the lights right on cue. They'll think we've blown the generators.*

Pistol shots cracked and echoed up the hillside. Men's voices rose in shouts, fading as the *pistoleiros* moved toward the mining pit and processing shed.

Time to move.

I ran toward the compound, strapping on my headlamp as I went. El Capitan's office was deserted, papers strewn across the desk and floor like the room had been hit by a tornado. The supply room behind it was empty.

Porfilio had said El Capitan's personal quarters were housed in the large building set to one side by itself, away from deafening clatter of the mining pit and processing shed. I headed that way, snaking between outbuildings. Twice, a *pistoleiro* ran across my path, his assault rifle at the ready, but neither one saw me.

The colonel's personal quarters were housed in the one cinderblock building in the compound. It was eerily silent, with only a nervous guard at the front door. Given the general state of uproar around the mining camp even before the festivities started, I had no real way of judging how many guards would be inside.

And contrary to popular belief, I was not a trained commando. That was one of the drawbacks of surviving the messes you made—people got the idea you knew what you were doing.

I skulked around the building for an unguarded way in. On the eastern wall I found a size-two window that wouldn't accommodate my size-eight ass. No good. I'd have to go through the front door.

If I could figure out how to get rid of the guard. I peeked around the house's corner. Uniform shirt untucked, sleeves rolled up over thin forearms, fidgety hands. The guard's attention kept flicking toward the processing shed. His nervousness could work for me, letting me get the drop on him because he was distracted. Or it might work against me, because his keyed-up nerves would add quickness to his reflexes, make him trigger-happy. My only weapon was the rifle I'd taken from the *pistoleiro* who'd guarded Rick and me when we first arrived, and three remaining shells.

I took a deep breath and hefted the rifle, hands steady. The wave of anger had grown until it felt like I was standing on an island, watching the ground fall away from all sides. The ground of goodwill. The ground of righteousness. The ground of happiness. The island got smaller and smaller, and the black waters got closer and closer.

What the hell.

I stepped around the house's corner and leveled the rifle at the guard. He leaped back, shouted something, threw down his gun and ran. I dropped to one knee, keeping my head down. No shots pierced the wooden door. No crowd of booted men descended on me.

What was going on?

I slowly rose to my feet. Around me, nothing but jungle noise and darkness. I gingerly pressed my ear to the door. No sound from inside. My toe eased the wooden door open.

Nothing. No shots, no click of cocking guns.

I slipped inside. The headlamp's lowest setting showed

me an anteroom in as much disarray as the office. An overturned desk, broken lamp, smashed armchair. Looked like the
guard wasn't guarding much.

A volley of muddy coughs scraped the darkness. The cold
tide welled inside me.

El Capitan. Take your medicine like a good boy.

Behind the anteroom, two rooms lay off a short, dead-end
hallway—if you could call it a hallway—that was about two
feet long. The coughing had come from one of those two
rooms. The west room was padlocked. The east room's door
was ajar. Hands clenched on the rifle's soothingly cool steel,
I waited for another cough. None came. I snapped the headlamp off.

With the rifle ready in my right hand, I pushed the east
room's door further open with my left. I snatched my hand
back. Silence. Crouching low, I slinked inside. My nose told
me this was storage. Cloth, maybe. Musty. The headlight's
dimmest beam cut a dusty darkness. Old linens, bags of un-
identified supplies, cockroaches sprinting from the light.

I stepped back into the hallway. If El Capitan was in the
west room, why was it padlocked from the outside? As a security measure, it sucked. No sound of movement on the other
side of the west room's door. No shuffling boots or cocking
guns. The cough rasped. El Capitan was definitely inside.

So much for subtlety. I'd have to hope the noise I made
went unnoticed in the general confusion outside. I struck the
padlock with the rifle stock a few times. No go. I lowered the
muzzle and squeezed off a shot. The padlock hung from its
busted haft. I quickly recharged the bolt-action. Still no noise
from inside.

I shoved open the door, then leaped into the pitch-dark,
windowless room.

The stench hit me hard—human feces and stale vomit, and
an underlying putridness worse than either.

"Whiskey." El Capitan's voice graveled in the distant darkness.

I'll get your whiskey, old man, and a little shot of something extra to go with it.

My hand reached for the vial of poison in my zippered inner shirt pocket while my headlamp cast a dim vee toward the voice. I froze.

The colonel lay naked on stained and bloody bedsheets, his body twisted at the waist as though he'd tried to reach for something on the battered bedside table and failed. Gaunt, his thin chest struggled to rise with each breath. On the bedside table, an overturned glass sat next to a nearly empty whiskey bottle.

"Amalia?" he rasped. He grunted, then added, "The cockroaches." He gasped for a breath. "Make them stop."

I raised my lamp's light level. The colonel's skin gleamed like wet, gray clay. Beside his head, a cascade of dried vomit caked his pillow. I looked around, wondering if his cockroach comment was literal or figurative. Probably literal. Judging from his state and the room's mess, he'd been desperately sick for several days, uncared for by anyone. Not even fed.

"Make them stop," he croaked.

Then I realized what was going on. The guard wasn't outside to keep anyone from getting in. He was there to keep the colonel from getting out.

El Capitan had been left here to die.

He was a sick old man, clearly too delirious to give orders or even know what the hell was going on. He hadn't ordered the attack on the village last night. He wasn't capable.

I couldn't kill this man. Not like this. I couldn't even hope he'd attack me so I could shoot him in self-defense.

I lowered the rifle's muzzle, defeated, hands and gut trembling with nerves. What was I supposed to do with the horri-

ble blackness in my heart? Where was I supposed to put the
rage? The hate?

Who would pay for Marcello?

The electric lights stuttered, then popped on. Outside, I
heard Porfilio talking to someone. The front door banged
open. Footsteps racketed off the wooden floor. The bedroom
door shoved back and Porfilio walked in.

"Jesus, Mary and Joseph," he said in a hushed tone as he
came to stand beside me.

The bare bulb overhead blazed. The bed, I realized abruptly, was much filthier than I'd thought, the smell worse.
The colonel shivered, sweating. I drew the stained sheet up
to his chest. The old man clutched it in clawlike hands,
opened his toothless mouth but said nothing, a fish gasping
for air.

"Do you know what's wrong with him?" I asked.

"Mercury poisoning," said Father João's voice from the
doorway.

I turned. The padre looked beat. His arm sling wore smears
he'd picked up hiking through the jungle. Bumping his broken arm must have hurt like hell. His good hand carried a
medical bag.

"What are you doing here?" I asked.

"I thought there would be wounded."

"Can we get the colonel to Boa Vista?"

"I thought you came to assassinate him." The padre moved
to the bed and laid a hand on the sick man's forehead.

"There's no need," I replied. "He's dying. Someone locked
him in here so he could do that alone." I jerked a thumb at the
busted padlock. "The colonel isn't the man we should be worried about."

"Indeed, he is not!"

I heard the words at the same moment my peripheral vision registered Goldtooth, pistol in hand. My rifle muzzle

came up. The *donos* fired a round that flew high and outside. I squeezed the trigger. Nothing. Jammed shell.

Porfilio leaped toward Goldtooth, grabbed his gun hand. The much heavier *donos* levered the pistol's muzzle toward Porfilio's face. I swung the rifle at the *donos*. The steel barrel caught him across the neck. He staggered. Porfilio ripped the pistol from Goldtooth's grip. The *donos* lunged for the revolver. My next swing hit the back of his knee. He dropped, grabbing at his leg.

Porfilio and I stood over him, both of us panting more with adrenaline rush than exertion.

I glanced at the doorway. "Did he bring any friends?"

"His friends are all gone," Porfilio said. "The *pistoleiros* were the colonel's men, not his. They are scared we will kill them."

"You don't have many buddies, do you?" I asked Goldtooth as I plucked the jammed shell from the rifle's chamber and loaded up my last one.

The *donos* levered himself to his feet. Porfilio's pistol clicked loudly as he cocked it.

I raised the rifle to Goldtooth's chest. "Stand against the wall."

Goldtooth's cheeks had gone gray with pain. A massive red welt was spreading just beneath his ear. It was a wonder I hadn't broken his neck.

"You're responsible for the colonel's condition, aren't you?" I demanded in Portuguese.

"When his superiors are angry with him, he blames me." His voice rose, tight with indignation. "The mine makes money because *I* make it so. He's an old man and foolish. *I* do what needs to be done. *I* keep his superiors happy."

"By bullying the *garimpeiros*."

"They would not eat if not for me!" He winced as his shout strained his neck muscles. "I feed them. I give them clothes," he said more calmly. "They hate me. Do not think I do not know."

Give the man a medal. "And the Yanomamo?"

A sneer cracked his fleshy face. "They are animals."

I thought of the village, constantly alive, constantly in motion with its twenty families. The men joking after a successful hunt. Women chatting and arguing. The children. Always the children, running in and out of the *shapono,* getting into everything. Laughing.

Marcello dancing along in front of me, his climbing harness tied around his little body. Batting his eyes. Grinning.

I lifted the rifle's muzzle to Goldtooth's face. Sweat oozed from his temples. No, I wouldn't shoot him. That'd be too quick. Too easy. I'd shot two dead men over and over but it hadn't helped, hadn't resurrected Marcello. Anger curled around my heart, sweeping me under, pouring down my throat. No. I had a better idea. I handed the rifle to Porfilio, who automatically took it.

I unsheathed the machete from its holster on my back. The *donos's* eyes widened. Fear. That's what I wanted to see. Fear and blood, like Marcello's blood, running all over—

I stopped. My God. What the hell was I doing? The machete felt suddenly heavy, hateful, in my hand. God help me. I wasn't an executioner. I slowly backed away.

"You deal with him," I told Porfilio.

He silently gave me back the rifle, not taking his eyes off Goldtooth. I holstered the machete and tried to breathe. Porfilio motioned for the *donos* to put his hands behind his head.

The padre stepped forward, silently contemplated Goldtooth for a moment before threading his fingers through the man's greasy hair and forcing his head up to look in his eyes.

"You will scream in hell for what you have done," Father João said in soft, slow Portuguese.

The *donos's* shoulders hitched once, then several times in succession. The bastard dared to laugh? His lips drew back in a teeth-baring smile. "No one cares about the Indians. The government does not care. The *garimpeiros* do not care. Not even your God cares," he said. "I don't believe in your hell, old man."

The cold rage I thought had drained away like water suddenly boiled, hot and fierce, in my chest. "But I assume you believe in the Roger prison in Paraíba." I glanced back at the bed, where the colonel moaned pitifully, like a dying animal. "You're guilty of trying to murder a respected Brazilian army officer."

The arrogance faded from Goldtooth's eyes as that sank through his thick skull.

I persisted. "You gave him the mercury, didn't you, trying to make it look like he'd inhaled the fumes or got hold of mercury-tainted water. But he'd have to drink a helluva lot of water to get that sick that fast." I glanced at the padre. "Make sure that empty glass goes to the authorities. I bet there are trace amounts of mercury in it."

The *donos's* eyes creased as he tried to smile, but his mouth failed him.

"I don't think they'll let you keep that pretty gold tooth for long in prison," I added as boots clunked on the anteroom's wooden floor.

Carlos led a pair of dirty-faced *garimpeiros* into the bedroom. Porfilio stepped back as the miners trussed the *donos* with lengths of rope.

"Do not disobey me!" the *donos* ordered the miners, who acted as if they'd either stopped understanding Portuguese or lost their hearing. "They are traitors! The colonel will be angry!"

Porfilio tore a strip off the colonel's nasty sheet and stuffed it in the *donos's* mouth. "Shut up."

The *garimpeiros* towed the gagging Goldtooth outside. I noticed they weren't being too gentle.

"Where are they taking him?" I asked.

"I'm flying him to Boa Vista at dawn," Carlos said.

"With the colonel?"

Carlos looked at Porfilio, who looked at Father João. Father João shook his head. "I don't see how he can survive," he said simply. "He's too far gone."

"We should try, even though he is not a good man," Porfilio insisted.

What no one was saying, or would say, was that Porfilio, in trying to save the colonel's life, would insure his place as head of the mine. We all knew the colonel would die before they reached Boa Vista, but Porfilio needed to look like a hero, someone the army could trust to run its operation.

"Leave him to me," Father João said. "I will clean him up for the journey."

"Have you got the camp under control?" I asked Porfilio.

He nodded, eyes bright but calm. "The *garimpeiros* are glad. Now we can do what we know is right."

And still make a profit, I added silently. At least with Porfilio in charge, the mine stood a chance of giving the desperate miners a living while leaving the Yanomamo in peace.

Carlos and Porfilio left me and the padre alone with the dying man. Father João didn't have anything else to say to me, but I did to him.

I tugged the vial of shaman's poison out of my zippered pocket, then dug around until I found the vial of morphine I'd once thought about giving Rick. I looked at them both for a moment, then handed one to Father João.

"Morphine," I said, "in case the pain gets too bad."

Father João's eyes widened as he stared at the vial I offered.

"I know you don't believe in suicide or mercy killing. I'm not suggesting that." I glanced at the colonel's skin stretched over his bony face. "He's an old man. The plane ride's going to be hell. This might make it easier."

The padre took the vial from me and tucked it into his shirt pocket. "Thank you."

That was probably the best I was going to get from him.

He didn't like me or "my kind," thought I was a cold-blooded murderer at heart, and clearly wanted me to go.

So I went.

Besides, it was time I gathered up my gear and hit the road. I left the colonel's quarters and headed for the airstrip. I was double-checking my duffel when I heard something shuffling through the underbrush toward me. I froze, then heard Carlos's voice.

"Jessie!" he hissed.

"Here." I watched him slink close and then asked, "Why are you sneaking around?"

"The other plane belongs to an Americano."

"Lawrence Daley?" I asked, my heart thudding with anticipation. I'd love to pound that guy into the ground.

"No, a customs officer. He's looking for you."

Shit.

Daley had probably alerted customs to my existence and my purpose, damn him. The last thing I needed was to try to smuggle not just my plants but me back into the States. My brain started firing in several directions trying to figure a way out. Would Carlos fly me into Paraguay or Venezuela so I could leave from there?

"What did you tell him?" I asked.

"He knew I brought you here. I told him I hadn't seen you since dropping you."

"Did you say anything about Kinkaid or the research station? The village?"

Carlos shook his head. "But you cannot come with me to Boa Vista now. He is watching the plane. He intends to search it before I leave."

"He can't do that," I argued.

"Not legally, no," he agreed, then shrugged philosophically. "But you know how it is. You play the game when the other player has…influence."

I stared at his handsome face. "He's got something on you, doesn't he?"

He shrugged again. "Listen, I will come back for you tomorrow. Go hide in the jungle and I will be back at dawn."

Scooter, I thought. *Five days.*

"We've got to be smarter than this guy," I insisted. "I've got to get back home."

"Then I will take you to São Paolo tomorrow instead of Boa Vista. That alone will save you a day. I owe you." He slid his hand over mine where it rested on the duffel between us. "I should not have left you. It's why I came back. After a while, I started thinking they might kill you." His smile in the faint light that reached us held chagrin and even a little surprise, as if he'd never expected to find himself doing something honorable. "I will make it all up to you."

Had I not been well aware of just how studly this guy was, I would have thought his admission almost gentlemanly. But as his thumb subtly caressed my wrist, I recognized the old game being played out once again. Like he'd said, you play the game when the other player has influence.

But you didn't have to play the game, I suddenly realized. Rick had refused to play it with me for reasons I didn't understand, and now I didn't have to play it with Carlos. Not again. Not to wake up once more to an aching loneliness and the realization that I'd given myself to a dream that didn't exist. I'd thought the sex would make the emotion happen. I'd been doing it bass ackwards all my life.

No wonder Rick didn't want to have anything to do with me.

Back at the village as I was leaving, Rick had looked me in the eye and said, "Do what you need to do, Jess." I'd thought he was talking about killing the colonel. Now I knew he wasn't. He'd meant I should go back to the States to save Scooter, or stay with Carlos if that's what I wanted. Or keep on doing what I've always done. Be the kind of person I am.

Problem was, I wasn't sure who that was anymore.

"I'll be here tomorrow morning at dawn," I said to Carlos.

He lightly kissed me on the lips, and when he tried to make it into something more, I leaned away. He sighed, then drifted into the underbrush. A few minutes later, I saw him stride from the colonel's office building toward the airstrip, where the tall Americano intercepted him. I put the field glasses on them. The crew cut American was definitely not the Brain from San Antonio. And I knew now it was unlikely he was the man called Noah. Noah, the Brain had implied, was a botanist like yours truly.

Carlos and the customs agent spoke briefly, then turned and walked toward Carlos's plane. And me.

I picked up my gear and backed deeper into the trees. Waiting in the jungle all day was going to be a pain. The agent, a burly, middle-aged guy with a stern face, waved at someone in the mining camp and three *pistoleiros,* apparently picking up fresh work for the American government, fanned out along the airstrip's edge.

Looking for me, no doubt.

A slight hiss caught my attention. I turned to see a Yanomamo warrior step out from behind a tree. A single hand motion invited me back with him.

And as I didn't really have a choice, I followed the silent warriors back to their home, to a place I didn't belong.

Chapter 13

I showed up at the village in the light of false dawn, dragging myself one more time along the trail behind my silent and swift Yanomamo escorts. One day, I thought as I stopped at the little hut, I was going to stop retracing my steps and actually get somewhere. My shoulders ached from carrying my duffel, my feet and ankles ached from hiking over uneven terrain for what felt like nonstop for eight days. The rage had finally drained out of me, leaving nothing but a heart aching from new hurts that had dragged up old hurts. Even the little detour for a bath hadn't soothed my nerves. I felt like I'd been on the verge of weeping for decades.

Inside the hut, Rick wasn't sleeping like I expected. He was meditating, I guess, sitting on a kapok-fiber-stuffed pallet, wearing only his pants, his bare back to the door and his legs pulled up in lotus position. My duffel's contents rattled despite my best attempt to set the bag down quietly. Rick turned his head. He wasn't wearing his glasses. Then he swiveled and rose somehow at the same time, his brow furrowed as he took the two steps to where I stood.

"Are you okay?"

His warm grip on my fingers felt too good. I couldn't say anything for a minute because I was trying not to burst into tears again. I just shook my head.

He tugged me into his arms. I latched on to him and held on for dear life. That's what it felt like, trying to save myself from drowning in all the pain left when the rage eased out of me. I could have stood there with his arms around me all day, but after I got hold of myself and thought I could talk without crying like a baby, I pulled away.

"Change of plans," I muttered.

He took that in, then asked, "What happened?"

I dropped into my hammock and pulled off my boots while he settled again on his pallet. I lay down, too tired to undress, and gave him the details, right down to the customs officer and Carlos's offer of a ride into São Paolo the following morning.

"So you didn't have to kill the colonel," he said.

"I don't know if I could have even if he'd been well." I studied my hands, innocent of shedding blood. "I've only killed one man in my life and that was in self-defense." I shook my head. "But the *donos*." I remembered the lines of terror around the man's eyes as I unsheathed the machete. "I nearly killed him. I wanted someone to pay. I've never been so angry in my life."

"But not just pay for Marcello."

"What do you mean?"

"Pay for Scooter, too."

I was too tired to be annoyed at his digging around. Besides, it kind of sounded right. "Yeah, I guess."

"Does Scooter know you're down here, trying to save him?"

"I didn't have time to talk to him. I left a message with a close friend of his, told him I was trying to find a cure, but I didn't talk to Scooter."

"Jessie," he said, then hesitated.

"Look, I know it was lame to come down here without—"

"What if Scooter doesn't want you to save him?"

"That's ridiculous."

"How old is he? In his sixties, seventies?"

My mouth clamped shut.

"What if he's ready to move on?" he persisted, more gently.

"You mean, what if I've come down here for no reason."

"Jessie, listen to what I'm saying instead of what you think I'm saying. Did you ask Scooter what *he* wanted?"

Tears abruptly spilled from my eyes. And in that moment Rick made me angriest of all, because I knew, damn him, that he was right. I hadn't bothered to ask Scooter what he wanted because I believed I knew what was best for him. I covered my face with my hands and tried to breathe.

"You don't have to save everyone you care about," he said gently. "Or get retribution. Sometimes terrible things just happen and there's no one to pay for it."

I could only let the waves of grief crash over me. Maybe Scooter didn't mind dying. Maybe he'd gotten into the Parkinson's drug trial despite the risks because he figured he had nothing to lose. Maybe that was why he never complained about what had happened, but just kept cooking up four-alarm chili and caring for his beloved orchids.

But if he weren't around, I'd be standing there in the middle of a dry cornfield, the noon sun beating down on my head and dust rising around my feet, no place to go. No Scooter. No home.

"I can't let him die." I mopped my face with my shirtsleeve. "I've got a possible cure in my hands. I can't stop now."

He seemed to accept that. "If Carlos takes you straight to São Paolo, does that give you time to get back to Scooter?"

"It's cutting it close. I'll call von Brutten from town and let him know I'm coming straight to San Antonio. He can fire up the lab and be ready for me." I sighed. "With the mine out of the way, that's one less thing for me to think about."

"You've done a good job," Rick said.

I met his eyes and looked at him, really looked at him, for the first time.

He wasn't gorgeous, but he was definitely attractive. He was the kind of guy you don't really look at twice until suddenly something shifts, either in you or in him, and for an instant, he becomes the sexiest man on the planet. Rick's inner bad boy lurked underneath his dark, expressive eyes. I could go on ad nauseam about his shoulders and pecs and how strong he was and all that, but the point is the best time I'd ever had in my life with a guy was waking up with Rick's arm around me.

"Are you tired?" he asked.

"Yeah. Finding the colonel like that—" I paused, seeing again the old man's frail body twisted on his filthy bedsheets. "The poison would have been mercy. Better than the *donos* leaving him to die."

"I know." He stared at me a moment, then stood and walked over. "Come on, you need some sleep." He stretched out with me in the hammock, tucking me into his arms.

And though he didn't say it or make any promises, I knew he'd still be there when I woke up.

A light mist hissed on the hut's thatched roof. I listened to the water splatting on broad leaves just outside, smelled the clean wetness, and thought, *I'm okay.* Sometime in the early morning while I slept, the clenched fist of anger and pain and grief had released its grip on my heart. The rain was steady, peaceful. In the distance, Yanomamo voices rose in muted laughter.

I opened my eyes. Rick's chest warmed my back, his legs lay comfortably against mine. I extended one leg to stretch and suddenly doubled up, pain knifing through my foot.

"What's wrong?" he asked, instantly alert.

"Muscle cramp."

He reached down and pulled my toes toward my shin. The hot knife in my instep stopped jabbing, but the ache reverberated through my foot and toes. He swung out of the hammock. "Come here and lie down." He gestured to his pallet.

"Why?" I scooted over and sat down, like he asked.

He knelt.

"Foot massage." His strong fingers pressed into the bottom of my right foot. "You've earned it."

I gave a fleeting thanks that I'd bathed before he pulled this stunt. My boots plus my feet plus an all-night tromp through the jungle equaled nuclear-powered noxious.

Then I forgot trivialities like baths when his thumb dug gently in just at my big toe's joint. Pure bliss. His hand cupped my heel. His fingers pressed between my toes, rubbing each in turn, taking his time.

I opened my eyes. He wasn't looking at what he was doing. He was looking at me. His slow smile quirked his lips like I liked and shot my blood straight to my sweet spot.

He switched feet. "How many miles do you think you've hiked since you got here?"

"On this trip so far?"

He nodded.

"About forty-eight."

"That's a long way." His fingers traced circles on the top of my instep and a gentle warmth started easing through my body. "I admire you for that."

"You hiked nearly all of them with me," I said.

His fingers stilled, then squeezed my foot. "Let me appreciate you, Jessie. You don't have to hold me at arm's length."

I would have agreed to just about anything at that point, but it felt awkward, his praising me.

"I know you don't like hearing it," he went on, and so did

his fingertips, reducing me to something slightly less jiggly than Jell-O. "And I know receptivity isn't something you're good at—" here he gave me his bad boy smile "—but try just listening to me for a while. No protests. No sarcasm or smart-alecky remarks. Don't push me away. Okay?"

I was about to tell him he had his head up his ass, but he raised my foot and pressed his lips to the sensitive, ticklish stretch of my instep. My temp shot up about ten degrees. Centigrade.

He gently set my foot on the pallet, then slid his hands up the sides of my legs, over my hips, to my waist. "May I?" he asked, his clever fingers poised to unbuckle my belt.

I propped myself on my elbows to watch. "I thought there were too many people here."

"Right now it's just us, isn't it?"

And for the moment, in this place, with a new day passing outside, it was.

I nodded.

He made quick work of the belt and slid my canvas pants down my thighs. When they were off, he folded them neatly and set them aside. What was this guy? A neatnik? He scooted around to kneel at my side and unbutton my shirt, brushing my fingers away when I tried to help.

"Let me. I want to do this for you. Sit up."

His warm eyes darkened as he slipped the shirt from my shoulders. He paused, letting the shirt hang from my elbows, to gaze at my neck, then my shoulders, in my muscle tee. After a moment, he swept the shirt from my arms, folded it, and stacked it on the pants without taking his eyes off me for more than a second. He rubbed the muscle tee's fabric between his thumb and forefinger before tugging it over my head.

Down to my sports bra and panties, I wasn't sure what he would do next.

He slid his forefinger between the bra strap and my shoulder. He looked me in the eye again, then cupped both hands around my arm and stroked it from shoulder to wrist, taking his time. Then again. And again. Then the other arm.

"Is this—?" I tried to ask, but he stilled my lips with his fingers.

"I'm looking. Don't interrupt."

"But you have the advantage." I glanced meaningfully at his pants where his gloriously cut abs disappeared into the waistband.

"Take this off," he said, tugging at my bra strap. "Turn around first."

I did as I was told, wondering why he could make me do that when no one else ever had. I pivoted to face my pillow, reached cross-armed, and swept the bra off as elegantly as a heavy-duty piece of underwear could be swept. I heard cloth rustling against his long legs. Then the inevitable folding. He folded my bra, too.

I wondered what his place looked like. Did he have an apartment or a house? A condo, maybe? What kind of furniture would he have in it? Was he a leather-and-glass kind of guy? Probably all hardwood from sustainable farming efforts if I had to put money on it. But light, like teak, or dark, like cherry? Mahogany, maybe?

"Lie down."

I stretched out on my stomach, now wearing only my sturdy and resolutely unsexy panties. I was still pondering whether he'd have solid or plaid cushions on his sofa when his thumbs found the small of my back, either side of my spine, and pressed.

Raw and entirely sexual energy exploded deep inside me. The little circles his thumbs made sent warmth flowing like a river of light up my back. I couldn't move, pinned to the soft pallet partly by the weight of his hands, partly by the intense sensations spiraling up my spine.

Why had I never tried massage before?

I lost time and space. All I can say is that his hands worked over every inch of my back, my shoulders, my neck, my arms. Wherever he touched, my body heated up until I was humming like a high-tension power line. His bare knee settled between my thighs as he moved closer, occasionally pressing up against me when he reached for my shoulders and neck. When his fingers started a deeper massage, really kneading, I thought I'd pass out from the pleasure.

"I was wrong," he murmured after a while, fanning his hands, sliding them down my back in long strokes. "You're *very* receptive." His fingers slid beneath the elastic on my panties, set my heart to pounding, then retreated. "Turn over."

Had he taken off his briefs as well as his pants? Had he left them on? I didn't know which I wanted, but I was about to find out. Anticipation surged in my core.

I rolled in place. When I saw the heat in his eyes, I quit thinking about his briefs. Drowning in his gaze. That was the way to go.

He put his right hand on my stomach just above my panties, barely touching me. Keeping eye contact with me, he slid his hand slowly up the center of my body to stop between my breasts. Moments passed while he knelt there, touching me, not moving.

"What are you doing?" I finally asked over my skin's nearly audible hum.

He smiled. "Synchronizing our breathing. You have so much energy."

Then his left hand made the sensuous journey from my panties and he started massaging the top of my chest, leaning over me, his left knee firmly pressing between my thighs, his body heat radiating onto my rib cage. I wished he'd stop playing around and get down to some serious action—my breasts were, after all, right there—but he seemed happy to just stroke and tease and keep me in a high state of hum. If you'd poured water on me I swear it would have sizzled.

"No, look at me," he whispered when my eyes closed.

I did. His brown eyes, so deeply dark, so warm, welcomed me in. Our faces were close enough his breath warmed my cheek. He smelled faintly of sandalwood. His fingers slid up my neck to gently massage the spot under my left ear.

Kiss me, I mentally begged. When I lifted my head slightly to steal a kiss, he caught my face in his hand and smiled.

"Not yet," he whispered.

He lowered my head to the pallet, all the while pressing his knee between my thighs. Evil, evil man.

Then he stilled, looking at my neck. His finger stroked his pendant.

"I forgot to give that back to you," I said. "Here—"

"Keep it." His lips tucked into a smile. "It looks good on your skin. Very pretty. I'm going to make love to you," he went on, keeping up the pressure as he leaned back and trailed his fingertips down my neck, across the top of my chest, and lightly skirted my breasts. "I bet no one's ever done that before."

"I've had some great—"

"I'm not talking about sex. Anyone can have sex." His fingers made lazy circles around my breasts. "You deserve better than that. And I want more than that."

I wasn't in any position to argue, so I didn't. I was too busy trying to keep from panting. My skin tingled all over, on the verge of bursting like overripe fruit.

"The men you've had, they haven't really appreciated you, have they?" He lowered his head and blew on my nipple. "Not really." Before I knew what he was doing, his tongue dipped out and licked where he'd just blown.

I groaned. "Nothing like this." And that was God's honest truth.

"A little more massage then," he said, his eyebrow cocked

and Mr. Bedroom Fantasy present and accounted for. When I opened my mouth, he said, "Don't complain or I'll make you wait even longer."

I clamped my mouth shut.

His hot hands slipped down my waist and burrowed between my panties and my skin. I lifted my hips obligingly. He eased the panties down over my thighs and calves, over my feet. I looked. He folded them. I sighed.

He stood then and looked down at me. He wasn't a huge man, but standing over me while I lay naked on the floor, he looked fantastic. Every lean, sculpted muscle slid beneath his tanned skin as he moved. His smooth chest went to a cut waist and abs, which below his navel went to a single dark arrow of hair aiming at what I wanted. His thighs and calves, which I hadn't noticed much before, weren't the gargantuan tree trunks of a bodybuilder but as long and lean as the rest of him, covered with fine hair. His body wasn't built for brute strength over short distances, but for endurance and versatility.

I took that as a good sign.

He slid his thumbs under the waistband of his black briefs and paused. I realized suddenly he was taunting me, teasing me visually as much as he had sensually. My gaze roamed all over him as I hadn't allowed it to the two other times we'd been naked together, drinking him in. That satisfying bulge wasn't all I wanted, I realized. I wanted to run my hands over every inch of his body the way he had touched mine, to give back what he had given me.

I studied his face and the overnight scruff darkening his cheeks and chin. I locked gazes with him and instantly felt the heat surge inside me. He lifted the waistband up and over his erection, slid the briefs down, and stepped out.

Fold all you want, I thought. *Take your time.*

He did. He let me look. And look. He moved the folded clothes from their place on the floor to the duffel bag. He straightened and peered outside for a long moment before making sure the door—a lightweight blanket he'd brought in his gear—was hung properly across the doorway. He walked from the door to the pallet's foot, then came to kneel next to my left hip.

I ached with imagining him inside me. What would it take to get this man where I wanted him? He stroked my centerline from chest to my stomach twice, then on the third time, passed my tummy and kept going. His right hand cupped me gently, put a little pressure on, paused, made a little circle, and so on until I thought I'd die.

"I want to touch you," I said.

"You have gorgeous breasts," he replied. His fingers kept moving, slowly massaging things I didn't know you could. "I haven't stopped thinking about them since I first saw them."

"I thought you couldn't see without your glasses."

"I can see large objects well enough," he murmured, sending a shudder down my thighs. "You should walk around in a wet T-shirt more often."

"You didn't seem very interested at the time."

"You wouldn't believe what I wanted to do with you behind that waterfall."

"Why didn't you?"

His fingers paused as he said, "I wanted to do this instead. Back then, it would have been just…physical."

"But you were ready."

"That doesn't mean I have to act."

I gathered enough breath to say, "I'm glad you waited."

"It wasn't easy." His attention drifted to my breasts again. He looked hungry.

"Aren't you going to touch them?"

He nodded. His fingers caressed. "Eventually." His left hand stroked down to my navel and rested on my tummy. "There's something special I want to do for you first," he whispered.

Two fingers slipped inside me. It was like plugging me into an electrical socket—the hum, the tingling, exploded into full-fledged heat emanating from someplace deeper than the sensitive nub he hadn't even touched yet. I could feel him exploring, testing, searching. His left hand, settled firmly on my tummy, made leisurely circles, somehow building up the heat from deep inside. My back arched. Then his left hand slipped lower. His outside fingers, teasing, found my sweet spot at the same time his inside fingers made a "come here" gesture.

And I did. Deep waves washed over my entire body, drowning me in sensation. My skin glowed with heat. I'd never believed in the G-spot until that moment, when he must have hit it and hit it good. The waves rode higher and higher with no end in sight. I clutched his hard forearm. His muscles rippled as he rubbed me. I forced my eyes open.

Rick's intense gaze rested on my face, and I had the crazy thought he was getting almost as much pleasure out of my orgasm as I was. He was doing something beyond touching me—it was like he was feeding that tingling heat into me, cycling it through his fingers into my body and back to himself. I was at his mercy, I realized, and he wasn't having any on me.

I raised up on my elbows, still overcome. A single drop glistened on his tip where he rested, hot and pulsing, against my thigh. I wanted that, but I didn't want this to end, either. My head fell back. The hut's thatched roof swam and blurred. Would it never stop? I felt I could keep going forever, flame waxing and waning through my body.

Then his fingers began to slow. It took a while, but I started to slow, too. When he finally slid his fingers out of me, I felt light, clean. Ordinarily I'm like a man—I want to roll over and go to sleep afterward—but this time my mind was clear. Even the physical fatigue of the long night and long hike had fallen away.

Nice massage.

Rick stretched out next to me on his side and pulled me close. Nice man. I struggled to catch my breath.

"Feel better?" he asked, his lips brushing my ear.

"Much," I managed. "What was that?"

"Healing massage."

"It felt like orgasm to me."

"That was a bonus."

I turned my head to look him in the eye, intending to be pert. The moment I met those deep browns, I felt the heat surge in me again. Had he so much as thought about touching my sweet spot, I would have come again.

"It felt…different," I said, unsure how to talk about what had just happened, how it made me feel.

"We connected." He ran a hand down my centerline. "Our energies are in sync."

"Does that mean I get a kiss now?" I asked.

He leaned in and took my breath away. How could he fire me up so easily? And that was my last coherent thought for a couple of minutes while he kissed me thoroughly amid sandalwood and his own musky scent. His hand found its way to the back of my head, threaded through my hair. I wanted more, but he didn't seem to want to give it to me. Instead, he wrapped his arms around me, letting his hardness rub tantalizingly against my hip. His lips teased mine until his mouth broke away and he nibbled his way to my neck.

"Please," I gasped. Desire spiraled down through my chest and stomach. "Don't." I dug my fingers in his hair to drag his mouth back to mine. He obliged, then his teeth nipped my neck just beneath my ear. "Stop," I whispered.

He pulled away slightly to study me. "Was that three sentences or one?"

"Just one."

"All or nothing, Jessie. Which are you going to give me?"

I met his gaze. He was asking for more courage than I had,

but I wasn't sure I had the courage to walk away, either. I guessed it came down to the fact that being afraid wasn't a good enough reason not to do something.

"All," I said. And as his eyes warmed and he leaned down to kiss me again, I opened my heart and gave him everything I had.

"How do you do this?" I reached down the tangle of our bodies and stroked him where we met. The charge of energy I'd spent the midafternoon riding had ebbed faintly but wasn't gone, not by a long shot. And Rick still hadn't finished. He rested, nice and thick, inside me.

He quirked his eyebrows at me, as if I'd asked him to share a secret. "Orgasm and ejaculation aren't the same."

"What?"

"They're not the same."

"You didn't come."

His smile faded into heat as he gazed at me. "I didn't ejaculate. There's a difference. A man can score a goal without having to leave the playing field."

"How eloquent. What are you talking about?"

He leaned down to whisper in my ear. "Tantra."

"This is one of your yoga things, isn't it?"

"Mm-hmm." He nuzzled my neck, sending a charge spiking into my breasts. "The important part is the connection we make. The intimacy."

Intimacy I could understand. What had happened with Carlos, that was screwing. What was happening with Rick—there wasn't a comparison. Words didn't do it justice. Screwing, I realized, had just fallen off my list of fun things to do.

"We're still connected," I reminded him. I stroked him again and smiled to feel him shiver. I knew what he meant. The body connection drove me crazy, but the other connection, whatever it was—heart, soul, spirit—made us one. The deeper we could get into each other, the better. "Are you going to come for me?" I asked.

"I have, every time you did after the first one."

"Swear," I challenged.

"I swear," he breathed into my ear.

I sighed. Of all the men I knew, the only one actually capable of keeping it up all night *would* turn out to be a bug nerd.

But that wasn't fair. He was much more than just a bug nerd. Rick, good idealist that he was, believed in something richer and deeper than I thought existed, whether that was this forest, or the dignity of humankind, or even how to treat a woman in bed. Maybe the shaman's medicine worked on him because he believed in the connection between all things. Maybe he connected with me because he believed he could, and I responded because his belief was big enough to carry me.

Now I just didn't know what to do. Ask him to come back to the States with me? Hell, I didn't even know what university he worked for. Did he teach or was he a researcher? He probably had co-eds hanging all over him every semester.

My first hint of jealousy twinged, followed by a quick prick of fear. Was he married? In a relationship?

His lips contentedly pressed my shoulder. No, he was single. He was too good a guy to two-time a wife or girlfriend.

"I want you to help me catch another moth before you go," he said.

I dragged my thoughts out of the interesting places on a college campus a Tantra-practicing entomologist and an orchid hunter might recreate. "I left a trap up in the canopy. I'll check it this afternoon."

"If there's a moth, my work will be done." He traced a circle around my breast, then gripped me gently. "I want to go back with you."

"You mean go back in general or go back in particular?"

"Go back in general. We can talk about particular after I've dropped off my moth and you've seen your uncle." He squeezed, making me squirm a little. "There's no rush."

My heart thudded hard. A protestation of eternal affection would have been scary and a goodbye speech hurt like hell, but his "let's see" felt just right. And because his grip felt so good, I simply nodded agreement.

I didn't know what I wanted for the rest of my life. All I knew was that I wanted Rick around longer than for just one roll in the hay.

He must have heard that thought because he started moving, sliding easily, creating a gentle friction in the way that made my skin tingle, and after a very short time, I stopped having thoughts altogether.

A Corpse Moth rested in the trap.

I studied its black wings and body in the afternoon light. "Beautiful thing," I whispered to it. It was doing me a favor, getting Rick to come back with me. Seemed a shame to have it end up mounted on a bug board.

I took the trap down and hung it off my climbing harness. Pausing for a last look around, I spotted a tiny pink *Cattleya delictabus* near the trap, clinging to the bark. Scooter didn't have one of those. A couple of quick swipes with the machete and I had the little orchid in my hands. I tucked it into Rick's backpack.

After that came the tricky business of taking down the slings without accidentally dropping myself a hundred feet. I fed the belaying rope over the *Pterocarpus's* bare branch.

"Here it comes," I said into the headset.

"I'm ready."

The rope fell. Rick took up the slack. "Got me?" I asked.

The rope tugged comfortingly on my harness, then his low, sexy voice answered, "You're safe with me, babe."

Ignoring the burn that comment started, I detached myself

from the slings and dangled, held only by Rick's grip on the rope. The slings slid off the branch and hooked onto my harness.

I double-checked to make sure I hadn't left anything, then asked Rick to drop me. He eased me down, controlled but not too slow.

The very first time I climbed, my belayer—someone I thought I could trust—chatted with friends while I was on the cliff. I struggled up a particularly rough stretch, panting, tired, a little scared, and glanced down to see a pool of rope lying on the ledge beneath me. My belayer had been too busy talking to keep the slack taken up. Had I fallen, I would have fallen only about ten feet, but I've not liked being belayed since. Sort of like life in general for me, I guess. I can trust myself, but not anyone else.

Not until now.

My boots touched down and I started unhooking myself from the harness. Rick stored his trap while I rearranged the *Cattleya* in my duffel. In minutes I had the rest of my climbing gear collected. For the first time in my career, I'd leave my gear behind. Father João would be able to string himself a new hammock, I supposed. Nice high-tech bed for him.

"I'm sorry," Rick said out of nowhere.

"About what?"

"I didn't show you what I wanted to do with you behind the waterfall."

My body hummed briskly. "You'll have to show me next time we're here."

He grinned and in the late afternoon light his glasses glinted mischievously. "Do we have time now?"

I was sorely tempted, but I didn't like the idea of yet another sprint through the dark. Especially not with the customs agent wandering around with trigger-happy *pistoleiros* in tow. "Next time. Promise me."

Sandalwood and musk enveloped me for a moment while

his clever lips and tongue promised, at length and in detail. If there was a loophole in that contract, I didn't find it.

"Ready?" Rick asked, readjusting his glasses.

I fleetingly hoped he'd never succumb to the temptation of contacts. "After I drop this stuff off at Father João's, you want to try navigating?" When he hesitated, I added, "It's good practice. If we run into the customs agent, we'll probably have to split up. I need to know you can get to the mine without me."

"But not leave without you."

"Preferably not."

He nodded. "Should we divide up your orchids? In case the customs agent shows up and one of us doesn't make it to São Paolo. I can take the Death Orchid to your lab for you."

I considered. It made sense, but Scooter was my responsibility. And I didn't know how many plants the biotech lab would need to develop its wonder drug, even if it could. If the Death Orchid was that toxic, the lab might need every plant I had in my possession to figure out how to turn its deadly alkaloids into the elixir of life.

"Better keep them together," I said.

And when we came across the customs agent a mile away from the mining camp, I was glad we did.

Chapter 14

I ran. Thorns and spiky branches tore at my long sleeves and pants. I ignored them. Dodging rocks and fallen logs, I tried to put more distance between myself and the big American pounding through the jungle behind me. He was fast, much faster than Daley could hope to be. And smarter.

Two hours of cat and mouse in the jungle wasn't my idea of entertainment. So far the agent had avoided a fire liana trap, a drop into a bog, and a low-hanging beehive. The man looked like he could break little ol' me in half with one hand. And he seemed to know which biologically hazardous trees and bushes to avoid. This guy wasn't a pencil pusher or a Tarzan wannabe. He was the real McCoy.

And I was getting tired.

It's not a good time to wear out, I told myself as I scrambled up a muddy embankment, heaving for breath. *Only eight more hours of this to go before dawn.*

The agent didn't bother me as much as the missing *pisto-*

leiros. I hadn't spotted any when this little jaunt got kicked off, which suggested they were either scattered over the jungle looking for me or maybe lurking around the airfield waiting for me to try to leave.

Why hadn't I thought to meet Carlos at the research station's airfield instead? I would have smacked my forehead if I'd had the energy.

With any luck, Rick had found his way to the mining camp. Down to my last day, I couldn't afford to go looking for him if he got lost. If I could still walk after losing the customs agent.

A little more time sleeping this afternoon and a little less time on the verge of total ecstasy might have been prudent, I reflected, splashing across a stream.

Ain't no Ladybug of mine goin' give up now, Scooter's voice whispered in my ear.

No, sir. No givin' up.

Pushing hard, I kept the hell-for-leather pace for another thirty minutes, circling wide back toward the mining camp. My best bet was to find a place where I could wait out the long hours until dawn. Porfilio's little cave, sheltered from casual sight by a manioc tree and practically nonexistent in the dark, fit the bill.

Staggering, I threw my duffel into the cleft and climbed in after it. Sweat poured down my face and back. I fought to control the gasps as my breath hitched. The agent might not be able to see me, but he could probably hear me wheezing for miles. I pulled my camo shirt collar up to cover my face and hunkered down to wait.

The jungle at night is the scariest place on God's green earth, even if you know what's making all those sounds. Clicks, hisses, howls, hoots, screeches. Hour after hour, day after day, of trying to pick out human noises—rifle safety click, snapped twig, low voice—from the jungle noise drove sane men crazy in Vietnam.

That's what I was up against now, straining to hear a footstep, a cough, anything that would tell me the agent had come close.

Chuff. Chuff, chuff. I froze, forgetting for a moment my jackhammering heart and aching lungs. The growling chuff moved further north, a little ways up the hillside, then circled back, crossing in front of the cave's mouth. Silence. Then scraping, like metal tearing wood. Then the chuffing again, a rhythmic pant with a hint of growl behind it.

Jaguar.

I'm not a fan of mixed blessings. I usually end up on the less desirable side of them. In fact, I couldn't think of a single mixed blessing that had actually turned out more good than bad for me. My track record strongly suggested I think of a plan. Fast.

If the cat was out there, the agent wouldn't be. But if the cat decided I resembled kibble, I literally had nowhere to hide.

Too bad I'd left the old bolt-action and the assault rifle with Porfilio last night.

I shrank a little deeper into the cave and tried not to smell delicious. The chuffing wandered back and forth across the cave entrance, each trip bringing it closer. My mental inventory of the gear I had with me confirmed I had nothing to use as a weapon. And I doubted I could climb a tree faster than a jaguar, especially in the dark.

What I really needed was one of those Hollywood moments: lone Yanomamo warrior emerges from the forest to shoot the cat with a curare-tipped arrow. The best I could hope for was the jaguar would get bored and go away. Heck, maybe it'd already had dinner. Maybe it was just curious about my scent.

Just in case, I dragged the duffel out from the deepest part of the cave and wedged it between me and the cave entrance. Pitiful barricade. I'd have to do better than that.

The chuffing paused. Utter silence. A snort.

I strained to see in the dark. But I didn't need to see. I suddenly smelled the dark, pungent scent of a wild animal. My blood iced in my veins. Over the duffel's top, the jaguar's silhouette filled the entrance. Dimly outlined by faint starlight, the cat's magnificent head turned. My hand clutched the duffel's strap.

The cat dabbed a paw at the duffel. I held on, feeling the paw's weight in the tugging motion. Did the jaguar want the bag? Or was it trying to get past the obstacle to its goal—me?

My heart thudded. I had to do something. I couldn't just sit there and be slowly mauled to death.

Jaguars aren't naturally aggressive with human adults, I told myself. *They attack only when provoked. They're spookable. Dangerous, but spookable. Okay.* I breathed deeply. Time to make a ruckus.

In a minute. My hands shook too hard. I couldn't move. I ordered my legs to scramble. They ignored me. Sweat poured from my neck despite the night's coolness. The jaguar pawed the duffel again. *Try,* I silently yelled at myself. I shifted one foot under me before my body froze up again. The cat was too big, too close. Its eyes gleamed, round and yellow.

The cat got a claw into the bag and pulled. My throat, long closed tight with fear, refused to open up enough to shout. The only part of me working reliably was the hand white-knuckled on the bag's strap. I held on. The bag scraped over the cave's uneven rock floor as the jaguar tugged it.

The cat backed up enough to clear some space in the entrance. It was the opening I needed. Time to stop being a wuss and get on with it.

No, Scooter, I ain't skeered.

"Get the hell out of my way!" I yelled with all the breath I had. My "Aaahh!" escalated from a mild growl to a roar as I scrambled out of the cave, charging. I jerked the bag around, swinging it wildly. The cat's paw got yanked right and left, then the jaguar released the duffel. It paused, took a swipe at my leg, growled. My pant leg tore at my calf but I felt nothing. All the pent-up panic came gushing out of me in a crazy dance. I spun and stamped and growled and yelled. I swung the bag toward the cat's head. The jaguar ducked and slunk back, eyeing me.

"You think you're tougher than I am?" I shouted at the cat's tensed form. "You better stay the hell away from me! I'm not backin' down!" The bag whirled in the air over my head. "I'm not your dinner!" I stomped my feet, advancing on the cat. It backed off, hissing, its teeth bared. "Get away from me!"

Two more swings with the duffel and the cat decided I was too much trouble to bother with. It turned its back on me but eyed me over its shoulder. Two fluid steps later, it faded into the night.

I dropped the bag, exhausted. Every ounce of spare energy I had left had just been screamed and danced out of me. I panted, trying to get some control over my shaking hands. My stomach churned. My leg started to sting where the jaguar had managed to get a claw in. My breath hitched.

"Dr. Robards," an authoritative American voice said from the trees. "Are you all right?"

Concern wasn't one of the top ten things I expected to hear from a United States customs agent, especially one who knew my work. Too exhausted to run, I dropped the pack and collapsed on the nearest flat rock.

"Yeah, I'm fine. Give or take cat scratch fever." I rolled my pant leg up.

A click, then a powerful light beam swept over my leg. The agent whistled. "You got lucky," he drawled, all peaches and Spanish moss.

"Unusual for me," I remarked.

But he was right. Purely superficial, the scratch ran a good eight inches or so from just below the kneecap halfway to my ankle. The bleeding had already slowed.

"You'd better disinfect that."

I never knew the word *that* could have two syllables or that such a short sentence could take so long to say.

The agent squatted next to me. His flushed and sweaty face accentuated his fairness, and a puckered scar furrowed his cheek. Broad features. Healthy country stock. "You won't mind if I search your bag while you take care of your leg." He reached for the duffel.

I snatched it out of his reach. "Damn tootin' I will," I retorted, wishing for the umpteenth time I'd kept the rifle. "Let's start with some basics. Who the hell are you?" I demanded.

"I'm very sorry, ma'am. I assumed you knew who I was."

I nodded. "Right. Big white man chases me through the jungle. That narrows the list of possibilities to, oh, about two billion. Try again, Atlanta."

He pulled his wallet from his pants pocket and obligingly held the flashlight while I studied his ID. Yep. He was definitely a customs agent. And I was up the creek without a paddle. He didn't have any legal right to be here, but I was certain his cronies would be waiting for me to touch down in the States. And where were his *pistoleiros?* Time to bluff.

"Mind if I ask why you're harassing me?" I asked as I dug through the duffel for a disinfectant wipe.

"I wanted to ask you some questions, Dr. Robards. That's all. You're the one who ran when I approached you—" he checked his watch "—three hours ago."

I shrugged. "Must have been the way you started the conversation by pulling your sidearm." I nodded at the gun butt sticking out of his shoulder holster. "Most gentlemen I know introduce themselves before whipping out the old six-shooter."

"Beggin' your pardon. Lewiston Shoemaker, Special Investigator for the U.S. Immigration and Customs Enforcement, Homeland Security." He put on a happy face, like he wanted to earn my trust. "Maybe we can have that conversation after I search your bag."

His hand rested gently, almost caressingly, on his revolver.

I sighed resignedly and handed over the duffel. Shoemaker started pulling stuff out. I tore my disinfectant wipe out of its pouch and mopped up my leg while he did his duty.

He looked carefully through my camo clothes, unfolding everything and shaking it out. Out came my plastic zippy bags of supplies. He stared for a moment at the cloves of garlic, then shrugged and put them aside. His fingers dug into the duffel's lining. He turned the bag upside down and shook it. Finally he set it to one side.

"There aren't any orchids," he said.

"Bummer of a trip for me," I replied, suppressing a smile. I'd put all my eggs, as it were, in one basket, and had handed that basket over to the one man in the world besides Scooter I trusted.

Shoemaker scowled. "You collect rare plants for a man called Linus von Brutten the Third."

"Is that a question?"

"This will go much easier, Dr. Robards, if you cooperate with me."

"I'm sure it would. But you've given me no reason to answer your questions, you've searched my gear without a warrant, and last time I looked, this wasn't our homeland. If you want my cooperation, you're going to have to tell me what you're fishing for."

"I'm investigating plant smuggling as prohibited by the Convention on International Trade in Endangered Species. I assume you're familiar with it, ma'am."

I crammed the used wipe back in its pouch, then retrieved my duffel and started repacking my stuff. "I know CITES."

"And you know a man called Lawrence Daley."

"Yeah, you just missed him. He's probably already in the States."

"Yes, ma'am, he is in the States, picked up by my team in Miami."

I felt a satisfied smile welling up in my soul but squelched it before it reached my face. Daley must be cursing his karma. Very nice, Special Investigator Shoemaker.

"He had on his person two specimens of a heretofore unknown orchid," he continued. "An orchid he tells me you know a lot about."

His eyes studied my face, but I'd played way too much poker with Scooter's wily retirement home friends. I kept packing. "I know enough about it to know it's illegal to transport it across an international boundary," I said in all seriousness. "Isn't it used in some of the native medicine?"

"That's what his employer thinks."

Surprise. "Constance Thurston-Fitzhugh is interested in ethnobotany?"

Shoemaker's lips pinched, like he'd caught me at something. "So you know something about Mr. Daley."

"Come on," I retorted. "You know how small this world is. He's been working for Thurston-Fitzhugh for three years. So he got caught orchid smuggling. It happens."

"It hasn't happened to you."

"All my orchids are certificated under CITES." The certificates were just usually forged, like the ones I carried for the Death Orchid.

"I can't let you back in the States with that plant," Shoemaker drawled. He shifted his weight back on his heels. "Daley wasn't working for Thurston-Fitzhugh. The British government picked her up in a raid on her nursery a month ago."

I struggled for a moment with the image of the heavily coifed Constance raking a tin cup across the steel bars of her dingy jail cell, demanding another splash of Dom Pérignon.

It was bound to happen. Occasionally a nursery or private collector ticks somebody off and the jealous tickee drops a hint about where a huge collection of illegal plants can be picked up. Next thing you know, the government descends in the middle of the night with automatic rifles and attack dogs. Don't scoff. It's happened. The plants all find their way either into the tickee's pet botanical garden stash or wilting in a windowless warehouse because no one has any idea how to care for them. Only God knows how many one-of-a-kind specimens had perished that way.

But I was curious about Lawrence. "So who's Daley working for?"

"Cradion Pharmaceutical."

My stomach clenched. Stunned, I could only stare at Shoemaker. "So *Daley* is Noah?"

"No, ma'am," he replied, not batting an eye that I knew the alias. "We have reason to believe Noah is here in Brazil, but we haven't been able to find him."

"Who is he?"

"I was hoping you could tell me."

"I've heard his name in passing, that's all. I take it you know his work?"

Shoemaker shrugged. "Hearsay says he's a collector like yourself, done a couple of one-off contract jobs for Cradion in the past. That's about all we know from our surveillance."

"Impossible. I know all the orchid collectors."

"He collects more than orchids. And he keeps an even lower profile than you, Dr. *Robards,*" he said, telling me he knew that was my current stage name. "The only way we figured out who you were was by running a check on everyone who'd participated in a Cradion drug trial over the past year. That turned up your great-uncle. We still had an interesting time connecting him to you."

Well, hell. That meant my mug and real name would end up pasted all over international airports. Changing my stage name every six months or so had helped me travel pretty much unmolested by customs. Most collectors did the same. The only exception to that general rule was Daley, and look where that had got him.

But I'd deal with that problem later. I rolled my pant leg down over the slash just beginning to crust over. "Why are you checking Cradion's patient list? It's a legitimate pharma, isn't it?" Knowing Scooter's wacky herbal tendencies, it wasn't.

He set the flashlight on the rock between us, pointing it up to shoot a swath of light into the canopy. "It's legitimate. It's produced several popular over-the-counter drugs in the last five years. All FDA approved. But a Cradion contract employee came to the FBI a couple of weeks ago with the story that a subsidiary biotech lab in San Antonio is creating bioterrorist weapons."

I knew the truth before I said it. "The lab that poisoned my uncle."

"Yes, ma'am."

"Were they testing one of their 'weapons' on my uncle?"

"We can't say that for sure." Shoemaker's closed expression said they were. Bastards. "I'm telling you this so you'll understand why we're so interested in the plant," he continued. "It's why we picked up Daley. Our technicians are running tests on the orchid now, to see just how potent it really is."

"You think it's being used to create this bioterrorist weapon."

"We can't let it fall into the wrong hands. That's why if you had one, I couldn't let you take it back."

I studied Shoemaker's broad, open face. There was obviously plenty he wasn't telling me, and I don't like plenty. Plenty gets peons like me killed in the cross fire. If people would just tell you the whole story from the get-go, things would be a helluva lot easier.

But it sounded like von Brutten might be in the middle of it. Von Brutten had told me his own pharmaceutical company, Lexicran, was in direct competition with Cradion over the Parkinson's cure, but that might have been only part of the story. Was his group formulating a bioweapon from the Death Orchid? Or had he told me the truth, that he was after a miracle cure, and it was Cradion that was after the bioweapon?

I zipped up my duffel and stood. My leg ached, but it was surface, pulling at the skin. Just enough to be annoying.

Shoemaker stood, too, watching me hoist the bag onto my shoulder. "We could use your help to track down Noah."

"You think he's down here for Cradion?" I asked, knowing the answer. Hell, the Brain had practically told me he intended to hire Noah. Which meant the Brain worked for Cradion as well. Cradion was serious if they'd sent two collectors, Daley and Noah.

"Do a little undercover work for us," Shoemaker said. "Be our eyes and ears. If we can find Noah, we can link him to the pharma and shut it down."

I laughed at the thought: Jessica Robards, Secret Agent. "You don't want me. I'm about as subtle as a jackhammer in a tin can."

"It'd be a chance to serve your country."

"Appealing to my higher motives," I said. "Very nice. I guess Daley didn't tell you I don't have any." I hooked my thumbs through the pack's straps and hitched them up a little higher on my shoulder. "My only goal right now is to get home and see my great-uncle before he dies. If I'm interested after that, I'll call you."

São Paolo's Guarulhos International Airport sported an extremely bleached and ammonia-smelling ladies' room. A wide table, presumably for changing diapers, was shoved up against the end wall. A short line of sinks sat under a long mirror that stretched the length of the wall facing the stalls. At just before noon, I expected the ladies' to be standing room only, but the last occupant, stylishly stilettoed as only Brazilian women can be, finished touching up her plum-colored lipstick and huffed out as I, the riffraff, walked in.

I hiked my and Rick's duffels onto the table to re-sort our stuff. After heading back toward Ixpachia Research Station at a leisurely pace for a couple of hours to throw off Shoemaker, then doubling back to the gold mine where Rick waited for me, I was too tired to do anything but sleep on the plane ride from the gold mine to São Paolo. Rick was pretty beat, too, but luckier than I was: I drew the short straw on the division of labor. While Rick arranged our flights to Houston, I was going to repack. I'd put my orchids in Rick's duffel for the run from Shoemaker, on the off chance I got caught and searched. Time to put things back where they belonged.

Still, I wasn't too annoyed. It gave me a chance to have a quick sink bath and put on my flowing *turista* dress for the ride back. I pulled the dress from Rick's duffel and draped it over a stall door to let the wrinkles fall out of it. At least I wouldn't look like an extra from a B-grade action movie starring The Rock.

I quickly transferred our gear into the correct duffels, pausing to admire the *Cattleya delictabus* I'd collected for Scooter. A tiny thing, its pink flowers reminded me a little of cherry blossoms. Scooter would love it. I eased it back into its cardboard cylinder, which I then shoved into my duffel along with the forged CITES certificate.

While I hit the high spots with the soap and a towel, I pondered the conversation with Shoemaker. He'd said a lot in a very short amount of time, none of it good. Maybe Rick and I could go over it on the flight to Houston.

Had Scooter really ended up in a drug trial that was testing a bioterrorist weapon? I couldn't imagine any terrorist worth his salt taking that kind of risk. What would be the point? If you were developing a lethal drug and wanted to test on humans, wouldn't you have the money to hide your testing activities? Or test on people whose deaths you thought no one would notice, like homeless people or drug addicts?

And would Marcus Donovan's CIA-powered lab information on the blood-that-wasn't-blood square with what Shoemaker had told me about a bioterrorist weapon? I didn't know how many contacts the FBI and CIA shared, but it'd be interesting to know how widespread the Cradion investigation might be. Not that Marcus would tell me but, with any luck, he'd at least have some information about Dr. Harrison. I hoped my old mentor was still alive. I wanted to see him after this little adventure, tell him I'd found his Death Orchid. He'd be pleased.

But that thought brought me around to von Brutten again. Too many things had happened at the same time: Scooter got sick, Harrison disappeared, von Brutten hired me to find the Death Orchid. Those were the good guys. Then, according to Shoemaker, Cradion also hired Lawrence Daley and Noah to go after the plant, and a Cradion contractor had turned himself in to the FBI. Had Harrison been kidnapped or killed by Cradion? And why? He wasn't a medical research scientist. I felt like I was still missing half the story.

And what did the Brain have to do with any of it?

I shook out my dress, then threw it on over my head. Regardless of what was really going on, von Brutten's lab had better be able to do something positive with this orchid, I thought, provided I could get it there in one piece. Thanks to Shoemaker, I knew to watch my back for Cradion's minions trying to steal my plants.

I brushed out my hair thoroughly for the first time in days. It had grown out a little and was starting to show a glossy, deep red at the roots. I kind of missed its real color, but it made me stand out like a sore thumb. Time to color it again. Or not. Rick would probably like it red—all natural, of course. I'd ask him. Heck, I could go buy some hair coloring and take it back to something close to its original red. I had time.

I studied my reflection. The tiniest of crow's-feet suggested I'd be leaving my late twenties behind soon. The rest of me looked lily fresh, with a touch of sunburn across my nose. Even without makeup, my eyes stood out, more green than gray in this light.

Scooter liked to say that every woman was beautiful at some point in her life, whether it was when she was a girl, a coltish teenager, a young woman, in middle age, or a senior. Knowing my luck, I'd be gorgeous at eighty-two. Better yet, I'd been gorgeous at five. No knockout right now, I decided, but I'd pass for kind of cute. I'd take it. Kind of cute had risen in my estimation since I met Rick.

A flash of metal caught my eye as I turned to check for a protruding clothes tag. Rick's medallion lay in the open neck of my dress. He was right. Very pretty.

Leaning forward, I studied it in the mirror. The side facing out was a moth of some kind, no surprise there. I turned it around and tried to read the inscription backward. Finally I unclasped it and took it off. The inscription was simply his full name: Alistair Richard Kinkaid.

Alistair? I could see why he went as Rick. Rick suited him.

Then every ounce of blood in my body went cold. I carefully pooled the chain and medallion on the porcelain sink.

I unzipped Rick's duffel bag again. Hands trembling a little, I moved his moth case and monitoring equipment to the side. There, in the bottom of his bag, safely sealed in a plastic bag, lay the remains of a Death Orchid, mostly intact but clearly dying. One of its original flowers had been pinched or cut off the stem, and its pseudobulb—the fat root where it stored sustenance—had been sliced open.

It must be the plant the shaman had used to concoct his poison.

In a pouch on the back of the bag was a folded CITES certificate. I took out the piece of paper and studied it. An excellent forgery, seals in the right color, expertly written signatures. Hell, it looked real.

Why would Rick have a Death Orchid in his gear? It was useless now for feeding his moth. There was no reason in the world for him to have it.

Except one.

I almost laughed. Low profile, indeed. He'd taken me for a ride I wouldn't forget. And would never forgive.

I picked up the medallion again. Alistair Richard Kinkaid. A.R.K.

Noah.

Chapter 15

I gripped the sink with both hands. Rick's necklace dangled from my fingers. I stared at my own stunned expression in the mirror, trying to make it all make sense, while my stomach plunged to my feet.

Was I that stupid?

I thought back, from the beginning, over what we'd talked about, things he'd said. He'd never told me who or what he worked for. His contact with Dr. Yagoda had centered on either their shared history, Rick's being Yagoda's student, or the gold mine situation. Rick had described his trip down as a hunt for the Corpse Moth.

But the clues were there. He knew the pharmaceutical industry processes inside and out. He'd argued with me over a little-known genus of *Streptocarpus* like he knew what he was talking about. He'd shown up in the Amazon at the same time I had. Hell, he'd said to me that first night at the research station: I think we're looking for the same thing.

I had simply assumed Rick worked as a researcher at a university. Rick had never said whether he did or didn't. He hadn't lied to me.

Unless you counted his silence when I bared my soul and told him about Scooter.

He'd said nothing. Absolutely nothing. I didn't expect him to tell me he was hunting the orchid for a bioterrorist group, but he might have said, "Oh, yeah, I'm working for a pharmaceutical company." Instead, he'd followed one of the basic rules of illegal plant collecting: don't let anyone know what you're after or why.

We were mercenaries after the same prize, just pursuing it in different ways. I used my botanical knowledge, he used a moth. Hell, I had used him and his moth to find the orchid. Then he'd turned around and used me to actually retrieve it. I couldn't fault him for being what I was.

But as my reflected eyes grew overbright, I felt the first hint of anger. I'd talked myself into believing he was a really good guy, a keeper, the one I'd stay with and maybe not just for a while. When it came to motives, he'd lied to me when I'd been straight with him.

Part of me wanted to argue. Rick had proved himself more than once to be a whole-earth kind of guy. He really had been upset with himself over getting the Yanomamo village attacked. Even now Marcello's death weighed on him like a millstone. He'd worked hard alongside Father João to tend the wounded. And he'd spouted all that verbiage about protecting the rain forest habitat.

Which a savvy field operative would do if he were interested in protecting his supply of Death Orchids.

That was true. He'd only need them around in the wild, or cultivated on-site, for however long it took his lab cronies to replicate the Death Orchid alkaloids. Hell, if the Death Orchid poison made assassination look like a heart attack—and turned out to be untraceable—how valuable would it be to terrorist organizations all over the globe? And what better place to test it than on a group of seniors suffering from Parkinson's disease?

A desperate part of me kept up the protest. Maybe Rick didn't know who he was working for. The Brain was only going to use him if the Death Orchid's location—which was recorded on the paper I'd stolen from him on the River Walk—hadn't turned up. Maybe Rick did his own work with the best of intentions and never knew he was being used.

But if that were the case, there'd be no reason not to tell me he was working for a pharmaceutical company.

Which meant he knew what he was doing. He'd charmed me, and sucked me in, and used me. Like no one ever had.

I'd given him everything I had, and look where it got me. Again.

I swiped my palms over my wet cheeks, hands trembling with rage.

Good. I needed that anger now. I wanted it to boil hard and then go cold as ice so I could do what I needed to do next.

Rick stood haloed in an oblong of sunlight, waiting for me in the lobby. Now a little after noon, tourists were arriving for their flights home. Voices ricocheted from the high ceiling. Wheeled suitcases and trunks clicked across the tiled floor. A few people headed straight for the ticket counter but the majority idled around, either trying to find other members of their party or figuring out where they could best stand to block the doors.

I stepped into the crowd, a duffel in either hand. The mob grew quickly, becoming a tide of bodies pushing to the security area and swirling in little eddies near the ticket counter. Rick's gaze swept over me twice as he scanned the human river, then he blinked and snapped back to me. His slow smile brought his bad boy straight to the surface.

Hello, Noah. Do I have a surprise for you.

I smiled back as I got close. I handed over his duffel, which he set aside to look at me. The little cosmetics shop I'd found had indeed carried a dye that would pass as my original color, and I'd taken the time to become a redhead again. It had also carried mascara and lipstick, which I'd gingerly applied, hoping I didn't end up looking like Bozo. Rick's expression said I didn't. His gaze wandered over the formfitting bodice, the flared skirt and Birkenstock sandals, heat building as it went. Even now, knowing who he worked for, my traitorous body responded, remembering how well we fit together.

"You look great," he said over the growing hubbub.

"How's our flight?" I eased my duffel to the floor.

"Nearly booked up." He handed me my ticket voucher. "You have to go check in yourself. Are you going to check your duffel?"

"Are you kidding? I'm not letting it out of my sight."

"Mine's too big to carry on."

We presented ourselves at the counter for formal check-in. My boarding pass read Row 42. Not very nice, and not useful for my plan.

"I hope you're going to be a gentleman and give me your seat if it's closer to the front," I said as we walked toward security.

He looked at my pass, cocked his brow and traded with me. Row 16. That would work out just fine, thank you very much. It meant I could deplane and go straight through customs without waiting for him. I winked and slipped through security without so much as having to take off my Birkenstocks.

Walking through the duty-free shop, buying a piece of local pottery as a souvenir, standing close to him and feeling his body heat, I managed somehow to radiate serenity instead of the churning anger I felt. I might not be able to save Scooter, but I could slow down Cradion. Old Shoe was going to owe me.

"I need to call Scooter," I told Rick as we walked toward our boarding area.

"I'll wait here," he replied, and dropped into a seat near the gate.

The phone bank was packed with yackers so I wandered around to the kiosks' backside. I spotted a luggage store on the other side of the terminal walkway. My luck was headed north again.

I bought a high-dollar wheeled leather case and hauled it and my duffel off to a crowded ladies' room. I took a stall next to the dingy white-painted wall and quickly transferred everything from the duffel to the new leather case. At the sink, I set the case near some little girls struggling to wash their hands. Water splashed on the case, giving it a nice weathered look.

Leaving the ladies', I scraped and bumped the case into every corner I could in search of the terminal's luggage lockers. Airport lockers had pretty much gone the way of the dinosaur in the States, but here, a nice broad wall of them waited to take my money. I stuffed the deflated duffel into an empty one and stuck my last *rials* into the pay slot.

Back at the phone bank, I scored a phone. The not-so-new-looking leather case wedged between my feet. Rick still sat right where I'd left him, people watching.

Minutes later Scooter yelled feebly, "How you doin', Ladybug?"

The landline connection was crap, but good enough for me to hear the fight in Scooter's voice. "Just fine. You won't believe what I'm bringing home to you this time," I said, trying not to yell back.

"I been worried 'bout you. You comin' home now?"

In the background, I could hear Hank's voice talking to someone. I imagined him and Marian in Scooter's trailer, Marian's famous lasagna in the oven while Hank and Scooter played checkers on the woodgrain Formica table. Yeah, I was ready to come home for a while. "I'm getting on the plane in about half an hour. How are you feeling?"

"Perty good today. Yes'day not so good."

I blinked back a sudden rash of tears. "I'm glad today's better. Hey, is Hank around?"

"Well, I reckon. I can't get rid of neither him ner Marian. You take care now."

"I love you, Scooter."

"I love you, too, Ladybug. Here's Hank."

A chair scraped, then Hank's voice boomed. "Jessie!" No problem hearing him over a bad connection.

"How's Scooter?" I asked.

"Doin' all right, considerin'. He has good days and bad days. You know. You headed home?" he asked.

"I gotta stop off in San Antonio first, but then I'll be right there. Couple of days, probably."

"Well, hell, we'll be in San Antone tomorra evenin' for Scooter's doctor appointment the day after. Why don't you just meet us there?"

Things were finally looking up. "Where're you staying?"

Hank gave me the motel information. Thank God he'd booked a motel room. Scooter was too sick to make the long trip to San Antonio and back in one day. He'd be exhausted.

"We're looking forward to seeing you," Hank yelled. "I know Scooter's glad."

"Me, too. Keep him around till I get there, all right?"

"Me and Marian been doin' our best. See you soon."

I hung up and had to stand there for a minute. My heart had just about stopped when Scooter answered the phone at the trailer. And now I'd get to see him sooner than I'd hoped.

I snatched up the receiver again and swiped my credit card, then dialed my voice mail's backdoor number. Two messages from Marcus at the San Antonio CIA lab. One told me what I already knew: the stain on Harrison's note wasn't blood, but an extremely poisonous extract from the Death Orchid. The second said only that he'd found Harrison.

Well, damn it. He'd found Harrison, but Harrison alive or dead? If he was alive, where the hell was he? What was he doing? Was he okay? Had he been kidnapped?

Or could Marcus just not tell me over the phone?

The intercom system blared over my head, informing me first in Portuguese and then in English that my plane was preparing to board. Out of the corner of my eye, I saw Rick stand up and look toward the bank of telephones where I was.

I fished the card Shoemaker had given me out of my dress pocket and dialed the number on it.

When Rick waved, I smiled and waved back.

Just as I expected, dark-suited agents swarmed the George Bush International Airport customs and immigration area. Shoemaker had taken my phone call seriously. I just had to get through before they nailed me.

I wheeled my leather case down the ramp toward the queues, trying to breathe deep and keep my cool. I'd arrived here sooner than anyone else from my plane; they were all stuck collecting their checked luggage. With any luck, I'd look like I'd come off whatever flight had landed before the São Paolo plane. If Shoe's agents were looking for me, they'd be looking for a brown-haired woman in outdoor clothes carrying a duffel, not a red-haired tourist in a flouncy dress with an expensive leather case.

Nor would they realize I had two Death Orchids taped to my calves.

"Anything to declare, Ms. Sutherland?" the U.S. customs agent asked, taking my declaration card.

I shrugged. "Just a piece of pottery."

He studied the dollar amount I'd scribbled in, 72 USD. His raised brow had *incredulous* written all over it.

A tingle of fear tickled my stomach. "I don't like things like that. It's for Aunt Ella."

He glanced at my duty-free shopping bag, then at my business-like leather case.

I gave him the tired smile of an exhausted tourist wanting to go home.

"Thank you, Ms. Sutherland." He waved me through.

I paused just this side of the double doors leading toward the airport lobby. Behind me, the lines of travelers coming through customs had stacked up with people declaring nothing, which was predominantly untrue, or just a little something, like me, which was almost true. Bored security guards waited at the lobby doors.

Down near the secured office area, a little flurry of activity suggested the Homeland Security agents were ready to go. I shouldn't have waited, but I couldn't leave. The São Paolo passengers started trickling in.

Rick looked ragged, his Patagonia shirt rumpled and his hair looking like he'd combed his hand through it too many times. He handed over his passport to the agent. The customs agent did a double take and waved over a plain suit colleague wearing an earpiece. The suit said something. Rick nodded and started to unzip the duffel, but the suit stopped him and gestured to a table off to the side.

The suit escorted him to the table where he was immediately surrounded by uniformed guards. The suit opened up the duffel bag and pawed around until he took out the Death Orchid specimen. Rick pointed to the CITES certificate. The suit nodded, then took out a single cardboard cylinder. He opened the cylinder, then drew out *Cattleya delictabus,* carefully supporting its strands of tiny, delectable pink blossoms.

There was, of course, no CITES certificate for that Appendix One beauty, because I didn't put it in Rick's duffel when I put the *Cattleya* in. Carrying that orchid across an international boundary meant jail time and a one-hundred-thousand-dollar fine.

Rick's head snapped around, his gaze searching the crowd until he found me. Even from this distance, our eye contact touched me to the core and the stunned hurt in his eyes brought tears to mine.

"I'm sorry," I said aloud. And I was.

Then I pushed through the lobby's heavy double doors and lost myself in the crowd going home.

"Talk to me about Harrison," I said to Marcus as I wrapped my brand new sweater around my chest. Jeez, did these guys never let the lab temperature rise above forty degrees?

Marcus pulled a file folder from a steel cabinet and laid it on the examination table between us. My elbows chilled the moment I leaned them on the table. He spread out the folder's papers and plucked one from the stack.

Marcus's deep voice echoed richly in the cold, barren lab. "The cursory test I just ran says the stain on the notebook page you gave me matches the shaman's poison sample in terms of the basic compounds. We're definitely talking about the same substance."

Dr. Harrison working on a *poison?* That didn't sound like him at all. "So what happened to him?" I asked. "You said you'd found him."

Marcus's chiseled lips curved in a classically handsome smile. "As impatient as ever."

I shot him an annoyed glance that must have verged on something else because his smile disintegrated. "I don't have the time for you to tell me how brilliant you are," I said.

"Then you probably already know what I was going to tell you." His voice held almost as much steel as the table. "You don't need this genius to fill you in."

I bit back a sudden spate of tears. Good God, I was weakening by the minute. Ten hours on the flight from hell and then a bone-jarring puddle jumper from Houston to San Antonio had worn my nerves paper thin. Besides, I'd lived my days and nights backward for so long my body clock thought I should be unconscious. "Look, I have to get this stuff sorted out. It's important." I pressed two fingers to my temple. "I'm sorry I'm being a bitch."

Marcus paused, studying me with his clear blue eyes. "You look like you've had a bad two weeks."

"I have," I admitted, and let it go at that. "I'm sorry. Go ahead and tell me what you have. I'll shut up."

His measuring look told me he wasn't sure whether to take me at my word or not. Then he turned back to his papers, leaving me looking at his virile profile, his dark hair lying longish on his collar.

Rick's hair looked just like that. I mentally shook myself and said, "How about the poison's effects?"

"They mimic a heart attack, as you suggested. It'll take me another few days to determine whether the poison is traceable."

That made sense. He'd have to poison some mice and study the corpses to figure out the chemical signature.

Marcus picked up the shaman's vial. "If this poison is untraceable, the Death Orchid is a far better weapon than the Danube violet. Did you see the shaman make it?"

I shook my head. "All shaman cooking is secret." I held out my hand for the vial.

Marcus watched me pocket it, brow cocked. "You aren't going to leave that with me for further testing?"

"You've got enough of a sample to play with."

"How about leaving me a Death Orchid to study?"

I shrugged, hoping I was as good a liar as I thought I was. "Daley stole them from me." I glanced at Marcus. No, I wasn't a good liar, but he wasn't going to argue. Yet. "What about Harrison?" I asked.

Marcus pivoted to face me, leaning his hip on the table. "It's all here." He tapped his long fingers on the stack of papers. "You can't take the report with you."

Great. I love reading while freezing my ass off. "Harrison makes an appearance in the report?"

"More of a *dis*appearance."

I sighed. "Well, yeah, he did that a couple of weeks ago."

Marcus shifted his weight, crossing his heavy arms across his chest. "He didn't disappear on his own. He went into FBI protective custody. We're working with the FBI on this one."

My conversation with Shoemaker fast-forwarded through my head. Shoemaker had said a *contractor* had rolled one of Cradion's subsidiary labs. That had been *Harrison?* "Harrison turned himself in to the FBI and implicated Cradion in a bioterrorism plan," I muttered aloud.

"How'd you know?" Marcus asked, surprised.

Harrison was supposed to be working for von Brutten's lab, Lexicran. Von Brutten's lab was supposed to be in direct competition with Cradion. A Cradion subsidiary lab had poisoned my uncle in a Parkinson's drug trial.

I put the pieces together and didn't like the picture. Either Harrison was two-timing von Brutten and working for both Lexicran *and* Cradion…or von Brutten had lied to me about his intentions and was running the whole show: Cradion Pharmaceutical, Harrison, and the deadly drug trials.

But which?

The Death Orchid was important enough to send me, Lawrence Daley and Noah down to the Amazon. Somebody—anybody—had to bring it back for the poison to be produced.

Did Shoemaker or the FBI know about von Brutten's connection to all of this? Did the CIA? Did anyone other than me?

Marcus touched my arm. "You okay?"

I thought of Harrison's pallid face, his weak eyes. "Why did Harrison turn himself in?"

Marcus shrugged. "Paranoia. He came in saying his unfinished formula could be the end of the world."

"Unfinished?"

"He was within a week of having it, he said. He'd exhausted his supply of test orchids and needed more, but was afraid to go after them." He paused. "It'll be ironic if you've got the formula in that shaman's brew."

I couldn't appreciate the irony because the one-week timeline hammered my chest. Von Brutten had said his lab would take a week to develop its miracle cure. But that was still circumstantial. Von Brutten's week didn't necessarily equate to Harrison's week, not if Harrison was two-timing von Brutten. My boss might still be innocent.

My voice started to work again. "Did Harrison give you the formula?"

"He said he'd put it in a safe place and would turn it over when he felt he could."

"Who did he think was gunning for him?"

Marcus shrugged. "That's where it gets tricky. There's no record of any wrongdoing at the main Cradion labs. The Cradion directors working on the Parkinson's drug are clean as a whistle."

"There has to be somebody," I retorted. "Harrison wasn't a medical research scientist. He had to have been working with someone to develop this poison."

Marcus flipped through a folder. "The only Cradion scientist he's had regular contact with is a Dr. Reginald Thompson. Thompson's worked for Cradion for eleven years, runs trials, works with patients, relays data and results back to the main labs, that kind of thing."

"And he's clean?"

"So far."

"So nobody at Cradion fits the bill."

"Nobody. Which suggests Harrison was working for someone else on the side."

And I knew exactly who. Von Brutten. But if Harrison was making both a poison *and* a cure, which was he making for whom? *Please, God,* I prayed, *let him be making the cure for von Brutten.* "He was really scared of somebody," I murmured.

Marcus nodded. "He was right to be. Less than forty-eight hours in protective custody…" Marcus made a finger-and-thumb motion of a gun going off. "Got popped."

"God." I remembered Harrison's wry smile and felt my throat close up. He'd been a good man. A top-notch professor. A challenging mentor. Something must have been very wrong for him to have gotten involved in all this.

"It was a professional hit. The men assigned as guards were killed at the scene. Internal Affairs is all over it but hasn't turned up anything yet."

"How about his lab? Did your guys look at it yet?"

"Agents scoured it, dusted for prints, but didn't find anything."

"No formula?"

"No nothing."

"Wait a minute. None of this makes sense," I said. "Why would Harrison roll Cradion if he was afraid of someone else? If Cradion's legit, there's no reason for him to implicate them. There's got to be *someone* at Cradion who's dirty." I liked that answer. It meant von Brutten was, if not a good guy, at least a neutral capitalist kind of guy.

Marcus shrugged. "Maybe. Or he just wanted federal protection and didn't care who he implicated."

"But if no one knew where the formula was, why would the murderer kill him? You kill him, you lose the formula for good."

"Not if he was working with a bioterrorist on the side. The

bioterrorist might have the formula already. And maybe Harrison had become a liability."

I could see Harrison losing his cool and going rabbity. I thought of his panicked stare when I'd startled him in his office years before. All he needed was a hint that he was in trouble. Leave him alone in his lab and he was fine. Put some pressure on him and he fell apart.

I still had the key to his lab, the key von Brutten had given me when all this got started. Maybe it'd be worth another look tonight after I saw Scooter. I figured the feds would have found something if there was anything to be found, but there was the slimmest chance they'd missed something. Something a keen graduate student who knew Harrison's habits inside and out might happen across.

"Now that I've given you all this information…" Marcus said casually.

Uh-oh. "What do you want from me?"

"You know what I want."

"I told you the orchids were stolen from me. If you want them, go find Special Agent Shoemaker and get the ones he took from Lawrence Daley."

Marcus smiled. "I'm due to meet with Shoemaker—" he checked his watch "—in an hour."

"Then I should let you get to it." I turned to the stack of papers.

"No, Jessie. I saw the wheels turning in your little head. You know a few things we should know."

Yeah. My employer might be a bioterrorist, but I'm not sure. He told me he'd use the Death Orchid to save my great-uncle, but I don't know if that's really why he wants it. And if he *is* a bioterrorist and senses the FBI, CIA and Homeland Security are on to him, he'll disappear forever.

I looked Marcus in the eye. "I don't know anything for sure. That's the truth."

"If you have the orchid, you need to hand it over. Give it to me or to Shoemaker. You let it go to anybody else, and it'll end up doing some really bad things."

"Yeah, Shoe's already told me that."

Marcus's fine, black brows drew into a frown. "Whatever's going on, we can help."

"There's nothing going on," I lied.

"Don't bullshit me, Jessie," Marcus snapped. "I've given you a helluva lot more here than I should have because of our history. Now it's your turn."

I heard Rick's voice. *It's all or nothing for you.* I gritted my teeth. I gave my all once and it'd gotten me nowhere.

"I need some time to think, okay? The orchids are safe. Just give me a day or two."

His blue eyes met mine. I could see him measuring, deciding. The civilized version of the Evil Eye, I realized. Putting the fear into me to make me behave.

"Just a day or two," I repeated.

He sighed and nodded, willing to take nothing for now.

I looked at the papers in front of me. "I need some time to read through this stuff," I said. "Can you turn up the heat a little?"

Marcus abruptly laughed, his rich baritone echoing around the lab. "You've spent too much time down south. It's a balmy sixty-eight degrees in here." He grinned as I pulled my sweater around me, then leaned close, laying his broad, caressing hand on my arm. "I can heat things up if you like. Just to take the edge off."

"We tried that once before."

"I'm not prejudiced against second chances."

His expensive cologne wafted over me. I glanced up at him, warm and sexy. He'd always been a nice guy, a total hunk, confident and cocksure of himself, but gentle. We'd been pretty good together that night, even if I had run away the next day.

But now, with him offering something like comfort, I realized that wasn't what I needed. Not from him. He just wouldn't feel right. Too big, I thought, studying his bare, muscular arms. Not lean enough.

Not Rick.

"I gotta get this stuff read," I said as my throat closed up. I pulled the papers toward me and stared at the words until he left.

Chapter 16

"How are you feeling?" I asked Scooter later that evening.

He sat propped up in his motel bed, a tray over his lap. Marian's fried chicken, mashed potatoes and butter-drenched asparagus sat, nearly untouched, on a plate. His skin had gone even grayer than the last time I'd seen him, the wrinkles more pronounced. The bed, with its crisp sheets and full comforter, swallowed him whole.

But what told me how bad he really was were his eyes. No fight. He lay there, a tired old man, picking at his food.

Scooter pushed the plate away and heaved a sigh. "I don't feel too good. I just don't feel too good at all."

"Seein' the doctor's what done it," Hank said from the chair across the bed. "We shoulda put that off till tomorrow."

Scooter's brow took on his characteristic granite furrow. That was the Scooter I knew.

"At least you're done and can go home tomorrow," I said in the best approximation of 'soothing' I can do. "Nice spread," I said, looking around the large blue bedroom and hoping to change the subject. "How many bedrooms total?"

"Two, with a full kitchen," Marian said as she breezed in with a half-filled water glass, full of young energy and efficiency.

Two? I guessed Hank's pot had found Marian's lid, as Scooter would have said. Hank sat like a rock on the other side of Scooter's bed: stable, still strong and good-looking. Good for Marian, I thought, getting the man she wanted.

"I wouldn't let my favorite man out of my sight," Marian said with a wink at Scooter, "so we got us a suite. And he sure didn't need to be eatin' no restaurant food."

Right. Heavily breaded and pan-fried chicken ranked right up there with raw fruit on the healthy-eating scale.

Hank took Scooter's plate from the bed tray. "And he can't remember which pills to take when."

Scooter humphed weakly. A bouquet of pills, all sizes, shapes and colors, sprouted next to his napkin. "If I wrote it down, I'd keep up with it."

"If you could remember where you put the paper," Marian teased. She dropped a kiss on his silvered hair, which he accepted with grudging grace. "Now take them pills." She set the glass on his tray.

Scooter put the first one in his mouth, then picked up the glass with both hands. Water sloshed with his shaking and a thin line of liquid ran down the outside, over his fingers.

"That's good," Hank said encouragingly as he walked to the bedroom door. "Only seven more to go."

"Here you go, let me help." Marian took the glass from Scooter, her tanned skin startlingly young next to his wrinkled, mottled hand.

"I'll do that while you wash up," I said suddenly. I was scared to death—nursing is not my bag—but it seemed like something I *ought* to do.

Marian handed over the glass. "Give me a holler if you need anything," she said on her way out, Hank right behind her.

Scooter fished the second pill, a blue one this time, off the tray. He juggled it into his palm, then raised his palm to his mouth. I held the glass to his lips, my hands trembling almost as much as his. He needed me to hold his glass right now and it was almost beyond me. The image of the dying colonel, naked and weak and alone, nearly overcame me. I clamped down on my tears and shame.

All the weeks and months Scooter had been fading from the stout, healthy, robust man I'd grown up with, I'd been running around in some jungle somewhere, not giving him a second thought. I guess I figured he'd always be around for me to visit. That every time I came back, he'd be exactly like he was when I left on my little adventures.

But here he was, having to rest between pills, and I had no idea how to take care of him, scared of doing something as simple as helping him take his medication. The grand gesture I could do: risk life and limb, talk big, strut around. But hold a glass steady?

Why hadn't I left well enough alone and let him keep going to Old Lady Fenster? The worst she'd have done was give him a pouch of herbs to stick under his pillow at night. Hell, doing nothing would have been better than this.

And now I carried in my luggage either the cure for all ills or the next terrorist's weapon of choice. I didn't know which angel—life or death, saving or avenging—von Brutten was. I wanted von Brutten to have told me the truth about saving Scooter. I wanted him not to be funding a bioterrorism lab, even though I knew in my heart of hearts he was capable of it. I wanted him to save Scooter because he said he would.

But there was more to it. There was what Rick had asked me back in Brazil. About whether or not I'd given Scooter a choice. Had I made that choice for him, when all along he might have just wanted me to be around for his last days?

"Scooter," I said softly.

He blinked his watery eyes and looked at me. "What's on yer mind, Ladybug?"

"If somebody came up with some medicine that could fix your heart tomorrow, would you take it?"

His teeth gleamed as he grinned. "You think seventy-four ain't old enough? 'Cause it feels plenty old to me."

"That's just because you don't feel well."

"I don't know 'bout that." His gnarled fingers played with the blanket's edge. "They's times I figger I've lived long enough."

"But you could have more time," I insisted. "Don't you want that?"

His brow furrowed as he thought. "It's been a good run, and I done ever'thing I wanted." He smiled feebly. "I reckon I ain't so special I deserve to see more than what my Creator intended I should see."

Tears slipped down my cheeks. "Your Creator didn't intend you to get hold of bad drugs."

Scooter gripped my fingers. His skin was hot, a little feverish. "Maybe, maybe not. But there ain't a whole lot I kin do 'bout that, is there?" He sighed and added, "You done growed up. I reckon my real work is done."

And there was nothing I could say to that. I laid my head on his thin chest and breathed in his vaguely mothball and spearmint scent. "I love you, Scooter."

"I love you too, Ladybug."

After a little while, his chest rose and fell evenly. I raised my head. Everything about him had gone colorless, as if he were about to disappear into the air itself.

I had the cure in my possession and wanted to use it, to

keep Scooter around for a little while longer. He might be at peace with his coming death, but I wasn't, and wasn't sure I ever would be.

I juggled a metal clipboard and stack of papers at the locked side door of Harrison's office building. The lab coat Marcus had borrowed for me to wear didn't quite reach the short gray skirt I'd bought. Absurd as it seemed, the high heels felt like they'd added about two inches to my thighs. Behind me, the parking garage sported my rented Lexus and a single Toyota that had just pulled in. The Toyota's occupant, a harried-looking lab tech, got out carrying a fast-food bag. His footsteps slowed when I dropped the clipboard and bent over straight-legged to pick it up.

"Let me get the door for you," the scrawny tech said.

"Thanks!" I stood straight and heaved a sigh that shoved more cleavage from the push-up bra into the opening of my pink silk blouse. "I hate these late evenings, don't you?"

"Not tonight."

He swiped a keycard through the card reader and held the door for me, blocking half the entrance. *Lecherous rat,* I thought as I smiled and brushed against him, full frontal. His smile stretched. That was probably as close as he'd been to a woman since birth. I felt his attention lingering on my legs until he peeled off down a side hallway leading toward the back of the building.

In the soaring foyer, the Spurs game echoed from a clock radio. My heels clicked on the polished brick floor as I walked past the spilling fountain and ficus trees toward the stairs. A guard's desk sat at the stair's base. The beefy guard grinned and turned down the game as I approached.

"Got to sign in? I just left!" I protested, shuffling the messy papers in my arms from one side to the other, pulling the blouse open a little wider.

"Aw, you know the rules," the guard said. "Especially after all that ruckus with the police."

I took a deep breath, bent low and scribbled an indecipherable name on his check-in list. It'd be a freakin' miracle if I didn't fall out of this blouse. "What's the time?" I asked idly.

"Nine-oh-five."

Of course it was. I'd watched this guard's predecessor leave at eight-thirty and waited for a late-working lab tech to return with dinner. Lucky for me, both the tech and the guard had been male. No woman would have let me just walk in and go upstairs.

"See you later," the guard said as I straightened.

I smiled sweetly and started up the stairs. The heels made me walk slow and put a lot of hip action into climbing the steps. After I walked around the landing corner, out of the guard's sight, the game started blaring again.

A couple of minutes later I found Harrison's fourth-floor lab. As far as I could tell, there were no surveillance cameras. Had Harrison rented a high-tech science lab in a down-market building? Anybody working in the pharma industry ought to have a protected environment. Maybe I'd drop old Shoemaker a note about the state of security in this place.

As a high-dollar contractor with an academia attitude, Harrison didn't use Cradion's facilities but preferred to keep his own. If he was working for both Cradion and von Brutten's Lexicran, I realized as I unlocked the office door with the key von Brutten had thoughtfully provided, the preference went beyond just his being a cranky highbrow. He needed his privacy for all his little extracurricular activities. My first browse through had yielded nothing because I was looking for a run-of-the-mill map to the orchid. But now I wanted the Death Orchid formula and I'd have to be more thorough.

His lab *had* been cleaned up, as Marcus had told me, but just barely. Residual light from the building's floods next door illuminated the office well enough to let me get a good look without turning on a light. The broken specimen glass that had graveled the floor during my first visit was gone and traces of powder still lingered here and there from the fingerprint dusting. Long, bare worktables loomed. The oak specimen cabinets sat empty along the walls.

The odor of alcohol, formaldehyde and propylene glycol took me straight back to long afternoons in school, when heatless New England sunlight shone through the tall windows onto a table covered with hundreds of incredibly boring North American specimens. I'd spent the better part of a semester cataloging the damned things for Harrison's herbarium. By the time he and I quit squabbling over the uselessness of the task—who needed yet another sunflower preserved for all posterity?—Dr. Harrison had finally decided I was better utilized in the field. I felt a stab of regret. I'd never see him again. Never work with him again. Never read his papers again.

"Okay, Doc," I said aloud. "There's no reason to hide anything like you did the medicine bowl. This time I want to know about von Brutten. What exactly were you doing for him? Did you hide the formula here? Throw me a bone, old man."

Two hours later, I leaned against one of the stainless-steel worktables and pondered. Nothing up his sleeve, nothing in the lab. But the Brain and the Whiner had clearly known where to look when they searched his home office. Hell, they'd destroyed a desk to dig up his map.

But the desk here hadn't been dismantled. Had the Brain come here first? And who was that guy? My bet was he was the medical science part of the team on the Death Orchid project, working for Cradion. Maybe this Reginald Thompson.

That idea made a lot of sense. Even if the Cradion directors were clean, it was possible Thompson was the bad seed, the bioterrorist connection. So when Harrison got scared and went to the FBI, Thompson was left without any orchids and without the man who was capable of finding more. Hence his hiring of Rick.

This theory still made Cradion responsible for the poison—and the drug trials. I made a mental note to ask Hank to remind me who the Cradion rep was attending Scooter's trials. Dime to a dollar it was Thompson.

Maybe all that theorizing was me grasping at straws to absolve von Brutten of any wrongdoing, but it was all the hope I had. My realism kicked in hard and heavy. I couldn't just make up an idea and hope it was right. I had to *know*.

I had to know whether my boss was out to save my greatuncle or out to poison the world.

First things first. The desk, a metal utility affair, had nothing to hide. I inspected each cabinet in turn, checking for hidden compartments, loose drawers, buttons, knobs, anything to press. Nada.

Then I looked at the untouched specimen cabinets. The Brain had torn the home office wooden desk apart, so could it be that one of these cabinets might need the same treatment?

I dragged one of them screeching out from the wall. The glass doors had already been smashed, leaving just the empty frames and a few dangerous teeth of glass. I reached inside and whacked the middle shelf from beneath with the heel of my hand. It gave slightly. Good old Harrison, using only real wood furniture. Another couple of whacks and the wood tore from the securing nails. I examined the shelf closely for seams, lettering, carvings—anything that might constitute a clue. Nothing.

Then I got the trusty minicrowbar from my oversize purse and methodically dismembered the cabinet. Still nothing.

This went on until I pulled out the last cabinet. I opened the useless doors and when I reached in to whack the shelf, I realized something was different. My stinging hand fell to my side as I looked. The shelves in this cabinet were a good inch narrower than the others. But the cabinet itself was the same size as its siblings.

I angled the cabinet around to look at its back. The wood was just as solid there as anywhere. Around front, I tugged on the middle shelf. It was loose. When I lifted its front edge, it pivoted up, attached to the solid back by a hidden hinge.

At the point where the shelf met the back wall was one of those four-digit combination locks where each number had its own dial setting, like on luggage locks. I looked closer at the back wall. A fine seam ran horizontally where the shelf had rested, then when the seam reached the cabinet's sides, it turned to run down nearly to the bottom shelf. Big enough to house documents if nothing else.

The lock was set to 2317.

Great. Like I'd be able to figure out which four numbers Harrison might have picked to protect his little treasure trove. I'd be here all damned night trying out numbers I could remember from his life—birthday, phone numbers, office number at the university, and so forth.

I guessed I could try breaking up the cabinet back, but half-inch-thick oak would take a heck of a wallop to crack, and I wasn't sure when the guard might be making the rounds. Knowing my luck, he'd overhear me kicking away and bust me.

The more I thought of ways to break into the cabinet, the more I became suspicious of that number. The anal-retentive Harrison I knew would have set that number to 0000 every time he closed up his little hidey-hole. He couldn't help it any more than he could help wearing his lunch on his tie or marinating in his aftershave.

I pulled a penknife out of my purse and inserted it into the hidey-hole's seam. Nope, 2317 wasn't the magic number. But I guessed it wasn't far off. If I were Harrison and in a hurry not to get caught, I'd have spun the lock a number off and dropped the shelf. The bad guys couldn't break into the hole if they didn't know it was there, and keeping the hole a secret would have been the top priority.

Reaching in to spin the 7 to 6, I paused. Harrison was left-handed. I spun the 2 to 3 and tried to pry the panel off. No good. Okay, turn the 2 to 1. Nothing. In disgust I reset the lock to 2317. Going through all the possible combinations would take a year.

But maybe I wasn't being patient enough. If Harrison had been in a hurry, he'd have spun the dial up because that's the easiest direction to get a good spin. I thumbed the 2 up as far as I could with one stroke. The 2 landed on 7. I pried with the penknife. On 8, the panel popped out and dropped onto the bottom shelf. I maneuvered the panel out of the cabinet and set it aside.

In a shallow compartment behind the panel, a manila envelope clung to wood by a thin strip of tape.

Heart pounding, I carefully peeled the envelope from the compartment. Inside the envelope lay two pieces of paper and a microcassette tape.

I spread the papers out on the floor, then dug my penlight out of my purse and knelt. Down here, the light shouldn't give me away to anyone watching the office from outside. Like one of Shoemaker's buddies in uniform.

The first paper was a summary printout of Harrison's electronic date book for the past year, detailing dates and times he'd met or talked with Cradion. But two appointments were with von Brutten, both occurring the week before von Brutten called me. On its own, the paper confirmed only that Harrison had had contact with both Cradion and von Brutten. It wasn't enough to exonerate von Brutten.

I moved on to the next page. It was another handwritten sheet, torn from a project notebook. A neatly printed chemical formula was written on it, with Harrison's trademark shorthand notes scrawled to the side. I scanned the margin notes. One read simply:

With the proper dilution, this formula has exactly the opposite effect—of healing heavily damaged heart tissues.

I caught my breath. The Death Orchid poison.

Nowhere were the "proper dilution" specifics mentioned. I checked the back of the page, the envelope, every scrap of paper within reach. No dilution details anywhere.

Tears welled in my eyes but I squeezed them back. I had the poison here, not the cure. Had Harrison taken the cure to his grave? Scooter didn't stand a chance unless von Brutten's lab had the cure formula.

If von Brutten's lab really was legitimate. I still didn't know and couldn't tell from the limited evidence in my hands. Was von Brutten the good guy?

I picked up the microcassette tape. My last chance to find out. Harrison's desk drawer held a microcassette player with, thank my one lucky star, live batteries. I snapped the cassette inside and turned the player on.

The conversation sounded like the participants were arguing in a bucket. The recorder must have been in Harrison's metal desk. But no mistaking the voices: Harrison and von Brutten, discussing due dates and timelines. Harrison's thin voice trembled and broke. The man was terrified. Von Brutten was his usual soft-spoken, austere, vaguely threatening self.

Then a door shutting and a voice I'd heard only once, two weeks ago. When I'd heard him before, I'd had my hands in Harrison's sock drawer as he'd said, "I don't want to pay Noah if I don't have to." Soon after that, I'd chased him all over the River Walk. The Brain.

On the tape he said, "I hope, Dr. Harrison, you've made your final decision about retrieving the orchid."

"And I told you, Dr. Thompson, I'll f-find another one." Harrison's voice wavered. "Th-That's not the issue. Another week after I have the plant and I'll have the cure Cradion's looking for."

"And the substance I contracted you to create?" von Brutten asked.

"Yes, th-that, t-too. The issue is k-keeping the C-Cradion directors in the dark. If they lose credibility, the whole p-p-project falls apart."

"Quit worrying about things that don't concern you," von Brutten said.

"I can handle Cradion's precious credibility," Thompson snapped. "Just get von Brutten's formula ready."

"I'm d-doing all I c-can."

"If that's true," von Brutten said in a soothing tone, "your little video collection will remain just between us."

Thompson snorted. "Video collection?"

"The stars are rather...young," von Brutten breathed. The tape barely caught his irregular, chuffing laugh. "Never mind, Dr. Harrison. We all have our weaknesses."

"All right," Harrison murmured. "I'll d-do what you want."

The rest of the conversation deteriorated into science-speak. I snapped the player off.

Absolute silence filled the abandoned lab. It filled my head. I breathed, waited for my heart to slow its pounding. I waited for the clenched fist that was my stomach to loosen.

I'd needed to know whether Harrison was working for two different labs, Cradion's and von Brutten's. He was. For Cradion to develop its good medicine, and for von Brutten to develop a biological weapon.

I'd needed to know whether von Brutten was involved in the bioterrorism lab Shoemaker told me about. He was.

Cradion hadn't poisoned Scooter. Thompson had. Thompson working for von Brutten in Harrison's lab.

I sat on the floor for a moment longer, letting the grief crash over me. I didn't cry. I was through crying for a while.

Time to decide.

I thought about Scooter, swallowed in blankets, taking his pills. He didn't belong there. He belonged in his little green-house with his orchids, or in the Slapdash's kitchen standing over a pot of chili, or out on the trailer's front porch holding a glass of cold grape Kool-Aid.

I thought about Marcello and that damned green harness tied around his little brown legs. The *shapono* burning, women wailing in the dawn. Porfilio's earnestness as he tried to convince Rick to help him stop the colonel. Rick's strong face in firelight. The shaman's unreadable black eyes.

I'd already made this decision once, I realized. That early morning I let Lawrence Daley walk away with the very orchids that could snatch Scooter from the brink of death, I'd turned my back on him and tried to save a village full of people I didn't know and would never see again. People who meant nothing more to me than what I allowed them to mean. Marcello. Rick.

Back then I'd thought I could somehow cheat time, change fate, get everything I wanted. And I had, a little. I'd eventually lost Rick, had been betrayed to the core, but I'd brought the orchid back against all odds.

But there was no cheating fate this time. This decision was for keeps.

Forgive me, Scooter.

Chapter 17

Von Brutten, I learned when I called him the following morning, leased a penthouse condo in San Antonio. It turned out to be a posh place near downtown, where parking sucked because all the money was in office and living space. My rented Lexus squeezed into the last parallel parking spot on the street behind a windowless cable repair van. Hitching my oversize purse onto my shoulder, I tucked a cardboard cylinder containing a Death Orchid under my arm and locked the car.

I rode the elevator to the twelfth floor, trying not to look at myself in the mirrored door. Lack of sleep, too many hours worrying. Too many hours grieving. Hank and Marian would have Scooter on the road for home, probably to die. The kiss goodbye I'd given him had felt like forever. I steeled myself to feel nothing. Nothing at all.

Linus Geraint Newark von Brutten III, you bastard, here I come.

The elevator hummed open on a black-suited butler. Not-

Sims. I felt a little sad. I'd probably never see my favorite butler again.

"Dr. Robards to see Mr. von Brutten," I said.

Not-Sims stared down his long nose at my blue jeans and walking boots. "Please wait here. Mr. von Brutten is with another guest at the moment." Not-Sims glided off to what I gathered was The Study and opened the double doors.

While he waited to be acknowledged, I studied the foyer's walls. Abstract art, brightly colored slashes and shapes, hung over a muted and classy wallpaper. A marble-topped antique table sported some kind of china bowl. A Waterford chandelier hung above my head. This ten-by-ten-foot room had cost more than I'd made in my three-year career. What was it like to have that kind of money? Did it make you think you had the power of life and death?

I heard a raised voice from The Study, arguing. Not-Sims stood in the doorway, still waiting. The raised voice was more than familiar. My heart stopped, then painfully jerked into motion again.

Rick.

Before I could get a handle on the four hundred thoughts clamoring for my attention, Not-Sims beckoned. "This way." He took a single step onto The Study's antique Oriental rug and announced, "Dr. Robards."

Inside, a cacophony of colors and shapes exploded over the walls and bookshelves. Every surface in the study held an artifact—cloth, bowl, weapon, pot, parchment, skin, figurine, totem, charm, dried specimen. Blankets and animal skins hung on the walls. An array of arrows from several different cultures weighed down the desk's glossy surface.

There was so much to see, in fact, that for an instant I had a hard time separating the men from the stuff. Von Brutten and Rick had squared off against each other in front of the desk, but both stared at me as I stalked inside.

"Welcome, Dr. Robards," von Brutten breathed. The doors clicked shut behind me.

"Am I interrupting?" I jerked my head in Rick's direction.

Von Brutten's goatee quivered with his frosty smile. "Merely a business transaction. I didn't realize you had yet another competitor."

Of course. Thompson had hired Rick to bring back the Death Orchid at the same time von Brutten had hired me. But I wasn't supposed to know that. *"Competitor?"* I asked. I shot a hard glance at Rick, who glared back. "You horning in on my territory, *Noah?*"

Rick shrugged his broad shoulders arrogantly, sending my stomach to my feet. "Fair play," he said.

"He brought me a specimen." Von Brutten waved a hand toward the desk, where the mangled Death Orchid Rick had salvaged from the shaman lay like a corpse.

I forced a laugh, my throat tight. "I did a little better than that." I uncapped my cardboard cylinder and carefully pulled out my Death Orchid still clinging to its raft of bark. It was perfect. Flawless.

Von Brutten plucked a pair of rimless glasses from his vest pocket and examined my orchid while Rick and I eyed each other behind his back. The lines under his eyes suggested he hadn't slept in a while. How could Rick be a part of this? This wasn't the man I knew. Anguish squeezed my chest. Rick's gaze dropped another five degrees.

"Very nice," von Brutten eventually pronounced. "Is this the only one?"

I broke my gaze-lock with Rick to smile. "Not hardly."

"You said you have something else for me."

"That's correct. And I'm more than willing to pass it along to you—" here I glared at Rick "—if you pass up offers by my *competitor.*"

"Forget it," Rick snapped. "I produced the Death Orchid—"

"After I cut it down for you." *After I trusted you. After I gave myself to you. After I let myself want you again.* I cursed inwardly.

Stay strong, Ladybug, Scooter's voice whispered.

Right. Time to get the job done. "Which is it?" I asked my employer. "I have another orchid *and* Harrison's formula. Shall I take them to another buyer?"

Von Brutten's thin lips parted to speak, but I cut him off.

"Or should I take them to Homeland Security? They started giving me a hard time after Harrison gave himself up and told them what he was up to."

Von Brutten plucked a cigarette from a silver case resting in the arrow cache. "Yes, I always had my doubts about Dr. Harrison. A weak sort. Morally weak." His pale eyes flickered red as he fired up an embossed silver lighter. He met my eyes, blew a quick stream of smoke. "Unlike you. Unlike me." He snapped the lighter shut and returned it to his pocket, then gestured to the loosely grouped leather chairs that formed a conversation area. "Please," he said to Rick.

"You're a woman of great loyalty," von Brutten said as I dropped into a chair and set my shoulder bag on the floor at my feet. He seated himself next to Rick. "I admire that."

"You made a promise. About my great-uncle."

"Yes. You know I always keep my promises." His pale eyes slipped to Rick, calculating.

I pulled a piece of paper from my jeans pocket and handed it to him. "A good chemist should get you where you're going. This is the formula Dr. Harrison created for you. I found it hidden in his lab."

He opened the folded paper and perused it. I hoped he hadn't been a chemist in a previous life because I'd copied Harrison's poison formula from the original notes and made a significant change. Knowing my luck, I'd just given him the formula for Listerine.

Rick's frank hostility cut me to the core. It was bad enough knowing he worked for Thompson, but to find him here, selling the orchid directly to von Brutten? There wasn't any room left in my heart for more pain. *Feel nothing.*

Von Brutten laid the paper on his cluttered desk. "And the other orchid?"

"It's in a safe place. I hoped you'd feel a little generosity coming on, especially after what your buddy Dr. Thompson did to my great-uncle."

"Unfortunate," von Brutten agreed. "I was not pleased when I found out. Still. The old man can be saved."

"Yes, now he can. Dr. Harrison may not have told you he had more than one iron in the fire. While he was working on your formula, he was working on something else as well." I fished the shaman's vial out of my pocket and set it on top of the formula. "I found this in Harrison's lab. Everlasting life."

Rick stared at the shaman's vial, clearly trying to make sense of what I was saying. The two things, I knew, were not computing. Time to distract him before he asked a pointed question and screwed up my plan.

I leveled a cool glance at him. "How did you get away from Shoemaker and his boys, anyway?"

His jaw tensed. "I posted bail."

"But customs didn't confiscate your Death Orchid." Which they should have, given Shoe's insistence that no Death Orchid make it into the States. Unless... My brain spun into overdrive.

"My CITES certificate cleared," he replied.

Von Brutten tapped his cigarette into a silver ashtray. "Did you happen upon your old friend in the field?"

"Daley? I took care of him," I said. "Did you know someone at Cradion hired him to steal the orchids from me?"

Von Brutten squinted through the spiraling cigarette smoke as he exhaled. "That's why I hired you. My confidence was

well-founded." His calculating gaze fell on Rick. "I didn't realize Cradion had hired you as well."

"It wasn't Cradion. It was Thompson."

Von Brutten's silvery eyes flashed with ire. I gathered Dr.
Thompson had his own private agenda.

Rick went on, "But he doesn't really understand market
need and market pricing. I follow the money. My not liking
what you plan to do with the orchid is my problem."

"And how do you know what I plan to do with my orchid?"
Von Brutten's squint darkened.

"The natives make a poison out of it," Rick replied smoothly.
"I have to assume you'll do the same. Kill innocent people."

The corners of von Brutten's silver eyes crinkled in amuse-
ment. "I assure you, Dr. Kinkaid, none of the people I intend to
kill are innocent. You know as well as I that progress in certain
areas can be held back by the unenlightened. Technological
progress, biological progress, even environmental progress."

"Not to mention political progress," Rick said dryly.

"Indeed." Von Brutten tapped his cigarette into a tray. "The
future of humankind depends upon strong leadership. Weak
leaders cause chaos. They defend the status quo. They sup-
press innovation. Progress requires risk. I'm merely making
progress possible."

Three things occurred to me simultaneously.

First, von Brutten honestly believed what he was saying.
In a sickening déjà vu, I thought of the *donos,* old Goldtooth,
justifying both his attack on the Yanomamo village and his
methodical poisoning of the colonel as necessary to
"progress." The difference between Goldtooth and von Brutten was only that of scale.

Second, if Rick was truly just trying to sell von Brutten a
priceless orchid, he wouldn't know about von Brutten's plans
for the plant unless he'd talked in-depth with Homeland Security. My memory flashed on the cable repair van. Window-

less, nondescript. Shoemaker must have talked Rick into setting up von Brutten in exchange for a lighter prison sentence.

Third, von Brutten would never be so stupid as to voice his intentions unless he knew Rick was trying to compromise him and was now toying with Homeland Security's freshly recruited errand boy.

Which meant Rick was in terrible danger. I had to get him out before von Brutten killed him. Shoemaker could handle the criminal side of things.

"Look, I just want to get down to the financial transaction," I said to von Brutten. "Have you guys finished your chitchat or should I come back later?"

"You and I can have our discussion now," von Brutten breathed. "Dr. Kinkaid will be staying." His pale eyes gazed mildly at me as if to say, *Indefinitely.*

"Then I just have one more question for Dr. Kinkaid," I said. "Does the wire you're wearing have a recorder?"

"What?" Rick sounded offended. To his credit, he didn't sound scared.

Von Brutten smiled his frosty smile. "A detail, I must admit, I was wondering myself."

"Stand up," I said.

"Please do," von Brutten invited.

"Homeland Security may know about von Brutten's plans for the orchid," I said, "but do you honestly believe they'd be able to *catch* him at it? With a *wire?*"

"Jessie," Rick said in a low voice. "I can't believe you're involved in this."

"Why not? You're working for Cradion."

"Not the way—"

"You lied to me. I told you why I wanted the orchid. I was the one telling the truth."

Rick took a single step toward me. "Yes, I worked for Thompson. But he didn't send me to the Amazon for the orchid."

"Bullshit."

"The moth, Jessie." His deep brown eyes begged me, but for what I couldn't tell. "I went for the moth."

"Touching but irrelevant," von Brutten murmured.

"Cradion—the real Cradion—wanted the moth for their research." His glance cut to the vial of poison sitting innocently on top of the fake formula. He raised his chin, daring me to believe him. "It was *important*."

"Unbutton your shirt," I replied.

While Rick did, von Brutten said, "Modern theaters and concert halls have started installing a special material in their walls and ceilings to block wireless signal transmissions. I've put it to a similar use here."

The wire and transmitter strapped to Rick's rib cage made him look like a hot-bodied cyborg. Von Brutten stripped the transmitter from him. No recorder. Then anger crept over me as von Brutten's hand lingered on Rick's chest. Rick's face was a study in granite. A single long lock of hair had fallen over his forehead and he was suddenly bad boy without even trying. "You're definitely staying with me," von Brutten murmured.

"I don't think so," I snapped. I didn't care if Rick was working for Shoemaker just to save himself some jail time. I didn't want to see him hurt. "Rick leaves. Now. Unharmed."

Von Brutten's brows tipped up in surprise. "I thought you were through with him. Don't you have a habit of throwing them back once you've had them? Oh, don't be angry, Dr. Robards." He stepped away from Rick and balanced his cigarette on the ashtray's lip. "You and I are very alike in that way."

"I'm nothing like you," I grated.

I dug my cell from my jeans pocket and tossed it to Rick, never taking my eyes off von Brutten. "Get downstairs or to the roof and hit Redial. Shoemaker's boys shouldn't be far away."

"Jessie—"

"Please do it, Rick."

I heard his footsteps on the rug, then the elevator door *shush* open. Von Brutten's pale eyes flickered with something like respect.

"Just like Dr. Harrison," he breathed. "Working for two masters."

"Not anymore. That's something else I wanted to tell you." I reached into my shoulderbag and pulled out Harrison's microcassette player, its wheels turning on a fresh tape. "I quit."

Von Brutten's face faded from pale to ghostly. "Well, Dr. Robards, I certainly didn't expect this *disloyalty.*"

"I'm a mercenary," I admitted, setting the recorder on the desk's edge, "but there are some things I won't do for money."

"Or for love, presumably."

"No," I replied, thinking about Scooter, and Marcello, then Rick. "Not even for love."

Von Brutten took a deep breath. "Then perhaps you are right. We are not very alike after all."

He reached behind himself for his cigarette and came back with a black-tipped arrow in his fist.

Curare.

He stabbed, lightning quick, at my chest.

I twisted to avoid the razor-sharp point. My left hand grabbed the arrow's shaft dangerously near the head. Von Brutten angled the arrow toward me at the same time he kicked out with his right foot, connecting with my calf. The muscle spasm threw me off balance, but I held on to the arrow and managed to get my right hand on the other end of it.

He braced his legs like a defensive lineman. Breathing hard, we leaned against each other, struggling for control. He was a small man, but he was still stronger than I was. I was going to lose.

No. I was *not* going to lose. I had the outside grip, von Brutten the inside. All I needed was to break the damn thing. I eased off the pressure, then abruptly shoved forward. The arrow shaft snapped in von Brutten's hands. The arrowhead, suddenly freed from resistance, dug through his suit coat and into his right shoulder.

I let go and backed off, panting. Von Brutten's breathing exploded into panicked heaving. A pained whimper escaped him. He gripped the little bit of shaft sticking out of his shoulder and pulled, stared at the reddened tip like he couldn't believe what had happened. The arrowhead dropped onto the floor.

"Ten minutes and counting." I kicked the arrowhead safely away as von Brutten collapsed, gasping, on the floor.

"Jessie!" Rick pounded back into the study, my cell in his hand, his open shirt waving.

"He's been cut," I said. "Call an ambulance." Before I'd finished the words, Rick was dialing on the landline.

I rolled von Brutten onto his back. He stared into space as though his brain had overloaded. Sweat sheened his graying face. I really wanted the bastard to live. I wanted to see him go to prison for all this mess. And the mess he'd wanted to make. My hands shook as I loosened von Brutten's impeccable jabot, but I didn't know whether it was from frustration that he'd gotten poisoned or relief that it hadn't been me.

"They're sending an ambulance," Rick said, putting down the landline handset.

"They'd better haul ass," I muttered. "But they probably won't have anything to treat him with. It's like he's taken a megadose of Tuberine."

Rick paused his shirt buttoning. "Skeletal muscle relaxant?"

"Yeah, but the curare won't stop at that. It'll paralyze the muscles and then he'll die of asphyxiation."

Von Brutten blinked. His goatee trembled.

"And you'll be awake the whole time," I told him. "Until you stop breathing."

I climbed to my feet and faced Rick's eyes, dark with concern. "Did you call Shoemaker?"

"Yeah, his guys are on their way up."

"Bully for them. How long for the ambulance?"

"I will not die," von Brutten gasped.

He levered himself to his stomach, then to his knees. He anchored his elbows on the desk and pulled himself along it. What was he after? Another poisonous arrow?

"Better give him room," I said as Rick moved to help him. "He may want to take us with him."

Von Brutten's shaking hand lurched and grabbed the shaman's vial sitting on top of my fake formula. His ghastly smile stretched his thin lips thinner in his white face. He wrenched the cap from the vial.

"No!" I shouted, leaping forward.

He threw the liquid back like a whiskey shot as I caught his hand. His pale eyes glittered. He swallowed.

"We have to get him to puke," I said to Rick, then realized it was too late.

Von Brutten slid to the floor, back against the desk, his eyes still locked on mine. One hand clutched feebly at his chest. His mouth opened slightly.

He was dead.

"Damn," I muttered. "Damn." When no words came from von Brutten's mouth, I elaborated. "I wanted you to pay."

"He did pay," Rick said softly.

"No, I mean I wanted him in prison. A bunch of people are going to die because of him. He should pay. At least for Scooter."

Body-armored men piled into the room, weapons drawn. Three of them spread out in the study, facing us, their guns pointed at our chests. I resisted the urge to raise my hands like a criminal. The adrenaline that had started draining from me surged again. I heard other men searching the condo, rousting out a protesting Not-Sims.

Another minute and Shoemaker strolled in, his revolver holstered. He surveyed the scene, studied von Brutten's body, the bloodied shoulder and the hand still clutching the empty vial, and turned to me.

"Poetic," he drawled. He looked at Rick. "You okay, son?"

"I'm fine, sir."

"Edwards!" Shoemaker barked. "Take Dr. Kinkaid to headquarters for debriefing. Dr. Kinkaid, I sure do appreciate all your help. I'll see you a little later."

So Rick hadn't been working off jail time after all? He was innocent in some way I hadn't figured out yet. The good man who would never forgive me for setting him up. Twice. Once at the airport and then here, when I'd practically told von Brutten he was working for the feds. The good man who'd tried to tell me he was innocent even while I was exposing him to von Brutten. The good man who'd asked for all of me when everyone else had been happy with what little I'd give.

Rick didn't look at me as the square-jawed, flak-geared Edwards ushered him out. He didn't know it, but he took what was left of my heart with him.

"Now, Dr. Robards," Shoe said, turning to me with a face full of steel and flint, "let's talk."

Two months later, I stood under a maple behind Scooter's trailer and looked down the little rise to the creek that ran through his acreage. Past the creek, the scrub grew slowly into pine forest that climbed stubby hills and shielded the Slapdash from the rare but cold northwestern wind. Here, you could just get a sense of what this land had been like before the farmers came and the oilmen struck it rich a hundred and fifty miles west.

"You picked a good spot," I told Scooter's headstone as I had every few days for the past six weeks.

It wasn't the Amazon—nothing was or could ever be for me—but it'd be home for a little while. I finally understood what Scooter had meant when he said there's nothing like the first orchid. For me, my first real love was Rick, and he and the Amazon would always be bound up together in my senses, in my heart.

The breeze kicked up, brushed my long, true-red hair over my shoulders. I settled cross-legged on the ground next to Scooter. The dew had long since lifted into the morning. A cardinal gave its distinctive snap of a call, then dipped from a young oak's lowest branch to the ground to rustle in the underbrush. Somewhere in the trees, his brown mate waited, hidden.

I missed Scooter like hell, but not as much as I thought I would. It was almost like I'd started letting him go that day in San Antonio when he told me he was ready to be let go. Knowing that you make your choices and suffer the consequences, good or bad. I'd cried myself to sleep like a baby for a week. But every day got easier. Scooter's little girl had finally growed up, as he would have said.

The greenhouse was flourishing, and it helped to be there, in his favorite place, working with his plants. I'd never have his obsession—or his success—with orchid growing, but for now, it gave me something to do. Hadn't stopped me thinking about Rick, though. Or regretting him. I didn't suppose anything ever would.

In the distance behind me, I heard car wheels crunching gravel. Doors opened and shut. The steady stream of well-wishing neighbors had just about spent itself, but the good friends, like Hank and Marian, who were up at the trailer now, kept coming around to see if I needed anything. I'd just smile and say no, thanks.

"They told me I'd find you here." Shoemaker's voice cut through the clear air.

I turned to look up at him. "I don't have to check in for another three days, Atlanta. You think I'm going to skip out on you?"

"That whole check-in thing was the judge's idea, not mine," Shoe drawled good-naturedly.

"Right. You just want to make sure I don't take off for parts unknown without you knowing about it. You've probably got my mug shot posted all over every airport in the States."

He chuckled and squatted down beside me. "Here," he said, handing me an industrial-looking box. "Today I'm a delivery boy."

The metal container had air holes and "Live Animal" emblazoned on the sides and top. I flipped the heavy-duty catch, lifted the lid. Inside sat a smaller, clear plastic box, also punched with air holes.

Black wings fluttered. Pearlescent black, the creature's body the size of a small bird's. My heart leaped. A Death Moth. My breath caught in my throat.

Every moth has its orchid, Scooter would have said, and I knew what this moth meant. Rick was looking for me, if I'd have him. The question was, Would I, after all that had happened between us? Could I forgive him for badgering me to open my heart while he withheld so much of himself?

"That the moth Dr. Kinkaid was looking for in the Amazon?" Shoe asked.

"Yeah. We found it before we found the orchid." I snapped the lid back on. "Did you catch Thompson?"

Shoe beamed a satisfied smile my way. "Day before yesterday. He spilled a lot more information than we thought he would. Confirmed what we'd already pieced together about Cradion's involvement."

"Cradion didn't know about Thompson's rogue lab."

"Nope. They're about to start Phase one trials on their new heart medication, too, using Dr. Harrison's good formula. Dr. Kinkaid's pretty happy about that."

It turned out excretions from the Death Moth provided the "proper dilution." The poison overstimulated the heart tissue, but the neutralizer reduced that effect to a constructive level. Ironic. I'd thought I was after a miracle cure but brought back a poison. It'd been Rick who'd brought back the real cure.

My throat closed. "I guess he is happy."

"Dr. Thompson confirmed a few other things, too," Shoe said. "He'd been the doctor responsible for administering those trials. He'd seen your uncle several times during treatment."

Most of my anger had already been grieved away, but I conjured up enough to think, *Bastard*. "Did he tell you how he knew me?"

"When we got around to you, he said your uncle had gotten talkative one day, flashed some snapshots of family."

After that we didn't say anything for a while. The sun raised the scent of hot, dry grass and pine needles while a handful of grackles squawked and screeched in the trees. I balanced the moth's case on my knee.

"Why Parkinson's patients?" I asked finally. "Why pick on a bunch of elderly people?"

"They counted on attending physicians to notice the heart disease symptoms and report back. In most of the diagnostic tests, the heart disease looked natural."

"Untraceable poison."

"A real world test," Shoe said.

"There's a bunch about Harrison that doesn't make sense. Why he implicated the Cradion lab rather than Thompson or von Brutten. Why von Brutten had him killed."

"Thompson says Dr. Harrison rolled the lab because he thought he'd get away with being in protective custody."

"Like von Brutten would say, 'Oh, Harrison didn't mention me when he screwed up my plan so I'll just let this slide'?" I asked, incredulous.

Shoe's grin flashed, then he said, "I don't think von Brutten had him killed. I think Thompson knows who did, but he's not telling."

"Great. So Thompson was working for yet another bioterrorist?"

"That's what we'd like to know. Maybe it was someone who wanted von Brutten out of the way."

"Thinking you'd trace the hit back to von Brutten and arrest him."

"Or that someone else would get to him first." Shoe's eyes, golden like a lion's in the growing light, glittered. "Thompson clams up on some things like a man afraid for his life."

"So we don't know who really killed Dr. Harrison."

"I don't know if we ever will." Shoe stood, then helped me to my feet. "We might have had a chance if you'd called me before you started your one-woman crusade."

I held on to my moth with one hand and brushed the seat of my jeans with the other. "Come on, Atlanta. He would have smelled me coming a mile away. He did Rick. You know I couldn't take the chance of him running. You'd never have caught him."

Shoe just looked at me as we started back to the greenhouse. We'd probably never agree on that issue. I'd paid for my crimes. They'd hit me with a CITES fine that pretty much put me back to zero savings, then told me I'd be watched for the rest of my life, my every international trip scrutinized like a crime scene. But I'd stopped von Brutten, horrific accident that it'd been. Shoe would just have to get over it.

"You never said if you'd come work for me," he said.

I laughed, for the first time in weeks. It felt good to do that. Freeing.

"Benefits are good, lots of travel," he persisted. "I'm gettin' too old to chase orchid smugglers."

"Jessica Robards, Secret Agent," I said as we rounded the trailer and stopped at his nondescript brown Buick parked in the drive. "I don't think so."

"Yeah, you'll probably get a better offer anyway." He jerked the driver's door open. "I hear Cradion's hiring."

That set me laughing again. Right. Like that would ever happen.

"No," Shoe said, nodding toward the front porch. "I'm serious."

I turned. Before I even saw him, my whole body went hot. Rick stood on the porch, hair tied back in a short ponytail, hands in his jeans pockets, all lean and hard and sexy. His strong face looked relaxed, serene. As I took my first hesitant step toward him, his lips curved into that slow smile I liked.

He didn't tell you the truth, I reminded myself. *He didn't have to lie.* My grip tightened on the moth's case.

"Jessie." His voice was a little deeper, a little softer, than I remembered.

I stopped before I reached the porch. "I got your message." I set the moth's case on the old hitching post Scooter had been so fond of. Behind me, Shoe's car growled back down the drive. "Shoe tells me you're doing well at Cradion."

He stepped down to meet me on level ground. "I'm running a sustainable resources program they've just started. It's a pilot project." His eyes gleamed and the dimple made him look suddenly shy. "It's why I showed up today. There's something I hope you'll help me with. If you don't have something else to do."

So the message had been about work, not about me. "My employer's a dead bioterrorist," I said gruffly. "I think I'm free for a while."

He smiled slightly, undaunted. "Cradion needs a stable supply of Death Orchids to produce the heart medication Harrison developed. It'll take months to synthesize the alkaloid it produces. I'm heading back to the Amazon to start a moth-orchid farming operation."

"Why not just mericlone the orchids here?" I asked. "They could have hundreds in a matter of weeks."

He shoved his glasses further onto the bridge of his nose. "The moths don't survive long in captivity and we haven't figured out why."

"So Cradion needs both orchids and moths." I was drowning in his eyes again, just like before, wishing it were for good this time. Knowing I wouldn't be more than a colleague if he asked what I thought he was going to ask.

Then he asked it.

"Are you interested in managing the orchid side of it? I'm thinking we could bring the Yanomamo into the project. I know there's no preventing them from being exposed to Western culture, but maybe we could incorporate their knowledge into what we're doing instead of the other way around. Learn some new things from them."

I took a deep breath, steeling myself to say no. Not because I didn't want to, because I did—and his idea about the Yanomamo was great—but because I would put myself through too much pain to be that close to him without being *with* him. Then again, maybe he was offering me a desk job here while he was in the field.

He added softly, "I want you to go back with me."

My heart stuck in my throat, making it difficult to get the next words out. "In general or in particular?"

His gaze warmed. "In particular."

"Rick—"

His lips caught whatever else I was going to say, which didn't matter because I forgot what that was the moment he threaded his fingers through my hair. His strong arms went around me and held me tight against his body. His kiss grew desperate, searching and needful, and I knew he'd missed me as much as I had him. But he'd been the one to keep us apart.

I broke the kiss and shoved him away. "You didn't have to lie to me, Noah."

His hands dropped to his sides. "No, I didn't. I let my job get in the way when I knew it shouldn't. But I'd dabbled in a few other things I shouldn't have and got the village attacked." His voice lowered. "I got Marcello killed. That was my fault." Before I could protest, he added, "I wasn't willing to take that chance with you."

"So you were going to tell me who you were when we got back?" I couldn't keep the disbelieving tone out of my voice.

"Shoemaker tracked me down before I ever left the States. When I told him I was after the moth, he let me go and told me to keep an eye out for you. He had to know whether you could be trusted with the orchid." That slow smile kicked in. "It turned out you could."

I felt my eyes go wide. Rick had been working with Homeland Security all along? "Wait a minute—"

"Why do you think you got away with only a fine for illegal transport?" he asked. "Who do you think's been in your corner all this time, helping Shoemaker convince Homeland Security not to send you to jail?"

"You—"

He caught me up in his arms again, grinning as I sputtered. "Hey, I was just doing a job when we met, exactly like the one he keeps offering you." He tightened his grip, nearly squeezing the breath out of me. "Nice trick with the *Cattleya delictabus,* by the way. Talk about blindsided."

I struggled a few seconds more until I realized just how good it felt to be in his arms again, to smell his sandalwood scent. "You stick with me and you'd better watch your back," I muttered, wrapping my arms around his neck.

His lips trailed along my jaw to my ear, sending shivers down my spine like no man ever had. "If I stick with you, I won't have to," he whispered.

I smiled and settled deeper into his embrace.

Damn straight.

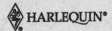

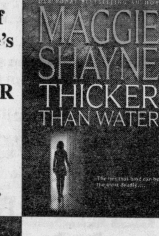

If you enjoyed what you just read,
then we've got an offer you can't resist!

Take 2 bestselling love stories FREE!

Plus get a FREE surprise gift!

BOMBSHELL™

COMING NEXT MONTH

#37 WILD WOMAN by Lindsay McKenna
Sisters of the Ark

Pilot Jessica Merrill's risk-taking actions had earned her the nickname Wild Woman. Now she'd been charged with retrieving a powerful Native American totem from the madman who would use it to gain immortality. But Jessica's doubtful partner, Mace Phillips, was less enthusiastic about the mission. It was up to her to save the tribe—and show Mace that sometimes you had to take wild chances to get what you wanted....

#38 COUNTDOWN by Ruth Wind
Athena Force

Time was running out for code breaker Kim Valenti. She had evidence that terrorists were planning to disrupt the upcoming presidential election, but when she thwarted one attack, the terrorists made her their next target. Racing to save herself, the president and his opponent, she'd have to rely on her code-breaking skills—and the help of one sympathetic member of the bomb squad—before time ran out for everyone....

#39 THE MIDAS TRAP by Sharron McClellan

Renegade archaeologist Veronica Bright knew myths were based in truth. But her professional reputation had been torn to shreds when she'd tried to prove her theories. Now the renowned Dr. Simon Owens had handed her the opportunity to fight back—on a hunt for the legendary Midas Stone. Was this finally her chance to validate years of hard work, or was it a trap?

#40 SHOW HER THE MONEY by Stephanie Feagan

Accountant Whitney "Pink" Pearl was in trouble. She'd exposed a funny money accounting scam by one for her firm's biggest clients—and the only evidence was locked in a box with a blow-up doll! Meanwhile, someone was stalking her, and when a top executive turned up dead, she realized she had been the intended victim. Only Pink's feisty determination—and the help of one savvy lawyer—could get her out of this mess!